Family
Matters

Family
Matters

Jan Duckland

PIATKUS

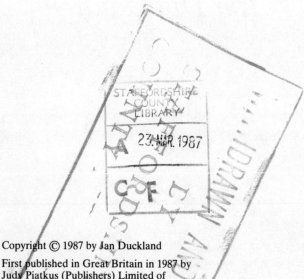

Copyright © 1987 by Jan Duckland

First published in Great Britain in 1987 by
Judy Piatkus (Publishers) Limited of
5 Windmill Street, London W1

British Library Cataloguing in Publication Data

Duckland, Jan
  Family matters.
  I. Title
  823'.914[F]   PR6054.U2/

  ISBN 0–86188–625–9

Phototypeset in 11/12pt Linotron Times by
Phoenix Photosetting, Chatham
Printed and bound in Great Britain by
Mackays of Chatham Ltd.

For my husband and especially my children,
who have made me what I am today . . . !

Teatime is the wildest time, mixing
tiredness with hunger, making
mountains out of molehills, stirring
dried-up rice pudding with a piece of old Spam.
The pushchair kept them quiet,
we stopped under the arches and had a chocolate drop each,
and that shut them up for a minute.
And when we were at the shop, I said, Tommy,
Tommy, stop hitting me. And down he went.
In the evenings, then you feel knackered.
I read much of the night, and drink cider and have a hangover.

What are the roots that clutch, what branches grow
out of this plastic rubbish? Son of man,
you cannot say, or guess, for you know only
a squeaky rabbit on skis, the separateness of socks,
Lego, Humpty Dumpty, a pig's head with a bell in it,
and the spectre of an omnipresent Raccoon.
Only, there is shadow under this gatelegged table
(Come in under the shadow of this gatelegged table)
and I will show you something different from
an infant with red hair grabbing your right leg
or an infant with blond hair grabbing your left leg:
I will show you dog hairs in a handful of blancmange.

                                        Barry Dennell

Part One

Chapter One

Barry and I were lying on the eiderdown on the bedroom floor, and panting. At least, I was panting. Gasping, in fact, like a stranded fish. Barry wasn't gasping but he was making erotic grunting noises. There was a smell of sweat and hot bodies and our skin was slippery and shone as if it were oiled.

I tried grunting too but it didn't help. I wondered resentfully why the hell I was doing this.

'Your body,' said Barry, 'is supposed to be parallel to the ground.'

I swore, and collapsed. 'It's not possible.'

'It's possible.' He scrambled to a sitting position and pulled the book towards him. 'Number 70, the *Nakrāsana*. There's the picture.'

I didn't look. I had already seen the picture and all the other, equally horrible pictures. Tortuously contorted limbs, legs crossed behind necks, feet in groins, heads under armpits, elbows in figures of eight. 'This one,' said Barry enthusiastically, 'represents a crocodile hunting its prey. See, you raise yourself on palms and toes – palms level with the waist, mind – feet apart – '

He resumed the *Nakrāsana*. I said nastily, 'Your body isn't parallel to the ground.'

'And then you – *lunge* – towards your prey – keeping your body – '

It wasn't bad, I thought critically, as his nose hit the floor. Certainly there had been a lunge of sorts. 'You have to keep practising,' he explained. At last he was panting. Just a little.

I stood up. We were both in our underwear and my bra was

1

soaked. 'I'm going to have a bath.'

'You've only done five minutes.' He was hurt, or disappointed, or both. 'You haven't given it a chance. Honestly, Amabel, it makes your whole body feel – once you've got past the pain barrier, that is.'

'Will you listen out for Drew? I'll leave a bottle by his door.'

He started to mutter about his concentration being broken by interruptions so I tiptoed out politely, went to the kitchen to prepare the bottle, then locked myself into the bathroom with my diary.

This was luxury indeed. It was the first time I had thought of writing my diary in the bath. I lay in the hot water, a shower cap spread across my stomach to protect the book which was balanced there and, while the pages curled in the steam, laid bare my soul for posterity.

March 12th. Today Drew used the potty four times and only wee'ed over the side once. Becky held his penis inside the other times. She is developing a penis fixation and made several out of pastry.

Becky dressed herself this morning, mostly back to front but it's a start. She told the milkman she was going to have a penis for her birthday.

Drew bit into eleven bars of chocolate at the shop.

Becky broke her recorder over Drew's head. Drew has a lump.

I paused to read what I had written and depression descended on me. Surely there had been more to my day than this? I had been keeping the diary for less than a week but already the sameness of the entries was beginning to disturb me. I thought, then wrote determinedly:

Listened to some Wagner on Radio 3. It was the final part of the Ring Cycle, just before Brunnhilde throws herself onto the funeral pyre. Very moving.

There. Culture at last.

2

*Becky said 'Get rid of that whiny woman' so we had Tubby the
Tuba instead.*

Oh God.

*Made a resolution to look more attractive about the house and
got out my pink crêpe dress. Drew emptied the potty over it.*

I slammed the diary shut and slid despairingly down into the
now tepid water. Loud howls were issuing from Drew's room
so I splashed about meaningly and listened again. Barry's
steps came out of our room, the heavy footsteps of mar-
tyrdom, and I heard Drew's door open. The howls stopped. A
moment later Becky, woken by them, screeched in her mind-
bendingly penetrating foghorn voice, 'I WANT A DRINK OF
WATERRR!!!'
    'Life,' someone used to say in *The Hitchhiker's Guide to the
Galaxy* when it was all the rage, 'don't talk to me about life.' It
had become a catchphrase.
    I sat up and made another effort on the now soggy page.
'*Joined Barry in his Yoga tonight. Very difficult.*'
    Very difficult? Was that all I could say?
    '*Hopeless,*' I added. '*Everything. All of it. Bloody
hopeless.*'
    Then, '*Don't talk to me about life.*'

Why couldn't I write the sort of diary I had planned? A proper
one, full of profound thoughts and flowery, philosophical
passages; a diary which reflected the Essential Me? I pon-
dered the question in bed that night while Barry made love to
me. (This would necessitate yet another bath in the morning.)
Glumly I concluded that there was no longer any such thing as
the Essential Me. It had been bleached pale by innumerable
packets of Napisan, ground small by fast liquidisers, sucked
out through the Great Teat of Motherhood and finally dispersed on the winds of a good drying day. What other explanation could there be?
    I used to be a literary person. Somewhere in my mother's
house were a dozen or so letters from a dozen or so publishers
testifying to my literary merit and assuring me that I was a

Writer of Great Promise. I even held an honours degree in English Literature and Language: second class, it is true, but then only original geniuses like Barry ever got a First. So why was my diary so – so *vapid*?

I gave a sigh, and inadvertently spurred Barry on to greater heights.

There was a time, during my travels abroad, when, unemployed, I used to write for several hours a day. Even when I was working (typist, usherette, waitress, shop assistant, milkmaid, sandwich maker, petrol pump attendant) there was free time, lots of it, to be filled as I chose by reading poetry, going out (going *out*!), writing novels . . . All those thousands of pages, all those literary aspirations; and at last a book, an actual published novel; which sold eighteen hundred copies and was remaindered a year later (free copies to all admiring relatives), leaving me a has-been who had been and come back in record time.

But it didn't matter. Much. I was a literary person. Enthusiastically I attended night school, took belated A levels, entered University as a mature student to read English. (More admiration from the same relatives.) And University, alas, made me so completely literary that I could no longer construct a sentence without immediately subjecting it to the dread process known as critical analysis. Disaster.

I became aware that Barry had stopped.

'What's the matter?' he whispered.

'Nothing,' I whispered back. 'Sorry.' I had been forgetting, I realised, to make the requisite sounds and movements.

'Are you all right? Are you getting sore?' He was concerned for me and willing, if I was uncomfortable, to make the greatest sacrifice known to man. One of the unsung heroes.

'I'm fine,' I said. 'Carry on.'

There was a pause. Then he did, though with less conviction, carry on.

Bloody kids, I thought venomously: sucking out my libido like leeches. It wasn't like this at University, when I used to break the rules and let Barry stay the night in my room at the students' residence. It wasn't even like this when I was heavily pregnant – not during the first pregnancy, anyway. But by the second . . .

4

Ah, those nights of boyfriend smuggling! The whole ethos of the students' residence, the academic discipline, the parties, the pressure of imminent exams, combined to make sex fun. Light-hearted and intense at one and the same time, with discussions about Eliot and Pound in between love-making, and a shared consciousness of the very special context in which it all took place. And plenty of leisure to catch up on *sleep*!

Sleep. Our marriage bed was three times the width of that nun-like bunk I had occupied. Barry and I used to lie there snuggled together like kittens, he (uncomplaining) with a hand on the floor to keep from falling out, I (complaining bitterly) crushed against the wall. Now, as we rolled apart (I hadn't noticed him finish: had he noticed that I hadn't noticed?) we settled down to sleep with a foot, or its metric equivalent, between us. This was comfortable. It did not signify estrangement. Indeed, I had read somewhere that when this manner of sleeping begins to occur in a marriage it denotes mutual security.

Instead of thinking about sleep, why, I wondered irritably, was I not practising it? It was that damned diary. It had set me thinking about the past, the irretrievable past (Never never never never never!) and now I couldn't stop. And yet I was dog-tired.

'Amabel,' said Barry, 'I'm picking up some very strange vibes from you. What's the matter?'

Barry and his vibes. 'Nothing, really. I'm just tired.'

'Yes,' he said expressionlessly.

'My mind's churning around. I was thinking of you in the communal kitchen at the residence, early in the morning, remember? Unshaven, with your scarf on, trying to look as if you'd just walked briskly across town; and none of the girls being fooled for a minute. Then you used to go off to your lecture with your books tucked under your aching elbows.'

Silence. He knew perfectly well what I was really saying. I wondered if he also knew (I barely knew it myself) that I was, cryptically, apologising. Probably he was not even aware that I felt guilty. But why should I feel *guilty*? Women, I thought suddenly, will never be fully liberated until they have cleansed themselves of their eternal guilt. It starts at the moment of childbirth and you're stuck with it for life. Guilt for not loving your man enough, for not loving your child enough, for loving man or child too much, for disciplining too little, for disciplining too much, for dirty floors, for apathetic sex, for seeking an identity through diary writing, for putting too few blankets on the cot, for putting too many blankets on the cot, for not taking the children out, for taking the children out because you need to go out yourself, for needing to go out, for making your husband get up to them in the night, for resenting your husband for not getting up to them in the night, for feeling resentful, for not being the warm, loving, giving, forgiving selfless, bloody doormat of a hundred Victorian novels.

Barry's breathing told me that he was almost asleep.

'I've put your cereal out for morning,' I said, 'and your clean socks are in the airing cupboard.'

Becky arrived at my bedside at seven o'clock. It was still dark. I squinted at her in the light from the landing and mumbled, 'Give the door a push.' She did, and in the softer glow I watched her struggling with something outside my line of vision. I was still half asleep. 'What are you doing?'

'Taking my (grunt) boots off.' More struggles. 'You do it.'

'*Please*.' I stuck an arm out into the cold and yanked off her red wellingtons. 'They're wet. Don't tell me you've been *out*!'

'I'll tell you in a minute,' she said primly. 'After I've had my drink.'

I shut my eyes again. We had discovered long ago that by the simple expedient of keeping drinks on the bedside table it was possible to postpone the moment of complete awakening. Becky climbed into bed on Barry's side (he had already left for the hospital) and lay quietly sucking her Ribena through her blue cup with the spout. Slow light began to seep through the curtains, to my infinite relief. I had always detested getting up in the dark. When Becky started school, of course, I would have to. No blessing is unmixed.

The drink finished, she wriggled until she lay fully on me, her face tucked under my chin. Our morning love. It wasn't a bad way to wake up.

'Shall I tell you now?'

6

'What? Oh, yes, if you like.'

'*Well*,' she began, 'Daddy said to stay downstairs with him because you were still asleep so I told him could I let Gin out and he said I could. So I went outside to watch her do her poo on the grass. In fact there was a spider in a cobweb in the hedge. When we get up and go outside,' she added, 'you must get the spade from the shed and move Gin's pooh before Drew treads in it.'

'All right,' I said obediently.

'If it rains,' she said severely, 'if it rains it will make a very sloppy mess.'

'Yes,' I said. 'All right. I'll move it.'

She sat up and planted one of her small, warm, gentle kisses on my cheek. I held her round little bottom in my two hands and thought how marvellous she was, how affectionate, how intelligent, how articulate. She had, I used to think, my temperament and Barry's brains. And whose beauty? Not mine. I looked at her in the dim morning light, as I looked often, amazed by her. Red-gold hair she had, the colour of cherry wood, thick and luxuriant although I never let it grow long enough to trouble her. Deep, receptive brown eyes, a small, mobile, vivid face. Even, absurdly, dimples in her cheeks. Her skin was a rich tawny rose, her legs had been gorgeous even when she was a baby. Someone had once said that I should enter her for the Miss Pears competition. She was a delight to look upon.

'There's a great big yellow wee-wee in my potty.'

'Good. Go and empty it.'

'Would you like to feel my dry bed?' she offered.

'In a minute. Empty the potty and don't trip on the way to the bathroom.'

She stood up on the bed, dragging the covers off me as she did so, and began to bounce energetically. 'Stop that!' I ordered. She carried on bouncing, laughing at me. The springs creaked. '*Stop* it! Do you want a smack?' From the next room there came an answering creak as Drew leapt into life, then a deafening, crashing, recurring ricochet as he started to rock his cot back and forth against the dividing wall. Becky slid nimbly off the bed as my hand threatened, and set off for his room at a run, grabbing his drink as she went. His

7

door burst open and crashed back against the wall. There was instant cacophony as both of them rocked the cot with mutual vigour and screams of laughter. I yelled at the top of my voice '*Stop that!*' but they were effectively deaf.

The day had begun.

Now the way to avoid this and the chaos and confusion which always followed was obvious even to me: I should get up earlier. My reason for not doing so was valid. It was that the day was long enough already. Quite, quite long enough.

I shivered my way into the bathroom, wondering when on earth the winter would end, and began the usual morning calculations. Whose pyjamas were thickest, who felt the cold least, in what order should I wash and dress the three of us? The wind blew through the gaps in the bare floorboards and wafted my nightdress about. I braced myself and flung it off. Becky came in and announced, 'I'm cold.'

'We're all cold,' I said unsympathetically. I stood among a host of goose pimples, running the hot water, and then I remembered that I needed a bath. Good. A soak after breakfast would kill part of the morning nicely. I donned a dressing gown.

I washed Becky as she teetered on the toilet lid and managed not to lose my temper when she repeatedly pushed my cold hands away, or even when she dropped the spare toilet roll into the water, but only when a new tin of talcum powder followed it. A couple of smacks warmed both of us up. Then I sent her off to find some knickers and went to see Drew.

The Other One. Becky had been, since babyhood, such a dominant character that Drew always seemed like The Other One. I was in love with him. Placid, amiable, with the sweetest of dispositions, he had borne all with a barely a protest when Becky had made repeated assaults on this unwelcome newcomer, when she had hit him with her metal lorry, split the press studs of his Baby-gro asunder with one forceful rip, forced the teat of his bottle down his drowning throat, and, finally, nearly asphyxiated him with the violence of her new and passionate love. He was devoted to her and she, though she bullied him unmercifully, to him.

I stood in the doorway now and surveyed his cot. Becky had been in generous mood this morning. She had given him four teddy bears of varying sizes, several books, a pink pig, a musical box, a spinning-top, a xylophone, a bucket of bricks, a large woolly Humpty Dumpty and a plastic vase full of dried hydrangeas. From beneath it all Drew's blue eyes beamed at me. He pointed sweetly at his Ribena-soaked sheets. I did not react. I heaved out him, the toys, the sheets. I said pleasantly, 'So you've been experimenting with the force of gravity and the natural tendencies of water. Fine.' I called after him, as he bumbled out of the room, 'I'm not going to shout at you. I have already shouted and lifted my hand in anger against your sister. Today,' I went on, gathering belief, 'I am going to be CALM. We are *all* going to be CALM.'

There was a thump and a clatter and wails broke out simultaneously from both children. I felt my blood pressure shoot up. Becky ran in, screaming hysterically, tears flooding her cheeks in preposterous quantities. Behind her hobbled Drew, his mouth wide with loud misery, one hand rubbing a tiny red mark on his knee. I knew immediately what had caused it. The bloody nails were working their way up through the bloody floorboards again.

'All right, my love, my precious,' I said, down on my own knees and hugging him hard. 'Oh, that *hurts*, doesn't it?' Meanwhile Becky went on screaming like a banshee right down my ear. 'What's the *matter*!' I snapped at her. 'It was Drew who fell, not you.'

Gone was the ability to articulate clearly. There came a sobbed incomprehensible sentence ending on a high note of Attic agony. Resignedly I said 'Show me', picked up Drew and followed her across the landing. She pointed tragically into the bathroom. 'It was *my* wee-wee!' shrieked Becky, '*I* wanted to empty it, it was *my* wee-wee!'

It was still only eight o'clock.

Perhaps I ought to explain about the floorboards. We were not newly resident in our house, nor were we in the process of packing up to leave it. It was simply that, judging by the standards of most people in England in the 1980s, we were very poor. This is not to say that our children were barefoot and swollen-bellied, that we ourselves often went hungry, that we lived in a cardboard-and-plastic-bag shanty and

9

fetched our water in buckets from an excreta-infected stream four miles away. No: simply that we lacked a car, telephone, television, video, vacuum cleaner, tumble-drier, dishwasher, toaster, freezer, food-mixer, micro-wave oven, electric hedge-cutter, power lawnmower and home computer. And upstairs carpets.

The reason for this dire poverty was that Barry had, after a few years of pushing insurance papers around on a desk, discovered his Vocation: he was now a second-year trainee psychiatric nurse. Thus our circumstances were, to say the least, straitened. When we needed clothes we bought them at Oxfam. Few people realise what a wonderful institution the National Health Service is. Not only does it benefit the sick people of Britain but also the Third World.

Barry was one of that rare breed which puts worthwhile work before a good salary. Fortunately we were at one on the matter, although I complained loudly, often and vociferously about the lack of that most necessary of mod. cons., a vacuum cleaner. Every so often I would break out in a passion of rage and frustration on the subject and Barry would sit down glumly with pen and paper, knowing the results of his calculations even before he started, and eventually announce that we could not possibly afford even a modest monthly payment. His glumness engendered in me guilty remorse and I would make brave resolutions about Doing Without and Never Mentioning It Again. Until the next time.

In theory I could have found some kind of part-time work to boost the funds, but in practice it was just not possible. There was a variety of reasons for this. First, our only transport was an aged and unreliable mo-ped, so any employment would have to be local. But the village of Lottabridge was isolated and its sole source of employment (also the reason for the isolation) was the hospital. I could, I suppose, have done what many of the nurses' wives did, and performed cleaning and other menial domestic tasks there in the evening. But to co-ordinate my working hours with those of Barry, who, as a student, worked very erratic hours indeed, would have been extremely difficult. And thank God for that. I had quite enough cleaning and menial domestic tasks at home. Often, too, Barry was sent to other towns, other

10

hospitals, to augment his training, and a baby-sitter was out of the question. So too was the job. The vacuum cleaner would have to wait, just as the automatic washing-machine had had to wait until, fortuitously, a great-aunt of Barry's died and small bequests were scattered around amongst the family. (Definition of *nightmare*: two kids in nappies and no washing-machine.) Thus, though not uncomplainingly, I did my part in fighting the good fight against mental illness.

I had to confess that it was a fairly negative role. But then I had become a fairly negative person and it was for that reason that I had begun the diary. With the first contact between pen and virgin paper would come, I knew, that old electrifying thrill (but one did not talk blithely of electrifying thrills when one's husband was in Barry's line of work); then slowly, inevitably, a portrait of the real Me would grow upon the page, as photographs grow from nothing when held in the developer. This sense of non-identity would vanish, and there she would be, Amabel Dennell: vital, confident, full of intelligence, razor-sharp wit and mental energy.

Well. But I would not give up, I decided bravely as I crawled round the kitchen floor with my dustpan and brush (I had allowed Becky to put the cereal into our bowls). Something more, though, was also needed. Some sort of project, some scheme not connected with children or husbands. But what?

I mulled it over in between scraping soggy lumps of Weetabix off the hairy floor and burning the toast. Evening classes? Too expensive. I remembered glancing through a prospectus the year before and recoiling at the fees. Even if we could afford it there would be the usual problem of fitting in the classes with Barry's shifts. It would be no good expecting a baby-sitter to cope with the children's bed-time – and again, we could not afford one.

Becky said, with her mouth full, 'Where are you going?'

I regarded her. 'I'm not going anywhere. What do you mean? And don't talk with your mouth full.'

I was made, justly, to wait while she deliberately masticated every last crumb, grinning at me with her eyes. The next lot of toast burned under the grill. While I was sorting that out she said, 'I thought you were going out tonight and somebody else would read my bedtime story.'

'Oh, you're at that game again, are you? Do you want honey?' She nodded, and I brought a new jar to the table and sat down. From his highchair Drew watched me remove the lid. As soon as it was off he leaned over, plunged his hand in clear honey up to the wrist, and smiled ecstatically. The subject of Becky's extra-sensory perception was not resumed.

When she was younger, Becky had had a most disconcerting habit of homing in on our thoughts. After the initial shock I put it down to her age. It seemed reasonable to assume that a very small child has not developed certain mental faculties at the expense of others and that, consequently, mild ESP or simply the receiving of her mother's thoughts are still possible to her. Later, as her mind embraces a multitude of information she loses this ability, much as she loses the ability to put her toe into her mouth or perform all the contortions illustrated in Barry's Yoga book. So I had theorised. When I mentioned this to other mothers, however, I found that none of them had experienced it. Immediately I knew that Becky was going to be different, abnormal, a freak, a victim of sensational publicity, an early suicide.

Then she stopped.

Until this morning. Was it all starting again?

Previous incidents had been fairly trivial. Just enough to pull you up short for a minute, before you forgot about it. But there had been two occasions which were rather more striking. One concerned our first visit to the nearest Health Centre, soon after we moved to Lottabridge. Becky had walked purposefully around the doctor's desk and started to open a closed drawer. I stopped her. 'But I want a Smartie,' she said plaintively. The doctor opened the drawer she was touching and took out a tube of Smarties. I remember that my mouth fell open and I just gaped. Eventually I managed to stutter, 'But how did she know?' The doctor said casually, 'Oh, all the kids know I keep Smarties in that drawer.' He seemed to have forgotten that Becky had never been in his surgery before.

The second occasion was when we met an acquaintance whose mother had recently died. This lady did not mention her loss at all, and greeted Becky smilingly. Becky, usually so gregarious, did not smile back. She stared gravely for some seconds before saying, with the utmost sympathy, 'I'm very sorry for the lady. Why is the lady sad?' That effectively brought to a close any conversation we might have had.

This, then, was my precocious, highly unpredictable daughter. And it was through her that I got my Great Idea.

I had washed the dishes. This may sound a small task, swiftly accomplished. It was not. During it, it was necessary to sweep up the remains of the breakfast bowl which Drew had kindly carried to the sink for me; wipe two bottoms, one of them three times (I had forgotten that Becky found the bottle of Syrup of Figs yesterday); clean the toilet; disentangle Drew from a chair leg which had somehow got jammed through the crotch of his training-pants; mop the kitchen floor (my own fault, I had forgotten to put the milk out of reach); and change Drew's shoes and socks after he stood in the bucket.

I am a *graduate*! I raged inwardly as I finally got into the bath at half-past ten; a *graduate*! I have a *brain*, I could be contributing something to the cultural life of the nation. And what am I doing?

'Can I go beep-beep on your nipples?' enquired Becky.

I submitted, but forebore to make the sound effects. This was a game which Barry had started long ago. It was all very well for him. Then Drew put his little shining face over the rim of the bath and he had to prod too. It was the most unsexual thing you could imagine.

So far, thank goodness, we had succeeded in keeping intact the children's innocent and frank curiosity about their own and our bodies without inculcating any awful sense of sin and shame. The occasional nipple prod was, I thought, a small price to pay for such a prize. So perhaps, after all, my brain was not being entirely wasted. I could think, and did think very carefully (most of the time) about what was healthy and constructive for the children's development. But oh, to put that brain to some other use! So much of it must be atrophying through lack of exercise.

And suddenly, there it was. My Idea.

I dropped the soap with a splash. I stared at Becky, now dragging Drew around on the bathmat and shouting 'Sorry' at intervals.

13

Brain: extra-sensory perception.

Brain: contribution to the cultural life of the nation.

Brain: centre of intelligence, consciousness, identity, imagination; self.

'That's it,' I said. 'I've got it.' I leapt from the tub with growing excitement and yanked Drew's pants down, just in time. 'Children, your mother is going to write a novel. At last, another novel! And *this* time – ' I grabbed a towel and attacked my skin as if all the apathetic motherhood in the world lay damply there – '*this* time it'll be a bestseller. You see if it isn't!' I rubbed away vigorously, hopping about a bit to keep warm. Two blue eyes and two brown stared worriedly up at me. I dropped to my knees and took Becky's serious face in my hands. 'And *you*,' I said fervently, '*you* my girl, are going to be in it.'

Her eyes filled. She opened her mouth and wailed.

Chapter Two

I couldn't wait to start. But I must. There was the day to be got through first, or what was left of it. But I was already finding that when a long-dormant section of one's mind wakes up, in this case the enthusiasm department, the longest day becomes bearable. A positive attitude is all. Unfortunately, positive attitudes, when you have two small children and one of them is Becky, suffer the same fate as the rock beneath the constant drip: erosion. It may take the rock a few million years longer but the end result is much the same.

Enthusiasm! I flew about the tasks I generally drudged through, I sang (loudly) Beethoven's Ode to Joy, ignoring Becky's command to switch to 'Twinkle, Twinkle, Little Star', and I refrained from screaming abuse at Gin when Drew went into the garden and trod in the dog mess. Poor Gin, it was not her fault but mine. Belatedly I got the spade and disposed of the horror in the bit of jungle at the bottom of the garden. I admit that my new positive attitude did wilt a little when I returned to the house to find that Drew's shoes, with him in them, had trailed the mess around the kitchen floor. It wilted even more when, having put the shoes outside, I turned round and saw him carefully retracing the same steps in his socks.

But I held on. Becky shouted at Drew and I shouted at Becky for shouting at Drew, and then we all regained our equanimity and I my positive attitude. Gin lounged in the doorway as she always did, obstructing my path while I went about collecting hats, mittens, coats, shopping bags and the pushchair and I didn't swear at her once. 'Are your pants still dry?' I gushed at Drew. 'There's a *good* boy. Let's have a little wee-wee before we go to the Post Office. Becky, I think he can manage his own penis now.'

I was all patience and maternal warmth.

Why had I never had such an idea before? I wondered, as I searched the house for Becky's wellingtons. Why had I allowed such deadness of spirit to grow upon me, wearing me down until I lost interest in practically everything? How silly I had been, how feeble, how weak-minded. One must not allow oneself to be so easily defeated. Why, I was a new woman already.

'Becky, where are your wellingtons?'

'It's not raining.'

'I know it's not raining, my love, but I need your wellingtons for Drew.'

'They'll be too big for him.'

'Now don't argue, there's a good – '

'Put his shoes on,' she ordered decisively. 'His new little red shoes which we bought for him last week when we went on the bus and the lady in the shoe shop said what bee-eautiful hair I had.' She preened.

'Becky, you know he stood in a bucket of water in those shoes. And his old ones,' I said quickly, forestalling her, 'are outside. Now where – '

'Well, scrape the poo off them.'

I broke. '*Stop arguing with me! Where are your bloody wellingtons?*'

'I don't know,' she said.

We managed to get out of the house at last, unbattered save mentally, and set off for the sole shop in Lottabridge, the Post office-cum-General Store. The day had warmed up and if I sniffed determinedly enough I thought that I could smell spring. A new season, a new approach to life, a new me. Better yet, the old me regained, but one couldn't have everything. Ahead of me the hills rose with a lovely, gently undulating line. Beyond lay a popular seaside resort and, nearer, our small market town and another village called Massey. All were hidden behind the hills, on which we could see sheep moving and hear the new lambs bleating. On a higher slope there grazed a herd of Highland cattle, unusual in this part of

16

England: graceful golden shaggy creatures with immensely long, near-horizontal horns. Mummy's favourite cows, Becky called them. They were, too.

It was a beautiful area in which to live, and I was grateful that the children were growing up here, but its very isolation was one of the negative factors in my life. Another was the hills themselves. If you have ever tried pushing a heavy tandem pushchair up a steep hill you know that one very soon ceases to appreciate beautiful surroundings. Even when I made Becky walk, which, despite her age, she did with very ill grace indeed, it was impossible to go very far from home.

Three women, wives of nurses who lived near to us, passed and nodded to me. I had learned by now not to stop for a chat. I did not fit in with these people and neither, though it mattered less to him, did Barry. Why, I was at first unable to fathom, for I had made friendly overtures in the beginning, I had not been standoffish. Nor had they, but we had all quickly found that we had no common ground at all – except children. And on the subject of children we differed so greatly that it was embarrassing. These mothers were contented with their lot, happy to gaze at the television every night after their offspring went to bed, while I wanted activity, creative thought, mental stimulation. Probably the mere knowledge that we had no television was enough to set us apart. My conversations with them, self-conscious and too eager, were greeted by bewilderment or amused incredulity. Too late I had discovered that it was not politic to speak of reading poetry to the children or playing games of fantasy and imagination with them. The women here were too busy being Good Mothers – cleaning the house, turning out the cupboards, sewing patches on dungarees – to have time for such non-sense. We were different and it showed. Not once had I been asked to one of their houses for coffee, and none of them had taken up my own invitations. Though I knew we would have little to say to each other, I would have liked such companionable visiting. We met weekly at playgroup, exchanged a few words, and that was all.

Then I saw Rose, who had at least favoured me with her enmity. Rose was an old arthritic lady who habitually stood in her doorway, rain or shine, to see what was going on, and who had been friendly to me until a fracas occurred concerning Ginny and her own dog. I had never been forgiven for it and now she steadfastly refused to acknowledge my presence, looking straight through me with a cold, bold stare even when I greeted her. I had persisted with the greetings for several weeks, thinking that she would eventually relent, but she did not, and ultimately I had given up. Now all three of us, for the children had somehow picked up the discord, returned her hostile glare.

It was all very depressing.

Further down the hill, however, was Gloria Griffith, out with her grotesquely obese Labrador and cheerily waving to me. She was a small, thin, vitally alive lady and how she had managed to retain her vitality and her lively personality in this village was something of a mystery to me. She it was who had told me Becky could certainly win the Miss Pears competition. Gloria was so uninhibited, so outgoing, that she cared nothing whether people were 'different' or not. She was herself something of an eccentric, dressing her fine-boned body in the clothes of a young girl and evidently still feeling like one, but with a face that was well into middle age.

We came level, she said '*Hello*, darlings', to the children, and let the Labrador lick them lavishly. Drew giggled, Becky was actually knocked backwards into his lap by the weight of the affection, and Gloria gave her lovely laugh and apologised. We talked, or she talked and I listened, enjoying her liveliness, and then we went our different ways.

'That's *much* better,' I said, cheered by the meeting. 'Isn't it nice, children, to meet friendly people? Not everybody is friendly, you know.'

'Why not?' enquired Becky. 'Are they sad?'

Were they sad? No, on the whole I thought not. Just – self-contained? Reserved? Afraid of contact? What was it that made people able to shut out other people? I was not at all good at it.

But the thoughtful mood was abruptly shattered, thoughtful moods being, after all, a luxury in this job.

'DADA!'

Drew had suddenly sent forth a piercing yell which echoed around the valley for several seconds. This was his usual way

18

of announcing to Barry that we were waiting for him outside the hospital. 'No, love,' I said, after my eardrums had stopped vibrating, 'we're not meeting Daddy now. We're going – '

'DADA!'

Joyfully and wickedly Becky joined in, although she knew our destination perfectly well. But it convinced Drew, who could see the hospital through the bare trees, that he was right. I winced at Becky's incredible voice and glanced apprehensively at the bedroom windows of night nurses. 'Dada! DADA! Dada! DADA!'

'Now stop it. Do I have to smack you?' I could hear my voice, high and ineffectual as some poor student teacher's voice drowning in a classroom of unruly adolescents. '*Stop it*! Why must I say everything three times?'

But I knew why. It was because I did not administer discipline quickly enough or harshly enough. The din continued as I pushed doggedly onward, each child egging on the other. I felt my positive attitude slipping. Again. There were so many ways you could handle this. There was an argument for allowing, even encouraging, high spirits, the life force, the shout that was like the morning star. There was another for knocking their heads together. I had, after all, told them to stop.

We were approaching the shop. Four-year-old Tommy stood on the doorstep waiting for us, half horrified by my patent lack of control, half enjoying, in a sniggering way, witnessing such licence. In the same way will the puritanical thrill to a glimpse of the lascivious.

The sight of his face decided me. I leaned over the pushchair and administered two swift, very hard smacks on two right legs. (You have to smack hard in cold weather in order to penetrate the layers of trousers and tights. It is sometimes difficult to adjust when the hot weather comes.)

The shouts of DADA stopped instantly, to be replaced after one second by equally loud roars of outrage, or pain, or both. I left them bawling in the pushchair outside the shop and went in, saying with bright hypocrisy, 'Hello, Tommy, how are you?'

He gave me his little suspicious, half-averted smile, and

19

remained outside to watch the show.

With equally bright hypocrisy, Marjory, the proprietor's wife, said, 'Dear oh dear, what's the matter with those two?' I was sure that she despised my two children as much for being loud, vital and free, as I despised her one for being furtive, secretive and sneaky. We had frequent warm friendly discussions about our children.

'Morning, Annabelle,' said Ivan jovially.

'Morning,' I said gloomily. I had given up correcting him. You would think that, stamping my Child Benefit book each week as he did, he would know my name.

I brooded on this as I made my frugal way round the shelves, mentally totting up pennies as I went. Names, I have always felt, are important. The use of one's given name is, or should be, an indication of friendship, warming the person addressed just as a more direct expression of personal regard would do. This opinion is not, I know, shared by the rest of the modern world which disdains to use the formal Miss or Mrs. (Ms, I concede, poses serious problems of pronunciation.) Jane Austen would have had a fit. Mr Darcy and Miss Bennet remained Mr Darcy and Miss Bennett right up to the moment of their betrothal. Imagine the intimate thrill experienced by both at the first use of their given names!

Advertisers of consumer goods know about this thrill. Circulars drop through your letter box, obsequious and insultingly personal: 'Dear Amabel, Here is the opportunity which you, as a housewife, have been waiting for. Amabel, our computer has given YOU the chance to be Mother of the Year! All you have to do . . .'

Computers apart, Barry was the only person I knew who had heard, and used, my name correctly the first time. People almost always said Annabelle, except my library ticket which said Mabel (misread from the form I had filled in). I was so disgusted by this that, perversely, I made no attempt to correct it. Amabel means 'lovable'. This is nutritious ego food and one of the reasons why I like people to get it right. Doubtless I was lovable once.

I had, naturally, investigated names for the children before we labelled them for life. Drew (Andrew) meant manly. He would probably turn out to be gay, just to spite me for being

20

so besotted with his little body. Rebecca – well, that was my master stroke. It meant 'charmer'. Or 'ensnarer'. Either was accurate; it all depended on your point of view.

I heaved my basketful of groceries on to the counter. Ivan was busy serving another customer and Marjory was in the stockroom, so I went outside. There was always the chance that one of the children had died of grief or exposure. But no.

'We're being *ever* so good,' said the ensnarer, in her most honeyed voice. Tommy watched me. I felt, as always, like some small squirming thing being peered at through a microscope by his cold, fishy eye.

I allowed them to come into the shop and Becky and Tommy immediately disappeared into the back whilst Drew remained seated in the pushchair, just out of reach of the sweets and in a puddle which I hoped no-one would notice. I began the lengthy process of asking for quarters of this and half pounds of that (the cheapest margarine, rubber sausages, plastic cheese, real dolly mixtures) and indulged meanwhile in my daily chat with Ivan.

When you live in an insular village like Lottabridge and all your neighbours have a 22″ colour television but no books, you find yourself somewhat starved of conversation. Occasionally Barry and I had a conversation. But Barry was not a chatterer. He was what they call quiet. Extremely quiet. Often the extremeness of his quietness drove me to distraction. '*Talk* to me!' I would demand. 'Tell me about your day. Recite little anecdotes: what the patients did, what the nurses said, how they said it!' Because that's what I would have done, if I'd had any decent anecdotes to recite. But such demands plunged Barry straight into purgatory and, as usual, I ended up feeling guilty for having made them.

Well, beggars can't be choosers. I would see no-one else that day, or the next, or the next, seemingly ad infinitum. Ivan didn't converse but he did chat. We chatted. Drew sang happily in his puddle. Becky had not yet emerged in tears because Tommy had hit/pushed/pinched her or pulled her hair. There were, for the moment, no customers. So Ivan told me, at length, about the walk he and Marjory and Tommy had taken on the hills last Sunday and I told Ivan how few country walks I managed because of tottering Drew. Ivan

21

reminded me that I had a pushchair, I reminded him that rough hill country and heavy pushchairs were irreconcilable. Ivan recommended a day at a particular beauty spot, I told him yet again that we had no car. Ivan mentioned buses, I mentioned bus fares.

I am becoming, I thought as I paid him an exorbitant amount, a sour, discontented shrew. And yet – people with cars! I would dearly love to see Ivan or Marjory climb unaided on to a bus with a toddler under one arm, a second small child held by the other hand, the enormous frame of a collapsed double pushchair clasped between the knees, and a purse with the correct fare in it protruding from between the teeth. Not to mention three bags of shopping. I would make sure the bus was full, too.

I smiled guiltily at Ivan to soften the impression I had probably made (in closed communities, as in prisons, one needs good opinions) and began to make noises signifying departure. Becky crashed out through the door marked Private, screaming that Tommy had hit her and pursued by Tommy himself, who was bent on dragging her back inside. Marjory emerged from the stockroom, her lips pursed tight in disapproval. She glanced briefly at Becky and uttered a significant silence. It was familiar. The silence said, 'Your child is a spoilt, temperamental, over-emotional cry-baby.' She was probably right. On the other hand, as my own loud silence retorted, *her* child was a repressed, aggressive and perverted bully.

We smiled affably at each other.

I was juggling in the doorway with all my paraphernalia when Ivan called me. I jammed on the brake and, since I couldn't hear a word over Becky's caterwauling, went back to the counter. 'Sorry, Annabelle, I almost forgot to say there was a telephone message for you.'

I brightened. A message, any message, was out of the ordinary and therefore welcome.

'Your visitors will be arriving tomorrow,' he informed me.

I looked blank. 'Visitors? What visitors? Becky, do be *quiet!*'

He looked at a scribbled note in his hand. 'Rayner Lamb?' he said doubtfully. 'Is that the name?'

I stared, incredulous. '*Rayner*! But they're in – oh Lord!'
Frantically I looked round the shop at all the food I hadn't
bought and should now buy but couldn't afford anyway. As
for booze . . . Patrick and Rayner were great drinkers . . .

Absently I thanked him and somehow got the pushchair
through the doorway before the queue that had formed outside became abusive. Becky quietened as we slogged our way
up the hill. She knew I would give her a love and a sweet as
soon as we got home. I always did when Tommy had used his
brute male strength on her. Now that she was quiet I could
absorb the astonishing news that Rayner (and Patrick presumably) who were supposed to be somewhere in Africa, were
going to turn up on my doorstep tomorrow. They were our
best, our oldest friends. Rayner, in fact, was the closest friend
I had ever had. The two of us had shared the same sense of
humour, the same enthusiasms, and sometimes even (until
we met Barry and Patrick) the same boyfriends. It would be
marvellous to see her again. But . . .

Yesterday the news would have been the most wonderful
tonic. Today –

I realised at last what was troubling me.

'But I want to write my *novel*!'

When we got home it was time to start cooking lunch. I had
been striving desperately for about three years to become the
sort of organised housewife who has a casserole in the oven by
nine in the morning. Needless to say I had never succeeded.
So I launched into the usual midday muddle of sausages and
demands, thankful that Barry was not coming home. Barry
was the most obliging and co-operative of men. He understood, although I frequently accused him of not doing, that
cooking was, for me, sheer hell; that cooking with starving
children fighting all round me was worse than anything
Lucifer had endured in the burning lake; and so he ate at the
hospital whenever I seemed on the point of hurling plates. He
would do this for a week or so (though we could ill afford it)
and then the unbroken loneliness of the days would begin to
tell and I would ask in a hurt voice why he never came home
for lunch anymore? So we would return to frantic lunch-
hours, watching the clock while I scurried round in a bad

temper. The situation was made considerably worse by my never knowing what time he was going to arrive, hospital administration being quite as disorganised as I was.

Today, however, we could be relatively relaxed. Nothing of any import occurred except that Drew decided it was more fun to suck his sausages and spit out the remains into Gin's waiting jaws than it was to swallow them; and that he had the most terrific erection during the rice pudding.

It was Drew himself who noticed it first, peering interestedly downward behind his tray. Becky, who missed very little, peered too. I would not have been human if I, too, did not crane my neck. 'Oh, look,' said Becky, tapping the protruberance through Drew's terry-towelling pants. Drew gave a throaty chuckle. 'That's his penis getting big. Shall I see if it's moving about?' She got down off her chair and stared fixedly between his knees.

'Well, is it?' I asked, just as fascinated as she was. After a moment she shook her head. 'No, not today.' She climbed up again and resumed her pudding. 'I used to have a penis,' she informed me, 'a long time ago, when I was in your tummy.'

I shook my head. 'No, you've never had a penis. At least – ' I stopped. I had already forgotten most of what I'd learned about early foetal development. At what stage did potential gender become actual? I had better clear this up now, for both our sakes, before I started attributing to Becky supernatural powers or uncanny feats of memory.

I got out the Baby Book. The rice pudding was abandoned. '"Chromosomes and Genes,"' I read. We all looked intently at the relevant paragraph. I paraphrased. 'Mummies have an X chromosome. Daddies have X *and* Y chromosomes. If Daddy's X chromosome meets Mummy's X chromosome it will be a girl baby. Immediately.' I shut the book.

Becky nodded comprehendingly. 'I used to have a penis.'

I sighed. So much for educating my young. Still, it was a great improvement on the bad old days when children were kept in anatomical ignorance and brides were horror-struck by what was expected of them on their wedding night. A patient of Barry's (an old lady in the Occupational Therapy Unit and of perfectly sound mind) had told him that not until the *moment of birth* had she realised where her first baby was coming from. She had believed throughout her pregnancy that her stomach would burst open.

'Did it hurt,' asked Becky, 'when your baby popped out?'

I eyed her. Definitely she was starting another phase of mind reading. 'A bit,' I said mendaciously. Then, quickly, in case she'd picked up the wrong thought, 'Look, you know where the baby comes out, don't you? I've told you before. Through the vagina.' I pointed to the place on her own body to make quite sure she understood.

'Did you cry?'

'I said "Ouch".'

She thought a little. I glanced at Drew, wanting to put him down for a sleep. But this might be important. I waited.

'If I don't have any babies,' Becky said ruminatively, 'I shall probably cry.'

Yes, I thought, sensitive intuitive child, you probably will. But if you do have babies you'll cry for the rest of your life, for one reason or another.

I pinned two nappies on Drew, kissed his infinitely kissable feet, and put him to bed.

The day was two-thirds gone. I had achieved nothing, but then I always achieved nothing. That was what was so mind-destroying. The only way to get a modicum of peace was to do housework all day long, non-stop. The moment you paused for a cup of tea they were on you like a horde of locusts, digging their knees into your groin and their elbows into your neck in an effort to unseat each other, poking storybooks under your nose and demanding games. I once had a friend who regularly took her morning coffee-break standing behind the kitchen door with the Hoover running noisily.

Doing housework all day, however, was no solution either. Dustpans were emptied over the dog and teddies dipped in buckets; sewing baskets became lethal ammunition; ironing was commandeered for dressing up or mopping furtive puddles; and *everything* was subject to endless interruptions. So I would find myself trying to look busy without actually committing myself to anything of importance. There is nothing more exhausting.

How on earth, I often wondered, did single parents manage? How did parents of handicapped children manage? How did our great-grandmothers manage with their nine or twelve or fourteen children? But that was easy to answer: they died at forty, and were probably considerably relieved to do so.

Drew asleep, I tried to think of some absorbing activities for Becky which would allow me to do a couple of jobs: wash the dishes, tidy up, make a blancmange. The problem was that there were very few absorbing activities left for Becky. Together we ran through the list.

'Can I have my recorder?'

'No. I've put it away. Remember why?'

She nodded, unperturbed. 'Well then, can I have my plasticine?'

'No. You kept treading it into the carpet so I threw it into the dustbin.'

'It was an accident,' she said, flagrantly fibbing.

'It was not.'

A histrionic sigh. 'All right. Can I have my make-up?'

'Absolutely not. You are not having your make-up again for a long, *long* time.'

'But what can I *do*?' she said plaintively. 'I've got nothing to *do*.'

I thought. Wooden skittles: confiscated (for hitting Drew with them); crayons: confiscated (for drawing on the walls and also for eating them); picture cards: confiscated (what was left of them).

'Well,' I said doubtfully, 'you could do some painting, I suppose. If you promise not to paint yourself again.'

'I promise.'

So I put a plastic apron on her, spread the newspaper, got out the paints, the brushes, the water and a sheet of drawing paper, pushed up her sleeves and left her seated at the dining-room table. Four minutes later, as I was starting the dishes, she came in and announced brightly, 'Finished.'

I looked at her. We had Words. I washed her face, neck, arms, apron, the paintbrushes, the sink, the table, the chair.

I finished the dishes.

Then I let her mix the blancmange into a paste with milk and sugar. The saucepan had dog hairs in it after being used as a stepping stone.

After that she decided to go out to the sandpit. A miracle!

So I grew over-confident and made myself a pot of tea.

'Mummy,' she said, appearing just as I raised the cup to my lips, 'come outside with me because I'm lonely and a hedgehog might come.'

Drew woke up. Two hours had passed since I put him in his cot. Do you know what it is possible to do in two hours? You could walk six miles, fly two-thirds of the way to New York, watch half of *Gone with the Wind* or all of *Waiting for Godot*, write several pages of a novel, listen to *Under Milkwood*, read the complete works of Confucius, or throw yourself from the top of the Empire State Building seven hundred and ninety-nine times.

An hour to go till tea and Barry's arrival. Thankfully Drew could now bear the brunt of Becky's bullying instead of me. I tidied the cot and re-made the beds which Becky and Drew had unmade while I was doing the cot; then I did the cot again because they had undone it while I was doing the beds. Then I shut them in the bathroom and sat on the stairs and calmed down.

Teatime. Boiled eggs, luncheon meat and bread and margarine. The first few mouthfuls were always consumed with silent intensity so I took advantage of the lull, threw some mince and onions into a frying pan and put some water on to heat for our rice. A piece of bread came sailing into the kitchen. Gin ate it. Becky shouted urgently, 'Drew wants to do a wee-wee!' I rushed in, hauled Drew from his highchair, put him on the potty, went back to drop rice into the boiling water. Becky said conversationally, 'No, not like that, Drew,' and I rushed in again. Too late. I got a floorcloth and mopped up. I put Drew back in his chair. The rice boiled over. Becky shouted, 'We're ready for our blancmange now.' I dabbed frantically at the top of the cooker. Gin burned her tongue licking up the drips and started to run round in circles. 'I – want – some – blancmange – please,' said Becky, very distinctly. Another piece of bread came in. I took the blancmange out of the fridge and inspected it.

'It's not set,' I said desperately.

'Let me see,' demanded Becky, and foolishly I took the bowl to the table.

'I want some.'

'Say "please",' I ordered.

'Please.'

'Well, you can't have any. It's not set. Look, it's all slithery.'

'But you said I could,' she began.

'No I didn't – '

'You made me say please! And then you said I – (starting to sob) *couldn't have any!*' (sobbing tragically).

I gazed hopelessly into the sloppy pink mess and extracted a dog hair. Drew pointed at the bowl and began to bang his spoon on the table. Becky stopped sobbing, grinned, and joined in. BANG BANG BANG. I shouted, 'Stop banging!' BANG BANG BANG BANG. I smacked them both. They screamed. The rice boiled over again.

Barry came in.

Chapter Three

I hate him, I thought passionately, banging things about in the kitchen. I hate him, it's not fair, why are they so nice as soon as he comes home? In the next room the children were crawling all over Barry, giggling, being tossed, being tickled, pretending to be lions and growling. I stirred the burnt mess of mince savagely. At least he had had a decent lunch at the hospital.

He came into the kitchen and sniffed. 'Smells good.'

'It smells terrible,' I said sourly. 'It's burnt.' I looked at him. So far I had barely spoken to him. All day I waited for him to come home, and by the time he came I was feeling too ill-tempered even to greet him.

'Bad day?' The tone was understanding and I felt an immediate urge to pour forth my sufferings. This was why he was, or would be when he was qualified, such a good psychiatric nurse. That and his own reticence. No wonder I talked his head off. For now, though, I contented myself with, 'No worse than usual. A life in the day of Amabel Dennell.' He laughed. 'How was yours?'

'Oh . . .' The laugh faded. 'A bit grim. Tell you later.'

'All right. Look, do you want to eat this muck?' I showed it to him and he hid his grimace well and said it was fine and said I was fine too for managing so well and gave me a hug. I was never sure if this kind of reassurance was genuine or if it was what his psychiatry books called Positive Reinforcement, but anyway it worked and I felt a bit better. Then he put on one of his horrible records while I dished up and I immediately felt worse again; but managed, for once, to keep quiet.

It was not simply because Barry was a few years younger than me that he liked the sort of shrill, grating, discordant music that brought out my most vicious murderous instincts. It was also because, artistically, he was more innovative, less conservative than me. I wrote, or used to write, 'straight' novels, nothing cryptic or obscure, the action taking place in chronological sequence and all the ends neatly tied up. He wrote deep profound blank verse full of hidden allusions and complicated, deliberate ambiguities. I liked Thomas Hardy, Tennyson, Milton, Henry James. He raved about Sam Beckett, James Joyce, Ezra Pound, and thought *Tristram Shandy* (which I had been quite unable to read at University) the cleverest thing ever written. Not unnaturally this cultural generation gap extended to music. I liked almost all music except the sort he liked best: the sort he was playing now.

I endured the wailing shrieks and repetitive threshings of a minor chord, remembering just in time that I had asked once before if the needle was stuck at this point and that it hadn't been, and then, thank goodness, it finished and Barry put on some Bach. We sat down to our feast and prepared to repel boarders.

'There's something I want to do tonight,' I said with repressed excitement, 'so let's do baths and bedtimes as soon as we've eaten.'

He nodded, mildly interested but not wild with curiosity as I would have been. We ate, swatting at hands as, in different circumstances, one might swat at mosquitoes.

'Guess,' I said, 'who's coming tomorrow.'

He thought, and I watched his lean, almost ascetic face. Some nights Barry was very handsome, and this was one of them. He had loosened his tie and opened his shirt to reveal a hairy chest, and this gave him a kind of devil-may-care buc-caneering look, especially as he also needed a shave. His hair was clean and fluffy and that was flattering too. Usually Barry suffered from excessively greasy hair, or rather, he didn't suffer at all but I did.

'You're looking very nice,' I said, and he smiled.

'Tell me,' he said, and I told him. 'Good God. I thought they were in Marrakech.'

'*I* thought they were in Kenya.'

30

'That was months ago. Oh, that's great news.' He was delighted, and I thought penitently that, his job apart, Barry must find life quite as dull as I did. Perhaps duller, since he had not had the chance to go gallivanting around the world, footloose and fancy free, as I had. Like me he had no social life at all. Barry was too quiet, too academic perhaps to make friends easily.

'I'd better give you a cheque,' he said. 'Get some bottles in.'

I laughed. 'That was my first thought too. Can we afford it?'

'Oh, they'll pay their whack. They always have before.' He pushed away his half-eaten meal. 'Is there any pudding?'

'Yes.' I got up. 'There's rice pudding left over from – Oh.' I stopped and looked at our plates. 'Oh,' I said, 'sorry. I don't suppose you want rice pudding after boiled rice.'

'Not really,' he said, quite gently. I stood there, biting my lip, while Becky leaned on the table, surreptitiously chewing. 'Don't worry. I'll have a honey sandwich instead.'

'Ah. Well, there was a little mishap with the honey.'

'There's some pink balange,' Becky informed him.

'Fine. I'll have that.'

'But it's not set.'

Barry sank his head in his hands. 'Just tell me what to eat,' he moaned, 'and I'll eat it.'

'I know,' I said brightly, 'let's bath these two first and get them to bed. The blancmange will be set by then.'

'But it's for the children,' protested the inconsistent Becky.

Barry swung her on to his knee. 'We'll leave some for you,' he promised. 'Now, what sort of bath would you like? An upside-down one?'

He got up and dangled her by the heels. She shrieked joyously. 'Yes!'

'Would you like ketchup in it?'

'Yes!'

'Would you like vinegar in it?'

'Yes!'

'Would you like salt and pepper in it?'

'Yes!' She was giggling helplessly.

'Right. Off we go.' He slung her over his shoulder and took her away, Drew staggering at his heels making noises that meant 'Me too'. I watched, smiling and faintly envious. It must be easy, I reflected, when you hadn't had them all day . . .

And now, at last, they were gone. Upstairs, wondrous silence reigned. Downstairs, the living-room curtains were closed and we sat cosily before the hearth in our battered second-hand armchairs, breathing in the fumes of the paraffin stove. Several months ago we had ordered a huge consignment of logs which filled the shed with heady smells of beech and pine and which we used to supplement the weekly bag of coal that was all we could afford. Now the logs were used up and coal alone got consumed at such a rate that we had been forced to cancel its delivery. If spring had only come when it was supposed to . . .

Barry had changed into an old pair of cords and a jumper with big holes in the elbows. Every time I saw the holes I was pierced with guilt. Once I had even gone into a wool shop, intending to do some darning, but for the price of one ball of wool I could have cooked two liver dinners. So I came out again and got liver instead.

'I'm sorry about that jumper,' I said, not for the first time.

He glanced at the sleeves. 'It's all right. The trick is to wear a matching shirt, then the holes don't show.'

His eyes returned to *Some Illuminating Aspects of Post-Victorian Theories Concerning the Lunar Phenomenom in Mental Health* so I fell silent. If I kept talking he would lay the book down on his knee without actually closing it, and I would feel (probably rightly) that he was dying to get back to it and that nothing I could say would stimulate his brain cells half as much as its pages did. Further, that what I was saying was actually *boring*: domestic trivia at its worst. Like listening to a tape recording of my diary.

So I put my feet up on a large woolly cross-eyed dog, and relaxed. In a minute, when I felt that Barry had wound down after his working day, I would tell him about my novel. A few minutes after that, when he went to play at crocodiles, I would actually *begin* the novel. I should manage, I reckoned, about two hours' writing time before bed.

I sat on. This morning I had been on fire with impatience to begin. Now the edge had been taken off, various parts of me ached and my mind felt like soggy cardboard. But that would pass as soon as I picked up the pen.

Barry put down his book. And closed it. 'Do you want any help with the preparations?' he asked.

'What preparations?'

'For Rayner and Patrick.'

'No, thank you. I'm not preparing anything tonight. I have other plans for tonight.'

As before, he nodded. It was maddening. How could he be so incurious? 'I'll get Becky's room ready in the morning. I don't know when they're coming but I'm sure there'll be time for that.'

He looked apprehensive. 'You're putting them in Becky's room?'

'I think that's best, don't you? The last time we moved Drew, when your mother came, he was upset all night because he was in different surroundings. Becky's old enough to understand what's happening. I expect she'll be quite pleased.'

'Oh, I see. You're putting Becky in with Drew.'

'No. With us.'

'Oh God,' he said.

'If I put them together they'll keep waking each other up.'

'I suppose so,' he said with a sigh. Then, 'How long are Rayner and Patrick staying?'

I glanced at him suspiciously. He hardly ever complained about sexual deprivation though God knows he suffered it quite often; but maybe I misjudged him: maybe he was merely thinking of an horrendous early-morning Becky waking up in a bed only feet away from ours. 'I've no idea.'

He got up. 'Well, if you don't need me I'm off for my session. Want to join me?'

I pulled a face. 'I'm still stiff from last night.'

'You'll get less stiff as you do more of it,' he assured me.

'I won't,' I assured him, 'because I'm not going to do more of it. Listen. Sit down again. I have a project I want to tell you about.'

He obeyed, eyes fixed on me in that encouraging way which came naturally to him and which made his patients open up their poor confused hearts. He had had this quality ever since

I knew him, long before he discovered that he could use it in a career. Sympathy and genuine caring for the weak, the outcast, the misfit. Tramps used to see him coming a mile off. I had often seen them veer towards him when, as students, we walked across the city together. Probably they thought him a soft touch. However they regarded it they recognised the quality instantly, sometimes even crossing the road to him, selecting him from hundreds of others and requesting the price of a cup of tea. He always carried loose change for just this purpose and his habit was to delve into his pocket and bring out some coins without looking at them. It happened repeatedly and seemed to me most uncanny and yet something to be vastly proud of. Especially as, because of it, we frequently lacked the price of a cup of tea ourselves.

'I'm going to write another novel.'

For all that I tried to keep my voice flat, my feelings showed and his eyes lit up in pleased response. 'Tell me,' he said, and leaned back, crossing his legs.

I was now sufficiently educated in the language of Non-Verbal Communication to recognise this move and to be amused by it, but not sufficiently inured to fail to succumb. (Actually I would have told him about it even if he'd put his head back into *Some Illuminating Aspects* but this reaction was undoubtedly better and anyway it was good practice for him.)

'Becky gave me the idea this morning. She's at it again, by the way.' I related the mind-reading incident and he groaned.

'I thought she'd finished with that.'

'She's having a resurgence. Is that the right word?'

'It'll do. Go on.'

'The novel will be about someone with ESP, someone who shows the first signs in childhood, like Becky; and his, or her, parents are surprised but don't really take it seriously. And then as the child grows up his, or her, powers strengthen. And he, or she, hides them, sensing that they make her, or him, different.'

'Just a minute,' he said. 'Is it a her or a him?'

I hesitated. 'I don't know yet.'

'Hmm,' he said.

'And then the rest of the story will be about, er, his or her experiences and attempts to fit into normal everyday life.'

He waited. He said, 'Is that it?'

'It's a brief synopsis,' I said defensively.

'But you have the details in your head.'

'Well, not yet,' I admitted, 'I'll get those as I go along.'

'Ye-es . . . Some authors work that way, I know. Is that what you used to do?'

I nodded eagerly. 'Sometimes. Sometimes I did.'

'And did it work?'

A pause. 'Sometimes,' I said again, less eagerly. He laughed. 'I got into a terrible tangle once or twice, but that was when I was writing mysteries, you know, who-dunnits. I couldn't always work out who dunnit, myself. But this book will be different.'

'How?'

How. 'Well – there's no plot, for one thing,' I said vaguely.

'No plot?'

'Oh, not no plot, but – you know – a gradual development of a situation rather than a series of interdependent incidents.' I was rather pleased with this last phrase, and he saw that I was, and grinned. 'What do you think?' I finished.

'I think it's got a lot of potential,' he said, and I beamed at him. 'But – ' He hesitated.

'But?'

'Well – how much do you know about ESP?'

'ESP? Thought reading – dreams of the future – knowing where dead bodies are when the police can't find them . . . Oh, that's clairvoyance, isn't it?'

There was a silence. I did not break it. People who had not known Barry for long did not always realise that his silences portended speech. You had to be patient. Sometimes the silence would be considerably longer than the utterance which eventually followed it. He called it marshalling his thoughts. For someone on the garrulous side, like me, this marshalling was a very great trial and often I failed and started talking again. Then, when I paused, the whole thing would start over. Worse still were the times when I imagined he was marshalling and waited, only to find that he had finished several minutes ago and was waiting for me.

At last he enquired, 'What was *Crows Flying Sideways*

35

about? The one that was published?'

'You know what it was about. You read it. So did your mother.' I was proud of that fact.

'Never mind my mother,' he said, amused. 'What was it about?'

'Oh, *Barry*. All right. It was about life on a farm. Milking cows, working the fields, wading knee-deep in muddy cow-shit in the winter, swearing at flies in the summer – '

'Yes. And how did you know about all those things?'

'I'd *done* them,' I said, exasperated. 'You know perfectly well I worked – '

'Right,' he interrupted, 'you'd done them. It was authentic and the authenticity showed. The novel was published.'

'And flopped,' I said resentfully.

'Doesn't matter. It was published.'

'You're saying I don't know enough about my subject to write this novel.'

He said nothing. I got up to fiddle with the wick on the paraffin stove. It was burning unevenly and smelling. 'You have a point,' I conceded. 'I'll do some research.'

'Fine. Good luck.' He came over and kissed me. 'I'm glad you've found something to be enthusiastic about.'

'Huh,' I said, and grinned. 'No, you're quite right. I don't know enough about it. But I will,' I promised. 'And in the meantime – '

He turned in the doorway. I remembered that Becky had recently lectured me about going on talking to Daddy when he wanted to go, so I didn't launch into a lengthy account of what I was going to do in the meantime. I said, 'I'll think.'

He smiled at me and went out.

In the meantime, I thought happily, scurrying about, I can certainly make a start on Chapter One. I found several pens, one of which worked, and no decent paper at all. After some rummaging I found a half-used drawing book of Becky's. I brought the paraffin stove into the dining-room and sat down at the table, the tools of my trade before me.

Now. Title?

I thought. No title came to me. Never mind. That could wait. 'Chapter One.'

I needed, first, a gripping opening, something that would

immediately catch the reader's attention and hold it. Something, perhaps, like the mother's stunned reaction to her daughter's (son's?) first indication that she (he?) had extra-sensory perception.

I decided on a boy. I wrote firmly, 'Jane Walthers' jaw dropped in amazement. She stared in horrified disbelief at her small son.'

No. Too melodramatic, and the second word was clumsy with an apostrophe in that position. I crossed it out.

'Jane Walthers stared aghast at the innocent face of her two-year-old son.'

Better. I crossed out 'innocent' and substituted 'smiling'; then crossed that out too and left the word 'face' without an adjective.

'Timothy had been talking fluently for only a few weeks yet already'

Rubbish. I disposed of that with one sweep of my pen. Gripping, it's got to be gripping.

'Was it really possible that this child, this baby, could *read her mind*?'

I stopped to have a chew at the pen. This was beginning to sound like a sensational article in a Sunday newspaper. Maybe a more gradual build-up would be better.

'Jane Walthers had been working in the garden while her baby son took his afternoon nap.' Now why did that sound American? 'It was an ordinary day, full of ordinary activities. There was nothing to suggest that this day was to bring bewilderment and fear to the young mother.'

I pushed out my lips in disapproval. Too many ordinaries, too many days, too many 'th' sounds.

Oh, not that again. Surely I was now far enough from my literature tutorials to have lost that awful compulsion to scrutinise and criticise every syllable?

I was, I thought dully, tired. It was nine in the evening. I suddenly realised that I had not washed the dishes. Why hadn't I remembered it earlier, when Barry had offered his help? Perhaps he would do them when he came downstairs. No. That wasn't fair.

I got up, put the kettle on to boil, washed up quickly, came back with my cup of tea and resumed.

I decided to change the whole approach.

'Timothy Walthers was only two and a half years old when his mother discovered that he had well-developed powers of extra-sensory perception.'

Too long. Most readers would not even bother to finish the sentence.

I drank my tea wearily. I had forgotten how tiring writing was. If I could only get past the initial stage of having to think, and reach the point where it just *came* in a long beautiful flow . . . It was, I remembered, rather like rowing along a river, straining at the oars, and then suddenly, blessedly, being caught and carried effortlessly along by the current. (And into the rapids, I added mentally, there to be dashed to pieces on the rocks.)

I must not get either cynical or disillusioned. It was simply that I was rather rusty and very tired.

Drew woke up. I swore, and went to find his bottle. Periodically we made feeble efforts to get him off it and on to a cup with a spout. He accepted the cup during the day but for his night wakings only the comfort of the teat would do. Barry had pointed out that Drew might stop the night wakings if he were refused the bottle but so far I hadn't had the heart to try it.

He had his leg stuck down a hole in the bottom sheet. The hole hadn't been there this afternoon. I changed the sheet for an equally threadbare one, gave him a drink, gave him a love, put him back in his cot.

After ten minutes away from them my few sentences looked worse than ever. As I gazed at them I felt my eyes blur with exhaustion. There was not a single creative thought in my head. All I wanted to do was sit down with a book, somebody else's book, some light escapism; or go to bed. But it was too early to go to bed.

Becky screamed horribly. I ran, and arrived at her door seconds after Barry. 'MY BEAR!!' screeched Becky in her raucous sleep-voice.

I retrieved the bear from the floor and tucked him in next to her. She fell asleep again instantly. Barry, underpants-clad and sweating, shook his head in wry amazement, and returned to the eiderdown on our bedroom floor. I went downstairs in a rage.

What's the use? What is the bloody use? I'm too bloody tired to write anything and it's no bloody wonder. Bloody kids.

I put away the drawing paper and poked around in the fridge. There was half a bottle of flat cider left. I carted the paraffin stove back to the living-room and sat down with the bottle. Above me the ceiling shook as Barry thumped about. I knew those particular thumps. They signalled the Final Position.

After a while he came down, washed and wearing only his trousers. I surveyed him. 'You're getting brawny,' I said admiringly. 'The Yoga's working. Look at that muscular neck.' Then, irritably, 'You'll need new shirts if you keep this up.'

'Which of those remarks am I supposed to respond to? The admiring one or the grumpy one?'

'I'm not grumpy. Yes, I am grumpy. Have some flat cider.'

'Thanks. Judging by my homecoming you had a pretty grump-making day.'

'They're all grump-making. That's what you never seem to realise. Can you imagine, really with your whole being imagine, never seeing anyone but the kids and the people at the shop and you?'

'No,' he said, after a moment. 'No, I don't think I can.' He regarded me seriously.

'I know it must be lonely for people who live alone, but at least they can do their own thing,' I complained. 'Whereas I – bloody kids! In one sense, you know,' I added hurriedly, 'I'm crazy about them.'

'I know.'

'It's just that there's *so much* of them.'

'Yes.'

He sat down and looked at the plastic mug in his hand. We had only one china cup left and I had it. All our glasses had gone long ago.

'Still,' I said, more cheerfully, 'I wouldn't want them to be like Tommy. That child is so repressed, poor little thing.'

'"Poor little thing" indeed! You can't stand him.'

'No, I can't, but it's not his fault he's the way he is. It's Marjory. Do you know, when I once asked her if she had

39

breast-fed Tommy, she shuddered at the very idea? Actually *shuddered*.' I shook my head in wonder. 'God knows how she managed to conceive him. Remote control, probably.' I stopped. Better not get on to the subject of frigid women. I was too frigid myself, these days, to joke about it. 'How was the Yoga tonight?'

He looked pleased. 'You know that position I could only get halfway on? The *Prasarīta Pādottānāsana I*?'

'Yes?'

'Well, now I can get halfway for longer.'

'Congratulations.'

'Thank you.'

A pause. I thought about preparing the morning drinks and going to bed. That reminded me again about frigidity. If Becky was going to sleep in our room from tomorrow I ought to be co-operative again tonight.

Perhaps I would postpone bed for a bit longer.

'You were going to tell me about something grim that happened today.'

His face clouded. 'Yes. We had a suicide.'

'Oh . . . Who was it?'

'You know I can't tell you the names of short-term patients. Actually I've never mentioned her to you, because – Well, because I thought her history might upset you.' I waited, watching him, trying to gauge his feelings about the matter. Even now, after several years, I often had no idea how deep his emotions ran. 'She was a depression case,' he said. 'Very severe, couldn't reach her at all.'

'ECT?' I asked. ECT was Electro-convulsive Therapy, electric shock treatment which sometimes had spectacular results despite its bad press. We were now well past the days described in *One Flew Over the Cuckoo's Nest* when ECT was administered with great zeal and often all too little reason. Barry had reservations about it, I knew, partly because it was thought to speed senile dementia in old patients, but he had also reported several cases of highly successful treatment.

Now, however, he shook his head. 'They wouldn't give ECT when the depression had a cause, I mean a cause in reality, outside herself. Years ago they may have done, but not now.'

'Did you know she was likely to be suicidal?'

40

'Oh yes. It was on her file. We watched her, of course, but – ' He shrugged. 'It happens,' he said.

I didn't ask how she had committed suicide. He didn't tell me. I did ask, however, what was the 'cause outside herself' which had led to the depression.

'She had lost her two babies.'

'Oh.' I took a breath. 'In a – in a fire?'

'No. Cot deaths, two separate cot deaths twenty months apart.'

A little, cold feeling in the stomach. 'Cot deaths?'

'Sudden Infant Death Syndrome. Death occurs during sleep but not necessarily in the cot. They just call them cot deaths. So far no-one can explain what causes them.'

'Yes,' I said, 'I know – I know about cot deaths. But – *two*?'

'Oh yes,' he said. 'There was a case recently where a mother lost four babies in six years. Four babies just died in their sleep, one after another. No medical explanation.'

I just sat there, staring at him, thinking of my children asleep upstairs.

'And – your patient?'

'Volatile,' he said, 'from what I can gather. Though I never saw her looking anything but – like this.' He hunched low in his chair, wrapped his arms around himself and dropped his chin down on his chest. He stared sightlessly at the floor and rocked slightly. I turned cold.

He sat up again. 'Her husband couldn't cope with her after the second baby died. The marriage broke up. She broke up. She was brought to us.' He shrugged again. I knew from the short, matter-of-fact phrases that he had been hit hard by this, that he was wondering if he could somehow have prevented it. He had been doing this for too short a time to take it objectively, to learn dispassion. But then maybe objectivity and dispassion precluded being a good psychiatric nurse.

It was not the patient's suicide which upset me. I was glad she was dead.

I went into the kitchen and filled Drew's bottle and Becky's cup. I stood looking at them: the well-chewed teat, the blue cup with the spout.

I leaned against the sink and cried.

Chapter Four

Rayner and Patrick Lamb arrived at noon in a cloudburst. I had been paying the penalty for my laziness the previous evening. There was a ton or so of washing to sort and throw into the machine, the bathroom to clean (Rayner and Patrick, having no children, were fastidious about bathrooms), the hole-less sheets to unearth, Becky's little bed to move, several pounds of fluff under it to sweep, and the double mattress to make up. After all that I was hoarse from roaring at the children, who had insisted on helping me, so I gulped down a cup of tea before going out to hang up the clothes.

The sky looked threatening. I glanced anxiously up at it and even more anxiously back at the house, where someone was trying to murder someone else who didn't like it. After a minute Drew's screams became thickly muffled and I shouted at the open door, 'Leave him alone!'

'I didn't hurt him,' called Becky piously.

'You're comforting him.'

'I'm not,' she said indignantly. 'I'm giving him a love.'

Silently mouthing imprecations, I put down the pegs and went inside, where I found, after a prolonged hunt, shoes and anoraks. I struggled with Becky's kicking feet until I lost my temper and finally got both children into the garden. By now I could have hung up the washing four times over.

The job done, we came back in. I crawled round the kitchen floor wiping up muddy footprints. Gin came back in. I crawled round the floor again.

The heavens opened. So did the back door. And there they were.

'Typical!' exclaimed Patrick, shaking raindrops off his head. 'English weather! Hello, Ginny old girl. Amabel, how are you?'

Immediately the kitchen was too small. I was engulfed in what they call a bear hug.

'My washing's out there,' I said in dismay, staring past them at the downpour.

'Sod the washing,' said Rayner, and shut the door firmly. 'Now, where are they?'

'They' were hovering half-fearfully in the doorway of the dining-room. Patrick said heartily, 'Hello, you two!' His voice was much too loud and Drew's lip trembled. His eye sought mine, but I resisted an impulse to scoop him up and protect him from the invaders. Rayner went towards them and dropped to her knees in one casual but very feminine movement and Becky, scenting a good source of attention much as an addict scents a supply, began to sparkle. I said, 'Say hello, Becky.'

She did, repeating verbatim the words of the assistant in the shoe shop. 'Hello love, my, what bee-eautiful hair you've got!'

Patrick choked. Rayner, blissfully ignorant, said, 'Oh, you little love!' and grasped Becky's hands. Becky grinned at her.

Such close proximity, however, was too much for Drew. His little face crumpled and he gazed across the kitchen to where I, his sole protector in this suddenly threatening world, stood apart and inaccessible. I swooped past Rayner, scooped him up and protected him from the invaders. 'It's just his age,' I said apologetically. 'He'll be all right in a minute.'

I started to do all the right things, taking coats, receiving luggage as Patrick brought it in from the car, ushering my visitors into the chilly living-room. 'Sorry it's so cold,' I apologised again. 'I meant to put the electric fire on . . . warm the place up a bit . . .' I fumbled around with the wretched thing, placing it on the hearth behind the fireguard. A dusty smell crept from the reddening bars. We hadn't used the electric fire for months, being all too conscious of the meter ticking away beneath the stairs. Drew stayed close to me, one arm hooked around my leg, and I looked down helplessly at the top of his head. 'I'll make some tea in a minute . . . Sorry . . .'

'No hurry. Relax,' Patrick said cheerfully. They sank into armchairs and smiled. I looked at them. Relax! If ever people were relaxed it was Rayner and Patrick. Their lives were crammed full of friends, activities, plans, parties, travel, and they scarcely ever flapped. They were adaptable to a degree I had forgotten existed, were comfortable in any company, accepted without question the surroundings in which they found their friends, and emanated warmth, vitality and a genuine interest in people, all people. They were confident almost to a fault, rarely knew self-doubt, criticised often and openly but with such affection that you forgave them everything.

They were brown, fit, glowing with health and enthusiasm for life. Rayner was beautiful as ever, tall, blonde and statuesque, her hair in lovely condition, her nails manicured, her clothes, if not new, looking that way. I had not looked in the mirror for several hours and if I had it would not have told me much for the only one we possessed was a five-inch shaving mirror: but I knew that my hair needed re-styling and probably conditioning too (washing-up liquid doesn't do a lot for the hair), that there were bags under my eyes, holes in my last year's Thermal tights and Weetabix on my Oxfam dress. If only I'd known what time they were coming . . .

Becky had inched her way on to Rayner's knee and was slyly poking her breasts. 'Is there milk in your nipples?' she enquired.

Rayner looked slightly taken aback, then laughed. 'No.'

Becky went on poking and Rayner was disconcerted. Patrick was laughing. 'Don't do that, Becky,' I said. Amazingly, she stopped. But, 'Drew's got a penis,' she informed them. She looked at Patrick. He stopped laughing. 'Have you got a penis?'

Patrick had to admit it.

'Drew's penis gets big and moves about.' A pause. She looked at Patrick again.

'I'll make tea,' I said, and went.

In the kitchen, with Drew still clinging like a limpet, I put the kettle on, looked at the clock, and cursed. I had not yet been to the shop, it was nearly lunchtime, and not only had I no food to offer my visitors but there was hardly even enough for the children. I looked without hope into the fridge: two sausages left over from yesterday, half a can of beans and some cold potatoes which I had intended to fry.

Worse yet: Barry had forgotten to give me the promised cheque. I would have to ask Ivan if I could owe him, and I hated doing that.

Why am I so *stupid*? I asked myself viciously, disconnecting my leg from Drew's clutch. Why didn't I go to the shop first thing this morning? Why isn't that mythical, never-to-materialise casserole cooking gently in the oven? Why am I so disorganised?

Rayner came in, delight all over her face. 'Isn't Becky lovely!' she whispered. 'I had no idea she was such a beauty. Last time I saw her she was bald.'

I tried to concentrate. 'Bald?'

'Yes, she was about ten months old, remember, and had hardly any hair.'

'I'd forgotten. I expect I thought she was a beauty just the same.' I looked furtively at the clock. Ivan would be closing soon.

'You sent photographs, of course, but they didn't do her justice. And Drew was just a tiny baby on the last one you sent.' She smiled winningly down at him and he wound himself round my leg again and tried to scowl. 'He's like Barry,' she said.

'*Is* he?' I too looked at him. 'That explains his sweet nature. Becky is like me.' She raised her eyebrows and I laughed. 'In temperament, that is. Look, Rayner, I'm in a bit of a muddle. There's no food and I'll have to run to the shop. I didn't expect you yet, so – '

'We've brought food,' she said dismissively.

'Oh. Have you?' I was more taken aback than relieved. Usually my problems were not solved so easily. Then, suspiciously, 'It's not foreign stuff, is it? The children won't eat – '

'Stop *worrying*. We picked up pasties for all of us, for lunch. Then there's – let me see . . .' She put her head on one side and I saw her mentally ticking off items. 'Two large tins of ham, a bag of rice, a bag of pasta, a frozen chicken which is probably defrosting all over my new djellaba, some winter cabbage from Dad's garden, a big fruit cake, a couple of pounds – '

45

'Stop,' I said.

' – of apples, a dozen eggs, an infinite number of bars of chocolate and a crate of beer. And oodles of wine, of course. I think that's all,' she said doubtfully. 'My mother might have put in some stuff too. I haven't looked.'

'You're a saviour,' I told her in a heartfelt voice. 'That's fantastic.'

She looked surprised. 'Well, I did say in my letter that you needn't bother to shop.' She saw my face. 'Don't tell me you – '

'All right. I won't.'

'Honestly? Didn't you get it?'

I shook my head. 'All I got was a message from the Post Office to say that you'd be arriving today.' I disconnected my leg again and turned to make the tea. 'I expect your letter will turn up tomorrow. It doesn't matter, does it?'

'I suppose not . . .' She sounded uncertain and I wondered what was in the letter. Doubtless I would hear soon enough. 'It's rather chastening. We got back to England expecting swift efficient Western service in all fields, and what do we find? A dock strike which kept us hanging around Boulogne for hours, my parents' phone out of order so that we had to send them a telegram – Why on earth aren't you on the phone, by the way? – and now the non-arrival of our letter. But,' she said warmly, 'it's great to be home. It really is. Everything's so *green*.' She looked approvingly out of the window at the sheets of rain cascading down on my washing.

'Let's eat these pasties of yours,' I said, 'then I'll put Drew to bed and with any luck Becky might let us talk.'

I started to get out the plates. Patrick came in, wiping streaming eyes.

'What's the matter?' I asked, alarmed.

'That daughter of yours,' he said, muffled through his handkerchief.

'Yes,' I sympathised, 'she reduces me to tears too.'

'I cannot, alas, repeat the conversation.'

'I can imagine it.'

'We've got presents for both of them,' said Rayner. 'Shall I get them out now?'

I looked at Drew. He was growing braver, and at the word

presents had actually begun to smile. 'Yes,' I said. He followed her to the hall, where she rummaged about in a suitcase. He followed her back to the dining-room and stood next to her as she placed two large, gift-wrapped boxes on the floor. His eyes shone but he made no move to touch either of them. Becky came in at the gallop, her powers evidently having informed her what was afoot, flung herself on the floor and grabbed a box. 'Is this for me? Oh, *thank* you, *thank* you!'

I winced, and wondered, not for the first time, if Becky ought to go on the stage.

Rayner had chosen for her a large set of Lego which was probably beyond her at present but which, if she could keep still for long enough, would doubtless help to channel her energies into more creative fields; and, for Drew, a Fisher-Price pull-along raccoon on wheels, which made the most hideous din, rather like unoiled roller skates. His crowning feature was a tail which flopped about behind him on a tight spring, making the kind of noise you might expect a tight spring to make. Repeatedly.

Drew loved it. We managed to get him away from the thing for long enough to eat his lunch, but afterwards he insisted on taking it upstairs and into his cot. He would probably wake up, I reflected, with a black eye. If not worse.

'Have a beer,' offered Patrick when I came back downstairs. Becky was already absorbed in the Lego, her red head bent intently over its intricacies, so the three of us settled around the electric fire in the living-room, the overhead light on to dispel the gloom of the rainy afternoon. For the first time since Rayner and Patrick's arrival I began to relax: to feel as I used to feel some years ago when we sat together like this, in Barry's flat or Patrick's or in my room at the residence. It was so long since I had been in the company of real friends that I had forgotten the warmth it generated, the comfortable feeling of being completely at ease, of not having to pretend to be something I was not, of avoiding saying anything personal about myself in case it was misunderstood or making jokes which would bring only blank looks.

'Go,' invited Rayner, and sat back expectantly.

I took an appreciative sip of beer. 'Drinking in the afternoon is definitely decadent. Let's have your news first. You're the adventurers.'

'Oh, we'll talk the ears off you once we start. When Barry's here,' she promised.

'All right. But it's all so boring. Kids and home and hearth.' I waved my hand to indicate just how boring home and hearth were. 'What do you want to know? We told you everything in our letters.'

'It's not the same,' Rayner said comfortably. 'Start from our last visit, when you were living in the furnished flat.'

'With a bald baby,' I agreed. I glanced at Patrick. He was lounging back, plastic cup in hand, apparently as genuinely interested in what I had to say as Rayner was.

Wonderful. Unbelievable. I had an identity again.

When we last saw the Lambs we had been living in the south of England for eighteen months and I was feeling I had made the most ghastly mistake in dragging Barry down there. He was a northerner born and bred; so was I, but my years abroad had knocked all sentiment for the north out of me, and after University I had a yearning to move south and enjoy country life as, despite the mud and flies, I had enjoyed it once before. I persuaded and cajoled until at last Barry agreed. After all, he had nothing better to do than languish unemployed in his bedsit, writing poems. Despite his excellent degree he had not wanted to do research, feeling, I think, that it was somehow artificial.

I was already pregnant and we had a year of miserable insecurity, moving from summer let to winter let and back again, with landlords looking askance at my growing belly and, later, categorically refusing house-room to such an unnatural phenomenon as a baby. Meanwhile, Barry had found work in humble capacity as an insurance clerk. (We discovered early that an English degree was more of a hindrance than a help in gaining non-academic employment.) At last, when Becky was a few months old, we were fortunate enough to get a permanent let: a flat in its own cobbled courtyard, complete with clucking hens and a macho cock or two. And there we were, sitting pretty at last.

And yet it wasn't so pretty, for I soon began to experience

the loneliness of a young mother at home with a baby all day; and Barry pined.

He pined for the north; he pined for intellectual stimulation, for the friends who had shared our common interests, for the literary pursuits now abandoned, for the tramps who used to touch him for twenty pence, for a worthwhile career. He read passionately in the evenings: Baudelaire, Nietzsche, Walt Whitman, books on Zen Buddhism, books of critical essays on modern poetry, anything that would keep his mind alive and some spark of artistic appreciation still burning. Later I understood his desperation, because what the insurance office did to him my incarceration with the children was to do to me. All I knew at the time was that he was not happy and I should never have made him come to this part of the country.

It was while we were in this situation, stale-mated and with no optimistic vision of a future change, that Rayner and Patrick came to say goodbye. They had taken a Postgraduate Teaching Certificate following University and were now going, they informed us, to get stinking rich in Saudi Arabia by teaching English to the affluent natives. They reckoned a year, maybe two, would do the trick, enabling them to come home and buy a house. (In the event it was nearer three years because as fast as they earned their money they spent it again, tearing around the world during school vacations.)

They stayed with us for four days, got pleasantly drunk every night, raved over the baby but declined to change her nappies, promised (and fulfilled the promise) frequent postcards, and departed.

Life suddenly seemed very small. Very grey, very straight, the horizons so close as to be claustrophobic. We missed them badly, the breath of fresh air and independence they brought with them, the aura of freedom and choice and decision. It was like standing securely but oh, so tamely on the paved sidewalks of the eastern states whilst intrepid pioneers boarded their wagontrains for the trek to the unknown West. I returned, sick at heart, to my buckets of nappies, and Barry, even more sick at heart, to his hated office.

By this time Becky was beginning to show her true colours. I spent my days moving our belongings higher and higher up the walls until it began to look as if we were living in a state of siege. Even then she constantly defeated me. When I draped the washing on the clothes maiden she pulled it off, item by item, and threw it all into the coal scuttle. When I made strategically-timed dashes into the larder, she got there before me to clear the shelves with one dexterous sweep of her small hand. She threw her shoes and mine into the bath water at every opportunity, blocked the toilet with my potted azalea, stripped the wallpaper from her bedroom walls, even managed to break a cupboard door off its hinges despite its being, like all our cupboard doors, tied up with string for just this reason. But her greatest triumph concerned the eggs. By now we had Ginny, rescued from a dog's home just before her execution. (Considering what Becky and Drew between them did to Ginny later, execution may have been kinder.) Becky's favourite pastime was luring Ginny into the hen-house, locating and dropping newly laid eggs, and then standing back smiling while Gin ate up the mess. Our landlord smiled too, at first. Soon he smiled less. Then he began to glower. A couple of parallel bars appeared across the hen-house door. Becky crawled nimbly under them. Smacking had no effect at all. It was not until Barry and I extended the scope of the barriers into something resembling a portcullis that we were able to put a stop to it.

Then I had a brainwave. Becky, I reasoned, was far too big for her size three boots. She needed taking down a peg. She needed to learn that the world did not revolve around her. She needed to learn to share. In short, she needed a brother.

That it would be a brother I never doubted. Barry, too jaded and downcast to care much one way or the other, agreed to try for a second child and almost immediately Drew was conceived.

I have already mentioned Becky's attempts at fratricide. Despite Drew's being totally adorable, the first couple of months of his life were so unspeakable for everybody, except perhaps Drew himself, and the flat so cramped with baby things, that we all, Becky included, grew daily more bad-tempered. My welcomes to a home-coming Barry got grumpier, he grew ever more silent and morose, and the guilt I had been feeling over luring him here swelled to huge propor-

tions. Something had to happen or there would be a disaster –
a child-battering or a divorce.

'I'm getting out of that place,' Barry said suddenly one
evening. We were playing with the delightful Drew, quietly so
as not to wake the currently less-than-delightful Becky.

'Oh?' I said nervously. It had reached that pitch: I knew so
little of what he was thinking these days that almost any
proffered remark made me nervous. 'You mean you're
resigning?'

'If they don't fire me first,' he said flatly.

'What will you do instead?' The thought of his being unemployed held, interestingly enough, no terrors for me. Anything was better than this draining, negative, unfulfilled misery of his.

He flashed a grin at me, his old grin, and I knew that it was
going to be all right. 'Mental nursing,' he said.

I remember that I just stared at him while the baby swung,
agonisingly, on my hair. He had been thinking about it, he
said, for a long time, ever since he had watched some mental
patients being taught to shop for themselves in a supermarket, and watched too the embarrassed, discomfited reaction
of 'normal' shoppers. 'It's a no-go area,' he said. 'The
reaction of most ordinary people is one of fear or revulsion.
And yet mental illness is just that, an illness like any other. It
can be treated. People who suffer from it need friendliness
and compassion, not the cold shoulder.'

I recognised that quality in him again, the one that the
tramps had always recognised: a willingness, even a compulsion, to identify himself with misfits. No wonder he had been
miserable in the insurance firm among the pin-striped suits,
the dolly birds, the twin sets, the legal files and the dust, the
conventional attitudes and the secret backbiting and the daily
discussions of last night's TV programmes. Of course he must
become a mental nurse, he was a *born* mental nurse with his
quiet listening, his patient understanding, his tolerance of
unpredictable behaviour (like mine).

He was interviewed and accepted, and began a three-year
course at a psychiatric hospital in Dorset. Somehow, with the
help of in-laws, we scraped together enough money for the
move and a minimum of secondhand furniture, as the hospital

51

staff house which we were allotted was unfurnished. Our landlord, out of the kindness of his heart or because he was so relieved to have his eggs unmolested at last, gave us a battered three-piece suite and an ancient cooker. And so we came to Lottabridge.

'You must love it here,' said Rayner, when I had got this far. 'It's so beautiful.'

'It's beautiful all right. But what can you do with beauty, except look at it?'

'Look at it again,' said Patrick, somewhat sententiously. 'It must keep changing all the year round. It's never the same for two days together, surely?'

I agreed. 'Two hours, sometimes.' I thought of the wind sweeping in across the hills from the coast twenty miles away, to fetch up in our bathroom; of distant black rain falling dramatically from one identifiable cloud and heading inexorably towards my washing-line; of struggling up our scenic hill with the bloody pushchair, my body stretched practically parallel to the road like Barry's *Nakrāsana*. Why didn't people understand?

'Look,' I said patiently, 'we've no car. Getting on a bus is murder and anyway I can't afford to go anywhere. I couldn't push the kids up a one in six incline for very long without bursting a blood vessel. So, yes, it's beautiful; but so, I'm sure, are parts of Siberia.'

There was a pause. Rayner and Patrick exchanged glances. 'Oh dear,' said Rayner.

'That bad, eh?' said Patrick.

I realised that I was getting heated, just as I had with Ivan yesterday. I must pull myself together.

'What's the village like?' Rayner again. I looked at her face, already sympathetic so she had noticed how neurotic I was getting. Not difficult, I supposed. This time I chose my words more carefully.

'It's not Ambridge, that's for sure.'

'Litotes, I presume?' Patrick put in quizzically. I blinked at him for a moment before remembering that the word meant a form of understatement. I had forgotten all that literary terminology.

'Litotes,' I agreed wryly. 'Lottabridge is an odd sort of place, you see. It's grown up around the hospital and practically all the inhabitants are, or have been, connected with the hospital in some capacity. Take our little road here: the occupants of these houses are all nurses, or auxiliaries, or porters. The better paid staff own cottages down the hill or houses outside the village. There are flats up the lane for patients who are learning to live independently. There's temporary accommodation for doctors who flit in and out of the place as part of their training. But there's no *village*, no community or community spirit.'

'I should have thought,' observed Patrick, 'that those circumstances would make for a perfect community. You're all involved in the same thing, you have a common bond.'

'Yes. Well, it doesn't work like that. For one thing, most of them *aren't* involved. For them it's just a job. Maybe they were involved once, I don't know. Barry says they get burnt-out.'

'I can understand that,' said Rayner. 'It must be a terrific strain, and carry very little reward.'

I shrugged. 'Barry seems to find it rewarding, but then he's new to it.'

'Are there no village activities?' she asked.

'Bingo,' I said dryly. 'W.I.'

'Is that all? No operatic societies, amateur dramatics, music societies, barn dances, keep fit classes, discos for the kids, youth clubs, rambling and nature walks, coffee mornings – ?' Halfway through this list I started to laugh, and she broke off, looking defensive. 'Well, *I* don't know, do I? I've never lived in a village, not an English village anyway. I thought they all did all those things.'

'So did I,' I admitted. 'My last village did. You know, *Crows Flying* – '

'*Sideways*. Yes, I know. All the farmers going to church in their dungy wellies. Well, why don't you start something yourself? You were a great starter-of-things at University.'

I looked at their faces, their alert, alive faces, the vitality shining out of them. I wondered glumly when my face had last looked like that.

'DONE A POO!'

53

Rayner and Patrick jumped several inches into the air. 'Good God,' said Patrick.

'There's your answer,' I said. 'That's why I don't start anything.'

'But surely – ' began Rayner.

'DONE A POOOOO!'

I got up. 'I wish she'd learn to wipe her own bottom,' I said, and caught the flicker of distaste in Rayner's eyes. But immediately she was smiling again, as one does smile about other people's children's offending actions; as I smiled about Tommy's every day. I felt the all too familiar depression returning.

Becky was lounging on the toilet seat singing 'Fearful symmetry, fearful symmetry', to a tune of her own invention. 'What does "fearful symmetry" mean?' she enquired, as I did the necessary.

'Ask Patrick,' I said sadistically.

She did, following me back into the living-room after the ritual hand washing. 'What does "fearful symmetry" mean?'

They stared at her, at a loss. I sat back to enjoy it. 'It means – well, it means – why do you want to know?'

'I've made a tiger,' explained Becky. 'With my Lego.'

Light dawned. 'Ah,' said Patrick approvingly, 'Blake.' He quoted:

> '"What immortal hand or eye
> Dare frame thy fearful symmetry?"

Marvellous, isn't it?'

'What does "fearful symmetry" mean?' persisted the un-deviating Becky.

A silence. 'May we see your tiger?' asked Rayner, and smiled sweetly at Patrick.

It was all right until Drew got up. Even then it was nearly all right because Becky went upstairs with Rayner to show her her room and help her unpack, whilst Drew was happily engaged in knocking down the towering edifices which Becky had carefully constructed. But after that, as teatime drew near, it began to get difficult.

'The Berbers are magnificent,' Rayner was telling me,

54

propping up the kitchen sink and enthusing about Morocco while I tried to do things with her defrosted chicken and simultaneously boil eggs, butter bread and lay the table. 'They're so erect and dignified and their faces are from another age: craggy and primitive and remote, you know, and somehow both ageless and ancient, even the faces of the young ones. Do you know what I mean?'

'Drew's got my Lego!'

'Once when we were driving home we saw a long line of them on horseback along the skyline, silhouetted against the sunset. It was like being suddenly transported to the Middle Ages.'

'Mummy, Drew's got my Lego! Mummy, *smack* him!'

'It made my stomach turn over, it was so lovely.'

'Becky, stop screaming! Drew, give her back her Lego.' I stepped around Rayner to get the salt and fell over the raccoon, who lurched away noisily, tail whanging. 'Sorry, Rayner. Go on.'

'There's such a shocking disparity between the economic situations of the people. The poor ones are really poor, I mean they consider themselves lucky if they can eat meat once a fortnight. And yet at the other end of the scale – ' I made a dash for Drew, sat him hastily on the potty, fell over the raccoon again on the way back – 'at the other end of the scale,' persevered Rayner, 'are the rich foreigners who work there, driving around in their big cars with expensive cameras round their necks. One camera alone would feed a family of – '

Drew tottered in, clutching the potty with his offering in it. I made another dash, abandoning Rayner to her rich foreigners. When I came back she was down on her knees beside Drew, playing with the raccoon. Just as he reached for the string, Becky shot in and snatched it from him with one of her maniacal howls of glee. Drew screamed. I said, 'Right: Drew can play with your Lego.' He did. Becky screamed. I turned my back and got on with the meal.

'Rabat,' resumed Rayner, a little more loudly, 'has the loveliest gardens, but I think the best souk was at Fes. I'll show you the djellabas I bought there, the colours are out of this – '

'Becky, leave Gin alone.'

' – world,' said Rayner, and compressed her lips.

'You're throttling her!'

Ginny was submitting with her usual patience to a strangle-hold which would have broken the neck of a lesser animal. She rolled her eyes at me and sighed.

Becky did not let go. 'Gin *likes* to put her head against me when she has a love.'

I did not argue, simply extracted her and whacked her bottom. Patrick sauntered in. 'Anyone seen the bottle opener? It's disappeared.'

'Try the toy box. Becky and Drew: go outside till tea's ready.' I got their anoraks on in record time, shoved them out into the cold and shut the door.

'Found it,' said Patrick, after some rummaging. 'Amabel, there are some very odd things in that toy box. Did you know?'

'What things?' I couldn't remember how long the eggs had been on but they must be done by now. I fished them out.

'Two toothbrushes. A pair of pliers. A pair of tights. A – er – '

'Well?'

'A Tampax,' he said apologetically.

'Oh, Lord. Unused, I hope?'

Patrick turned pink. I had forgotten that men with no children could get embarrassed. He said stiffly, 'Naturally. I wouldn't have mentioned it otherwise.'

'What *would* you have done?' Rayner asked interestedly.

I rescued him. 'Patrick, go away and drink your beer.'

He grinned, started to go, turned back. 'Barry's got some very interesting psychiatry books. I've been reading the old theories about the effects of the moon on certain of the mentally disturbed.'

'Yes,' I said distractedly.

'How is Barry getting on, Amabel? I must say I was surprised to hear he'd taken up this line of work. We always thought he'd go for a PhD. Seems a waste of a First, somehow.'

'Yes,' I said again. Eggs in egg-cups, bread cut into soldiers, blancmange ready but not yet on the table or they wouldn't eat the eggs . . . Spoons . . . But what about the chicken?

56

'Will he mind if we question him about his patients, do you think? I mean, it's not confidential or anything?'

'Rayner, sorry, could you do something with this chicken for me? I must feed the – '

Loud wails from without, followed by a cheerful 'Sorry!' I jerked open the door and Drew limped in, his cries already diminishing. He had not Becky's capacity for prolonged hysteria.

She followed him in. 'He fell down. But I picked him up by the bladder.'

'Did you push him?' I demanded.

'No!'

'Then why did you say "Sorry"?'

'We were holding hands,' she explained.

I waited.

'We went down the garden very fast.'

Smothered giggles from Rayner. Becky promptly joined in and started leaping about, laughing in the silly show-off way she had recently acquired and which made me thoroughly dislike her. Patrick, after a further valiant attempt at conversation, retired to further peruse Barry's books. It was no use expecting any domestic assistance from him. Patrick had always been notoriously chauvinistic in that respect and I often used to wonder why Rayner put up with it. Eventually I had done my wondering aloud and Rayner had said simply, 'I enjoy cooking.'

Well, let her cook. I left her in the kitchen, searching my forlorn cupboards for exotic herbs I did not possess, and got on with pumping yet more energy into my young.

We had just reached the end of the initial lull when Rayner returned, looking totally relaxed, and joined us at the table. 'The chicken's in the oven,' she said easily, 'surrounded by veg and bits of mouldy onion.'

'Oh,' I said. 'Sorry.'

She laughed. 'I trimmed off the mould. And I made a kind of patchwork cover out of odd pieces of silver foil. There didn't seem to be a new roll.' She looked at me enquiringly.

'No.' I spooned a bit of egg off Drew's chin and popped it back into his mouth. Becky was at the stage of hammering her empty shell into a scrunched-up mess at the bottom of the egg-cup.

'What time will Barry be home?'

'Becky, that's enough, you'll break the egg-cup. About quarter to eight. He's on a twelve-hour today.'

'Twelve – ? You mean he's *worked* for twelve hours?' She looked aghast.

I nodded. 'Seven-thirty to seven-thirty.'

'But that's *awful*! How often does he do that, for God's sake?'

'Two or three times a week. Becky, I won't tell you again! Tomorrow he'll work from seven-thirty till five.'

'It's barbaric. Patrick,' she called, 'do you know what kind of hours poor Barry is working?'

Obediently Patrick came into the dining-room, still holding one of Barry's books. I peered at the title: *Body and Mind: A Synthesis*. 'I expect they work him into the ground, don't they?' he said absently. 'Rayner, this is fascinating stuff. Did you know that by analysing what your body is doing you can learn what your emotions are?'

'I know what my emotions are without doing that.'

'But you don't. Not according to this. Listen.' I got up to remove the eggy dishes and edged past him to the kitchen. The dining-room was blessedly silent save for his voice, reading aloud the relevant passages. I came back with two bowls of blancmange, edged past him again and set them down before the children. 'Do you see what that means?' Patrick was going on. 'You may be in a state of confusion or fear but not recognise it, especially if you've been pretending to yourself for years that nothing is wrong.'

'Eat your blancmange, please.'

'Under treatment,' he went on, 'they teach you to concentrate on your body, find out which bits are tense and when, so that you can recognise what it is that's troubling you and also gauge when you're becoming able to cope with it. Look – '

'Drew, stop playing with that blancmange and *eat* it!'

Patrick had struck a pose, obviously an uncomfortable one, and was staring into the middle distance. Both children were riveted. 'Here I am,' he said, 'tense as hell but somehow managing to believe that everything's fine. Now someone like Barry comes along and says "How does this bit feel?"' He flexed. '"How does that bit feel?"' He flexed again. 'Now

58

Barry takes me away from the cause of the tension, tension I'm not even aware of, remember, and says again, '"How does this bit feel now? Different, huh?"' He straightened up, looking enormously impressed with himself or the imaginary Barry. 'That's a rather loose paraphrase, of course, but do you see how it works?'

'*Becky* – '

'Amabel,' interrupted Rayner, 'why do you keep trying to make them eat the wretched stuff? They've obviously had enough.'

I caught myself glaring at her. I could scarcely point out that both children would be gobbling up the blancmange if it were not for these distractions. I said, 'They'll be hungry at bedtime if they don't eat now.'

'You worry too much.'

'Um,' I said.

'Let me read a story to them,' she suggested. 'Then you can wash the dishes in peace.'

Too late to argue. Both children were already making a rush towards the bookshelves, and I bowed to the inevitable and let them go.

'You're not a bit interested – ' began Patrick.

'Oh, let's leave psychiatry till Barry comes home,' said Rayner. 'I want to play mother.'

By the time Barry actually did come home I was mentally and physically exhausted. I didn't need the book to tell me how to analyse my tight and aching muscles. My head throbbed from trying to concentrate on too many things at once and I longed only for a quiet read and an early night. But I had not seen Rayner and Patrick for three years; I dearly loved their company; I would thoroughly enjoy an evening of drinking and talking with them; even if it killed me.

Chapter Five

Bedtime could have been worse. If Drew hadn't been such a smiley child I would not have spotted the bottle-top in his mouth and he would have choked to death during the night. And Becky did herself no real injury on Patrick's razor, which he had left on the bathroom basin: there was very little blood. And it only took a minute to find the cheese crackers when Becky shouted that she was hungry, another five minutes for her to clean her teeth again and not more than quarter of an hour to resettle Drew.

Downstairs, however, Barry, Rayner and Patrick were well into a bottle of wine and there was a chicken dinner magically ready. I accepted my drink much as the drowning man grasps his straw, and immediately the world was saner. And after the meal (how had Rayner made it *taste* like that?) it was almost the old Amabel Dennell who followed the others into the paraffin warmth of the living-room.

Barry looked tired, but eager. Usually when he came home after a twelve-hour stint his face was devoid of expression, and his mind (he assured me) of thoughts. There was little in my all-too-familiar company to stimulate him, but Rayner and Patrick were a different matter. I watched him as he sat in his armchair in the corner, still in uniform, his eyes red-flecked but alight and interested. Then I saw that the eagerness was a form of being keyed-up: a tension like my own, not a relaxation.

We see too few people, I thought; we are not good at socialising any more, we have become insular.

Patrick and Rayner, on the other hand, were as relaxed as

60

ever, drinks in hands, legs crossed, totally in command of themselves and, one felt, their lives. In the artificial light Rayner's tanned face glowed with health and her eyes were clear: no broken nights for her. She had changed into a golden-blue dress that suggested tropical skies and she had done something to her hair, too; I wasn't sure what, but it looked special, as if she had taken trouble to look nice for an evening spent with old friends. I looked exactly as I had when they arrived. A good deal more jaded, probably.

'That was a fabulous postcard of Tutankhamun's tomb,' Barry was saying. 'We pinned it on the kitchen wall but Becky got hold of it.'

'It was a fabulous experience,' said Patrick warmly. 'I think the only comparable experience was when we saw the moon rise over the Sphinx, don't you agree, Rayner?' He turned back to us. 'I've got some excellent pictures of the Sphinx, taken at night. It's floodlit, you know, absolutely breathtaking. We'll show you the slides. I spent a fortune on a new camera, extra lenses, light meter, the works. It was worth every penny.'

'I'm not sure I agree with you,' said Rayner, as soon as he gave her a chance, 'I thought the cheetah was our best experience.'

'Oh Lord, yes, the cheetah. In Kenya,' he explained. 'Our driver had stopped the Land-Rover for a minute, and there she was, under a bit of straggling bush about ten feet away. You could hardly see her at first, she was so well camouflaged, and she had a young one with her. Neither of them moved, just looked at us with those unblinking eyes. I used up half a roll there and then.'

We listened, fascinated, as he went on, 'Then there was that damned elephant. A great bull elephant, roaming about a safe distance away, or so I thought. I'd got out of the Land-Rover to take some photographs. Our driver had told me to heed the warning signals. If he flaps his ears, he said, he's probably going to charge.' Patrick laughed incredulously, lounging back in his chair. 'Well, I thought he'd flap his ears first and *then* charge. But that brute hadn't read the rule book! I hadn't even got the camera to my eye before the ground was shaking under my feet and he was coming at me like the QE2, flapping all the way. Christ! I jumped back in the Land-Rover and we got the hell out of there.'

They talked on, sometimes Patrick regaling us with their adventures, sometimes Rayner. Another bottle was opened and remembering Drew I memorised the position of the cork. They talked about Egypt, the pyramids, the great monuments of the monumentally (according to Patrick) egocentric Rameses II; about the sordid back alleys of Marrakech, the historical architecture of Meknes; about the traffic in Athens and the museum at Heraklion. They told us about the visual cleanness of the Jeddah streets and the olfactory foulness caused by daily feeding of the plants with sewage. They told us of the camels on the beach outside Jeddah, and 'Did you know,' said Rayner, 'that female camels are forced to use the equivalent of a coil? An Intra-Uterine Device?'

'You're kidding,' I said.

'I am not. They have a stone placed in the uterus, poor things. It performs exactly the same function as a coil and also prevents camel riots on long caravan journeys.'

'Well, I'm blowed,' said Barry, and held out his cup for a refill. I glanced at him. He was looking rather rosy. What the heck, I thought, and held out mine too.

'Tell us about the teaching,' I suggested. 'I assume you *did* some teaching in between all this gadding about? That was the object of the exercise, wasn't it, to come back filthy rich?'

Patrick grimaced. 'We're not as rich as we'd hoped. We've spent rather a lot. I think we've got about twenty thousand left, invested of course.'

I blinked. 'Of course.' I looked at Barry. 'How much have we got?'

He grinned. 'About twenty-five quid.'

Rayner said quickly, 'Look, we've worked very hard for that money. We put in a lot of extra teaching time and it wasn't easy, believe me.'

I glanced again at Barry, at his eyes red-rimmed with tiredness. 'Tell us about it. Why are you here in March, for a start? I thought you had to see the school year out?'

'You've forgotten, we left Jeddah last summer,' Patrick pointed out. 'Since then we've been travelling. That's why we've only got twenty thou. left.'

'Ah.'

'The most difficult thing,' persisted Rayner, intent on justifying her statement, 'was sticking to the regulations.'

'It always is,' murmured Barry.

'We were told at our initial interview in London, before we even left for Saudi Arabia, that we would be expected to teach very formally, to avoid references to sex or politics or religion. But when you try to put that into practice – well, it's damn near impossible. Can you imagine teaching *Paradise Lost* without touching on either the erotic or the religious content? As for D. H. Lawrence. . . ! Even the most apparently innocuous stuff has unsuspected pitfalls when you come to talk about it. The poor kids had to make do with expanding their vocabulary and learning about rhyme and metre. That's what I meant,' she added, 'when I said the teaching wasn't easy.'

Barry looked thoughtful and I recognised his marshalling process at work. In a moment, I knew, we would be on to literature and I wasn't sure that I was up to it after several years of housebound stagnation. But he must have thought better of it, because after glancing, very discreetly at his watch, he said merely, 'What were the kids like?'

'Delightful,' said Patrick promptly. 'Yours too, eh, Rayner? Separate schools, naturally,' he told us. 'Segregation of the sexes.'

'Naturally,' said Rayner dryly. 'Don't let me start railing against the repression of women or I shall be at it all night. Shall I tell you about my delightful pupils instead?'

She did, and after she had finished extolling their virtues, their exquisite manners, their industry, their punctuality and desire to please, Barry said in a concerned voice, 'You're going to find it very difficult adjusting to English delinquents again. Have you got jobs yet?'

They shook their heads, looked at one another. Something passed, unspoken. 'We're looking,' said Rayner.

'So are thousands of others.'

She shrugged, said confidently, 'Patrick will find a post.'

'Patrick will? What about you?'

'Oh, I may do supply teaching for a while.' Then, casually, 'I'm ready to start a family now.'

I groaned. 'Oh, Rayner.'

'What?'

'After the sort of life you've been leading – to tie yourself down with babies?'

'But I want babies.'

'Yes,' I said glumly. 'So did I.'

There was a pause, during which the bottle went round again and Barry cast another furtive look at his watch. 'Well?' said Rayner at last. 'Out with it.'

'I've said it. There isn't anything else to say.'

She laughed. 'What a tragic face!' she teased, 'And what a mournful voice! Amabel, it *can't* be that bad. If it was, people would have stopped having babies long ago, and a fine mess we'd all be in.'

I sipped my wine and looked sorrowfully at her. 'Once, when I was a little girl,' I said, 'my father and I watched a thrush. The thrush was stamping about on the grass, then standing still, his head on one side. I asked my father what the thrush was doing. He said, "He's knocking on the ground to attract worms. In a minute a worm will pop up to see who's there and the thrush will eat it." He was right: a worm did come up and the thrush pulled it out and swallowed it. Then he started stamping again. I remember that I stood there puzzling over this. Eventually I said, "But why do they keep coming up? Why don't they learn to stay hidden?" And he said, "Nobody ever tells them. By the time the worm has found out who was knocking it's too late to go back and tell them."'

I paused, then added, 'Well, *I'm* telling you.'

They were looking at me very oddly. Barry was laughing approvingly. He said, 'Amabel's drunk.' It was not clear whether the approval was for my drunkenness or my parable.

But Patrick missed the point completely. 'Surely,' he said, frowning, 'the worms think it's raining?'

There was a general laugh at this and the hint of tension which had been developing dissolved. Patrick asked me, 'Amabel, what are you up to these days, apart from Bingo and W.I?'

'I don't – ' I began indignantly, saw that he was laughing, and laughed too. 'Well, maybe I *should* go to their wretched

W.I. meetings. The singing of "Jerusalem" to an untuned piano puts me off.'

'They don't!' exclaimed Rayner.

'They do.'

'Are you doing any writing?' Patrick had always wanted to write a novel himself – who hasn't? – and when he first discovered that I was a published author his admiration, tinged with envy, had been quite gratifying. Later, of course, as he got to know the muddled labyrinth that was my brain (muddled even then) the admiration faded, but his interest continued.

I told him, briefly, of my current plans and of the difficulty I had experienced in making a start.

'And now we've come along and interrupted you,' Rayner said penitently

I shook my head. 'I probably rushed it. A little more fermenting time will result in a better brew. I hope.'

'What's it about? Have you got a title?'

'I've got very little so far. Just an idea based on Becky's talent for thought-reading.'

They hadn't heard about that. We told them and they were suitably amazed, sought as we had sought for explanations, and failed to find a satisfactory one.

'My real problem,' I complained, 'is a child-clogged mind. I've been stagnating mentally for so long that I've hardly a ripple of thought any more.'

'But a mean talent for metaphors,' said Patrick with a laugh. 'Look, why don't you try private coaching? O and A levels are coming up next term. You could give some kid a hefty push through his exams, tone up your stagnant brain and earn a hefty fee at the same time.'

'Splendid idea,' approved Rayner, and they all looked expectantly at me.

'Oh, I don't think I have the confidence.'

'Rubbish,' said Rayner briskly. 'You had oodles of confidence at University.'

'It kind of seeps away. Being stuck in the house, you know, not talking to people, not exchanging ideas.'

'Well, it won't come back on its own. Don't be so defeatist. You never used to be. Go out,' said Rayner with an extravagant gesture, 'and embrace the world.'

There was only one thing to do with that suggestion, and that was laugh at it. So I laughed. If they only knew! They had worn me to apathy, those children, to non-thinking, non-caring, blank, negative apathy.

'It's not just the confidence that I lack,' I tried to explain, 'it's the intellectual ability. I suppose, somewhere inside me, some thoughts are lying dormant; thoughts not concerning children or cooking, I mean. But how the devil do I excavate them? I don't even *care* if I don't excavate them, except sometimes when I'm angry. Survival and retention of sanity seem more important. I imagine that's why I had so much trouble with Chapter One.' With the first line of the first paragraph of Chapter One, I added mentally, but I didn't say it.

Rayner had her strong-jawed look on. 'For God's sake, they're only *children*!'

'One of them is,' I conceded. 'The other one – '

'Is six children,' said Barry.

Rayner shook her head impatiently, reached for the wine and poured herself another drink. 'I can't believe this is you, Amabel. Here, have a drink. Why, a few years ago you would have – '

'Do any of you know of Maslow's Hierarchy of Needs?' Barry enquired suddenly. It was so unlike him to interrupt that we all stared at him for a moment before shaking our heads. Patrick, scenting something interesting from the psychiatry books, asked, 'What is it?'

'It's a theory. Maslow structures it as a triangle, rather like the old feudal system was structured. You know, serfs at the bottom, monarch at the top. According to Maslow, our most basic needs are physical and must be met before anything else can even be considered. So at the base of the triangle you find oxygen, food, water, and such things as safety and security; shelter; sex.' He looked round at us. 'Only after those needs are met can we go on to develop and satisfy social needs: belonging, acceptance, self-esteem. By now we're getting near to the top of the triangle. Its apex, its pinnacle, is what I would call roughly philosophy: thought, abstract thought, the fulfilment of the intellect. This, you see, is the thing we need

66

least; but also the thing we most aspire to. We cannot gain it unless and until those other, more basic needs are met.' He smiled at me and, gratefully, I smiled back. 'Whilst Amabel is trying to survive she will have difficulty in thinking about her novel.'

'Is all this stuff set reading for the course?' Patrick asked.

Barry shrugged. 'I read everything I can get my hands on.'

'You always did,' said Rayner admiringly.

'Almost nothing is irrelevant. If I don't use it now I'll probably use it at some time in the future. There is so much new research being done, new discoveries or ideas, some of them controversial, some so obvious they should have been thought of years back. The thing is to try and look at everything, not to get trapped in one school of thought. That can be disastrous. For instance, it's only very recently that institutionalisation has been recognised as a sort of disease in itself. They should have seen that long ago.'

'You mean, the patient becomes dependent on the institution?'

Barry nodded. 'I was horrified when I first worked on a Long Stay ward and discovered that some of the patients had been there twenty, thirty, forty years. Whatever was thought to be wrong with them initially had long since been forgotten. They were simply institutionalised, couldn't possibly cope in the world outside without a great deal of training; were in fact terrified of the world outside.' He smiled, rather grimly. 'People are frightened of mental hospitals. If they only knew how much more frightened the patients are of coming out! Amabel spoke of loss of confidence after four years of limited communication with other people. Well, imagine what forty years would do!'

He went on to tell them about his work. I tucked my feet under me in the chair and sat there in our shabby room that smelt of paraffin and wine and, slightly, of dog. Our own smells, produced from free choice in a free if economically straitened life. Not the smells of hospital: disinfectant, incontinence, industrial floor polish. I tried to imagine forty years without choice, and could not.

Then I found myself remembering last year's visit to the hospital fête. Barry had been working so I had taken the children along. The day was hot, the grounds colourful with hydrangeas in full bloom and escallonia ranging around the edges of the sweeping lawns. There was a brass band playing, cake stalls and book stalls and plant stalls, plate breaking contests, sponge throwing, a dog show and games for the children. Patients, nurses, relatives and people from nearby villages were there, eating ice-creams. Most of the patients were elderly, from the Long Stay or Geriatric wards. The younger ones, the short-term patients with different kinds of problems were not in evidence.

We wandered about, Becky charming all and sundry with her uninhibited chatty friendliness. I knew enough of hospital policy by now to be confident that those patients attending the fête were either completely harmless or, if at all unpredictable, safely contained by the wonder drugs which had so radically changed the face of psychiatric medicine. Nevertheless, when one has children there is a small element of anxiety ever active, so when I saw Drew crawling across the grass towards some patients I was after him like a shot.

The group he was heading for consisted of three very old men and a young male nurse. As I saw just how ancient and obviously feeble the men were, I relaxed. Two of them had that blank, empty stare that I had met before: you could let off a firecracker under their noses and they would not react. The third was watching Drew's swimming motion with expressionless but not unintelligent eyes. All three were sitting passively on the grass, their nurse with them. I caught his eye and he smiled at me: Nothing to worry about.

Drew chose the third man and paused before him, considering the matter. The two of them looked gravely at each other. I saw now that this man was not so ancient as I had thought, despite the bent posture and white hair. Sixty, perhaps.

Drew made up his mind. Inch by painful inch he hoisted himself to his feet between the man's knees until at last he stood triumphantly erect, each fat hand clutching a thin, immobile knee, his little calves trembling with the effort. And he smiled.

I had always thought that when Drew smiled, it was like the sun coming out. This one was a special smile, aimed straight at his chosen friend and filled with all the guileless joyousness that only someone his age could achieve. There was a pause of perhaps three seconds, during which the patient did not move or respond at all. Then slowly, gently, he too smiled.

Drew was satisfied. He climbed down the man's shins and crawled back to me. I picked him up and hugged him hard, terribly pleased with him. I turned to give my own smile to the man, but the indifference had returned to his face, so I went to look for Becky and found her helping an old lady in a wheel-chair to eat an ice-cream.

A few minutes later I ran into a nurse I knew slightly, a girl called Sally, and asked her about Drew's friend. 'What's the matter with him? He looked quite *compos mentis* to me – compared with the others, that is.'

She looked across at the little group. 'Oh, you mean Mr Howarth. He's deaf and dumb.'

'Is he? But what's the matter with him?' She stared at me. 'I mean, why is he here, and looking as if he's been here forever?'

'He's here,' she said crisply, 'because he's deaf and dumb. And he *has* been here forever. Over thirty years, I believe.'

It was my turn to stare. 'You mean there's nothing wrong with him mentally?'

'Oh, there's plenty wrong with him now,' she said dryly. 'He's totally institutionalised. He'll never leave this place till he leaves in a box.'

I was horrified. That sweet, gentle smile . . . I thought I must have misunderstood her, misheard her, so 'Let me get this straight', I began.

She cut in. 'It's no good agonising over him. It's too late. He's happy. He's at peace.'

'But he could be taught sign language, he could be taught to read – *Has* he been taught to read?'

She shook her head. 'Look, I don't run this hospital.'

'But you work here, you could protest!'

She looked at me pityingly. 'I get on with the job I'm paid to do. I haven't time to protest about all the patients who shouldn't be here. There are too many of them.' She saw my face. 'Look,' she said kindly, 'Mental patients have been getting a lousy deal for centuries. It's changing now, but until the old ones die off all we can do is look after them as best we can. Most of the patients on the Long Stay wards are too institutionalised to be helped in any other way. They're remnants from the bad old days when, if you were different, if you had fits or visions or had an illegitimate child at fourteen and shamed your family, you got shut away in a mental hospital. A lunatic asylum, as they called them then.'

'You don't *mean* that about having an illegitimate child?'

'It's been known,' she said grimly. I looked down at the heads of my own children, too shocked to speak. At that time I was still learning about the various horror stories that Lottabridge Psychiatric Hospital had to offer.

'That one,' she said, looking over to where the men were shambling away, 'Mr Howarth, he came in when the last of his family died and there was nobody left to look after him. He'd always been kept at home, never been taught to look after himself.' She shrugged. 'What can you do?'

'Teach him sign language!' I said passionately. 'Teach him to read!'

'Don't you think that would be rather cruel? Now?'

There was a silence. I turned away from her, tears of anger in my eyes that such things should be allowed to happen, now, in the 1980s. I picked up Drew and we went home, leaving the cheerful music of the brass band behind us.

Barry was talking about rehabilitation. 'It's quite the best section I've worked in,' he was saying enthusiastically. 'No, I'll amend that, my present ward is the most interesting, but rehabilitation was the most satisfying. They're Long Stay patients, you see, those few who are thought to have retained some degree of initiative and have a chance of standing on their own feet again. It's the only way to combat institutionalisation, and it doesn't always work, but my word, when it does!'

The drink had made him talkative and he was wide awake again. I wondered apprehensively how wide awake he would feel a few hours from now, when he had to go to work.

'How are they rehabilitated?' Patrick asked.

'There's a section of one wing given over to that. There are a couple of self-contained flats which two or three patients

70

share while they try their hand at looking after themselves. Before they can do that they have to be taught to cook, to shop, to wash and iron their own clothes, to use a vacuum cleaner . . . All the things you and I take for granted. They have to *want* to do it, of course. Some of them don't, and that's when it doesn't work. In that case they go back to the ward, where they carry on giving good service.' He gave a reminiscent laugh. 'I ran into one ex-patient the other day, who'd been successfully rehabilitated and is now living in a hospital-owned flat in the village. He was extremely irate about it. "Seventeen years of my life I've given to that place," he said, "and now they've thrown me out! There's gratitude!"'

The others laughed delightedly, and Barry went on, 'Taking them shopping was great fun. You never knew what they'd do next. Just like children. You remember the first time I saw patients learning to shop, Amabel, and how uncomfortable all the other shoppers were? I suppose you can't blame them. I had one chap in my group, six feet four and built like a battle ship. He had the social training of a baboon, not unnaturally, and if he couldn't see what he wanted on the shelves he'd simply grab the nearest shopper by the arm and boom "CHOPS?" A grip like a vice, he had, too. He could empty a supermarket quicker than anyone I ever knew.'

Patrick was writhing about in helpless laughter. I said, 'Tell them about the shoes.'

'Shoes? Oh, that!' Barry was well launched now. 'Well, I'd taken one of our men to buy new shoes. We let them do everything themselves, you know, as far as possible, so this chap had chosen some shoes he liked, had his feet measured because he hadn't the faintest idea what size he was, and tried one on. You know how the assistants bring just one shoe to start with? He surveyed this shoe on his foot and asked, "How much is it?" The assistant told him. So my patient thought for a minute and then said, "How much is the other one?"'

This time we all roared. 'Stop,' gasped Patrick. 'Oh, open another bottle, someone.'

I was alarmed. 'It's awfully late.'

Rayner was all compunction. For Barry. 'Are you very tired, Barry?'

Barry had gone past being tired. 'Last one,' he assured me cheerfully as I watched another cork pop out.

'It can't all be fun and games, surely?' enquired Rayner as she lifted her drink. She looked, I noticed with resentment, as fresh and bright-eyed as ever. I supposed they were used to this life-style.

'Yes, tell us about your dramatic cases,' said Patrick.

There was the inevitable pause while Barry thought about this. I saw him look at me, and knew that he did not want to mention yesterday's suicide and did not want me to mention it either. I had no intention of doing so.

'Dramatic cases,' Barry said slowly. 'Well, mostly they're not very dramatic. Just rather sad. At present I'm working on an Admission ward. There's a great deal of variety and occasionally someone absconds or tries to slash their wrists. Is that what you mean by dramatic?'

Patrick had the grace to look slightly ashamed. 'Sorry. I sounded like a peeping Tom. Just tell us what you find most interesting.'

Barry considered. 'I have a phobic girl at present,' he said. 'She's terrified of dirt. Her definition of dirt is not the same as ours. For instance, she cannot pick up a telephone, touch a doorknob, handle money, sit on a seat in a bus . . .'

'How awful,' said Rayner.

'Her worst fear concerns old people. They're associated in her mind with dirt, for reasons which I won't go into. She had an unpleasant experience, let's leave it at that. She can't even bear to be near an old person, let alone touch one.'

'And this is real?' asked Rayner. 'I mean, it's not just in her mind?'

'Of course it's in her mind,' said Barry irritably.

'What's the treatment?' asked Patrick.

'Letting her talk, first. Then gradually introducing her to "dirty" objects. Persuading her to open a door without immediately rushing to wash her hands. Making her aware of tension in her body so that she recognises what's happening to her under what circumstances. Tomorrow I'm going to ask her to walk with me down the corridor to the Geriatric ward. Lots of praise if she does it.'

'Positive Reinforcement,' I put in knowledgeably.

72

'How old is she?' asked Rayner.

'Twenty-five. She has a baby in care.'

'I suppose babies are the dirtiest thing of all.'

'Oddly enough, she had no trouble with the baby, nor with changing dirty nappies. It was the general running of the house, shopping and so on, that she couldn't handle.'

I chewed my lip ruminatively. Somewhere in this story was a moral. I supposed it was "Count your blessings". All the domestic things I hated must seem the blessed occupations of some unattainable, halcyon paradise to this girl who could not perform them.

Barry went on to tell them about other patients, taking care as he always did, to retain their anonymity. The tense eagerness of a few hours ago was gone and now he was relaxed, intent on his subject. Barry rarely talked at length, probably because he felt himself ill-informed – a consideration that would not have stopped most people, including myself, from holding forth – but when it came to his specialised areas of English literature or, as now, psychiatric nursing, he spoke confidently and well. He told them about the young anorexic whose family problems were far harder to cure than her eating habits; about the fifty-year-old man who had turned into a dependent child upon the death of his mother and whose brother had subsequently housed him but not spoken to him for five years; about the highly intelligent professor of Egyptology whose elderly mother had asked that he be sectioned because his full-voiced, intellectual discussions, held interminably whilst quite alone in his bedroom, frightened her. ('Nice guy,' said Barry. 'He's just so damned clever that he's on a wave-length all of his own, so he addresses the only mind that can comprehend him: his own.') He told them of the numerous alcoholics who came and went and came again because whatever had started them drinking in the first place was still there, waiting for them when they left the hospital. He talked about the many kinds of schizophrenic patients, about the confusion inherent in the term. One factor common to many, he said, was the hearing of voices. He tried to make us imagine holding a telephone to each ear, hearing two voices simultaneously and trying to make sense of either of them. That, he said, must be how some of his schizophrenic patients felt when someone addressed them.

'How awful,' said Rayner. Barry stopped. 'I do admire you,' she added.

'Yes. Well.'

'It's a far cry from Shakespeare,' Patrick observed.

'Oh, I don't know. The same kind of analysis is needed, the same search for ambiguities, just as in studying literature. And don't forget Shakespeare had his share of madmen. Lear, of course, driven to madness by his daughters. And Hamlet, perhaps? How sane was he? If you pushed his sense of being under pressure, his intellectual ramblings and questionings just a little further he'd be on a par with my professor. Then of course there's Ophelia, driven to breakdown and subsequent suicide, again by too much pressure from outside. Shakespeare had the right of it, you know. Mental disturbances are commonly caused by outside circumstances, by the failure of others to understand or communicate or help, or simply be kind. Pressures, rejections, hostilities. People become rather peculiar if they're badly treated. Like dogs. Remember what Gin was like when we got her, Amabel? It's not enough to cure the patient. You have to cure or at least educate his parents – very often the cause of pressure – his friends, his colleagues. That means,' he said wryly, 'everybody. The world.

'Here endeth the lesson,' he added, and grinned.

I was proud of him. I always was when he talked like this. It didn't matter then that he forgot to pay the electricity bill, that he practised Yoga instead of plastering the bit of wall Becky had wrecked, that he left bits of food in the plughole after washing up, forgot to put the dustbins out on Wednesdays, left his dirty socks on the bedroom floor and played god-awful records too loud. This, I said to myself, as Mark Antony had said before me, was a man.

Chapter Six

'Becky, Gin's barking. Will you let her in, please?'

'You let her out, so you should let her back in.'

'That's true, but sometimes we do favours for one another.'

'Well, you do me a favour.'

I sighed. Indubitably she had won that one. I walked sideways towards the door, having discovered that my head hurt less that way, averted my face from the daylight as Gin ambled in (all the curtains were still closed) and staggered back to the sink.

'Drew!' said Becky severely, 'cover your mouth when you sneeze. Why must I say everything three times?'

Drew sneezed again. It was all I needed. If he had a cold we would all have colds before the week was out. With any luck mine would turn into bronchial pneumonia and I would have to be hospitalised. I could lie in bed all day, being waited on, and nobody would shout 'Wee-wee!' or 'Done a poo!' or 'I'm hungry!'

The children were eating digestive biscuits for breakfast, the grilling of toast having been too much for me. As it was, I was nearly undone by the noise of the cellophane.

'Why,' asked Becky, 'are these ladies dancing on the biscuit tin?'

I suppressed a moan and squinted dutifully at the tin. Old-tyme couples in breeches, bonnets, rosy cheeks, were square dancing on a village green surrounded by improbably idyllic country cottages. 'It's to make people buy the biscuits. We're meant to think that people who lived a long time ago made much nicer biscuits than we make today.'

'And did they?'

'Probably.' I strove to clear my head. 'They didn't use chemicals, artificial colourings, preservatives. No,' I said, 'on second thoughts, their biscuits were probably crawling with maggots.'

'What are maggots?'

'Maggots are little wriggly worms that come out of tiny eggs left on food by flies. That's why we don't like flies.'

Becky nodded. 'Also,' she said, 'they have poo on their feet.'

'What?'

'Off Gin's – '

'Oh, I see. I don't think I feel like talking about that, Becky.'

'Why not?'

But that was as much as I could manage for the time being. It was more than I had imagined I could achieve when I first dragged myself out of bed this morning. Not only had I a rip-roaring hangover but I was crying out for sleep. We had crawled to our rooms at two-thirty and collapsed into immediate stupor. At half-past three Drew had woken up. Somehow I managed to give him his bottle, and fell moaning back into bed. At ten-past four Becky had a nightmare and refused to be consoled by any means other than coming into our bed. When I stuffed her in between Barry and myself it was half-past four. At five o'clock, having been kicked, kneed and elbowed black and blue by her soundly sleeping limbs, I struggled out of the warm crowded bed and into her cold empty one. My head was splitting, my skin about to burst, my throat parched. But at last I slept.

At half-past six Barry's alarm clock went off only inches from Becky's head.

It was now seven-thirty. Barry was at this moment starting work, poor soul, and of Rayner and Patrick there was, naturally, no sign.

'When I was a little baby,' remarked Becky, 'in my cot and I didn't know where you were when I wanted to do a poo, I just squeezed it out into my knickers.'

All things considered I preferred her penis fixation. 'Nappy,' I said wearily. 'You wore nappies then.'

76

'I just squeezed it out into – '

'All *right*, Becky.'

She came to me at the kitchen sink and looked at the mountain of last night's dishes which I was doggedly and with closed eyes working my way through. 'I like having visitors. It makes me ever such happy.' She kissed my elbow with a loud smacking noise.

'You want something. What do you want?'

'Can I have all the little oysters getting eaten on the beach?'

Oh Lord. 'You mean "The Walrus and the Carpenter". Can't it wait?'

Bad phrasing. Two minutes later I was seated on the couch with a child on either side of me, discoursing poetically upon the ease with which the unwary run headlong into traps.

Heaven knows what she made of that poem. She had never yet asked for explanations and I proffered none, reasoning that since she liked it her imagination had evidently provided its own. After that we had one or two more favourites, and then it was only fair that Drew have something he liked, so we read one of Richard Hefter's utterly mad, totally captivating fantasies.

'Pears on bears,' I read, enunciating slowly and carefully, 'Bears in chairs; Pairs of bears with chairs going up the stairs – '

'Hairy pairs of bears running down the stairs,' cried Becky, who knew it by heart, 'and out of the door!'

And heaven knows what Drew made of *that*. But he liked the pictures. No wonder, I thought as I put the books away, that so many of us ended up in psychiatric hospitals. We probably spent our subconscious lives striving to find the reality of hairy pairs of bears and feeling that if we could only get to Yellowstone Park everything would be all right.

I was beginning, against all the odds, to feel slightly human. As we seemed to be having one of our cultural mornings I put Tchaikowsky's *Romeo and Juliet* on the record player, turned it up loud in a vain attempt to arouse the sleepers, and told Becky the sad story while I finished the dishes. She sat in unwonted quietness until the music finished and then plagued me with concerned questions which I was hard put to answer. Why *did* people choose dissent in preference to harmony?

Why *did* they sacrifice the happiness of their children for an ill-founded principle? I didn't know, and said so.

After the idyll the usual chaos resumed. Becky built a barricade of chairs and left Drew's potty on the wrong side of it. Drew found a new packet of margarine. Becky tried to clean up the mess with a corner of the curtain. I tried to listen to some charming Italian Petrarchan-inspired love songs on Radio Three whilst both children screamed at full volume. Gin went out to eat grass and was sick on the back step. Drew trod in it. I brought in yesterday's sopping washing, spun it, hung it out again five minutes before the rain began anew. A normal morning.

By half-past ten I was more or less myself again. I wondered about taking morning tea to my visitors but hesitated, knowing what a hot sex life the pair of them had and loath to risk interrupting anything . . . Although, I thought bitterly, Barry and I used to be interrupted often enough by the children, and it had mattered to me then . . .

I put the kettle on.

Becky called from the hall, 'Mummy, Drew's found a spider.'

'Oh. A big one?' I asked brightly.

'A *great big* one,' she said with relish.

'Oh,' I said again. Then, hopefully, 'You mean a big dead one?'

'No. It's running about.' A pause, then I heard Drew give one of his little pleased grunts. 'It's dead now,' said Becky.

Upstairs a door opened, there were bathroom noises, and then Rayner came down, looking fresh as the pearly dawn and wearing a floaty purple thing with wide sleeves. She fought her way through the welcoming committee with an 'Ugh! No, I don't want it,' and came into the kitchen wrinkling her elegant nose in amused fastidiousness. Becky followed her in. 'Would you like a biscuit?' she offered. 'All the maggots are gone now.'

I looked at Rayner's purple robe. My own dressing gown, which I was thankful I was not wearing, was eight years old, a large stout masculine affair of wool so heavy that I could only wash it in the summer and consequently it was indescribably filthy. I made a mental note to keep it out of sight during

Rayner's visit. 'Aren't you cold?' I said.

'Not in the least. Are you?'

'I'm always cold,' I said gloomily.

She laughed. 'What an old misery you're becoming. Any chance of a bath?'

I nodded. 'The water's hot. Wait a minute and I'll cut the soap in half.'

She watched in disbelief as I found a serrated knife and hacked my way through a bar of cheap nameless stuff that was guaranteed to make the toughest skin crack, dry up and fall off in defeated flakes. 'Barry gets washed in the kitchen in the mornings,' I explained.

'How very working-class of him.'

I glanced at her. It was a joke. I hoped. 'That way he doesn't wake the children up. Today of course Becky heard the alarm, so . . .'

She took the half of soap I handed her, torn, I think, between horror and laughter. 'There is a titchy bit in the bathroom,' I added, 'but not enough for a bath.'

'I think you're very courageous, both of you. I couldn't live like this.'

'No.'

'I like a few luxuries. A stock of soap in the bathroom, for instance. Incidentally, Amabel, I noticed yesterday that you buy small sizes of everything. Why on earth don't you buy your food in bulk? It's much cheaper.'

'Now why didn't I think of that before.'

She looked hurt. 'Don't be sarcastic' I'm only trying – '

' – to help. I know.'

She went off for her bath and returned presently, hair damp, no make-up on, but still managing to look exotic. 'There's no lock on the bathroom door,' she observed, with a glint of humour.

'Ah,' I said. 'I'd forgotten about that. I wondered why the children were leaving me in peace.'

'Oh, they didn't come in. Not all the way, anyway.'

'Sorry, Rayner – '

'Hands kept appearing in the gap, offering me things. It was quite amusing. Becky kept up a running commentary concerning the various parts of my anatomy as I washed them.' She helped herself to cereal and I reminded myself to order extra milk. 'She really is into bodies and bodily functions in a big way, isn't she?'

'Mm,' I said, and waited. I had been expecting this since yesterday. Rayner leaned against the counter, casually spooning Weetabix into her mouth.

'Do you think it's healthy?'

'Perfectly healthy.'

'Some people might find it embarrassing.'

'Look,' I said, determined not to show exasperation, 'they're tiny kids and they've got the rest of their lives to learn about embarrassment. They haven't been in the world very long and the most important thing in it is THEM. The first two words Becky learned to say were "me" and "mine". Well, "me" to a child means, above all else, body. "Here I am, this wondrous machine, things come out of me, they're mine, they're important, they're fascinating. Some parts of me feel nice and they're fascinating too. Drew's got something I haven't got, things come out of that too, and *he's* fascinated, therefore so am I." Don't you see? A small child lives in and for his body, much more than we do despite our sexual obsessions, and his prime, his paramount concern is self-gratification. That means food, attention, the satisfaction of the senses and particularly the satisfaction of curiosity. If that involves poos and penises, so be it. I'm damned if I'll sacrifice their natural development for the sake of other people's sensibilities. It *is* natural, it is healthy. Crush it and you have adults with severe hang-ups, particularly sexual hang-ups.'

I added in a lighter tone, 'Anyway, it's funny. Even artistic. Do you know that Becky gives names to her stools? "Look, Mummy, that's a moon poo".'

I ended with a broad smile, and Rayner smiled with me, rather apologetically. 'You feel strongly about it. Sorry. I expect I'm a bit squeamish.'

'You'll have to get over that if you're going to have babies.'

'Oh, I'm sure it's different with one's own,' she said confidently.

I didn't answer that. 'Toast?'

She shook her head. 'Cup of tea would be nice. I'll take one up to Patrick, if I may?'

'I'll come with you,' Becky volunteered. 'I'm very good at waking Daddy up when he's not going to work.'

I had forgotten that she and Drew were still standing there, waiting, quietly for once, for that precious commodity which would have been near to the base of Maslow's triangle had he bothered to include children: attention.

So Rayner said that they could come and while I made the tea she moved briskly about, picking things up off the toy- and clothes-strewn floor, packing bottles back into their crate (I had collected the corks last night) and generally making the place look a lot more civilised than it usually did. Then the three of them disappeared upstairs with Patrick's tea and Rayner left him lying there defenceless and returned alone.

'I'll clean your floors,' she said cheerfully. 'You won't be offended, will you? There are dog hairs everywhere. You should brush Ginny more often.'

I wasn't offended, I was delighted and said so. 'It's so difficult to do the floors with the children around. Thanks, Rayner.'

'Of course I'll help. Where's the vacuum cleaner?'

Oh. 'I haven't got a vacuum cleaner,' I said.

A pause. 'Oh. But you had one at the flat.'

'It belonged to the flat, like everything else.'

Another pause. 'Well, I'll take Ginny outside and give her a thorough brushing instead, shall I?'

'It's raining,' I said sourly.

'In the back porch, then.' She was not to be thwarted a second time in her desire to help. I found Gin's brush and comb and she took the dog away. Meanwhile there was a lot of excited shouting and thumping going on upstairs so I went up to rescue Patrick.

'Can I come in?' I bawled over the din. Various entangled bodies heaved themselves apart on the double mattress which lay on the floor, and Patrick sat up, hairy-chested and built more like a rugby player than an English teacher, and grinned at me. He was tousled and happy and there was a faint odour in the room which I recognised and which infuriated me out of all proportion. To make love in the *morning*! Barry and I had attained that miracle perhaps three or four times since Becky was born. What made it all the more frustrating was that mornings were now the only times I was sufficiently relaxed to feel any respectable degree of desire. But to exploit it was *totally bloody impossible.*

'Why are you glaring at me?' Patrick enquired mildly.

I pulled myself together. 'Sorry. Actually I came to take the brats away so that you could get up. Come on, you two.'

'But he likes us,' said Becky indignantly.

'Not that much. Out!' I dragged them away and shut the bedroom door on a lazily grinning Patrick, wondering with some embarrassment if he knew that I knew. Not that it mattered. Well, it shouldn't. It is only when one's own sexual activities are less than satisfactory that other people's matter.

Ginny greeted us self-consciously. She looked sleek and shining and considerably thinner. 'Why, she's quite good-looking,' I said.

'She's beautiful,' said Rayner, and hugged her. 'You neglect her, Amabel. How often does she get a real walk these days?'

I waited a moment before answering levelly, 'Not often, I'm afraid.'

'We'll give her a good long run,' she promised, 'won't we, girl?' And Ginny got very excited and began to yelp and rush at the door. 'In fact,' said Rayner, 'let's go out right now. The rain's easing off.'

'All right. I've got to go to the shop anyway. I'll just get the washing in.'

'Leave it.'

'But we'll have no clean clothes. I'll just give it another spin and hang it on the – '

'Amabel,' said Rayner impatiently, 'stop *worrying*. Stop *fussing*. Get your mac on and let's go for a walk. We'll leave Patrick to look after himself.'

So we did, though it wasn't quite so swift as that. There were bladders to empty, missing wellingtons to locate, anorak zips to unjam. Eventually, however, we were ready. Patrick appeared just as I was bringing the double pushchair in from the back porch.

'Good God,' he said. 'Where'd you get that thing? Job lot from *Ben Hur*?'

I surveyed it. 'It is monstrous, isn't it? Terribly heavy on the hills. But it's strong, and it was very cheap. Second-hand, naturally.'

'Of course it's heavy,' said Rayner. 'You need one of those light squashy things that fold up and hang over your arm like an umbrella.'

I nodded. 'A buggy. We had a single one for Becky. That was second-hand too. It fell apart.'

'Then get another. A new one.'

I eyed her coldly. She said, 'I know they're expensive but it would be worth the outlay for the effort saved. This thing must weigh a ton. And how on earth do you get it on a bus?'

I said slowly and very distinctly, 'Rayner. We – have – no money. *No* money. Do you understand?'

'I'm horribly boring,' said Becky plaintively.

Rayner laughed suddenly. 'Sorry, Becky. Sorry, Amabel. I was tactless as usual. Let's go.'

'What about me? I've had no breakfast.'

'You should have got up earlier,' I said heartlessly. 'Do you want us to wait for you?' I looked at the clock.

But Patrick was more interested in delving again into Barry's books than in wandering about in the rain, so we left him to it. The rain, in fact, had eased to a not unpleasant misty drizzle, and I realised when we got outside that our hilltop was once more sitting in a cloud. It spent much of the winter in this condition, looking charmingly remote and mysterious from a distance, but merely damply depressing when one got inside it. Drew sat snugly below the rain cover and Becky tramped along beside him, dragging on the chair handle as she always did, so that her weight might just as well have been inside it. 'We'll shop on the way back,' I decided. 'No point in adding to the load. Where do you want to go?' I knew the answer, of course.

'The hospital.'

'It's there.' I pointed through the bare trees to the Victorian expanse of dark red brick.

'Heavens. I'd no idea it was so close.'

'I like it. It's about the only thing I do like about living here.'

'Why? I should have thought you'd find it – well – disturbing.'

I shook my head. 'Barry's so close, you see. He can get home for lunch, and if there's a crisis he can be there inside five minutes. Once I let Drew fall off my knee and he cut his gum and lip and bled quite badly. I panicked, rushed to the phone-box with Drew bleeding all over me, and Barry was there in no time.'

She looked at me queerly. 'Just for a cut lip?'

'I didn't know,' I said defensively. 'He was crying so hard . . . His jaw might have been broken. I'm no good at these things and Barry is excellent.' I glanced at her, wondering whether to go on; but I wanted to recapture the mood of yesterday, when I had thought myself at last able to say what I felt without fear of being misunderstood. 'I need Barry a great deal now. In fact, I suppose I've become rather heavily dependent on him. You remember I used to be almost fanatically *in*dependent? Well, it's different now.' I hesitated, wondering how to explain the difference.

But already I had said too much. 'That must be very hard on Barry,' Rayner observed calmly. 'I imagine he has enough weight to carry without a clinging wife.'

I almost turned and went home. For a moment I stared straight ahead into the mist, my throat tight with hurt and rage. That, I told myself, was it. That was my last, absolutely my last proffered confidence.

'Can we go inside the grounds?'

I stopped. We had already reached the hedge that formed the boundary. Beyond it the green lawns swept up to the series of open verandahs which fronted the hospital and which were, as usual, empty. Even on fine days there were rarely any patients sitting or strolling there and I used to ask Barry, with some anger, why the staff did not encourage them to take fresh air and exercise. He would merely shrug and say, 'Too few staff, too many patients, too little time.'

Answering Rayner, I said, 'We usually cut through the cemetery. There's a little rose garden beyond it, and some seats. The children quite often play there and people walk their dogs.' I looked down at Ginny. She was walking along very politely, not pulling at all at the lead which Rayner held, but her head and tail were well up, her ears pricked and new life sparkled in her eyes. Rayner was right, I thought guiltily: I

84

neglected the poor old girl. 'Take her lead off, would you?'

She was gone, Becky after her, the pair of them rushing joyously ahead of us into a walled grassy enclosure and along the strip of paving stones which ran through its centre. 'There's our little garden,' I said, pointing beyond the long enclosure.

Rayner looked around. 'But where's the cemetery?'

'Here. You're standing in it.'

We came to a halt. Drew began to struggle and make determined noises so I undid his harness and lifted him out and he tottered off happily across the green wet graves of the insane dead.

'I don't quite understand.'

I bent down and pushed some grass aside. A small metal plate was revealed with a number on it. I stepped to the other side of the path and found another plate, another number. I let her see for herself how the grass grew lushly over the plots, how, if you looked carefully, you could see the slight dips between them where the earth had sunk, dip after dip stretching the length of this quiet place. Around us the trees dripped gently and the mist shifted.

Rayner shivered. 'How awful.'

'I find it very moving.' Already I had forgotten my resolution. 'Here they all are, forgotten, nameless, as if we were ashamed of them. Lost, hidden, yet always here, beneath our feet.' I watched Drew fall, face down in the soaking grass. He got up again, still smiling. 'I suppose there are record books somewhere, names attached to the numbers; histories, dates of death.'

She said, 'Do they still – ?'

'No.'

'It's spooky. Let's go on.'

'You wanted to see the place,' I pointed out. 'You wanted the experience.'

She gave me a look, and said nothing. I left the pushchair where it was and we followed the children.

The little rose garden was bare and bleak, the roses pruned down to dead-looking sticks. It always amazed me that such savage butchery resulted in luxuriant blooms year after year. In the centre was a paved area with a couple of wet wooden benches. We perched on the edge of one and watched children and dog going mad on the lawns beyond the rose bushes, Drew being frequently flattened by one or other of his companions but taking it like a soldier. A hundred yards away lights gleamed in the windows of wards and one or two figures passed behind them.

'What are they doing in there?' Rayner asked curiously.

'That depends on the ward. On Geriatrics they're wiping bottoms and mopping the floor. On Long Stay they're handing out drugs and trying to do Reality Orientation and then wishing they hadn't when the patient starts crying. On Admissions – '

'I meant, what are the patients doing?'

'Watching television, probably. Or the wall.'

She shook her head. 'It must be terrible. Every day the same. I couldn't stand it. I hate being bored. There was a period in Saudi when Patrick was working and I wasn't and I nearly climbed the walls, stuck in the flat all day with nowhere to go. I like lots of company and variety and activity and things to look forward to. I suppose that's childish of me but I do.'

I didn't say anything. There was no point. If she couldn't hear for herself her potentiality for being exactly as I was now . . .

Every day the same. Sometimes I felt a kinship with the people inside those walls, people who began by wanting to get out, like me, and ended be being afraid to get out – like me. I too was institutionalised. We were trapped by circumstances in the same old daily round, the same frustration and erosion of initiative, leading inevitably to the same apathy. But I always felt vastly ashamed of myself after thinking like this, for I had my health and my freedom and my children. My children, who were the cause of all the frustration, who were effectively my warders, but who were also the centre of my being, the reason for my life. Odd, maddening paradox.

Rayner, of course, even with children, would make sure that she was never trapped at all. They were rich, for one thing, or rich by my standards. They had that passport to freedom, a car. Rayner would make sure that she never struggled up hills with a Ben Hur chariot, and she would make *damned* sure that Patrick never subjected her to anything resembling poverty. She would get her company and variety and activity, I supposed, although nothing would be able to prevent her from climbing at least a few walls during those awful years when the children were small. I thought that I would like to see Rayner climbing walls.

A scream of the most intense rage rose into the mist. It was followed by a long garbled sentence shouted at full pitch and filled with raw hatred, and it came from a man who had appeared on one of the hospital verandahs.

'You're in luck,' I told Rayner. 'Here's a real madman for you.'

'I don't think I deserve that.' She was hurt again, and annoyed too this time, as well she might be. 'Had we better go?' she added nervously.

I shook my head. 'It's all right.' Nevertheless I turned to check on the children. They were heading towards us at a rapid pace; Gin too, with her tail well down.

'FOR CHRIST'S SAKE!' Another stream of invective as the man strode about, sometimes stopping to listen, sometimes starting angrily forward.

'Is he shouting at us?'

'At his voices, I think,' I said soberly. I had never witnessed an attack like this, although I was familiar with many of the patients as they went about the village, some of them behaving very oddly indeed. I knew this one. He was young, very handsome, with clean, strong bone structure, and I had admired him often. It had not been obvious, as it usually was, that he was a patient, but after seeing him a few times I had known from something indefinable in his face. I had not known he was subject to this.

The children were not frightened, only cautious. Becky leaned against me and when the young man was quiet she remarked, 'That man is shouting at himself.'

'Yes,' I said, and we were silent. After a minute he started again, raging at those goading him, and I thought of the agony of him and his kind over thousands of years: not understood, cast out, feared, except by one man. And now, though we had some knowledge and some medicine, we still had the fear.

'What would happen if we went to comfort him?' asked

87

Rayner, adding, 'That's an academic question, of course.'

'Of course,' I said dryly. 'I think Barry would say approach with caution and don't approach alone. You never know what his voices are telling him, you see. They might be saying that you're going to attack him.'

I looked at Becky's small beautiful face, the glorious red hair standing out around it. I had once asked Barry if schizophrenia was hereditary or if anyone could develop it. He had said that it was thought to be a form of stress but had added (I remembered the line because it had amused me) that to call it 'a response to environmental factors in those who are already predisposed' was a scientific way of saying we didn't know. But he had also told me, I remembered with relief, that all schizophrenics were thought to have been abnormally biddable children. So Becky was safe.

'Mummy,' said Becky, in response to my intent stare, 'my tummy's greebling.'

I laughed, gave her a hug and picked up the sopping wet body of Drew. 'All right. We'll go now. Half a minute, Rayner, I'll just water the boy.'

I pulled down his pants and held him aloft while he sprayed a rose bush. Behind us the argument raged, the voice lashed through the mist, tormented and unable ever to defeat its opponent. Poor man.

Poor man. Did he who made the Lamb, make thee?

On the way home we stopped at the shop where Ivan behaved idiotically at the sight of Rayner's face, showing off like a schoolboy and making schoolboy jokes. Marjory appeared and made a smilingly catty remark about my green eye-liner, which I had applied that morning while Rayner was in the bath and which constituted one of my bi-annual efforts at attaining alluring beauty. Then I let Rayner flog herself into an unbecoming perspiration by pushing the chair, with both children in it, back up the hill. Halfway up I relented, made Becky get out, and took over. 'Good grief,' said Rayner with feeling, 'how do you do it?'

'I don't. I pace up and down my little rat-trap with my little rats, and pray to the Almighty to send me a car.'

'I still think you should buy a lightweight pushchair. Even if it meant selling some books to do it.'

'We've sold all the books we're prepared to sell.' That horrified her, I could see. She and Patrick collected books as squirrels collect nuts, often several editions of the same book, and they had boxes of the things dumped with friends and relatives all over the country. They would never, I knew, have sold a single one except under very dire circumstances indeed.

The pushchair argument continued and I was trying to explain how hard to come by were secondhand double buggies, and anyway Becky would not need to ride for much longer, when I saw a man lurching down the hill towards us. Lurching was not quite an accurate description but I doubted that any verb would be truly accurate. Sam Beckett in *Watt* describes a progress rather like this man's, but in Beckett the progress is deliberately ridiculous, here simply tragic. The man was about fifty, thin, with an expression of concentration on a tired, grey face. His walk consisted of swinging his body forward with an obvious effort of will, whilst one leg was determinedly trying to turn into the centre of the road and one arm flung itself about erratically as if trying to stop the traffic. Not that there was much traffic in Lottabridge at the busiest of times. At present only we and he occupied the road and consequently neither party could be unaware of the other. I heard Rayner break into a gabbling kind of speech and recognised acute embarrassment. Finally we came level with the man, and I smiled and said hello, and he said, 'Hello, nice day,' which it wasn't, and we passed.

After a decent interval Rayner said softly, 'Who was that?'

'A patient. I don't know his name.'

'Is he ill? Mentally ill, I mean?'

'I don't think so. He has Huntingdon's Chorea, Barry says. Don't ask me what that is because I don't know, but what you saw are the results of it.'

'Is it curable? Will he always be like that?'

'Till he dies,' I said calmly, 'Which will probably be quite soon.'

'But shouldn't he be in a proper hospital?' I looked at her. 'I mean – oh, you know.'

'Apparently there are one or two centres for people with his condition. Apart from those, no, general hospitals haven't the beds to spare for that kind of thing. The victims, if they have no-one to care for them, get shunted off to places like ours. All wrong, but there it is.'

I waited for her to say 'How awful' but this time she said nothing. I too said no more. I was not going to tell her how that man wrung my heart with his courage every time we met, how I had never seen anyone else even wish him good morning, how he walked miles and miles, day after day in all weathers, fighting his disease with all the strength he had and with no company, no visible moral support: quite the reverse, in fact, for Barry had heard that he was frequently stopped by the police, who believed him to have absconded, and taken back to the hospital. Barry knew the man only by reputation. It was I who saw him, worried about him, tried to greet him cheerfully and wondered often but without reaching a decision whether I ought to invite him home for coffee. If I did so it would be out of pity, which I thought this man would not appreciate. And yet he must be so lonely.

When we got back there was the usual lunchtime rush to fill greebling stomachs, eased this time by Rayner and Patrick, who read stories to the children while I cooked the meal (without burning it, for once); but then Barry came in unexpectedly and I had to start all over again. He managed to swallow a nasty-looking mess of underdone sausages and tepid baked beans whilst simultaneously listening to Rayner's technicolour account of the morning's encounters, and then he dashed off again. Becky threw herself into a half-feigned tantrum, as she always did when Daddy came home for lunch and then went away again, and Drew wet his pants. The kitchen was strewn with dirty dishes and my sleepless night was beginning to catch up with me. So when Rayner offered, 'Where would you like to go this afternoon?' my response was not exactly enthusiastic. 'Bed' was what I would have liked to answer.

'I can't go out in the afternoons. Drew goes to sleep,' I said.

She looked disappointed. 'I thought it would be a treat for you. You were longing for a car and now that there's one at your disposal you don't want to go anywhere.'

'It's not that – '

'Can't Drew miss his nap for once?'

Yes, he could, of course. Of course he could. He had missed it before; and whined miserably, desperately, all afternoon, stubbornly resisting sleep because he was not in his own cot; being perfectly hellish at teatime, crashing out into total oblivion immediately afterwards, and waking us all up at dawn the next day.

'I suppose so,' I said lamely. 'All right. I'll just wash the dishes . . .'

'We'll wash up when we come back,' said Rayner firmly. 'You mustn't let your life be ruled by dishes and children.'

'No. I'm sure you're right.' I was, too. For years I had been sure of it but I hadn't yet figured out how *not* to be so ruled.

So we went out. Where we went I have no idea, but the scenery was lovely once we got down out of the clouds, and it didn't rain too hard and Becky was only sick once. We had an impromptu picnic of Mars bars and oranges by a river and my wrists ached for days afterwards through fighting Drew's manic efforts to throw himself in. Drew himself held up pretty well till about four o'clock, when he began to grizzle and didn't stop. Useless to try to explain the unhappiness this caused me as well as him, the cold anxious ache in the womb wherein Mother Nature had planted her damned maternal instinct immediately the foetus vacated it. It was not a happy outing.

We returned to an ecstatic welcome from Gin, who had been left behind because Rayner didn't want dog hairs in the car, and sardonic remarks from Barry, who was locked out and sitting in the shed. I lost my temper during the children's teatime, as I almost always did: this time because they were tired, hungry and screaming incessantly, and there were no clean plates. Rayner and Patrick retired with tact or disgust, I didn't know which, and Barry and I washed up and fed the children. There was one warm relaxed moment when they had begun to eat, and I put my arms round Barry who was peace personified and who understood me, and said 'I love you very much' and he knew that it had all been awful and smiled at me.

Then at last we got them to bed and when we came

91

downstairs there was Patrick with a twinkle in his eye and a corkscrew in his hand.

'Now this,' said Patrick enthusiastically, 'is the one I was telling you about. I'm really proud of this one. See how the sky is green in the background and the stone-work seems purplish? Absolutely remarkable colouring. It's all due to the sunset, of course.'

We sat in the dark living-room and gazed at the thrown image of the Sphinx gazing impenetrably back at us from the wall. Beautiful, wondrous, yes. I was too tired to care. I held my drink in numb fingers and tried hard to stay awake. The dinner which Rayner, bless her, had cooked, the wine which I had sworn to forego tonight, the warmth and the darkness, relieved only by the light from the projector, were all having their effect. The slides clicked on hypnotically: tombs, monuments, wall paintings; desert creatures whose names I had never heard; Rayner standing tinily before some vast Arabian sculpture; Rayner with a camel, both of them looking unhappy about it; Patrick hanging out of a Land-Rover, wearing a khaki hat and a broad grin. On and on. I was not bored – at any other time I would have been fascinated – I was simply exhausted.

At midnight Patrick said uncertainly, 'I *think* that's the lot . . .' He rummaged, and Barry sat up. Quickly we both made loud noises of appreciation and Patrick was suitably gratified. Rayner switched the light on. 'I hope we haven't kept you up too late. This was your last chance to see the slides because,' she threw in casually, 'we're off tomorrow.'

'Off?' Barry repeated, startled. 'Already? Where to?'

'Salisbury,' said Patrick, oddly self-conscious. 'There's a temporary teaching post at a school there, just for a term. I've got it. It'll keep the wolf from the door while I look around for something permanent.'

'Salisbury,' repeated Barry. 'That's fine, you'll be able to come over quite often. But why on earth didn't you tell us?'

Patrick spread his hands, glanced at his wife. 'You know how it is.'

We didn't, but let it go. Something, I thought, is going on. Something funny is happening. It's not like them to be secretive.

92

'I'd better say my farewells, then,' said Barry. 'I don't suppose I'll see you in the morning.' He said them, and we began to clear up the mess of equipment and bottles. In a fog, I removed the corks, set the tray with night-time and morning drinks for the children, let Ginny out and back in. The others had gone upstairs. Then Barry came down again and peered helplessly around the kitchen.

'What are you looking for?' I enquired, yawning.

'Clean socks and underpants. There are none in the airing cupboard.'

I interrupted another yawn to swear feelingly and at length. Barry looked interested. 'The bloody washing,' I said viciously, 'is outside on the bloody clothes-line. That's where it bloody is.'

I marched to the fridge, opened it, banged it shut. 'Furthermore, there's no bloody milk left so you can't even have cereal or tea in the morning. Oh, *shit*!'

'Poo!' said Barry.

'Penis!'

We stared at each other. 'Feeling low?' said Barry in a soothing voice. 'Unable to cope? Come to Lottabridge Psychiatric Hospital! We have: mahogany-veneered drug trolleys; ECT *twice* a week! And specially trained staff to make your stay memorable.'

We started to laugh, really laugh at last. And on that mad note we went to bed.

Chapter Seven

They left the next day, but not without leaving their mark. Rayner's mark, that is.

They got out of bed at about ten o'clock, by which time I had been up for three and a half hours. The first thing Rayner said when she appeared was, 'About that letter. You haven't mentioned it so I assume it still hasn't arrived?' I assured her it had not, and she frowned. 'It's very odd. In Morocco you half expect letters to vanish en route, but not in England. Still.' She shrugged it off. 'If it comes, will you post it back to me? Unopened?'

I blinked at her. 'All right, but – why?'

She hesitated. 'Oh – I wrote something ill-advised and I'd rather you didn't read it.'

'I'm intrigued.'

'You promised,' she reminded me.

'I didn't promise, but I'll promise now if you like. I've written some pretty stupid letters myself in my time.'

There was protest in her face, but she said no more and presently she and Patrick were bringing down their belongings and fending off Becky's manifestations of grief. My own feelings about their departure were mixed, concerned primarily with a resumption of reasonable sleeping hours and of course my novel, but, too, there was a deep regret that this friendship was not what it had been, a wish that I could now, at the eleventh hour, improve things and return our communication to its old footing.

Rayner, I thought, must have felt something similar, for she sent Patrick off to the shop with a long list of things they could not possibly need today, and which they could certainly have bought more cheaply in any town; and then she produced two particularly chewy toffee-and-chocolate bars to keep the children quiet, and sat me down at the dining-room table with a cup of tea.

'I want to talk to you,' she began purposefully. 'I want to know, before I leave, what you meant the other night by that spiel about the thrushes and the worms. When I said I was hoping for a baby. And I want the truth.'

She fixed me with her eye and I saw the light of battle in it. Me, I thought wearily, and my big mouth. She had evidently been brooding over my remarks ever since I had made them, thinking that I believed her incapable of motherhood.

'Rayner,' I said, with as much sincerity as I could muster, 'I'm sure you'll make a marvellous mother. Don't listen to me: I'm a chronic complainer.'

She was not deceived. 'You think I know nothing about looking after children. It's not true. I have several nieces and nephews.'

'Rayner, of course. I'm sorry, I – '

'I don't believe any woman is truly fulfilled until she's a mother.' An involuntary snort escaped me and she looked defiant. 'That sounds like women's magazine mush, I know, but I believe it.'

'Well, if you believe that – ' I refrained from saying, 'You'll believe anything' – 'you'll probably make a lovely mother. No, all I meant by that silly little story was that none of us knows quite what we're letting ourselves in for.' I gave a rueful laugh. 'I read all the books when I was pregnant and they made everything seem so rosy, mothers and babes glowing with happiness, you know the kind of thing. Even the sections about bored children, fractious children, children going through the "negative phase", even they don't really prepare you for the reality: the frustration and boredom of it all. I wanted to prepare you a little, myself.'

'But there needn't be any frustration and boredom,' she said decisively. 'There should be communication between you, constructive creative activities that you can enjoy and that stimulate the children's minds and imaginations and increase their self-esteem.'

95

I smiled, I hoped not ironically. 'Of course there should. If I had a cook-housekeeper there probably would be. That's what I meant by reality. I've tried doing projects with the children but they always end up throwing their musical shakers at each other or crushing the eggshells they're supposed to be painting or cutting up the curtains and glueing the bits to the dog. You may be lucky and get placid kids. God help you if you get a Becky.'

In some strange perverse way my words, meant to be helpful, were hardening her resolve to be right in this matter. I could see it in the set of her jaw, hear it in the increasing aggression of her voice. She was angry, I realised too late, because I had a whole world of experience which she lacked. Hence a feeling of inadequacy, hence the aggression.

'If I had a Becky,' she said clearly, 'I would handle her firmly, consistently, with love and discipline.'

'Mm,' I said. I picked up my cup and sipped tea thoughtfully. 'I suppose we all think we'll never do the things we end up doing. I never believed I'd lose my temper and yell the way I do. I used to think other mothers' behaviour was nothing short of disgusting.' I grinned at her. 'I understand now. You will too.'

A mistake. She said, rather coldly, 'Amabel, your type of person makes your type of mother. But I won't be like you. For one thing, I shall *enjoy* my children.'

'Oh, I enjoy mine sometimes. Quite often, in fact. On the other hand,' I added cheerfully, 'I hate them sometimes too.'

I heard her breath go in sharply. '*Hate* them?'

'Oh, yes. For short periods.'

She looked at me as if I were evil beyond belief. I paused, knowing I ought not to pursue the subject for Rayner never took kindly to suggestions that she was ill-informed, but aware too that she had her well-groomed head in the clouds over this fulfilment business. I said carefully, 'It's just another of the things the books don't tell you. Of course mothers hate their children sometimes. Why do you think there's so much baby battering?'

Her eyes widened. 'Amabel, you *don't* – You *haven't* – '

'No. I get rid of it by screaming. Look, I know mankind cannot bear very much reality and all that, but you're far too intelligent to believe that being a mother equals being in heaven. The more intelligent you are, the more hellish it can be. *Can* be.' Her face was stubborn, she thought I was making it all up or something, though God knew she had seen for herself this reality I was talking about. Of course one always thinks it will be different for oneself. I added with feeling, 'I wish people had warned *me* what to expect. You think you're the only one, you see. Everyone else, all the shining radiant women in the adverts, they've achieved this magnificent fulfilment and you haven't. It can make you feel pretty wretched to believe that.'

Mentally I girded my loins, braced myself, and went on, 'You also think you're the only woman who ever lost her sex drive. That's – disturbing. You suffer the most awful guilt, your husband suffers physically and feels rejected, you don't know how long it will last, maybe forever – and *nobody else* is going through it. Or so you think.'

But she was smiling her confident smile. 'Oh, that won't happen to me.'

'Yes, I know you two have an ecstatic sex life and that's why I'm – '

'Amabel,' interrupted Rayner, 'don't be so wet. Women don't go off sex just because they've had babies. If you've gone off it there must be other reasons.'

I began to get annoyed. 'But don't you see, that's precisely why it's so upsetting when it happens: because we believe it doesn't happen? Not one book that I've read, and I've read a lot, has mentioned it. Loss of libido in pregnancy, yes, but nothing about its loss whilst bringing up young children.'

'Then how do you know you're not the only woman to suffer it?' she asked, obviously enough.

'I've asked questions.'

'Of doctors?'

'No. Women at the babies' clinic. Strangers. You fall into quite intimate conversations under those circumstances.'

She smiled again. 'They were trying to make you feel better.'

I leaned back in my chair. I thought, Oh well, I tried. It was not my failure to convince Rayner that depressed me – she would find out in due course and with any luck her experiences would be happier than mine – it was the gigantic, unbridgeable gap between us, the entire lack of that empathy we had once known.

In the next room the children were being remarkably quiet. I called, 'What are you doing in there?' and Becky replied sweetly, 'Lego, Mummy.'

I raised gratified eyebrows at Rayner, who did not respond. 'Bringing the Lego was an inspired move,' I said.

But Rayner was not to be deflected by flattery. She pushed her untouched cup away so abruptly that the tea slopped over the brim. She didn't notice. I watched it trickle to the edge of the table and begin to drip.

'All right,' she said suddenly, 'you've had your say. Now I'll have mine.'

'Fair enough,' I said equably. 'Go ahead.'

'I wasn't going to tell you this. I thought you'd be hurt. But now I think I must. Amabel, you've changed. You're different, and for the worse.'

'Oh,' I said, 'if that's all . . . I know that.'

'Then why don't you do something about it?'

I looked into her determined eyes and didn't answer. I too used to have that determined, positive attitude to life. Why, I had wandered all over the Americas alone, allowing nothing to stand in the way of my independence, my freedom. I knew all about that attitude. Inherent in it was the inability to understand those who lacked it, and why.

'Let's start with basics. You've let yourself go shockingly,' Rayner told me. 'I know you're poor but that's no reason to go about with *food* on your clothes, for God's sake!'

'My clothes get grabbed,' I said mildly, 'by food-y fingers.'

'Then wipe the fingers. And stop being so defeatist. You've given up trying. You don't even keep your hair clean.'

'I do. It's the washing-up liquid, it makes my hair – '

'You've become lazy. You should take the kids out more, even if it's only to playgroup. They need it as much as you do, it's not fair to keep them shut up, you all get on each other's nerves. They need stimulation.'

'I do take them to playgroup,' I said, 'one morning a week. It's all there is.'

'Then start another. Organise the local mothers into some

kind of rota so that each of you has several kids for a morning while the others get a break.'

'The woman here aren't *like* that – '

'So change them. Honestly, Amabel, I'd never have believed you could become so negative in your outlook. All you do is worry about those kids, but you don't *enjoy* them; you spend half your time yelling at them. You get agitated about dishes and washing and naps and getting meals on time, and then you wonder why you're exhausted. You should make an effort and get out, get yourselves on a bus, take a picnic, and go off for the day. Go out alone sometimes too. Go to evening classes. Organise a baby-sitter and make Barry take you out in the evenings.'

'We can't afford – ' I began, but she swept on.

'And that's another thing: your attitude to Barry. I notice things, you know, I notice more than you imagine, and the way you treat him is – Well. You barely bother to greet him when he comes in, you just complain about having to cook another meal. Do you ever give him a big hug, just for nothing, just because you feel like it? You're too tied up with the children's demands. You haven't even listened to *us* these two days, you've kept jumping up and down because Becky's hit Drew or Drew's fallen over, and it's been impossible to hold a conversation with you, especially at mealtimes. *I* didn't like it so God knows how Barry feels. No man likes to come second to his children. Patrick will always come first with me, I shall make sure of that. Why, you don't even iron Barry's shirts. They're all crumpled.'

'They're hidden below his uniform as a rule,' I said dully. 'There doesn't seem much point.'

'But there is a point. It shows you care for him. *Do* you care for him?'

I looked down at my cold tea. 'Yes.'

'It's not obvious. And you're even depriving the poor man of sex. This loss of libido theory is just plain rubbish, you're simply making excuses because you can't be bothered. I know you get tired, your eyes are a mess, and I suppose that's natural, but he has rights too. He has a right to a decent meal occasionally, for one thing. If you'd given me what you gave him yesterday I'd have put it straight into Ginny's bowl.

Amabel, you don't have to live like this. Just organise yourself, get a proper routine; organise your money too. Use some of it to enjoy yourself and you'll be a nicer person to live with. You'll never catch me slaving away all day like you do, worrying about bills and filled with anxiety over the children. You've become boringly domesticated and so damned joyless that, frankly, I don't see how Barry puts up with you.'

A silence.

'There,' she said, with a little breathless apologetic laugh, 'I've finished. Now don't be offended, will you? I had to tell you, as a friend.'

'Of course,' I said, and got up.

'You must know I'm right.'

'Doubtless,' I said.

She bit her lip. 'You've gone all stiff.'

'You should reserve that line,' I said, 'for Patrick.'

She laughed relievedly. All was well, Amabel had made a joke, Amabel was not annoyed.

Patrick came back. The bustle of departure began: taking things out to the car, running back for things forgotten. I stood out in the road, Drew held in my arms, Becky clasped tightly by the hand as Patrick started the engine and the wheels began to move.

'Thanks for your hospitality, Amabel,' Patrick called. 'Be seeing you soon, I expect.'

'Good luck in Salisbury.' Hurry up, hurry up, *go*. It was an eternity.

'Lovely to see you again.'

Rayner put her head out of the window. 'Next time,' she said, smiling, 'I might be pregnant. Then we can really share experiences.'

'I hope so. I do hope,' I said fervently, 'that you have children, Rayner. I hope you have *lots* of children.'

She smiled radiantly and the car drew away.

My curses on her!

I seethed. I raged, I boiled, I felt I could do murder. Never, never in my life had I been so angry. The arrogance! The overbearing, damned conceited arrogance! Who was she, with her freedom and her bank account and her self-confidence and her sharp tongue, to tell me how to live, how to bring up my children, how to treat my husband! She, who knew nothing of childbirth, nothing of parental anxiety and broken nights and perpetual tiredness, whose worst experience of pain had been toothache or a bad period, who would not even soil her manicured hands with a nappy change; who was she to dictate to me as if I were one of her forelock-tugging pupils? My curses on her!

It wasn't true.

My raging ceased. It wasn't true, it couldn't be true, but – There was a sudden question mark.

The hurt of it hit me and I began to cry, standing in the kitchen with my face in a dirty towel, trying to cry quietly in case the children heard me. I made for Rayner all the excuses I could find: she was a teacher, accustomed to lecturing her subordinates: she had a critical mind which always saw room for improvement in others; she lacked, through no fault of her own, sensitivity and imagination, so she had been unaware of the pain she was inflicting; she had wanted to help me to a more satisfactory, as she saw it, life. But, the excuses made, the betrayal remained. She had said unforgivable things, unforgivable even if some of them *were* true . . .

Were some of them. . . ? Yes, for why else had I begun a diary and a novel if not because I realised I was becoming 'boringly domesticated and damned joyless'? (Oh God!) But I *did* realise, I *had* tried to overcome it. She simply didn't understand the difficulties. Or had I made too much of the difficulties, was I a defeatist as she said?

Was I as bad a mother as she said?

The tears began again. Weak tears, making me furious with myself and her. She doesn't understand, she doesn't understand . . . I knew my cooking was shameful, I knew we lived in a muddle, but surely, surely I gave to the children things worth having, valuable intangible things amidst the penny-pinching chaos in which we lived?

I thought of Becky and Drew standing together on one chair at the kitchen sink, the three of us watching intently the light reflected on the water in the bowl: shaking it so that the water trembled, tracing the glimmer of reflected sunlight on the ceiling back to the water. Weren't those things more important than cooking and efficiency, didn't they constitute that vital stimulation of mind and imagination? I remembered myself lying full-length with the children by a stream, a local one we visited often, and trying to identify a suitable hole which might house Toad or Rat. Would Rayner have done that, or would she have considered it too muddy an occupation, too damaging to the clothes? I thought of the three of us returning through the trees, myself carrying each child in turn as their legs wore out, panting but pleased when Becky bid me, 'Say "The woods are lovely", Mummy.' And myself saying it:

'The woods are lovely, dark and deep,
But I have promises to keep,
And miles to go before I sleep.'

'Say it again, Mummy.'

No, Rayner was wrong, I was not so bad as she painted me. And yet – I *did* lose my temper, I did shout and smack and fuss over trivial things, I *was* poor company when the children were present; or even – yes, I had thought it myself quite recently – even when they were not.

And that brought me to Barry.

Sex. She hadn't believed me. Fool that I was to have told her. You can't be bothered, she said. And it was true, I couldn't, but it was more than that. It was as if all my passion had somehow gone into the children. When I did 'bother' it was with an effort, without desire, with boredom even, and yet with ever-growing anxiety over what was happening to me . . . detached from the whole act, examining my responses during it as if I were some inquisitive sexual therapist. Trying. Nothing. I must have stopped loving him.

Guilt.

It was the guilt more than anything else which had driven me at last to open the conversation with the girl in the clinic, a placid-looking girl with three children under five. My heart had quailed at the sight of them. It was in fact quite easy to throw in a casually humorous remark about what kids did to your sex life, and her prompt and compassionate description of her sister's sufferings in this respect had told me all I wanted to know: I was not alone.

102

It had taken the sister two years to return to her normal self.

Two years!

Rayner, however, hadn't believed me.

And the rest of it – being cold to Barry, unwelcoming, uncaring, crumpled shirts, food fit only for the dog. Lazy, letting myself go. Boring. Joyless.

Oh Rayner. How could you?

The day passed in grey misery. I remembered, assessed, re-assessed, argued mentally, with Rayner, with myself; defended, prosecuted, convicted, acquitted. When I had completed the cycle once I began it again. Round and round, all day, until my brain was sick of it. Barry was working late. Like an automaton I moved Becky's bed back into her own room, fed and bathed the children, read bedtime stories. I knew nothing about myself anymore, nothing about Barry, whether he was unhappy or happy, and what small sense of humour I had had left was utterly gone. By the time he came home I was a mental wreck.

He was talkative, for once. 'Amabel, it's working, I'm actually having some success with that phobic girl I told you about. Remember, the one who was afraid of dirt and old people? Yesterday she stood in the corridor outside the Geriatric ward, today she went right in with me and stayed there for five minutes. She was in a cold sweat, mind you, but she did it. She's a trier, that girl, she's determined to conquer her problem.'

'That's fine,' I managed. 'Well done. It wouldn't have happened without you.'

'No, I really don't think it would.' He was animated, slightly abashed by his own pleasure. 'She responds to me. The problem now will be to encourage her whilst discouraging too much dependence on me. Apparently that's a common problem, especially with patients of the opposite sex. Still, I'll worry about that at the appropriate time.

'A new patient came in today,' he went on, throwing off his uniform jacket. 'Twenty-two years old, and he's been having psychiatric treatment on and off since he was *eight*. Heavy pressure from a domineering mother, apparently, because the poor kid wasn't as clever as his sister. God, some parents have a lot to answer for!'

He loosened his tie, yanked it over his head, and gave me a hug. 'You look tired. What time did Patrick and Rayner leave?'

I told him, pressing my head hard against his shoulder. He held me quickly away from him, searched my face. 'What's the matter?'

I forced a laugh. 'You and your vibes. Nothing. Want anything to eat?'

'Just a sandwich. I must catch up on my Yoga tonight and then early to bed. They've worn me out, those two. Seems quiet without them?'

'Yes,' I said.

I made his sandwich, a thick one crammed with Rayner's ham. Why had she brought so much food for a two-day stay? Why such kindness and warmness of heart followed by such. . . ?

'Amabel. What is it?'

This time his voice undid me and I started to cry again. How *could* she ask if I cared for him? I found myself sobbing like a child. I had not cried like this for ages, not since I was pregnant with Drew and subject to those terrifying emotional storms. 'Amabel . . . Oh love, what *is* it?' He was growing agitated in his turn, and I remembered Rayner's words: 'Barry's got enough weight to carry without a clinging wife.' More guilt, more and more guilt.

'It's not bloody *fair*!' I exploded suddenly, wrenched myself from his arms and reached for the toilet roll I always kept in the kitchen. 'Why was I born a bloody *woman*?'

He gave a relieved chuckle. 'Good,' he said. 'Now come and sit down and I'll eat while you tell me about it.'

At least he was not going to relinquish his sandwich, so I was not being treated like a patient. Not yet.

I told him. All of it. I left nothing out and I tried hard to put in nothing that had not been there. Chewing vigorously, he heard me out, and once the sandwich was finished his face was able to show concern. But –

'Well, never mind,' he said comfortingly, when I had come to the end. 'You know Rayner: can't stop once she starts.'

104

It seemed inadequate, to say the least. 'Is that all you can say?'

'What do you want me to say?' He regarded me. 'You're upset, but that's partly a result of being tired and tense. You and Becky are very alike, you know. You both leap up and down the scales of emotion an octave at a time, hitting notes of high drama at every possible opportunity.'

'Never mind the fancy metaphors,' I said bitterly. 'Just tell me in plain English that you think I'm dramatising and then I'll know where I stand. For God's sake, Barry, I thought I could count on you for support!'

He frowned. 'I'm sorry.'

'Everything about me has just come under attack. My whole way of life. My ability in practically every field. And all you can say is "Never mind!" What I want you to say is that Rayner is *wrong*! Or,' I added illogically, 'that even if she's right, it doesn't matter to you; that you *like* me this way.'

He smiled. 'Well, now that you've said it for me, I don't need to, do I?'

'Don't evade the issue. I suppose you agree with everything she said?'

'Let's say I think she showed a degree of insensitivity,' he said cautiously.

'Fine. Let's say that. And now let's say that you agree with her.'

'But, Amabel, you know these things yourself. You're always saying that you've become narrow and uninteresting, that you're a rotten mother, that you can't cook – '

'Stop it!' I shouted. 'I *know* I'm no good but I do *try*! Can't you see I want reassurance, not a goddamned recapitulation of the whole – Oh, hell!'

I couldn't believe this was happening. I had been so sure he would sweep me into his arms and pour into my ears a list of all my good qualities, my unusual qualities, those that compensated for the ones I lacked.

'Rayner has no children,' Barry was saying equably. 'You must make allowances for that.'

I grasped at it eagerly. 'That's right, she doesn't understand. So you *don't* agree with that she said.'

'I didn't say that.'

105

'*Barry*!'

'If you'll just calm down for a minute you'll see that it's your own shortcomings, or what you consider shortcomings, which are upsetting you. They've always upset you and they always will unless you can come to terms with them. Or unless you can do something about them, as Rayner seems to think you can. I don't know if you can or not. There are practical difficulties which she doesn't appreciate, but then she wouldn't, she's never experienced them. Amabel, you are the way you are. You're not a housekeeper; at heart you're a writer, and as such you do wonderful things with the children. You talk to them as intelligent beings when they let you, you even read poetry to them after breakfast. How many mothers do that, do you think?'

This was better. I said wretchedly, 'I spoiled their visit. I had no time for them.'

'Of course you had no time, but that wasn't your fault. It will be different when the children are older.'

'And – what about you?'

'What about me?'

'Those things she said – '

'Well . . .' He gave a wry smile. 'Again, you are the way you are.'

I said nothing for a moment. It was unsatisfactory. And yet – what more could I expect? He was so patient, so uncritical. Back came the guilt. I did not deserve him. 'She's right, you know,' I said sombrely.

He shook his head. 'Not all the way. She'll qualify it some day.'

'God,' I said feelingly, 'I hope her baby teethes for months on end. I hope it's hyperactive. I hope it gets up at two in the morning and doesn't go to sleep again until six. I hope it's sick all over her expensive dresses. I hope it grabs her gorgeous hair with custardy fingers. I hope her stitches are so damn painful that she can't make love for three months. I hope – '

'Stop,' he said. He was still smiling, but there was a gravity in the smile and I did stop. 'Rayner,' he pointed out, 'is also the way she is.'

We looked at each other. I had a brief flash of insight, a moment of illumination. If only people would stop criticising

106

each other, stop trying to force others into a different mould, understand that each person had his own method of living. Like Barry's patients we had somehow to come to terms with what life had done to us, with what we had done to ourselves and to one another. We all had the minutiae of daily life to contend with, battles large or small, with wailing children or phobias. To deal with them one needed courage for oneself and also compassionate understanding of the problems of others. Above all, acceptance and a willingness to make the best of what there was.

It was gone in an instant, but I had seen it and I would try to remember it. I would try to use it. If I could, I would find some way of enriching my life so that my own petty complaints ceased.

Why, I would be a perfect little Pollyanna.

Part Two

Chapter One

The first week of April. Through the open window of the dining-room, where I sat struggling with the second chapter of *Out of the Mouths of Babes*, the heady scents of spring floated in: earth and rain and new buds tearing stickily into life beneath one of those gently hurtful skies.

Rhapsodising over the spring was all very well but it didn't help my novel. I chewed my pen in time-honoured fashion and tried to be objective about what I had written. Difficult. I was by now so thoroughly convinced that I would never again write anything even mediocre, let alone good, that every word seemed doomed to certain destruction before I wrote it.

The doorbell rang. Gin, ferocious guard dog that she was, wagged her tail. I said 'Damn', and got up, not really sorry to turn my back on the lifeless Timothy Walthers. It would be a salesman of some sort, I reflected as I kicked my way through bits of Lego, for no-one ever visited us socially and I had paid the milkman last night.

'Who is it?' shouted Becky, before I had even got the door open.

'The milkman. Go to sleep.' I opened the door.

And gaped. It is not every day you find Mr Universe standing on your front step. 'Hello,' he smiled, 'Mrs Dennell?' I nodded, transfixed. Young, he was, not more than twenty, but built like an ox and handsome with it. He had thick dark-blond hair, very clean, which fell half across his forehead; clear, penetrating blue eyes, the sort that melt female cinema-goers everywhere; and the kind of tan that ought not to be allowed in April. The smile was good, a real one, friendly and open, and the teeth were even better. I stared up at the vision and thought, Drew will look like this one day. On the thought I beamed at him adoringly and his smile faltered for a moment.

'I saw your advert,' he said, well-spoken but not overwhelmingly so, 'and I wondered if you'd take me on?'

'Take you – on?'

'I'm doing my A levels this summer.'

Light dawned. I had almost forgotten the ad that I had placed in a newsagent's window in town. In truth I had been sure no-one would bother to track me down in person, since I had been unable to give a telephone number. However, this young Adonis *had* bothered . . .

I panicked, and was about to gibber when I was saved by my daughter. 'But the milkman came *last* night!' (And I had thought she was quick-witted.)

'Go to sleep! I'm so sorry,' I said to my visitor, with the stately smile I hardly ever used. 'Come in and let's discuss it. You've taken me by surprise, I'm afraid.'

I shut the door and followed his huge bulk down the hall, wondering what on earth to do. Now that I was faced with an actual flesh-and-blood pupil it was clear that I had to back out somehow. I had forgotten all I ever knew of literature, I should make a fool of myself the moment I tried to utter a learned statement and, worse, he would fail his exam.

There was an agonised whanging clatter and a raccoon shot away across the kitchen floor. My visitor apologised, I apologised. 'Come through. Sorry about the mess . . .'

He was the type of young man who is interested in things, in people, in surroundings. He looked about at the litter of domesticity, smiled at the toys, stared attentively at the books and finally lowered himself, at my bidding, into a chair. I felt relieved that he was at last at a manageable level, but even so I didn't know how to manage him. If I had imagined anyone coming it would have been a – well – a gangling, schoolboy sort of person . . . with glasses . . . When had they started making them like this?

I pulled myself together. 'I'd better tell you that I've been having second thoughts about coaching.'

His face fell. 'Oh, what a shame. You were the cheapest.'

112

I heard myself give a burst of appreciative laughter, and he blushed and laughed too. 'That,' I explained, 'is because I'm not sure that I'd be very good at it. You see, it's several years since I left University and I'm probably rather rusty.'

'Oh, is that all?' He was not at all put out. 'I expect it'll come back to you. One of our teachers came back to school after years at home. She said she was rusty too, but she's a good teacher.'

'Are you – are you still at school?' I asked hesitantly. 'You look older.'

'Sixth form,' he replied cheerfully. 'It's my size. It's deceptive.'

And your manner, I thought, and your unconscious charm. 'What's your name?'

'Francis. Francis Blake.' He scowled endearingly. 'My mother is from Plymouth. It was the closest she could get to the name of the local hero.'

I laughed. 'I see.'

'Look, Mrs Dennell – '

'Mine's Amabel.'

'Oh. Oh,' he said. Then, 'Amabel. That's pretty.'

He'd got it right. I was won. I went into the dining-room, tore a sheet of paper from my new and barely-used pad, got the pen and came back. 'Tell me what books are on the syllabus.'

'You mean you'll take me on? Oh, great,' he said boyishly. He *was* a boy, after all. '*Macbeth*,' he began to recite, '*Tess of the d'Urbervilles* – that's Thomas Hardy, you know. Sylvia Plath – she's a poet – '

'Yes,' I said.

'*The Duchess of Malfi*; Wordworth poems; Chaucer; and there's a modern novel called *Kes*. That's about a boy who trains a – '

'I know it.' I finished scribbling and looked critically over the list. 'Well, that's all right,' I said. 'We've got all of those, I think.' I sat and thought. Yes, I could handle it, I was sure I could. Why, even without opening the books I could give a kind of mini-lecture on most of them. And Barry would help me if I got stuck. 'How many evenings a week would you like?'

113

'Oh, just one. I'm quite busy. I'm a Venture Scout, you see, and my group does a lot of canoeing. I'm a kind of unofficial coach, actually,' he said with a self-deprecating laugh, 'so that makes two of us.'

Canoeing. I looked at him admiringly. So that was where he got his physique and his tan. 'Where do you canoe?'

'On club nights I coach some kids in the swimming pool in town,' he said, 'and at weekends we practise on the local rivers. But we go on trips too, canoeing and camping trips down in Devon and Cornwall. The River Lyner, the Tamar, the Dart . . . the Dart is quite intimidating,' he said, with evident satisfaction.

'It must be exciting,' I said enviously.

'It's great fun. You're flowing with adrenalin at the start, you know, then once you get going you just concentrate like mad. You're scared silly of going sideways or capsizing. But the whole experience is – kind of stimulating.' He smiled at me, rather self-consciously, but I was enthralled.

'Isn't it cold? You must get very wet?'

'We have wetsuits, of course, and spray-decks on the canoes, and life jackets and crash hats. We're very well-equipped, and physical exertion keeps you warm too. But rolling or capsizing are shockingly cold all the same, because the water shoots straight down your neck.' We laughed, and seeing my interest he went on, 'Most of the discomfort comes from cramps, after quarter of an hour or so. That and aching limbs. And terror, naturally.'

'Really?' He didn't look as if he knew the meaning of the word.

'Oh yes.' He gave a reverent shake of the head. 'There's a place in Devon on the Lower Dart, they call it the washing-machine – '

'Don't tell me.' Briefly I shut my eyes as, in my imagination, Drew hurtled towards this death-trap whose nickname alone was terrifying. Yet I was filled with admiration, for after all this was not Drew but a very competent canoeist who obviously knew exactly what he was doing. Marvellous boy!

And boy he then became, for 'I'm miles behind with my studying,' he said frankly, 'because of that. That's why I need some tuition. I'm hoping to go to University, you see. I'm

114

taking Sociology and History as well, and my dad is paying for private tuition for those too, so I owe it to him to give it my best shot.'

'Lucky you,' I said, 'with a father like that.'

For the first time his face showed an expression I didn't like. 'He's too pushy,' he said abruptly. 'It's all right for me, I don't mind it, but – '

The words fell away. I ignored them, got to my feet and said, 'Well, pick your evening. Not Tuesday or Friday.'

He thought for a moment and we settled that he would come on Wednesdays. His first visit would be in three days' time so I would have to get cracking. Bang went the novel.

At the door he turned. 'Er – how do I pay you?'

By looking like you do, I very nearly answered, and by telling me about your canoeing trips. 'Any way you like,' I said. I had a sudden, hotly embarrassing vision of a whore in a seedy room: 'Payment first, love, then the goods.' 'Sort it out with your father,' I said, my face burning. 'I don't mind at all.'

I shut the door on him and said, 'Phew.'

'What a GREAT BIG man,' Becky remarked from her position on the stairs.

'Get back into bed this minute! What do you think you're doing? And don't wake Drew!'

She trudged away but immediately changed direction and crashed downwards again as the back door opened and Barry came home from his late shift. I let her run through to the kitchen to meet him and he swung her up in the air and kissed her. 'What are you doing up at this time?' he said sternly.

'There's been a man,' Becky told him, 'an ENORMOUS large man, and Mummy's face was ever such red.'

'Was it indeed?' He put Becky down and glanced enquiringly at me. I went over to him and gave him a tight hug. My new policy. When I had finished he said, 'I thought I saw someone leaving. Who is he?'

I told him, briefly, and then sent him off to return Becky to her bed. When he came back I was poring over my book of names. 'Do you still do that every time you meet someone?' he asked in surprise.

'Not every time.' My finger went down the F's.

'What is his name, anyway?'

115

'Francis.'

'And what does it mean?'

I had found it. 'Free,' I said, and shut the book.

I had not, of course, become a Pollyanna in the three weeks since the Lambs' visit. The abiding memory of that last traumatic day was, alas, not of my almost visionary moment of understanding, but of the hurt inflicted by Rayner. Its effects had been severe. I had found myself doubting the wisdom of everything I said and did, whether administering discipline to the children, talking to Barry, making decisions about minor things such as what to wear, what food to buy . . . I even doubted whether they were minor things. I examined every word I uttered, fearful that I was being negative or defeatist or joyless or child-obsessed. I analysed my reasons for every action and then criticised the analysis. As for sex – poor Barry! Desire was never deader, and the more I tried the worse it got. By the end of that first week I felt ten times more inadequate than I had felt before, and ten times guiltier. I began to believe that everything I had done in these last few years had been a total error of judgement – particularly marrying Barry, who was obviously miserable with me, and having children, whose lives I was ruining by my mishandling.

These the fruits of Rayner's good advice.

Ultimately, of course, common sense prevailed. After a week or two I managed to stop composing defensive monologues in my head and to sleep instead of going nightly over and over my failings and the impossibility of rectifying them. When I felt that the treadmill was about to start turning again I reminded myself of those realisations that had, fleetingly, come to me, and attempted to think positively. I did not become a Pollyanna but I did manage to stop feeling sorry for myself. I even ironed Barry's shirts. And I stopped complaining about the unpredictability of his lunch hours. And I stopped screaming at the children (for a day or two).

I advertised myself as a tutor in English Literature.

And I joined a drama group.

This last occurred almost without my volition. I had had one of those days when resolving to spend time creatively and constructively with the children was utterly futile, because the

116

children flatly refused to be creative and constructive. Rain poured unrelentingly from a black and scowling sky and there was no outlet for Becky's wild energy but furious misbehaviour. She ran about like a lunatic, trying to scream it out of herself and luring Drew, her ever-faithful imitator, into most uncharacteristic waywardness. All the good intentions in the world are not proof against this kind of thing.

So all day long the noise of battle roll'd. By bedtime Becky and I were thoroughly hating each other, and even a long and mutually penitent cuddle on her pillow did not fully alleviate the effects of the previous hours. Then there was the evening, the dull nothingness of the evening: Barry moving from his psychiatry books to his Yoga practice to his bath, myself unable to write a word owing to the accumulated tension. Life? Don't talk to me about life.

The next morning I determinedly left Barry to enjoy what would doubtless be a completely trouble-free day off (it always was when I wasn't there) and rode our old mo-ped to the nearest town, four miles away. There I went straight to the newsagent's and placed an ad in the window, offering my tutoring services. Flushed with triumph, I went next to the library, and while I was there a girl rushed in and pinned up a notice close to where I was standing. Naturally, I read it. She paused and asked hopefully, 'Interested?'

'I might be . . .' I said slowly. 'Massey Drama Group urgently needs new members.' I had done some acting at University. It was fun, it was escapism into a land of fantasy, it was donning a new identity. Should I do it? Meetings took place, the notice said, at eight o'clock in Massey village hall, so I could get there more or less on time even when Barry was working late; always assuming the mo-ped co-operated. I knew that a notoriously steep hill separated the villages of Lottabridge and Massey, and the mo-ped felt much as I did about steep hills.

Dare I do it? I had already taken one rash step today.

But the girl seemed to take my hesitation as positive assent. 'The producer will be terribly pleased to see you,' she said enthusiastically. 'We're short of women at present. Two of them went off to have babies. You know how it is.'

'I do,' I said. That settled it. 'All right. I'll come.'

'Fantastic! It'll be Tuesdays only at first, then Tuesdays and Fridays as we get closer to the production date. Sorry, I must dash. My name's Miranda, by the way,' she added, over her shoulder.

'Mine's Amabel.'

'Annabelle. Good, see you Tuesday.' And she rushed away.

That's done it, I thought, somewhat bemused. I wanted action and I've got it. I was half excited, half nervous. It was so long since I had been amongst people that I had no idea how, or even if, I would cope with being suddenly plunged into a crowd of drama enthusiasts, all of whom, presumably, had known each other for some time. I never used to be shy . . .

And I would not be shy now, I resolved. I could and would hold my own amongst these people. I had a life to live, and life, surely, meant fun, varied experiences, fulfilment beyond that of reproducing oneself and tending the result. Despite my initial exhilaration over *Out of the Mouths of Babes*, the writing of it had not changed my life at all. If anything, it had made it even deadlier, pinning me as it did to the dining-room table night after night. Whereas this – *this* would take me out of the house, out of myself. And what had Miranda said, about the group's being short of women? That meant there was a surplus of men. Nothing like a surplus of men for giving one's flagging ego a boost.

I rode home through spring rain, considering the possibilities of playing Juliet to some local stripling's Romeo. No, perhaps I was a bit mature for that, and anyway Shakespeare was probably too highbrow for Massey villagers. Major Barbara, then, strident in Salvation Army uniform. Or even Lady Bracknell in *The Importance of Being Earnest*. No, on second thoughts I was too *im*mature for that.

By the time I got to Lottabridge, soaked through and brimming with anticipation, I had made my choice. The play should be *Pygmalion*, and I was to play Eliza Doolittle.

Alas! The play was the dated and improbable *Murder at the Manor*, and I was the maid. Rather a vital maid, being heavily involved in villainy, but a maid nonetheless. Shattered were

118

my visions of tripping, gorgeously clad, about Ascot.

I had made my announcement to an astonished but self-lessly encouraging Barry, laden my face with unaccustomed goo and urged the reluctant mo-ped over the hill to Massey. It was difficult to look glamorous on such a machine but I had done my best and it was not my fault that a tractor came out of a gloomy gateway at the wrong moment and placed me muddily but harmlessly in the ditch. Doubtless it was my subsequent streaked and dishevelled appearance which landed me with the part of the maid, instead of the dignified mistress of The Manor. It had also the effect, however, of doing away with any shyness I may have felt, for all members of the group were so warmly concerned about me that by the time we came to my informal audition I felt quite at home.

There were only half a dozen of us in the hall that first evening and I was able to get to know everyone quite easily. The one who was to concern me most, on stage anyway, was the leading man, ruggedly handsome and obvious hero material. His name was Godfrey and he smelt virilely of aftershave lotion, the sort which even I, with my lack of access to a television, knew was advertised with near-pornographic lust. I discovered later, when I was able to read the script right through, that when I was not saying, 'You rang, ma'am?' or answering the door to tweedy detectives, I was seducing this hunk of masculinity (the dignified lady's brother) with all the wiles of a Mata Hari. I wondered what Barry would think about that. Godfrey struck me as a type who was not only accustomed to being seduced, on stage or off, but had actually come to expect it. Not my type at all.

Then there was the lady herself, to be played, unexpectedly, by Miranda whom I had met in the library. She turned up late, flustered, wearing tired jeans and a t-shirt which enquired WOULDN'T YOU LIKE TO? and until she read the part aloud I couldn't believe she could do it. She could. Somebody (I didn't yet know who) did away with her at the end of Act I so perhaps the maid was a better part after all.

A dark, bearded man with an engaging manner played Miranda's husband, the master of the house. His name was Don Last and he was a night nurse at the hospital. Talking to him later I asked him about this, and he told me with charming frankness that he did it for the money. He worked three nights a week, he said, twelve hours per night, and when he told me what he earned I nearly fell over. If Barry was willing to do that when he qualified . . . But no. I would miss him too much. We chatted for some time about his work and Barry's training and I found myself, not without amusement, blossoming under such attention, concentrating on the conversation and taking care to be interesting, to appear intelligent. Judging by his manner I succeeded, but Don seemed a gentleman and could not, in all probability, have behaved otherwise in the company of a female.

He had, of course, a wife. His wife was the producer and I saw immediately that as such she was going to be a veritable tartar. Good. That meant a decent production, however feeble the play. The play, she told me regretfully, had been chosen with the village in mind. For themselves, they would have liked something more ambitious, Pinter perhaps, or John Osborne, but the village wouldn't have come, and anyway the royalties were so high . . .

As an evening out, I supposed, it was pretty poor stuff. But to me it felt like a night at the Ritz: heady, exciting, novel. All the self-conscious, garrulous over-friendliness which I had developed in Lottabridge fell away and I was myself again, had a personality again, one which quickly remembered how to reveal itself and win liking. These were delightful, intelligent people. Godfrey was a graphic designer, Mrs Last a teacher, Miranda an art student, the man who played the detective (I had not caught his name) a solicitor. The graduate in me, or perhaps the snob in me, found satisfaction in this. It was good to be with people who cared about drama, art, literature, who could make casual references to modern playwrights and expect to be understood. It was what I had missed in our own wretched excuse for a village. For the first time I saw that it was not solely motherhood which had changed me (for the worse, as Rayner said) but isolation.

But it was more than intellectual stimulation which I gained from that evening. It was self-respect. I *could* contribute intelligently and humorously to a gathering, I *could* communicate with people, I was not the dreary complaining failure I had felt myself to be. I was as vital, as alive, as Rayner herself.

Only I had forgotten that I was.

And – of course – there were the men. Godfrey, who must have learned on the Continent how to give those long, lingering glances that made one feel so desirable, for they were most un-British; Don Last, with his quiet, attentive manner and steady eyes (and disappointingly mercenary attitude to money, but one couldn't have everything); the detective, rather elderly it was true, but with a hint about him of the flame still burning.

Things were looking up. Things were definitely looking up.

I urged the groaning mo-ped ever more slowly up the dark narrow lane that led over the hill. A jogger overtook me, which was humiliating. Going downhill I got my own back, roaring past him, and he shouted something cheerfully insulting and waved. I laughed behind my visor and waved back, wobbling madly.

No, it wasn't just intellectual stimulation. It was freedom. It was living. It was activity, people, the rediscovery of Self. I recalled that speech in Henry James' *The Ambassadors*, the one about living life to the full, but all I could remember of it was the end, where Strether, half-hypnotised by his own intensity, simply keeps repeating one word:

'Live.'

And now there was Francis.

'Don't you think you're going to the opposite extreme?' enquired Barry, an hour after his departure.

'Mmm?' I was already absorbed in my old lecture notes. 'I'll need some A-level papers from previous years. I wonder if Francis has any? I've forgotten what kind of questions they set.'

'The obvious ones: "At heart Macbeth is pure as the driven snow: it is Lady Macbeth who is the embodiment of evil. Discuss." I said, don't you think you're going to the opposite extreme now? Writing a novel, coaching, going to rehearsals. Are you sure you can handle it all?'

I scribbled down a note. 'Half a minute. I want to get this down, about child imagery. Do you think they might use that?'

'The naked babe striding the blast, you mean? And Lady

121

M. plucking her nipple from boneless gums? I don't know, they might. You're doing this, not me. Look, Amabel, I'm trying to talk to you.'

Triumph sprang in me. At last! I refrained from pointing out that I had been asking him for years to talk to me, and said demurely, 'Yes, Barry?'

'You're taking on too much.'

'It'll enrich me. I'll be a nicer person to live with.'

'I shall hardly see you,' he said, mock-grumbling. 'You'll have your head in some book or other all the time.'

I looked pointedly at the book that lay on his own lap: *Anorexia Nervosa: Case Histories*. He said, 'That's different. I don't do this for pleasure.'

'Oh, you lie." I laughed at him. 'Anyway, do you begrudge me some pleasure?'

'Not in the least, so long as it *is* pleasure, not an ordeal by exhaustion. I know of old how involved you get in these things. Remember when you were producing the University pantomime? It was impossible to get any sense out of you for weeks.'

'I shall be very moderate in my approach,' I promised.

I looked thoughtfully at him as he sat in his corner, postponing the moment of beginning to read. Most unusual. I had realised very soon after the day of Rayner's lecture that Barry had given absolutely nothing away concerning his own part in it. I had no more idea now than I had had before whether I made him as unhappy as Rayner believed. 'You are the way you are,' he had said to me, and that could be interpreted in any number of ways. I supposed that when a man made love to an inert lump of flesh he was justified in being a little reticent. He understood the causes, or said he did, but I would probably never really know what he thought, for discussing his thoughts was not Barry's forté. Yet here he was, strangely edgy but, for the first time since he began this course, apparently finding me more interesting than his psychiatry books.

And I *was* more interesting than I had been. I had at my fingertips topics of conversation which, at last, did not concern the house, the children, the unpaid milk bill, the burnt rice-pudding bowl left to soak, the shirt that had turned pink in the wash, the wet patch on the carpet, the shortage of tea bags, the blocked sink, the broken washing-line, and all the other scintillating subjects I had verbalised on seemingly ever since Becky was born.

Then he said, 'I shall be working nights in June. Did you remember that when you arranged to attend all these rehearsals?'

'No.' I was annoyed, briefly: my new bubble, though not actually pricked, had been dented. 'You might have reminded me.' He said nothing. He was always silent when I criticised him, however obliquely.

A pause. 'One of the cast is a night nurse at the hospital. Don Last. Know him?'

He frowned. 'Bearded chap? Yes, I've met him. Bit of a ladies' man.'

'He's very charming.'

'Precisely.'

Another pause. I glanced down at my notes, but still Barry did not open *Anorexia Nervosa*. He just sat there, looking glum. I said uncertainly, 'Do you really mind me doing this? It's quite true that I'll have my head in a book much of the time, but *you* do, so . . .'

'It's not that,' he said. 'No, of course I don't mind. I was joking.'

'Well then – '

'Sorry, love. I'm in an odd kind of mood, I guess. There's rather a silly problem at work and it's bothering me. My anorexic girl. I told you and Patrick and Rayner about her.'

'I remember.'

'Of course you do.' He smiled, rather abstractedly. 'Sometimes I think you take more interest in my patients than I do myself. Well, if I'm grumpy, she's the cause. Nothing to do with your activities.'

'Oh.' So he had not, after all, found me more interesting than his book. He had just been making idle conversation while his brain, set on some kind of automatic pilot, tackled a different problem. I gave an involuntary sigh. Why did I not yet know, why had I never learned to know what was going on inside him? He knew me inside out. It wasn't fair.

'Do you want to talk about it?'

123

'No. Not yet.' Then he cheered up. 'I have a success story, however: my phobic patient is going home for the weekend. A kind of trial run. She's gained a lot of confidence, grown less dependent on me, thank heaven, and we think she's ready.'

'Home? To her husband, you mean?'

He nodded. 'He's very supportive. Very keen to have her back.'

I didn't answer. Presumably Barry was less obsessed, mentally anyway, with the question of sex than I was; but my first, my immediate thought, was, How on earth will the poor girl cope with *that* messy business? Someone, some very genteel lady, I could not remember who, had once said, 'Sex is not for the fastidious.'

I wished her luck, and immersed myself once more in *Macbeth*.

Almost immediately Barry, who plainly could not stop thinking about the hospital, said, 'I ran into Sal Jones today. She gave me a message for you.'

'Who's Sal Jones?' I asked absently.

'You talked to her at the fête last year, about a Mr Howarth? Deaf mute?'

I remembered. 'Has he died?'

He shook his head. 'Somebody has decreed that he should be taught to read.'

I sat bolt upright and thumped the table jubilantly. 'Hurray! At last!'

'Hold on. There's more. Sal said she had told you he was happy, docile and so on?'

'At peace,' I said, bitter again at the memory, 'was the phrase she used.'

'Well, he's not at peace any longer. He's becoming troublesome. "Extremely difficult," she said.'

I stared at him. 'Since starting to read? But I thought it would open up a new world for him?'

'I imagine it's doing that, yes: just as he's about to leave it.'

After that I couldn't concentrate on Shakespeare. I kept remembering that gentle smile which Drew had received, the passive light of acceptance in the old man's eyes. And now . . . Yes, Sal had said it would be cruel and she had been right.

124

I left my notes and went into the kitchen, scene of my personal reality. It seemed to me sometimes that all reality except that concerning the children came to me secondhand. There they were, just a few hundred yards along the road: the phobic, the anorexic, the deaf mute, the man with that terrible crippling disease, the handsome schizophrenic, a hundred, two hundred people suffering the most terrible misery, or, perhaps worse, suffering nothing at all; there too had been Barry's suicide case, the girl whose babies had died. It was all harsh, stark reality and I knew nothing of it. I trod my protected, limited little path of normality and domesticity and heard about these other things only through someone else's lips. I was the Great British Public, the man in the street who might want to know but certainly did not want to touch; who kept these people at arm's length, who said we don't want them in the community, for we had our own preferred version of reality. But how real was it when we rejected all unpleasantness, anything that made us feel uncomfortable, when even I with my trivial problems felt the need to escape into fantasy and make-believe? My novel was make-believe, that cheap silly play was make-believe, even Macbeth was magnificent make-believe.

Somewhere, somehow, I was missing something, failing to grasp some essential concept. Experiencing reality at second hand? Was that it? Was it that their lives, the patients' lives, were somehow more real than mine, more real than most people's, because less bland, less superficial, less pretentious?

I didn't know.

The next day I met my Huntingdon's Chorea victim again. The children were walking this time, Drew toddling along on his reins as we came back up the hill from the shop. I saw the familiar, grotesque movements in the distance and I made the decision: Today I will ask him over for coffee. On he came, lurching towards us, arms flailing with every step. He's worse, I realised; much worse. A few months ago I had thought his own determination had somehow forced his limbs to co-operate, so much more direct were their movements, but now there had been an obvious relapse. Yet he was stubborn, not

125

giving in, not feeling sorry for himself. Guts. Guts.

I didn't ask him. I said hello, he said hello, Becky said hello. For some reason Becky had never commented on his disability and she didn't now. Perhaps she hadn't noticed.

I let him go past.

Why? I didn't know. Something to do with conventional behaviour? After all I would not, on the strength of half a dozen 'Good morning's' issue such an invitation to a healthy man. And there were all the unknown factors: What was he really like? Would there be conversation, or strained, awkward silences? Would he keep appearing at my door, becoming dependent, becoming – a nuisance?

I was ashamed, but there it was. I was too afraid of the small things to risk the big one, the one that might, just might, have lightened his day and even what was left of his life.

And that was not much. His face was greyer, his eyes dead-looking. He was losing this last, tremendous battle and losing it fast. *Do not go gentle into that good night*. The words came fiercely, unbidden.

'Ba-ba,' called Drew suddenly, unexpectedly, and turned, pulling on his reins, so we turned too and watched the man going away. 'BA-BA!' bawled Drew with determination.

I shouted too, eagerly. 'He's saying bye-bye to you!'

We waited. For several seconds there was no perceptible check in the man's progress. Then he stopped and after another few seconds swung himself round. Drew, with great patience, was still waving. Up came the man's arm, slowly, stiff-jointed and jerky like a puppet's. But it was undoubtedly a wave, and the expression on his face was undoubtedly a smile.

We went on, I despising myself. If Drew could talk – Drew would not hesitate, falter; Drew would not be held back by silly fears.

If only we were all children.

Chapter Two

Barry was thumping about on the floor upstairs, doubtless trying to get more than three-quarters of the way down on the *Prasarīta Pàdottànàsana I*. The children, incredibly, slept through it all. They were saving their awakenings until I was soundly asleep myself. I minded this less than I used to. I minded a lot of things less than I used to. Today, for instance, when Becky had commanded that I come and see the House of the Three Bears which she and Drew had built out of Lego, I hardly batted an eyelid when I saw that they had also built the forest; and that all my potted plants were stripped bare of foliage. In fact, so crazily hiliarious did it seem, I sat on the floor and laughed. The lecture I eventually managed to deliver probably lost much of its efficacy as a result. But we were all very happy and we all thought the forest was extremely beautiful. A few weeks earlier I would have damn near burst a blood vessel over that.

I had got back my sense of humour. I had got back my interest in life. More, I was *beginning* to get back something else, equally important . . . There had been moments . . . short-lived, but promising. How many of those moments were due to the attentions of Don Last and the obligatory weekly seduction of Godfrey, I did not care to consider.

As usual I was seated at the dining-room table but this time I was neither learning lines nor preparing lessons; nor was I writing my novel, which had been put aside, not without relief. I would take it up again later, when my other activities ceased, and perhaps in the interim Becky would inspire me anew by some feat of thought reading. Her powers seemed to have waned again.

I picked up the pen and wrote,

Wednesday, 11th April. Francis has just left after a successful first session, during which I ascertained where his weaknesses lay and we worked out a rough study plan. He was wearing cream-coloured cords and a safari shirt and looked browner than ever. It must be the wind which tans him. It's almost impossible to believe he is still at school. Only his reluctance to call me Amabel reminds me of it. His teacher!

We did some Chaucer and I grew quite animated talking about The Parliament of Fowls. *Fascinating if all we humans met annually to choose a new mate! Chaucer sustains a clever duality throughout: the two gates, of bliss and sorrow, both leading to the same garden – love; the two types of love: courtly, chivalric which never actually gets around to mating, and the practical, procreative love which is that of Nature. I'm not sure whether Chaucer felt that courtly love is valueless because it leads nowhere or whether it's still a vital part of life. Doesn't matter – the thing is to get Francis thinking about it for himself, and that I did, although digressions threatened constantly as we found ourselves discussing the merits of the various birds' attitudes: some advocating the creation of jealousy, some fidelity, some avowing that a brief love may be just as intense as a long-standing one . . .*

I stopped and frowned down at my diary. Previously I had been upset because I could not write it interestingly and fluently. Now, the first time I had touched it in weeks, the words came in a positive torrent. Perhaps it was my very garrulity which had suddenly disturbed me.

I decided to change the subject.

Last night I went to Massey for a rehearsal of Murder at the Manor *and ran out of petrol, fortunately when I was already quite close to the village. Don said he could let me have half a gallon from the can in his garden shed, so after the rehearsal I went with him to his house, and he pushed the bike for me. He lives close to the village hall. Dorothy had gone to the pub with*

*the others, which rather surprised me. We filled up the tank and
then he asked me in for a drink. I said, 'Aren't you going to join
your wife?' and he said, ever so casually, 'Oh, Dorothy goes
her way and I go mine. It suits us.' There was one of those
heavy silences. I could smell the spring and the thick scents of
the garden all round us.*

Again I stopped. What was I writing here, a diary or a novel
for starved, romantic hearts? Just because nothing like it had
happened to me for years, just because I had thought that part
of my life was over . . . I was building it up into something it
almost certainly was not. It was the mention of the thick
scents, I realised, which had suddenly made the little episode
seem pregnant with possibilities. A point to remember when
next I tried to create atmosphere in my novel. If I had noticed
a smell of petrol instead the thing would read very differently.

And what *had* happened? Absolutely nothing. My heart
had given a little scared flutter and I had declined politely,
donned my crash helmet and ridden away. The man was
hardly likely, I reflected ruefully, to come the impassioned
lover when his wife was only a few hundred yards off.
Besides, I was fresh from Godfrey's fragrant arms.

I gave a chuckle of pure enjoyment and wrote, in a more
sensible frame of mind, '*Barry says Don is a lady's man. He
may be right.*'

I put the diary away and went to boil a kettle for our
bedtime drink. While I waited I stood before the mirror which
I had recently bought and hung above the sink, and looked at
myself. It was surely my imagination, but I looked younger.
Perhaps it was just that my eyes were brighter, livelier in
expression. And I was not drooping at the shoulders. I had
noticed already that I now strode about the house instead of
trudging, that I took the stairs two at a time. Interesting.
Evidently it was not a balanced diet and a good night's sleep
which determined vitality (not that I ever got a good night's
sleep) but something more subtle, some mental process which
revved up the hormones. It was the same process that had
allowed me, aeons ago, to stay up half the night, partying, and
yet be fresh for work or lectures a few hours later. I remembered the morning after Rayner and Patrick's first night, and

laughed aloud. Well, perhaps not quite the same process.

I heard Barry falling over the raccoon, then he came in, bare-chested and hot from his exertions, as I saw from his reflection in the mirror. 'That damned animal,' he said, then, 'What are you looking at?'

'Me.' I smiled at him in the glass. 'Me,' I repeated. 'Myself.'

He smiled back, his nice warm closed-lipped smile that I had always liked. 'You're happier. I'm glad.'

'*Are* you?'

'Yes.'

'I wish you had something too. Some interest other than the hospital.'

'Do you?'

'Yes.'

It was a typical exchange. I could never decide if such brevity denoted an intimacy which had no need of elaboration, or a lack of intimacy which no amount of elaboration could overcome. His patients, I often suspected, were far less unsure of him than I was.

'BLANKET!'

Becky's night-time roar shook the rafters and we both jumped. Barry said, 'Good grief. How does she do it, coming straight out of sleep like that?'

I laughed. 'How does she do *any* of the things she does?'

Becky was sitting up in bed, awaiting services like a queen. 'Will you put my blanket back on?' she croaked.

I picked it up off the floor and put it back on the bed.

'And the other one.' She pointed to a spare.

'You want two? Are you sure?'

'Yes, two blankets.' I put on the second one. 'Tuck it in.'

'It's tucked in.'

'Only on one side.'

'There's a wall on the other – '

'It'll fall off again.'

'It won't fall off.'

'Blankets fall off if they're not tucked in.'

'IT WON'T FALL OFF!'

She was asleep again in three seconds and I returned to the kitchen, not irritated, not railing against these intrusions into my free time, but amused. Definitely I was a more level, more stable person these days.

I repeated the exchange, verbatim, to Barry, and after he had laughed over it he asked, 'Were you writing, earlier?'

'Writing, yes, but not my novel. I've abandoned that for the time being. I'm too busy.'

'Want to make a note of Becky's latest, for Timothy?'

'Lord, yes.' I went for my pen. 'Has she done it again? When?'

'Tonight, when I put her to bed. You were busy with Francis.'

'Go on.' I didn't think it was a rebuke but you never could tell. I waited, pen poised.

'"If I didn't eat my dinner I'd get very thin. I'd get thinner and thinner and thinner, wouldn't I, Daddy?"'

'Oh.' So he was thinking about this girl, this patient of his, even while tucking his daughter up in bed. I put the pen down without writing anything. 'Coincidence,' I said flatly.

'"And then I'd have to go to your hospital, wouldn't I?"'

I shrugged. 'Logical deduction. She is logical, you know.'

'Maybe. I just thought I'd tell you.'

'It's not one of her devastating ones.'

'True.'

I had hurt his feelings. I said, 'Thanks for telling me,' and he didn't answer. For a few minutes we did our bedtime chores, let the dog out, got Barry's breakfast things ready for morning. '*Is* she very thin?'

'No. Her weight's improved a lot. It's – other things, now.'

'Oh.' He still did not want to talk about it. I said wistfully, 'I wish you'd tell me colourful anecdotes about your patients, like you did when Rayner and Patrick were here.'

'When I get some colourful patients,' he said lightly, 'I'll tell you some colourful anecdotes. Let's go to bed, and for God's sake mind that bloody raccoon.'

'You *must* believe me, Sebastian, I knew nothing about it, nothing! She always treated me so kindly. Why should I want to kill her? She was like a mother to me. Sebastian, I never knew my mother.'

'Forgive me. I said the first thing that came into my head.

Of course you couldn't have anything to do with it – You, with your gentle eyes . . .'

'You're so understanding. So kind. Oh, I *wish* I were your social equal!'

'When you look at me like that, social inequality ceases to matter to me.'

'Mummy, I'm sick of this tape.'

I switched it off, still muttering my lines. I had recorded all the scenes of *Murder at the Manor* in which I took part, and the cassette had been playing and replaying for most of the day. It was working. I was now near word-perfect, knowing not only my own but everyone else's part. Dorothy would be pleased with me. She had reached the foot-stamping stage at last night's rehearsal: '*None* of you can possibly *act* while you're having to consult the script! You can't *look* at each other, you can't handle *props*, you can't do *anything* convincingly until you've got rid of those *books*! The only person who knows *any* of her lines *at all* is Annabelle.' Fired by such praise from a producer notoriously difficult to please, I had hit on this method of learning the rest of my lines; much to Becky's disgust.

'All right, my love. You're quite right, it's unfair. Would you like "Peter and the Wolf"?'

'No. I want to look at photographs.'

She had been rummaging about in a cupboard and produced an album of her own old baby pictures. Every so often Becky had a photographic phase, during which she went about with a broken camera, snapping everything with her eyes tight shut. She was having one now.

Drew being safely asleep, I co-operated and we settled together on the couch, the album open on my knee. I began my commentary.

'That's me, with a fat tummy full of baby.'

'Becky.' She always spoke of herself in the third person when referring to her baby pictures. It makes sense, when you think about it.

'Yes. And there you are in the hospital, just a few days old.' She praised the baby's beauty in glowing terms. 'And there's Daddy, holding you.' I had forgotten that soft, giving-his-all look that Barry used to wear. I hardly saw it these days. My fault, probably. 'And there's – '

'How does a baby come out of Daddy's penis and into you?'

'Not a baby. Very tiny seeds. One of the seeds grows into a baby inside its mummy's tummy.'

'Well, how does a seed grow into a baby?'

She had got me there. 'I don't know. It's a very wonderful miracle.' I thought about it and gave up. 'How does a seed grow into a plant?' I countered.

'It just does that – ' unfurling closed fingers – 'and that – ' opening her hands wide – 'and grows up into a great bee-eautiful flower.' The arms went upwards, gracefully.

'Well, that's what a baby does,' I said gratefully.

Drew woke up and the afternoon, Wednesday afternoon, wore on. I might be less short-tempered now but I was still lonely. I longed for some close friend, an understanding ear, someone to drink coffee with, see the funny side of things with. It was a futile longing. Instead of drinking coffee with the sympathetic, humorous friend, I went into the garden and did things with washing and washing-lines, while Becky sat in the sand pit and ordered Drew about. He, affable and unflappable as ever, toddled about at her bidding, submitted to unexpected, passionate hugs and equally unexpected shoves, and all was well for a while. Then I went back in the house with the washing and Drew (was he becoming a mummy's boy?) followed me.

'Can I stay out?' asked Becky.

'Yes.'

'Why?'

'Because you just asked – '

'Why do you want me to stay out?' she asked indignantly. '*Drew*'s come in!'

I sighed. She came in. Knowing beforehand that I would regret it, I got out the paints.

'I want black, please.'

'You know black won't wash out?'

'I'll be ever such careful,' she promised.

She was shrouded from head to foot in plastic aprons and I'll swear I watched her like a hawk. Nevertheless, after ten minutes: 'That's the last time *I* have black paint,' she said severely.

What does one do with her? I wondered helplessly. Why is she like this? Drew isn't like this, why is *she* like this? I had once said to Barry, after one of Becky's particularly wild escapades, 'Why, when the pressure is being continually released, is she so like an erupting volcano?' And he had laughed and said, 'You've got the wrong metaphor. If a sprinter doesn't sprint for a year he doesn't run twice as fast when the year is up.' 'You mean,' I had said, 'regular practice makes him sprint faster.'

Becky was quite a sprinter, I thought, watching her ride her empty pram frame repeatedly and at speed into the concrete wall of the shed, accompanied by the kind of manic yells only she could produce. What *does* one do with her?

I switched on the radio and found Offenbach ballet music. Drew and I danced round the kitchen, his small solid body clasped in my arms. CRASH! CRASH! went Becky and her pram, outside. As we danced I watched birds through the window: seagulls gliding by in the distance whilst the music drifted smoothly, crows flapping past during the livelier section, a robin bobbing about on the grass in time to the can-can. It was a happy and oddly creative five minutes. Drew and I, I thought, were extremely compatible. Becky and I would be at battle stations until she left home. Then, too late, I would cry my eyes out and she, also too late, would become sentimental . . .

'Drew wants to come outside with me,' Becky said authoritatively from the doorway, and Drew, obedient as ever to his sister's edicts, struggled from my arms. 'I'll keep a nine on him,' she assured me, and towed him away.

Peace and quiet! Spring sunshine and the kids outside! Grabbing the moment, I got out my notes on the poems of Sylvia Plath for Francis' lesson tonight. ('That ought to be right up your street,' Barry had said, when I told him Francis was doing Sylvia Plath: 'Children and desperation.')

'Love set you going like a fat gold watch.'

Marvellous, marvellous line. You could hear the watch ticking in the last three words. Fat-gold-watch. (How *does* a seed grow into a baby?)

134

I read the poem through, pen in hand. But I didn't really need to make any more notes.

'. . . And now you try
Your handful of notes;
The clear vowels rise like balloons.

I had read the poem to Becky once, then talked it through in very simple language, until she leaned back, eyes wide and absorbed, and actually *watched* those balloons rising into the air. Strange, miraculous child. She would never, I knew, experience the placid contentment that would be Drew's. But what a priceless treasure she would know instead! I remembered her own first handful of notes, her clear vowels rising . . .

'This is my brother,' I heard Becky say formally. 'His name is Drew.'

I broke out of my reverie and went outside. Standing at the gate, looking over the gate at the children, was a stranger: a patient. He stood there, looking, with his blank, expressionless stare. An old man, in years anyway; something childlike about his creased face, about the way he stood, hands behind his back. A trilby hat sat correctly on his head. His trousers were too short, showing somehow vulnerable ankles and solid, sensible, childlike shoes. His expression was harmless, vacuous. He had come out for a walk and wandered down our little road, and now he was looking at my children.

But anxiety rose in me; irrationally, for did I not know that these people were safe, rendered safe by their drugs? This was probably a Long Stay patient suffering nothing worse than institutionalisation. But if he was institutionalised, would he have left the protection of the hospital?

I said politely, 'Good afternoon,' then, firmly, 'Come in now, children.'

'My brother is learning to talk. Say hello, Drew.'

'Lalloo,' said Drew cheerfully. The patient was unmoved.

'Come *in*! Time for a dolly mixture,' I added, and they came. I shut the door.

Dolly mixtures distributed, I looked out of the front window. The patient was wandering away, apparently undisturbed either by Becky's overtures or my own briskness.

Briskness? Call it what it was: rejection. I was very good at theorising about acceptance, tolerance, compassion; but when it came to putting those things to the test . . . Yet I knew that to encourage the man would have been foolish. I had heard of patients who, once having been offered a cup of tea, could not be got rid of. True, they tended to be the compulsive talkers, which this man patently was not, but still . . . I was not happy with my reaction, which had been purely instinctive. It was such instincts, deep-rooted and old as time, which had held back psychiatric medicine for so long.

Watching the silent visitor make his way down the road, I realised that I was not being altogether fair to myself. I had my children to consider, and the instinct to protect one's children was perhaps the strongest instinct of all. It was that which created the anxiety, the guilt, the constant worry which ruined your own life but ensured the safety of theirs. Why, if anyone ever tried to lay a finger on my children . . ! I had read in newspapers of the most horrifying incidents – babies snatched from prams and held at knifepoint while mothers searched desperately through handbags . . . Terrible, nightmare incidents. No, I would not reproach myself for wanting to protect them.

I turned from the window and absently watched Becky and Drew dismantling the coffee table. Becky was unscrewing the legs with expert efficiency, Drew fumbling it, as he fumbled most things, charmingly. Musing upon the nature of parental love, I barely registered their actions.

Why did one love one's children so differently, so much more intensely than one's parents? The one kind of love was active, the other passive; the former giving, the latter receiving. Parents – they were a safety-net, a security blanket, a foundation stone. You expected them always to be available, always to care what you were doing, always to stay in the selfless roles you had created for them. And, if you were lucky, as Barry and I had been lucky, they did all those things long after you had flown the nest. Later, as a parent, you did them too, but still you could not cross the abyss which separated parental love from filial love. Parent gives, child takes, through the generations. The arrows all go the same way. You could not conceive of your parents feeling about you the

136

way you felt about your child – and yet, somewhere inside, you knew that they did for why else would you expect the permanent availability and caring?

It all went back to that damnable Dark Lady, Nature. Nature did not care tuppence whether or not your ancestors survived. What mattered was that your offspring survived. She programmed you much as you would programme a computer, to ensure that your offspring did just that. While you were imagining scenes in which psychiatric patients leapt gates to threaten your young, you were forgetting to phone home or write home. Nature had decreed it. It meant the survival of the species – for what that was worth.

One day I would be the one not written to, not telephoned. I supposed that it would hurt. I supposed also that I would not mind being hurt.

'Screw those legs back on.'

'Can we go out again? Now the man has gone back to Daddy's hospital?'

I eyed her. 'How did you know he was from the hospital?'

'I just knew,' she said serenely. 'Mummy, I need some help with this leg.'

'You didn't need any help to take it off.' Nevertheless I went down on my knees and put the table back together. Then I exhumed a resigned and immobile Gin from a mound of blankets just before she expired (Gin had never been overly intelligent) and when I had finished folding the blankets into the laundry basket Drew came along and, for some reason best known to himself, carefully watered them. The laundry basket was the same colour as the potty so my new, stable self gave him the benefit of the doubt and I held my peace. Becky did not. Outraged, she berated him soundly and then hit him with a lump of rock-hard plasticine which she had unearthed from somewhere. It was time to go out.

On the way to the shop, old arthritic Rose scowled at me from her doorway. I scowled back. A couple of playgroup mothers nodded coolly to me and I coolly nodded back. I no longer cared about these people, I did not need them. Ivan talked at length about a series of wildlife programmes currently running on the television, and a customer heartily endorsed his recommendation and told me I absolutely must

137

let my adorable children stay up to watch it. I told her that we had no television and her face assumed an expression of sympathetic grief. 'Oh, I'm *so* sorry.' Marjory appeared with some of Tommy's outgrown vests and I thanked her effusively, not minding any more that I was a hyprocrite. Becky went into the back where she could be heard singing "The farmer's in his wife" to Tommy's bemused ears, until Marjory rushed in and silenced her. Drew opened several jars of Vaseline and scooped out a lump from each. I squashed all the lumps back in and discreetly replaced the jars. Tommy hit Becky who ran back to me, and when he followed she cried passionately, 'Oh, I *wish* I were your social equal!' Which brought trade to a standstill.

I explained, and Marjory showed amused interest and mentioned with an air of superior patronage that *she* had once been a member (an indispensable member, one gathered) of an Operatic Society. I considered returning the vests, but didn't. (In the event they were far too small for the strapping Drew. Tommy had always been puny.)

Returning, we met glorious Gloria Griffiths, the one person in this village I was always glad to see. She was atrociously made up and said, as always, '*Hello*, darlings!' Her dog doled out his usual licks to the children. I wondered why I had never asked Gloria round for coffee. Perhaps because, in her half-eccentric zeal for life, she treated everyone with exactly the same gushing warmth as she treated me. It was not a measure of her feeling for me. Nevertheless I decided that, later, when the play and Francis' exams were over, I would ask her. I had asked others and they had not come. Perhaps Gloria would.

I mentioned the man who had been looking over our gate.

'Oh! My dear, I'm sure he's perfectly harmless, quite a sweetie really. He looked over *my* gate while I was hanging out the washing. Poor doddery old love. I do think we should feel sorry for them, don't you?'

I agreed, and she bestowed impassioned farewells on the children and went on. Dear old Gloria. She didn't even know our names, but simply loved everybody. Even grouchy Rose, I noticed, waved to her.

And so home to tea. It had been a typical day and it was a typical teatime. I was no less muddled than before, in fact I

138

was twice as disorganised, because instead of making shopping lists or baking I was now usually to be found (if anyone had cared to find me) delving into my literature notes. But the children had been used all their lives to odd meals and they didn't at all mind that their boiled eggs were practically raw (much entertainment can be had from raw eggs) or that I had forgotten to put sugar in the custard. Scattering spoonfuls of sugar around the dining-room was *fun*.

Barry came in, took off his jacket and submitted to my warm embrace in a preoccupied manner. I leaned back and looked at him, and he produced a smile but did not quite meet my eyes.

'Trouble?'

'Nothing much. Any post?'

'Is there ever? Even Rayner and Patrick have abandoned us.'

'The postman's got an oval nose,' Becky put in. 'That's why he never brings us any letters.'

'I see. And your mother thinks you are logical.'

'Will you look after them while I do my face?' I requested. 'I'll bring you a cup of tea in a minute.'

Obligingly he got a cloth and went to wipe chins. 'Rehearsal tonight?'

'Nope. It's Wednesday. Francis.'

'Shall I make myself scarce again?'

'Please.' Barry had made himself so scarce last week that Francis had caught no more than a glimpse of him, nor he of Francis. I had not introduced them. I didn't know why I wanted to keep them apart, perhaps something to do with this being my own pet endeavour, unconnected with house and home; but for once Barry's retiring temperament suited me.

Becky wandered in to watch me put on my make-up at the kitchen mirror. I had started this quite recently and it still fascinated her. 'Why do you put make-up on your face?'

'It's to make me look beautiful.'

She accepted this, and went on watching. She was still watching me several minutes after I had finished. At last she asked, 'When does it start to work?'

'Is there anything to eat?' Barry broke in, with commendable tact.

139

'Pasties,' I said, 'in the oven.'

Barry's face didn't flicker. But Becky said indignantly, 'Daddy had pasties at lunchtime.'

We both stared at her. '*Did* you?' I asked Barry, but he only laughed. 'Becky, how did you *know* Daddy had. . . ?' But I shook my head and let the words tail off. Futile question. She didn't know how she knew. She just knew.

Later, tidying up while Barry put the children to bed, I wondered if I was being fair to Becky. She must be suffering the same frustrations I had suffered, the same sense of being imprisoned in boringly familiar surroundings with boringly familiar companions; the same sense of *sameness*. It was not surprising her wildness got the better of her. I had looked for and found interests to alleviate my own frustration but I had done nothing about hers.

I will think of something, I promised myself, as the doorbell rang; but not now. For this is where the day, at last, starts.

The day starts here. I gazed at Francis' bent blond head as he read aloud a few lines of the poem we were discussing. I had persuaded him to overcome his self-consciousness in this respect for often it is only by reading aloud that you can fully appreciate metre or some subtle consonantal rhyme. I had discovered this myself at University after hearing our tutor read aloud some Gerard Manley Hopkins, a poet I had detested until that moment. Francis conceded the point after trying it once and even made a few rapid notes on the subject. Whenever he made notes I felt a terrific fraud, for surely nothing I said was worth writing down? But he had confidence in me. I must learn to have it in myself.

What did he think of me? How did he see me? As an interesting, experienced older woman who might in different circumstances be alluring? As a drab housewife, child-ridden and lacking in any sense of fun or adventure? But I wasn't. I would dearly love to canoe down the most dangerous of his rivers, to sleep afterwards tented on its banks. I never would. Some other girl, young, streamlined in a black wetsuit, would do that.

'I don't really think,' said Francis honestly, 'that I shall choose to answer a question on Sylvia Plath. Not unless the other questions are completely impossible. Her poems are too – too intensely female. Too personal.'

'That's why they're good. You might even say so, if you do write on her: so long as you can produce a few quotations to back up your statement. You must always do that, you know.'

He grinned at me. 'I know. You keep telling me.'

'I shall keep telling you,' I said severely, 'until the day of your exam. Now, what do you want to do next? We'll have plenty of time to look at all your books more thoroughly but I want to do some quick groundwork first.' And there was arrogance for you: what had his school been doing for the last year and a half but groundwork?

'Hardy, please. Let's have a rest from poetry.'

So I got out my copy of *Tess of the d'Urbervilles*.

The eternal triangle. Tess, the warm-blooded child of nature, trapped between her two men: Angel Clare, the husband, the idealist, the thinker; and Alec, the lover, the pursuer, by whom Tess's eyes were 'dazed for a little' and her life ruined. I talked about the symbols of primeval nature and pagan superstition, about the inexorable triumph of a malignant fate, about Hardy's crescendo of language in passages such as the baptism of Tess' illegitimate baby; about the use of landscape to reflect mood, about nineteenth-century society's intolerance of fallen women; about love; about sex.

'There's an irresistible chemistry between Tess and Alec, compared with which Angel's gentle and poetic idealisation of her is – well, tame, to say the least. He knows a dream, an idea; Alec knows a woman. Alec stands by her in all her troubles – never mind that he caused them – except the one she doesn't tell him about; but what does Angel do when he discovers she's not "pure"?' I restrained myself and turned the rhetorical question into an actual one. 'Well, what *does* he do?'

'Rejects her.'

'Before that.'

Francis didn't know. 'He *thinks*!' I said, exasperated, not at Francis but at Angel. 'He *thinks*, for God's sake! Alec would have swept her into his arms and said "The hell with it!"'

He was laughing. 'You don't like Angel. I thought he was rather a gentleman.'

'He's short on reality, that's his problem. Has his head in too many books.' We smiled at each other. 'There's a neat little parallel with *The Parliament of Fowls*, have you noticed? Courtly love versus – well.'

He nodded and said, blushing slightly, 'But they do eventually – er, Tess and Angel – I mean, there are those few days together at the end . . .'

'Yes.' It was foolish to look beyond the words of the novel, of course, but I had often wondered how Angel compared with his predecessor in the marital bed. Pretty poorly, I suspected. But I had better not say that to Francis. 'We don't hear much about it, do we? They are discovered lying chastely asleep. Of course we're meant to feel that at last Tess has found peace and fulfilment. But how much more erotic that early scene where Alec crams her arms with roses and her lips with strawberries!'

I stopped. 'Sorry. I'm wandering. Self-indulgence.'

'No, you make it all come alive, Mrs Dennell.'

'Amabel. Do I? I'm glad.' I was, too; thrilled, in fact, that this thing I had taken on with such trepidation was succeeding so well.

I glanced at the clock and was about to utter dismayed apologies when the living-room door opened silently and a small red head appeared. 'Hello,' croaked Becky to Francis.

As so many before him, he fell instantly. 'Hello there,' he responded, and his eyes were delighted.

Becky came right into the room, nightdress-clad, ignoring me completely. 'My brother looks like you. My brother's name is Drew. His hair is blond like yours.' Oh God. If she was going to start listing Drew's physical attributes . . . 'My brother is a boy,' she added, ominously.

I got up quickly. 'Becky, what do you want?'

'Today he did a wee-wee on the washing. Usually he sits on the potty and – '

'Excuse me, Francis.' I scooped her up and fled before she could say penis. 'What's the matter? Why did you come downstairs?' I was carrying her up again as I spoke.

'I just wanted to see the big man,' she explained. 'Daddy woke me up snoring ever such loud and I heard the man talking.'

'I didn't realise Daddy had gone to bed,' I said, surprised and somewhat put out. She pointed to our bedroom door and grinned, and I heard it. Barry had temporarily bowed out from the too-exciting tempo of our life and was now having one of his roof-raising nights.

I tucked Becky up again, gave her a kiss and went back downstairs. I had expected Francis to be ready to leave, but he was still sitting at the table, surrounded by books and papers. 'We've gone well over our allotted time, I'm afraid,' I said. 'Sorry.'

He jumped up. '*I'm* sorry. You must be dying to get rid of me.'

'Not in the least. Have some coffee?'

He relaxed, and accepted, and followed me into the kitchen while I made it. 'My husband seems to have gone to bed. He works long hours at the hospital.'

'Oh, he's at that place, is he?' His face shadowed.

'It's very interesting work, but tiring. The strain, you know.' I was making excuses for him. To Francis or to myself?

'I suppose so. I hadn't thought of it that way.'

We settled at the table again with our cups. He trusted me, liked me, or he would not stay like this, beyond his time. I was flattered, and tried not to be. After all, he was only a boy. If it were Don Last, now . . . I pictured him sitting across from me, those warm, interested eyes, that air of attention which made one feel so important. Francis wasn't at all like that. He was not practised in such things. Perhaps that was why he was so endearing.

'Your little girl is lovely.'

'Isn't she? If only she were so lovely inside as she is outside!' I talked about the children for a while and he listened and laughed and was sympathetic, at all the right moments.

'They're lucky,' he said presently, 'lucky in their parents, I mean. It sounds a happy household, despite the ups and downs, and you're relaxed about them.'

'Relaxed?'

'Yes. Compared with my own parents, that is. My father is very ambitious for us.'

'Oh. I see.' That meant he was ambitious on his own behalf. I remembered that Francis had said once before that his father was 'pushy'.

143

There was a little pause and I thought he did not want to pursue it. So I said, 'I'm glad you liked Becky. Have you any nieces or nephews?'

He shook his head. 'There are just the two of us, my sister and I, and she's – ' He hesitated. 'My sister is not married yet,' he said.

'Engaged?'

'Sort of.' He was looking unhappy, and I was wondering whether to wait and let him get it off his chest if he wanted to, or whether to change the subject, when he took the plunge. 'She's not well,' he said abruptly. 'She's up at the hospital. At your husband's hospital.'

'Oh, Francis, I'm sorry.' I didn't ask why she was there. One didn't.

'I've been to see her a couple of times,' he said wretchedly. 'It was – It's an awful place.'

'Yes,' I said. 'I suppose it is.'

He picked up his cup and drained it. When he set it down again he was smiling and looking like his old self. 'I didn't mean to bother you with that,' he apologised. 'I was going to tell you about the canoeing trip we've planned for the summer.'

But I looked again at the clock and commonsense prevailed. 'Tell me next week. They'll be wondering where you are.'

He got up obediently and I saw him to the door. 'You'll just catch the bus if you run.'

'Bus? Oh, I jog home,' he said casually.

'What? Four miles? And all those hills?'

He just smiled. There was no swagger, no boasting about how fit he was, how fit he needed to be for these canoeing excursions. He was a lovely boy.

I brushed aside his thanks and off he went, loping steadily away into the darkness. I let Gin out, let her back in, made drinks for morning; smiled at the mess of books and papers we had left strewn across the table; then leaned in the doorway looking at it all, lost in reverie; and finally went to bed.

I was dreaming. I knew that I was dreaming and felt pleasantly guilty about it, but was able to dispel the guilt and retain the pleasure because one is not responsible for one's dreams. I was in a garden and Don Last was giving me not petrol, but roses. The garden was thick with them, lavish, opulent with them, and all over my bare arms as I held the blooms to me I could feel the sensual touch of the petals. There were no thorns on the roses. Then the touch of the petals became the touch of Don's hands, cool and smooth and lingeringly caressing on my bare skin, moving now through roses that no longer had substance to my neck and throat. I gazed at him, and as I gazed I began to melt with love, the way one can in dreams, impossibly, yearningly, every pore of me adoring him; but also as I gazed and as my body began to move towards his, his dark beard faded and his eyes changed colour and his hair changed colour and with a glad cry of recognition I saw that it was not Don Last at all but Francis.

Chapter Three

During the next few weeks almost everything became infinitely better than I could have hoped. For a start, it was spring. Hedgerows were fecund, birds frantically active, and we went into May with that budding promise of new life that is every year a surprise. The evenings were long, the sunsets red-rich over the hills, and day after day the sun shone down, metamorphosising everything so that I felt I was in another country. In a domestically practical sense, this meant that the children could play outside, that my washing dried, that I could go shopping without the daily battle with hats, coats, mittens and boots. In a more spiritual sense, it was uplifting, prompting smiles for no reason and a general feeling of well being.

Barry made several trips into town and brought back the mo-ped heavy-laden with fresh sand for the sandpit. He got out our ancient manual lawnmower and set about hacking through the grass, raising gorgeous scents that hung heavy and half-drugging on the air all the evening. He spent his free days walking with us through woods and across farmland, instead of lying comatose in bed for hours, as he did in the winter. We taught Becky the names of trees and filled her and Drew's bedroom with hawthorn blossom. Drew began to make serious attempts to talk. Francis came weekly, regular as clockwork, and I managed to suppress all memory of my dream. We covered *The Duchess of Malfi* and Wordsworth's poems with indecent speed, and then settled down to study Shakespeare. Rehearsals for *Murder at the Manor* became twice-weekly as the production date had been set for the end of June.

146

Life was eminently satisfactory. I contrived to get a pale tan by dint of sitting out in a straight chair and craning my neck at the sky while the children splashed hardily in their plastic paddling pool. I spent some of Francis' father's money on a good haircut, the kind that falls into carefully jagged, infallibly perfect disarray whatever you do with it; I also bought for myself some hair conditioner, nail polish, perfume, new summer make-up and another dress from Oxfam.

There were two flies in the ointment of my contentment at this time. One was Barry, who had now been gravely preoccupied for several weeks and was quieter than ever. I enquired about his work and he was taciturn. I asked more specifically about his patients. The anorexic girl – still there, he said uncommunicatively; the phobic girl – returned, he said, after an unsuccessful stay at home with her husband. Our eyes met at this point and I thought I knew what had gone wrong, but forebore to pursue the subject while he was in this mood. Ironically it was now Barry who turned away from me in the marital bed, and this, naturally, accelerated what was now my rapidly returning interest in things sexual. I was happy to wait, however, having gratification in all but the physical from several sources these days. What with Godfrey's stage embraces and Don's lingering looks I was riding quite high enough. Barry would get over whatever it was eventually, and when he did I would be ready.

The other fly was Becky. There was no doubt that her behaviour was deteriorating badly. She bullied Drew now with malice, not affection; she disobeyed me constantly, so that I found myself, half a dozen times a day, shifting from a quiet request that she perform some small task to a screamed command or a hard smack. Whereupon she became hysterical and sobbed all over me. Barry attended a lecture on behaviourism about this time and informed me that short periods of isolation and withdrawal of attention would probably be more effective than smacks, which were themselves a form of attention. I tried it, and it helped but did not cure the problem. Nothing seemed to do that. When Becky was in one of her exhuberantly happy moods it was as if I had a mad hare loose in the house: she ran and leapt, yelled joyfully, wrecked things, threw things, was virtually uncontainable. It was all in the highest of spirits. I walked her until Drew and I were worn out, and ultimately she would collapse amid emotional scenes of exhaustion. If I had not been experiencing the most fulfilling period of my maternal life thus far I am sure that she would have driven me to some act of desperation and violence. As it was, I took it all with as much phlegm as I could muster, and I read as many books as I could find on the subject of children like her.

She was not hyperactive. Hyperactivity included all kinds of symptoms which she did not have. She was not maladjusted. In new environments, even at Tommy's, she behaved well and sociably. She was not being affected by junk foods, crisps, orange colouring, or by an excess of tannin or sugar or any of the other astonishing possibilities.

Barry spoke to a child psychiatrist who happened to be visiting the hospital. The psychiatrist, daily seeing very severe cases of trauma, was interested but unconcerned. He said casually that it sounded to him as if Becky was very bright and simply bored to death.

Bored! I had gazed at Barry in comical amazement when he reported this. Of course, of *course* that was it. I had even realised it myself once, recognised her frustration, and then something had put it out of my mind.

And so I began a programme of intensive study for her. Becky would not have called it study. To her it was play. We kept tadpoles in a jar and read an illustrated book on the life cycle of the frog. We planted seeds in pots of compost. We had lessons in knot tying and bow tying. We made flash cards and she learned to read a dozen or so words. We bought a geometry set and learned about shapes, drawing them, naming them correctly.

It didn't work. For one thing, I couldn't keep up with her. She got tired of things so quickly, or absorbed them so fast, that almost as soon as I invented something new she had exhausted it – and me. Worse, that destructive element in her led her to shred, break, tear, chew or simply squash whatever she was working with as soon as it began to bore her.

Impasse.

By this time Drew was himself becoming starved of attention, the house was filthy, the nails were standing up in the bathroom again, the fridge was permanently empty and the top of the cooker looked as if it was rife with typhoid bacteria.

I bade a regretful farewell to thoughts of any more dresses and allotted Francis' father's money to a worthier cause.

'Mummy,' said Becky primly, after her first afternoon at nursery school, 'I would like a little hook to hang my apron on, please.'

I simply stared at her.

'I can never find it,' she explained. 'The kitchen is in such a muddle.'

I recovered. 'True. You shall have your hook. Where would you like it?'

She chose a place, and I got a nail from the bathroom and hammered it in. We made Drew stand under it to ensure that it would not catch his head, and then Becky hung up her apron.

'Thank you.' She looked around critically. 'Also,' she said, 'I would like more room for my toys. Mrs Thompson says things should not be crammed together and all falling out. Mrs Thompson says that that makes you untidy and itti – irritti – '

'Irritable. True again.' I hardly knew whether to laugh or tear my hair. If things were muddled, crammed, falling out and untidy, it was largely because Becky herself had been ripping her home to pieces since she first pulled herself to her feet at the age of six months. But certainly my prowess in this respect was nothing to boast about.

I emptied a cupboard and we re-organised everything, Becky directing with self-assertive gravity. Drew sat on his potty, sucked at the spout of his cup, and watched.

'Anything else?' I enquired.

She thought. 'My books,' she said, 'need sticking up with Sellotape. They're all in bits. Mrs Thompson says – '

'If your books are in bits,' I said acidly, 'it's because you tore them up.'

'But I *shouldn't* have done,' she said sternly.

It was as easy as that.

I had managed to cajole Mrs Thomson into taking Becky immediately by making her sound a challenge. Mrs Thomson,

I rapidly perceived, loved a challenge. She ran her little nursery school in town with precision, efficiency, and loads of love. The children adored her. She was formal with them, polite, but always genuinely delighted to see them and they knew it. She spoke quietly and so did they. She taught them to be considerate, to be tidy, to take a pride in their work. She believed in learning through practical experience, and so the children polished shoes, polished silver, learned to use kitchen scales and made biscuits and pastry, sanded and oiled wood, grew vegetables, made clay bowls, wove book markers, threaded bead necklaces . . . and learned to read and write.

For the summer term Becky was to be in the introductory class. I could manage the fees for that, but later, when she moved up . . I had a blind faith that we would find the money somehow. She was going to stay at that school until she was five even if it meant living on baked beans. Already it had wrought a small miracle in her. The question now was whether I could live up to her new and exacting standards.

'Mrs Thomson says she's extremely quick, highly intelligent, unusually creative, and no wonder she's such a devil,' I paraphrased to Barry.

'Did you tell her about – ?'

'No. There didn't seem any point. Do you think I ought to?'

'No-o. No, probably not.'

'She'll grow out of it soon,' I assured him. 'Especially now she has these new experiences to occupy her mind.'

He grunted, unconvinced. 'How are you going to get her to town twice a week? And back? And kill two hours in the interim, with Drew who ought to be asleep, and afford the bus fares?'

'The venerable Mrs Thomson,' I informed him blithely, 'has arranged a lift for Becky with another mother. I needn't go at all. In fact Becky has ordered me *not* to go.'

'Independent,' he remarked. 'Well, you'll have some freedom now. Satisfied?'

I frowned. 'It's for her, Barry, not for me.'

'Are you sure?'

'Of course I'm sure. She was desperately frustrated and none of us recognised it.' I added in annoyance, 'What's the *matter* with you?'

150

'If you mean why am I criticising you, say so.'

'I did mean that, though it was hardly a criticism. Still – it's not like you to be unfair.'

He shrugged. 'You seem to have been gratifying your own desires rather a lot lately. That's all.'

'But I was becoming a bloody vegetable! Boring, narrow, joyless – all those things Rayner said.'

'I thought you'd dismissed what Rayner said.'

'I have, but she was right in some respects and you know it. You knew it at the time. I'm less edgy, better tempered now. Don't you think I'm a nicer person to live with?' Silence. 'Barry?'

'In another minute,' he said, 'you'll be saying that you're doing all these things for my sake.'

'Barry, *stop* it.'

He got up. 'Sorry,' he said abruptly, and went out of the room.

Two things of special interest occurred the next day, not counting the evening rehearsal. The first resulted from my having a kind of mini-period, what the baby books call spotting; most unexpected and at altogether the wrong time of the month. I thought little of it at first, for I used a progestogen-only birth control pill which was known to affect periods slightly, although it had never affected mine before. It was only later that morning, sitting on the grass and watching, unmolested for once, as the children played in the sandpit, that the horrid suspicion came to me.

I'm pregnant!

Terror. I thought back fast and hard, over the past few weeks. Yes, there had been a couple of occasions, not notably passionate on either side but passion was not a vital part of the proceedings, any old ejaculation would do the trick. Had I forgotten to take my pill at all, even once, had I even taken it several hours later than usual? That was the trouble with the damned progestogen-only, you had to be so well organised, and I *wasn't* . . .

After a minute of sheer panic I started to calm down and convince myself that I was imagining things. It was then that Becky got leisurely out of the sandpit, strolled up the garden to where I was sitting, and said in a kindly voice, 'You'll have a bee-eautiful little baby which you can love. Won't that be nice?' Then she patted my tummy with the utmost tenderness and went back to what she was doing.

I sat there, stunned. In a daze I remembered the other incidents, examples of her foolproof powers: the doctor's Smarties, the sad lady, the hypothetical baby-sitter, the very thin girl, the pasties; those and a host of others. She must be right. She was always right.

I sank into despair. Just as I was finally seeing the light at the end of the tunnel! Just as I was getting rid of nappies, preparing to jettison the pushchair, just as I was starting to spread my wings again! What a rotten, rotten trick!

But underneath all that – something else. A little glow. Just a little glow. Mother Nature was at it again.

The second thing was Rayner's letter. At last. It came in a distinctive cream-coloured envelope, embossed, no less, and she wrote that they had temporarily rented a very expensive furnished house in Salisbury, that Patrick was enjoying his exclusive private school, that she had not yet been called on for supply teaching and was miserably bored and lonely sitting in the house all day. There was also a long paragraph of complaint about money and the difficulty of managing on one income, for their capital was still tied up in investments. She bewailed the size of the electricity bill, the telephone bill, the food bill, the cost of petrol, the cost of a colour television licence . . . Quite a boring and joyless letter, in fact.

I put it on the kitchen counter, less jubilant about her obviously inevitable come-uppance than I would have been before Becky's announcement, and started to think about lunch. Life, after all, had to go on (though I would have preferred a less appropriate cliché). The children traipsed in, leaving gritty trails all over the kitchen floor, and I scraped the sand from between Drew's teeth and gave both children a drink. Becky, Ribena-smeared, said, 'Oh good, another one. I'll put it with my other one, shall I?'

'What are you talking about?'

She picked up Rayner's letter and waved it at me. 'This bee-eautiful –' (The word that followed was meant to be

envelope: one of the few words she found unpronounce-
able.)

I frowned at her. 'What *do* you mean?'

'My *other* one,' she said impatiently, 'my other birthday
card.'

'That's not a birth – ' I stopped. Light dawned. 'I – see.
You like those envelopes and you're collecting them. Is that
it?' She nodded, still holding Rayner's letter. I extracted the
letter itself and gave her the envelope. 'Will you show me
where you keep them?'

'Please,' she said reprovingly.

'Please,' I said humbly.

We went upstairs to her bedroom. Inside a box of old
Christmas and birthday cards was the lost letter from Rayner,
torn, presumably during Becky's clumsy opening of the envelope. For some reason it was the envelope itself which was the
treasured possession.

I looked uncertainly at the two torn pieces of paper in my
hand. I had promised to return the letter unopened, but I
couldn't do that now. If I returned it as it was she would never
believe I had not read it. Obviously I must destroy it, now,
unread, and say nothing about its discovery.

Too late. Even as I hesitated my eye had caught a phrase:
'stay with you for a term?' After that I didn't need to read it. I
knew what the request had been and I knew too why Patrick
and Rayner had preferred not to repeat it in person, had been
secretly relieved that the letter had vanished. How ghastly it
would have been, they must have exclaimed to each other,
thank God the letter never arrived, what murder to have lived
in that house for a whole term! Amabel screaming at the
children, Amabel boring and joyless, up to the eyes in dirty
dishes and washing, Amabel no fun any more. Christ, what a
lucky escape!

I shredded the letter and flushed the bits down the toilet. I
was filled with hatred, not for my own shortcomings but for
Rayner. I'd thought I had got over all that, but I had not. I'd
thought I was winning the fight against mental stagnation and
domestic narrowness, and beginning to come alive at last. But
I was not. For now I would have to start all over again . . . All
over again, from the moment of that first enraged howl which

marked the cessation of physical suffering but forged one
more link in my chains.

'It's intolerable! I thought you loved me, I was prepared to
take you into my life and fight tooth and nail to make my
family accept you. Now I find you're nothing but a scheming
liar and, to all intents and purposes a murderess!'

'Sebastian! Please!'

'Why did you do it? Money? Revenge?'

'Sebastian, I do love you, I do. In the beginning – yes, my
actions were calculated, I admit it. I had instructions to turn
your head and blind you to what was going on. But later – I
meant those things I said.'

'Soften your voice,' shouted Dorothy. 'Wind yourself
round him, make him melt. You've got to extrictate yourself
from this mess somehow.'

Obediently I wound my arms around Godfrey's neck,
pressed my body against his and whispered, 'But later – I
really meant those things I said.'

'Now I can't hear you! Project your voice. And Godfrey,
try to look less like a tailor's dummy. You're anguished,
remember.'

He certainly was. I controlled the grin that threatened, but
he must have known I could feel his condition. Randy Godfrey. I had thought only Drew got erections this easily.

'You're lying. You won't fool me a second time, my girl.
Which one of them is your lover? My brother-in-law? The
chauffeur? Tell me!'

'Shake her! Put some *passion* into this scene!'

I found my upper arms grasped brutally hard and my head
began to bob back and forth on my neck. 'My brother-in-law?
The chauffeur? *Tell* me!'

'Sebastian, please! Please let me go. They'll hang me!'

He dropped his arms abruptly, pushed me away and turned
from me with a nice gesture of contempt. I admired it from
the rug, where I had managed to fling myself in a final effort to
win his mercy. 'Oh, they won't hang you,' he said bitterly.
'You're only an accessory after the fact.'

The wail of a siren. I leapt up, ran to the plywood window
and stared with hunted eyes at the prompter. 'The police are

154

here! Let me go, let me at least leave the house. I can get out the back way. Oh, give me a chance!'

'Your back's to the audience.'

I swung round and went on beseechingly, 'Just one chance! In memory of all that we shared together!'

'You didn't give my sister a chance.'

'But I didn't kill her! It was – ' I broke off. The library door opened with a loud creak, the door knob came off, and through the laughter Don, my lady's husband, said, 'Well, my dear, are you ready to face the music with me?'

'Where's Peter? Peter, fix that blasted door knob at once, will you? We'll have a comedy on our hands if it does that on the night. And oil the hinges.'

A local lad came leisurely forward, grinning his head off, and I wondered if he had loosened the door knob on purpose. We stopped for coffee while he attended to it, and sat round the hall in a big circle while Dorothy spoke to each of us in turn, being constructively critical but obviously growing very tense. She made no distinction between her husband and the rest of us when it was his turn, and he took it with an easy smile and an affable nod of agreement. The smile was still on his face when he turned to me and asked, 'Getting nervous yet?'

'Not yet. I expect the butterflies will start at the first dress rehearsal.'

'You're doing very well.' His eyes caressed me and I felt that I was doing very well indeed. 'I liked your fall. I once saw an Ophelia do it in just that way after "Get thee to a nunnery".'

I was delighted. 'Have you seen many Shakespeare productions?'

'Not many. Awful coffee, isn't it?'

Miranda, seated on the other side of him, caught the remark and gave him a jovial jab in the ribs. She had made the coffee, having been dead for one and a half Acts. Don laughed at her and I saw her eyes laugh back in sparkling response. He had that rare quality of making every woman feel special, not just in the narrow sexual sense that Godfrey's look suggested: it was much more subtle than that. I like your mind, his eyes seemed to say; you have character; your face

155

shows it, it is a face that, unlike the empty, pretty faces of young girls, has experienced Life. That, anyway, was what I read in the look. Miranda was a young girl, and a pretty one, and doubtless she received a different but equally satisfactory message. Don was gallant enough to pretend that inexperienced youth was just as enchanting as ripe, mature womanhood.

I was finding Don particularly attractive tonight, and myself particularly susceptible, since the day's events had reminded me of that other Amabel whom I had tried to quash, but who was to issue forth in triumph after all. Godfrey's flagrant masculinity seemed to have aroused in me more than amusement.

'Don, let's have your entrance again, this time without the doorknob.'

We took up our positions.

'Well, my dear, are you ready to face the music with me?'

'It was you!' gasped Godfrey. 'Why, you scoundrel!'

I had already flung myself on to the murderer's chest. 'You stayed! I was so afraid you would leave without me!'

His arms encircled me. They were not like Godfrey's arms, which went round women as instinctively as they went into shirt sleeves: these were slow-sliding, somehow suggestive arms, which communicated all along their length the pent-up fire within. The trouble was, I could not tell if it was genuine or assumed fire, and he, I guessed, had equal difficulty in deciding how much of my own fervour was for stage purposes.

'Oh, but I will,' said Don in a tender, sinister voice, 'I will leave without you, my darling. And you will help me.' And he turned me round sharply, dragged me against him and pressed the pistol to my neck. Godfrey had some lines here which I always missed because I was so conscious (in the beginning, so nervous) of where those two arms were going to land after this swift manoeuvre was completed. We had practised and practised it and it was surprisingly difficult.

There followed several minutes during which I was locked into Don like a Siamese twin, stepping where he stepped, moving as he moved. I had no more lines, but a considerable amount of concentration was required if I were to appear convincingly terrified. To make it more authentic, Don gripped me hard: left arm around the front of my waist, right arm around my neck, forcing my chin up, while the gun dug in just below my left ear. What with doing this repeatedly at each rehearsal, and being shaken and flung away by Godfrey at least twice a week, my body was turning into a mass of bruises.

It was over. The murderer was led away in handcuffs and Dorothy gave what was, for her, high praise. 'Not bad. Not bad. It's coming, at last. We'll finish there for tonight. Next time,' she went on, 'I want all of you to wear something appropriate for your part, so that you get a better feel of the character you're playing. Annabelle, have you got a short, slinky black dress?'

I gave an incredulous laugh and she made a note. 'I'll try to find one for you. It must be sexy. There's an apron and cap in the props box, I know. Miranda, what about you?'

I hung about while people discussed their costumes. The hall seemed crowded with new people: members of the group, I assumed, whose functions came into being only as the production date approached. It was partly this which kept me there, for I wanted to meet as many people as possible, and partly a feeling of recklessness which had been with me all the evening. It was nice to feel reckless. Rare, thrilling. Why should I not, for once, stay with these people, go for a drink with them, live just a little more before my belly began to bulge? I remembered that passage in *A Room with a View*, in which Lucy Honeychurch is likened to a kite straining against its string. 'I would like to be there,' one of the characters remarks, 'when the string is cut.'

And so I waited, and presently they made for the door in little groups, and someone said, 'Coming, Annabelle?' and I went.

It was an old pub, low-beamed, unspoiled by arty décor or computer games, and the bar was full of farmers. I recognised the tractor driver who had been indirectly responsible for my getting the part of the maid, and he grinned at me and asked after the mo-ped. Most of the locals knew most of the drama group members and reminiscences were exchanged, enquiries made about the forthcoming production. Our group gradually dispersed until at last I found myself sitting at a table with Godrey.

'I like to see a woman drinking a pint,' he said approvingly.

'This is my second. Let's hope I don't meet a zealous policeman on the way home.'

I raised the pint of bitter to my lips, enjoying the weight and the feel of cold condensation on the glass. It made me feel like a student again. I still was a student at heart, but all the pints in the drayman's lorry could not make me look as Miranda, who was a real student, did now. She was standing talking to Don, whose head was slightly bent beneath the low ceiling, and she was holding a gin and tonic which accorded oddly with her outfit. I decided I must get some jeans, then remembered Becky's school fees and sighed.

'Well?' said Godfrey, following my look, 'what do you think of us all?'

'I think you're all lovely,' I said largely, and downed more bitter.

He laughed. 'If you weren't a married lady I'd take you out to dinner for that.'

'Just for that? You're easily pleased.'

'What about our Don? Do you think he's lovely too?'

'He's *especially* lovely' I said with a smile.

His eyes rested again on Don and Miranda. 'They have a funny relationship, those two. I mean Don and Dorothy. It raised a lot of eyebrows when they first came here but the village has got used to them now.'

I said uncertainly, 'You mean they live independent lives?' I had noticed Dorothy was not in the pub tonight.

'More than that.'

'Oh,' I said, and took refuge in my glass. I was still not entirely sure what he meant, but could make an educated guess. Don himself had virtually told me, the night he gave me petrol.

'Like another?'

'I should fall off the bike. No, thank you, Godfrey.'

He went off to the bar to get one for himself and I sat there, musing. Why had Godfrey mentioned Don's relationship with his wife? Evidently he had noticed our mutual attraction: was he telling me that I could indulge my carnal desires with a clear conscience? Or was he warning me, thinking I might be chastely shocked, of a probable proposition? Knowing

158

Godfrey, the former was more likely; yet he had made that remark about my being a married lady and therefore not available . . .

Interesting, and barely believable, that I should have such thoughts, that I should be exposed to such possibilities. I wished it seemed more real. I had been too long amongst bibs and plastic pants to respond with the proper degree of excitement. I had been excited earlier, but that feeling of recklessness, of wanting to cut the string, had gone. Coming to the pub had not resulted, as I had imagined it would, in either mass conviviality or discreet intimacy. I would have liked either. That warm feeling of belonging to a group, of sharing laughs and experiences around a crowded table had not materialised. Nor had the legs-touching, eyes-meeting flirtation in a dark corner, for Don had, rather ostentatiously, kept well away from me. I appreciated his delicacy, but the fact remained that I was sitting alone in a pub while the indigenous population chattered all around me and even Godfrey had not come back. True, I had talked to several people and in a mild way had found the last hour or so pleasant; but mild pleasantness was not what I had expected and I felt let down. Barry had said I leapt about on the scales of emotion, seeking dramatic notes, and no doubt he was right. Middle C was deadly dull and it was playing now.

I finished my drink, picked up my crash helmet, and made for the door. People said good night. Don was just disappearing through the door marked MEN.

I walked slowly back to where I had left the bike, feeling a fool, feeling disappointed, wishing I had gone straight home after the rehearsal as I usually did. Hadn't I got enough excitement in my life now, without chasing more? Wasn't a quiet drink in a friendly pub enough of a novelty without seeking – Well, I didn't know what I had been seeking. Something to blast away the day's events and the impression they had left, I supposed. Anyway it had not happened. I no longer wanted it to happen. Recklessness and motherhood were not compatible.

The bike wouldn't start.

I set it on its stand and pedalled vigorously. Nothing.

I stood and thought. I crawled about, trying to locate

anything that looked different underneath the machine, wires hanging loose, anything.

I got on and pedalled again.

'Balls,' I said at last, panting. This was to me the ultimate in rude words. I pulled off my helmet, for I had become unbearably hot, and hung it over the handlebars while I mulled over the possibilities. I could walk home with the mo-ped. No I couldn't. I could walk home without the mo-ped. I could go back to the pub and beg a lift from – someone.

'Night, Annabelle,' called a voice, and I turned and waved to Miranda, who was walking away across the village square. From this distance she looked about twelve years old.

I had better make up my mind quickly. It was almost closing time and if I wanted a lift . . .

But I didn't want a lift. No. The silly mood was gone and I simply wanted to get home without any dubious complications on the way. I knew perfectly well that there *would* be complications if Don drove me, and I could hardly say, when he offered, which he certainly would, that I preferred someone else.

'Oh, get on with it,' I said aloud, and I hung the crash helmet over my arm and set off walking. Barry would have to come over tomorrow night and push the mo-ped back, as I certainly couldn't get it up the hill.

In the quiet village street footsteps sounded, running lightly and catching up with me. I knew, of course, I had known from the moment the bike refused to start that this was going to happen, I had known from the moment I thought of Lucy Honeychurch's kite string.

'Broken down?' asked Don Last.

I stopped. 'Apparently.' I wondered if he would offer to look at the bike, but he didn't. Naturally.

'I'll run you home.' Nothing in his voice. The nothingness and my own silence said all that needed saying. I didn't utter a word, simply walked with him to his house and got into his car. There were lights on upstairs but he didn't go in to explain to Dorothy where he was going.

The car slid effortlessly up the hill and I leaned back in the luxurious seat and watched the night sky. Still neither of us had spoken. The silence was thick and charged. Carefully I

160

examined my emotional condition, much as I used to examine my sexual condition with Barry. Am I nervous, anxious, guilt-ridden, confident, excited, full of anticipation or apprehension? Am I even (chastening thought) being over-imaginative and is he going to drop me tamely at my front door?

We rose to the crest of the hill, swooped down the other side. A mile to go. And, surprise surprise, here was a cart-track . . .

He slipped the car inside it, switched off the headlights, left on the dashboard light and in its glow regarded me. Slowly his hand moved to the catch of his seat-belt and the sudden loud click was absurdly erotic. He leaned over, not hurrying, and kissed me. Thoroughly. I analysed the kiss and my own reactions to it. He was very different from Godfrey. I half-expected Dorothy's voice to shout, 'Put more passion into it!' For this was not a passionate kiss, but a slow, exploring, sensuous one, the kind that turns your knees to water, that cuts all strings and makes all systems go.

Only it didn't.

His hand slid inside my blouse. He said huskily, 'Undo your scat belt.'

And I started to laugh.

I moved my head away from him and laughed properly, with delicious abandon. It was suddenly terribly, terribly funny. I got into one of those self-perpetuating laughs that start again the moment you think they've stopped, and after a couple of minutes of this I had to delve into my pocket for a yard of toilet paper, which I used to wipe my streaming eyes and blow my nose. Throughout this procedure Don sat stiff and silent on his own side of the car and looked expressionlessly through the windscreen. I had no idea at all of what he was thinking or feeling and I didn't care.

But good manners asserted themselves. I said penitently, 'Sorry, Don, that was very rude of me,' and promptly started to chuckle again. He said 'For Chrissake,' started the engine and backed viciously out of the cart track, hitting a granite gate-post on the way. There was a crunching noise and it sobered me and made me feel responsible, though I wasn't. I repeated, 'I really am sorry,' and he didn't answer for a minute. Then he said wryly, 'You had me fooled.'

'I had myself fooled,' I said with a sigh.

'Ah well. I'll accept it as a salutary lesson. Do you know you're the first woman to do that to me? I've had my face slapped, but I've never been ridiculed.'

He sounded so downcast that I felt suddenly affectionate towards him, and strangely protective. He was just a great, spoiled, charming boy, a slave to his phallus, a victim like so many men. I had thought it was Godfrey who was the compulsive seducer but it was Don. Or maybe (was I interested enough to find out?) it was both of them.

I told him where to stop the car, and got out. Then hesitated, holding the car door open. I did not want bad feeling between us, and he would not have played Don Juan if I had not encouraged him. 'Friends?' I asked, smiling.

He gave a little laugh and spread his hands hopelessly. 'Friends,' he said, and drove away.

Barry was still up, reading *Anorexia Nervosa: Case Histories*. He glanced up as I came in and gave me his new, detached smile.

'What an evening!' I exclaimed in great animation, dropping into an armchair. 'I've been battered black and blue by Those Men, nearly got drunk, bust the mo-ped, accepted a lift from Don Last, and was damn near raped!'

He raised his eyebrows. 'Did you fight him off?'

'No. I laughed. So he stopped. I mean I *really* laughed, Barry, I rolled about and cried, you know the sort of laughter – '

'Poor devil,' he said with feeling. Then, 'What's the matter with the bike?'

I waited, watching the calendar, watching my figure. Daily I examined my breasts but they were the same as always – small, limp, defeated. I had had nice breasts once, before I started feeding babies. The lack of swelling or pigmentation change, however, meant nothing. I had had no early symptoms of pregnancy with Drew, other than a missed period, although Becky had made herself known from the moment of conception. But then Becky would. I would just have to be patient.

I told Barry about my fears and repeated Becky's prophecy. To my surprise he seemed unalarmed and I realised that he simply did not believe I could be pregnant. Perversely, I was annoyed rather than reassured by this, for already the irrational part of me was cooing over my imaginary newborn babe. It *was* irrational. Common sense told me that all too soon the cooing would turn into something less pleasurable, both for cooer and cooed-to. Tiny babies have one aim and one aim only, and that is to turn into people as quickly as possible. And people, particularly little people, are notoriously complicated, selfish, and greedy beings, no longer satisfied by a mere feed but continually fixing their sights higher and higher up Maslow's Hierarchy of Needs. Even Drew, that sweetest, most amenable of creatures, was now beginning to test his powers, state his rights, make demands and even (unbelievable occurrence!) lie on the floor and kick and scream when they were not met. The first time he did this I laughed so hard that he got up and went away looking embarrassed, but it didn't stop him from trying again.

No, Nature might fool me once or even twice, but no more. Irrational desires for the warm smells of babies and milk must be suppressed, for the sake of my own sanity.

So I counted the days of the month, and occupied my mind with *Macbeth* and with slinking siren-like about the house, perfecting my hip-swaying walk. I bought some sheer black tights with seams down the back (not from Ivan: Marjory would never have countenanced his stocking such an item) and experimented with outrageous styles of make-up. I borrowed heated hair curlers from the props girl and created a wildly abandoned, flagrantly voluptuous hairstyle which was obviously meant to be seen against the background of a pillow-case. And my spirits soared. I had not revelled in life so much for years. I even started getting up early, going outside in my nightdress and treading barefoot through the dew-soaked grass. I encouraged the children to do the same, and even Gin joined in and turned her small hard paw-pads baby-pink in the process. Spring mornings, sunshine, and at last, however illusory, however short-lived, a sense of freedom!

163

I was not quite foolish enough to attribute this new life-force solely to broader horizons and mental stimulation. Much of it, I knew, stemmed from being playfully half-in-love with a man, or two, or was it even three? Dear old Don had done me a better turn than he knew: he had caused my female ego to shoot sky-high and stay there; so had Godfrey, with his involuntary springing to attention during our love scenes; and so had Francis with his trusting, almost reverential blue-eyed gaze. But it was Don who had done me the greatest favour by proving to me that the only man I really wanted was Barry.

Barry, however, was something of an enigma at present. I couldn't imagine what was the matter with him and, for the first time in our life together, I had no time to devote to finding out. This was probably fortunate for nothing riled him more than anxious and oft-repeated questions: What's the matter? Why are you so quiet? What are you worried about? I had asked them before when he had been feeling low and they made things considerably worse – as I knew; but I had never been any good at holding my peace.

The difference in him was hard to define. He played with the children, smiled at all my antics concerning my appearance, babysat uncomplainingly during rehearsals, and was only slightly detached during love-making. But to be even slightly detached was not like Barry. Sometimes, when he went out of the room, he would blow me a kiss in his old fashion from the doorway, but his eyes were strangely distant. It was as if Barry himself, for all his apparent normality, were not actually there.

At last it occurred to me that he was undergoing some kind of transition from student nurse to professional, with all the adjustment of emotions that that entailed: the searching for a balance between efficient indifference and a too-deep involvement with his patients' problems. He had always veered towards the latter and had, I knew, worried about it in the past. Once I had deduced this I felt a little easier in my mind. It was not, as I had once or twice feared, jealousy or resentment of my own activities but something quite removed from me. So I did my very best to be quiet and tactful and leave him in peace.

The week after I had flown my kite and hung on to the

string, Barry announced that he was going to the hospital social club to meet fellow students and discuss current placements. This the ostensible reason. The real one was probably that they were fed up to the back teeth with long hours and nutty patients and needed a good booze-up. Fine: they deserved it. I was genuinely pleased that he was to have a night out at last, for his only recent outing had consisted of a walk to Massey, armed with a plug spanner, and a triumphant ride back again.

So, as this was a Wednesday, I was alone and feeling virtuous, because unselfish, when Francis arrived.

'You look terrific!' were his first, admiring words.

'Do you like it? I've been experimenting. For the play, you know.'

'It makes you look quite different.' He was uncertain and kept looking at me, trying to identify what, exactly, had changed.

I laughed. 'It's the hair. And the make-up.'

His face cleared. 'Of course. You've painted some eyelashes on. It's great, Mrs Dennell.'

'Amabel. Thank you.'

Becky, inevitably, appeared. It was a ritual now, this coming downstairs to see Francis, and since she had never yet said penis in front of him I allowed her to come. They exchanged pleasantries and, satisfied, she went back to bed. Francis beamed at the door whence she had vanished, as he always did. He liked Drew, whom he met occasionally, but he was smitten with Becky.

I had had what I hoped was an inspiration some days ago and decided to put it to the test. 'I can't think what to do about the children,' I said, getting out my books. 'Barry starts working nights next week and I've got to go to rehearsals every Tuesday and Friday evening. The play goes on in three weeks so I can't possibly miss any.' I stacked the books on the table and added casually, 'I don't suppose you know some girl who'd be willing to babysit?'

He frowned and looked as worried as I. 'Can't say I do.'

'Oh well. Never mind, I expect I'll manage somehow.'

He thought, tapping his jaw with a rhythmic finger. Then he brightened. 'What about me? Would I be any good as a baby-sitter? The kids know me, so . . .'

'Francis, you're a marvel! I hoped you would offer.'

'Did you?' He looked pleased. 'Just a minute, though. Let me think.' He sat down at the table and scowled intently, muttering to himself. I watched, fascinated. I had never seen this side of him before, the one that, once it had decided on a course of action, determinedly removed whatever was in the way. At last he decided. 'It should be okay. I'll change my History night, I'm pretty sure the tutor won't mind, and I know someone who'd love to take over the canoe class for a few weeks – '

I was horrified. 'Oh Francis, no! I'm sorry, I'd forgotten about your other commitments. Of course you mustn't change anything.'

We argued, he was adamant, I was vanquished. 'I'd been thinking I ought to drop the canoeing anyway,' he said cheerfully. 'Just till the exams are over, of course.'

Of course. But I felt better then, and we arranged that he should keep his fees for my coaching as payment for the baby sitting (and the Lord alone knew how I would now pay Mrs Thomson; but I didn't say that.)

'To work,' I commanded at last. And, because we were saving our final assault on *Macbeth* till just before the exam, we sat down with our copies of *Kes*.

Freedom. The untameable freedom of the wild kestrel symbolising the spiritual freedom which the boy Billy fleetingly attains: freedom from a dreary, loveless existence, freedom which Kes herself lends to him. The bird encouraged to be whole, to fly; the boy suffocated, earthbound, trapped. The terrible lack of understanding, from Billy's mother, brother, his schoolmates, even or perhaps especially from his careers adviser. The rich potentiality of Billy, the impossibility of that potential ever being realised. The boy's painfully simple dreams – merely to have a father, warmth, food and Kes. His understated, often not stated at all, passion for this one free, real thing, this trainable but not tameable creature who demands and deserves respect in a way that no person of Billy's acquaintance can. There is a long, wonderfully evocative passage in which Billy tells his class about the training of

166

Kes: a slow, faltering start, short phrases dragged from him one by one until his reluctance diminishes and his words pour out in a great torrent, unstoppable, like Kes herself on her first heady flight into freedom.

I picked out words, images, comparisons. The kestrel feasting on scraps of beef and on sparrows which Billy has shot for her; Billy himself going hungry, until he buys, with stolen money, his own feast of fish and chips; and so, indirectly, causes her death. The building of panic, the search, the heart-rending calling of her name. Kes! Kes! Kes! The ultimate discovery of her body in a dustbin. The proud, the haughty. In a dustbin. Billy's journey through the past for one warm memory, one crumb of comfort. Written factually and without a shred of emotion and all the more effective for that.

'It's not just Kes who has been destroyed, you see. It's the boy. If Billy had received just a fraction of the love and care that he lavished on Kes, *he* could have flown. As it is – well, there are dustbins for people, too.'

I had talked myself hoarse. Francis' pen had been whirling, the pages of his book flapping about as I went from passage to passage to illustrate what I was saying. We were both flushed and deeply involved in this crime of Billy's non-life. I flopped back in my chair and grinned at him, which meant not that I was happy but that I was satisfied. 'That'll do,' I said.

'Gosh, Mrs Dennell,' he said, suddenly boyish, 'you can't half go.'

'I hope you're not going to use language like that in your essays.'

He laughed. 'Shall I put the kettle on?'

We were familiar with each other now, and Francis often made the coffee after the lesson was over. A couple of weeks ago he had met Barry in the kitchen and the two of them had finally introduced themselves. Afterwards Barry had remarked to me, 'Maculine type. I see why you're keen on him,' and I had said that I was not yet reduced to cradle-snatching.

Francis brought in the coffee and biscuits and we pushed our books to one side and sat talking about non-literary things.

Francis told me about the fibre-glass canoe he planned to build after the exams and I told him about the entertaining things that happened at rehearsals (some of them). He told me which Universities he had applied to and what were the conditions of his acceptance – the University of his choice, he said glumly, wanted two Cs and a B – and I talked about my own student experiences (some of them). Eventually, our cups empty, there came one of those silences into which the clock ticks very loudly and I broke it by asking how his sister was.

'Better,' he said after a moment, toying with his cup. 'Better in one sense. Worse, in another.'

I said 'Oh', trying to sound neutral and wondering if I had blundered. But I had not, for he added, 'It's a relief to hear her mentioned openly. At home we don't talk about her. My father is ashamed of her, I think, at least that's the only constuction I can put on his reluctance to mention her. I'd like to think it was guilt, or at least awareness of his own responsibility, but – well, he's not like that.'

Thoughts of incest went through my mind. I said cautiously, 'Responsibility?'

'She's clever, you see. Always has been. She can pass exams with her eyes shut.'

'That,' I pointed out, 'may be simply a facility for exam technique.'

He grinned wanly, taking my point. 'My father pushed her, even when she was very young. Pushed and drove and nagged. She's sensitive, quiet, very gentle. She never fought back, just did what he wanted her to do, got top marks in everything right through school and went on to Cambridge. She did brilliantly for the first year and then – ' He lifted his hands a little, let them drop again: a gesture of helplessness. 'I guess it all caught up with her.'

'You mean she had a breakdown?'

'Sort of. She stopped eating.'

I heard my breath catch. He looked at me and went on, 'I'm not telling the truth. Not all of it. The truth is that she'd been having psychiatric treatment during that first year and none of us knew. Trouble with boyfriends. Not ordinary trouble.' He became awkward. 'I don't really want to go into – er – details . . .'

I hastened to reassure him, and he continued, 'Well, she turned into a kind of skeleton and was taken into a general hospital, where they fed her up. Have you heard about the methods they use, incidentally? It's interesting.'

'Yes,' I said. 'Deprivation and reward. The patient starts out in a room completely empty except for a bed. No company. If she eats something, a piece of furniture is brought in. If she keeps eating, more furniture. A television. The door is left open, people can come in and out.'

He was surprised. 'You know a lot about it. Yes, that's what they did. Only the rewards are not for the eating but for weight gain. Caroline used to eat and then vomit.

'Anyway she did gain weight, and she was allowed to sit her second-year exams right there at the hospital, and passed with flying colours, of course, despite all her troubles. She came home for the summer. And it was the same old thing from Dad, persistent pressure, ambition for her. When she went back to her final year she starved herself again and this time there was a steady boyfriend on the scene too, and . . . Well, I'll cut it short: she dropped out of University, came home in a hell of a mess and ended up in the psychiatric hospital here.'

Being nursed by Barry, I added silently. This was almost certainly the girl he had mentioned. But I mustn't reveal that I knew anything about her. Patients' anonymity was supposed to be preserved.

'You said she's better, in one sense?' I prompted.

'And worse in another. Yes. She's eating now, you see, but – Well, they've cured the symptoms, not the disease, haven't they?'

'And the disease is?'

'Lack of childhood,' he said promptly. 'I've read about anorexia. The specialists think it may be caused by a fear of growing up. There are, er, physical symptoms that support that theory. Caroline never had a real childhood, she was always swotting. Maybe that's stimulating for some kids, I don't know, but it wasn't for her. So now – ' He jerked his head, eloquently, in the direction of the hospital. 'I've only been to see her twice. I'm a coward, I loathed seeing her there. She loathes it herself, although I gather there's one very good nurse who makes her feel human without expecting things of her all the time . . .

'So now they're having something called Family Therapy groups. She's supposed to get rid of all her pent-up resentment, you see, tell my father right to his face that she feels he's ruined her life. She can't do it. They think that if she could do that she'd be all right again. My parents go every week for this damned session . . .'

'Oh Francis,' I said, as he broke off, 'I am sorry. It must be terrible for you.'

'Not for me. *I'm* all right,' he said bitterly.

'Is your father ambitious for you too?'

'Not in the same way. I haven't got Caroline's brain. I'm not like her at all, I'm not a bit docile, never have been. If Dad had tried to push me as he pushed her I'd have simply laughed at him, or pretended to agree with him and then done my own thing in my own way.'

'But you're taking tuition for your A levels,' I pointed out, 'and he's paying.'

'I'm not being pressured. That's the difference.' A pause. 'It was all so pointless. She'd have done it anyway, if she'd been left alone. And done it happily.'

He packed up his books soon after that, and I saw him to the door. 'Thanks for letting me talk to you. It was a relief to get it all off my chest. I brood about it, rather.' He looked out into the still light evening. 'It's just occurred to me – which ward does your husband work on?'

I thought – oh, well, it can't be helped, and he needn't know that Barry has talked about her – and told him. His expression of relief puzzled me, and it was not until I had shut the door behind him that I realised I had mentioned not Barry's current ward, but the Geriatric ward where he was to have his next placement. It was a genuine mistake, for Barry had been talking about it only last night and the name of the ward was fresh in my mind.

At least I thought it was a genuine mistake; but the tricks played by one's subconscious were so many and so devious that one could never be completely sure . . . Anyway it was done and there was no point in undoing it.

I went to tidy up my notes and realised with a slight shock

170

that only half an hour ago I had been deep in *Kes*. I seemed to have been through a new, vicarious experience in that half hour. Poor Caroline. I had said of the boy Billy that, given different circumstances, love, understanding, he could have flown. Barry had said the same thing a hundred times in a hundred different ways. He had said it to Rayner and Patrick: that mental disturbance was so often caused by the failure of others to understand, or to help, or merely to ease off on the pressure; that it was not enough to cure the patient, you had also to cure or at least educate the relatives . . . And yet Caroline's father must have believed that his own motives were of the very highest: selfless, disinterested. The trouble was that you never knew what your real motives were. ('Well, you'll have some freedom now. Satisfied?' 'Barry, it's for Becky, not for me.' 'Are you sure?')

I gave a long sigh. Every time I thought I had got life taped so that I was able to enjoy it, along came a big invisible hand and knocked me over. Similarly, every time I perceived the shallowness, the unreality of such head-in-the-sand enjoyment, there appeared some alluring carrot which led me, braying, astray again.

An octave at a time, Barry had said. From highs to lows, comedy to tragedy; from total oblivion of anyone but myself to heart-rending recognition of the whole world's suffering. If one could somehow achieve a balance of perception, recognise that the top and bottom notes of the octave were connected by a lot of tones and semi-tones, and walk steadily up them looking both ways at once – making that connection – Barry seemed to have that facility but it was a rare one. Seeing life steadily and seeing it whole. *Only connect.*

I smiled then, as, I put the books away. How literary I was becoming again. Only connect, that was from *Howards End*, my old E. M. Forster favourite. What would he have made of this life we were living, with its half-mad children and half-sane patients? Only connect them. But how?

Barry was late coming home. Before he came I dipped into his *Anorexia Nervosa: Case Histories*, reading passages at random. Caroline's case seemed to be a classic one, even to the 'boyfriend problems' about which Francis had been

171

understandably reticent. Periods may stop for months, years . . . infertility may result . . . fear of sex . . . marriages unconsummated . . . divorces often result . . . spiral sets in . . . heart seriously weakened even if normal eating habits resumed . . .

Parents, look to your children.

Chapter Four

The next day we saw the schizophrenic patient whom we had last seen screaming out his soul at the hospital. He was in the shop, gazing with trembling nervousness at two packets of cigarettes, different brands, which lay on the counter challenging him to choose between them. Ivan knew him and called him by name, was too chatty, too self-consciously nonchalant with him, but how else could he be? He served me while the handsome, rather ascetic face with its lovely bone structure agonised over the choice he had to make. Only he knew why the right choice mattered so much. I watched him furtively as Ivan scooped back practically every penny of the Child Benefit money he had just passed to me through the Post Office grille. It was the patient's youth and beauty that worried and, to be frank, fascinated me. What pressures, in his twenty-odd years, had brought him, perhaps already predisposed, to this? And would I have cared so much if he had been ugly?

Ivan was good with the patients, skilled at cheerfully answering the meaningless or incomprehensible sentences that often came his way. I was not, possibly because I got no practice, more probably because I was too embarrassed to try. The healthy humans of Lottabridge seemed to fall into three distinct groups: those who felt deeply for the patients but did nothing about them; those who did not feel deeply at all but could and did work with them efficiently; and those who felt deeply and communicated that feeling with most positive results. Into the last group fell Barry and those few with not only a genuine vocation but also the right personal qualities – whatever they were. Certainly disinterestedness, the ability to put oneself and one's ego completely aside, was one of them. From the little that I knew of my neighbours and other hospital staff I judged that many of them were in the second category. But who was I – being in the first – to criticise them for that? They at least were looking after these people. I was doing nothing and would probably always do nothing.

I left my shopping with Ivan and took children and dog for a walk. It was almost June now and very hot, and I had dressed Drew in tiny shorts and t-shirt, Becky in a pink feminine little number that made her look like someone else's daughter. She wore sandals but no socks. A mistake, for within minutes she was complaining that her feet were slithering about. I said hard luck; we were not going back up that hill simply to get her socks.

I was trying now to manage without the pushchair, and this, on a narrow road with no pavement, required the organised control of an Eskimo sledge-driver. Dog lead in left hand, dog on left, Becky on far left holding the same hand that held the lead, Drew on right and my right hand holding the reins as well as his left hand. It worked well enough so long as nobody tugged or changed direction, but as soon as a car came along everybody did both and it took several minutes to get sorted out again. By which time another car was coming along.

So it was a relief when we finally got down to the fields beyond the main road, and the little wood with the stream running through it, and I could let go of everyone and pray that there were no close encounters with cow-pats. It was lovely down there, green canopies springing overhead and the sun glowing gold through the green. The field was full of buttercups and we picked them and held them under our chins and Drew trod in a cow-pat. So I let them paddle in the stream and waited for Drew to fall face down in the water but he didn't.

'It's very near today,' said Becky, splashing.

'What is?'

'Today. It's very near.'

'Well, yes. In fact it's here.'

'*No. Near* means it's warm but the sun isn't really shining.'

I was mystified for a moment. then, 'Oh, *close!* You mean

174

it's close. But Becky, the sun *is* shining.'

She frowned at me. 'Mummy, I'm trying to use my new word.'

'Sorry.' I subsided.

'Harry,' repeated Drew, and chortled. Becky kicked a spray of water over him and he stopped chortling. The water was sharply cold, as I had discovered when I too tried paddling, and I was sitting now on the shallow bank among the ferns, watching. Becky splashed Drew again and for once he retaliated quite effectively. Wet and enraged, she shouted, 'Drew! Go away and stay there!'

I sighed. I had hoped for a period of quiet reflection, seated among the beauties of nature. 'Becky, don't start being naughty again. Are you naughty at school?'

'No. I'm very good at school.'

'Then why are you naughty at home?'

'Drew bullies me.'

Gin barked a welcome and looking round I saw Marjory approaching with Tommy held by the hand. Go away, I told them silently, but they came on, Tommy gazing avidly at my wild children. 'Good heavens,' said Marjory, 'Do you let them do that?'

'Do what? Hello, Tommy.'

'Paddle.'

'Why not? It's only water.'

'And mud,' she said, with one of her shudders.

'It'll wash off. Let Tommy have a splash, he'll enjoy it.'

The three children were now standing motionless, my two looking at Tommy who looked back with incredulity in his pale little face. He was wearing wellington boots. No cowpats on *his* sandals. I added encouragingly, 'He can go in in his wellies.'

'Oh, I don't think so,' said Marjory with a comfortable smile. 'He'd be certain to get water inside them.'

I gave up. If they hadn't come for a paddle why didn't they just – 'I saw you from across the field,' Marjory said, 'and came over to tell you that I've got a couple of woolly jumpers for Becky, if you'd like to collect them.'

'Thank you,' I said, deflated. She was kind, in her way. Why wasn't kindness enough?

Tommy had managed to free his hand and move closer to the stream, where Becky and Drew were now splashing and kicking with crazy abandon. 'They'll be *soaked*.'

'Doesn't matter. It's a hot day. Anyway,' I added, 'try stopping them.'

'Ah,' she said. 'Well, I'm afraid I tend to be rather forceful.'

'Goodness,' I said admiringly, 'do you?'

With impeccable timing, Tommy stopped, picked up a large broken branch that was lying at his feet, and hurled it at Becky. Fortunately it missed. 'Hey,' said his mother with an admonishing tap, 'don't do that.' Tommy looked up at her with his furtive eyes and said nothing, and Marjory added, 'Now you tell Becky you're sorry. Go on, say "sorry" to Becky.' He continued to look at her, nothing in his face, and she turned to me.' 'How's the play going?'

I hesitated, still waiting for Tommy's apology, but apparently she had finished being forceful. So I said, 'Fine. We're on in three weeks. Are you coming to see it?' It was her turn to hesitate and I said in a jocular voice, 'Do come, if only to see me. Mine is a terribly sexy part.' Her face changed. 'I play a nude scene,' I added mendaciously.

'Oh. No. I don't think so. We're so busy in the evenings. Stocking the shelves. Say goodbye, Tommy.'

Tommy didn't, and she dragged him away from us before he could become infected.

Poor Tommy. Poor kid. He wasn't allowed to play with sand because it got all over the house, he wasn't allowed to play with water at the sink because the kitchen floor got wet, he wasn't allowed to play ball in the garden because the plants got damaged, and now he wasn't allowed to paddle. All he was allowed to do was vent his frustration on other people, mostly people smaller than himself. If Marjory had had any choice in the matter he probably wouldn't have been allowed to defecate. I had once seen her looking positively bilious after overhearing one of Becky's blithely unselfconscious remarks about human anatomy. It seemed to me that such an attitude towards the body and its functions boded very ill indeed for Tommy's future development.

But, again, who was I to criticise? I might be frank and

open concerning bodily functions, but I was far from being the perfect mother – whatever that was. I had been hysterically screaming at Becky for the last three years or so – driven to it, it was true, by unbearable and incessant provocation, but nevertheless . . . What had that done for *her* development? But guilt can make as bad a mother as repressiveness or thoughtlessness. You just have to get on with the job as best you can. You may be creating a potential psychiatric patient, you may not, but there's little doubt which it will be if you spend all your time worrying about it.

Becky did it at last: gave Drew an exuberant flying shove which left him prostrate and gasping in four inches of freezing water. I leapt to my feet, smacked her bottom, snatched up Drew and took him into the hot sunshine. Becky followed, giving her token wail. Drew was already so wet that the dipping had made little difference and he was merely shocked and offended. I took off all his clothes, and Becky's too, and spread them on the grass to dry; then took off my own underskirt and gave them a rub down with it. (Ever unprepared, Amabel had brought no towel.) Within a minute they were both thinking it was all a great joke.

'Now go and frolic,' I ordered.

'What does frolic mean?'

'Run. Play. Gambol amongst the buttercups. And watch where you put your feet.'

Off they went, stark naked, and frolicked and gambolled. (Little lambs, who made you?) They were perfect, physically flawless, their strong bodies already brown, limbs and hair flying about as they ran and fell and ran again through the blanket of buttercups, small showers of gold marking their path and their laughter rising up to the clear blue sky. I wished with all my heart that I could get Tommy to do this, just once. Marjory and Tommy had called at the house about something one day, and found Becky and Drew naked in the paddling pool. I had urged her to let Tommy join them, waving aside her anxiety about swimming trunks, and eventually she had taken off his clothes. He stood in the paddling pool for several minutes, white-skinned and anxious. Then he sat down. Otherwise he made no move at all. It was only as Marjory was preparing to dry and dress him that he began to come to life, and by then it was too late. At least, I thought, watching mine race through the thick grass waving gathered buttercups above their heads, at least they will have this; whatever kind of mess I make of them in other ways, they will have this sense of freedom inside them forever and nothing can take it away.

Unlike Caroline Blake.

I had not thought of Francis' sister for the last hour, though I had gone to sleep thinking about her and woken up thinking about her. It had been a most strange experience last night, hearing semi-intimate details about the life of one of Barry's patients, and not hearing them from Barry himself; knowing that I would never tell Barry what I had heard, and not knowing why. I now had two distinct concepts of her. She had become, in fact, two people. One was Caroline Blake, who was clever, and had a loving brother and an over-ambitious father; the other was Barry's "anorexic girl". Unless or until I told Barry what I knew, the two would never meet.

I mused on the coincidence for a moment, but it was not really so great. Probably half the population within a radius of five miles had some sort of connection, however indirect, with the hospital. What was stranger was that Barry and Francis had not yet met on the ward – but that was not so strange either, for Francis had only visited his sister twice and Barry's days off, though irregular, were frequent. And as far as I remembered I had never mentioned Francis' surname to Barry, so there was no reason why he should ever discover what, for some reason, I wanted to keep secret.

I looked around to check on the children. They had gone back to the stream and were standing at its edge, throwing sticks in and watching with squeals of excitement as the current took them away. Becky was organising a contest, Drew muffing it, and Ginny ruining everything by darting after the sticks. I reminded myself to call them back into the warmth of the sunshine in a few minutes, and returned to my thoughts.

I had had an interesting and probably, in the light of the earlier conversation, predicable dream the previous night. There were no roses this time but I was again in a garden, a big landscaped garden with rises and dips and decorative hedges. I had thought myself alone until I became aware of a horse

178

behind one of the hedges and, nervous, I moved away. The horse followed, slowly, not threateningly, but my nervousness suddenly turned to fear and I went quickly down into one of the dips so that I was out of sight. But very soon the creature appeared above me and looked down at me with great patience and persistence. I became resigned then, knowing that to walk away would merely result in more pursuit. I turned my back on the horse and shut it out of my mind. Either it would go away or . . . Then I knew that it was quite close, behind me. I turned to face the thing and saw Francis smiling at me, and I smiled too, and said with all the welcome in the world, 'Hello, Francis.' And woke up.

I had scrutinised the symbols in this dream, which was unusually clear in my memory. Horses, I knew – who didn't? – represented something sexual. As for running away from, turning my back on the "something sexual" – it was of course Caroline who was doing that; not me. And Francis' presence was easily explained away this time as it was he who had told me about her. It was not often that I could account so satisfactorily for all the details in a dream and I was rather pleased with myself.

It was difficult *not* to be pleased with oneself or with anything else on a day like this. I squinted lazily up at the sky, incredibly blue against the trees which rose steeply banked up the hillside. Oak trees. In the autumn we would come and collect acorns and try planting them in a pot of compost. They just might grow. It would be nice to leave an oak tree behind me for Drew and Becky and their children and grandchildren.

I wasn't really such a bad mother.

We struggled up the hill, hot, tired and rapidly becoming bad-tempered. Drew cried to be carried and pulled on his reins; Gin pulled on her lead; Becky said her legs were tired and pulled on my arm. I remembered I had to collect the shopping and two woolly jumpers, and swore. Somehow we got home, just in time to see the old man in the trilby hat (in this weather!) and the half-mast trousers, coming slowly away from our gate.

Alarm struck at me as it had before. But there had been nothing for him to look at today. He passed us, impervious to my polite greeting or Becky's silent stare, and we opened the gate, fastened it again and went into the house.

'I don't like that man,' said Becky.

'Why not?'

She shrugged, a mannerism she had lately picked up from Barry. I smiled at her, trying to dispel her alarm which she had doubtless, and with equal facility, picked up from me. I said, 'Do you remember saying Mummy was going to have a beautiful little baby?'

She nodded. 'In your tummy,' she said knowledgeably, and patted it.

'Is it still there?'

She looked surprised. 'Has it popped out already?'

'Oh, Becky,' I said, laughing, 'I'm being very silly. Sorry.'

'Harry,' said Drew, and lifted his arms irresistibly. I picked him up to give him a love and he took my face in his hands, deliberately and very firmly, and with great care placed a small, sucky kiss on my cheek – his first ever.

'You kissed me! Oh, Becky, Drew kissed me!' I was rapturous, more rapturous than I had ever been over any man's kiss.

Becky was as pleased as I. 'Kiss me too!' she demanded, and Drew did. 'Ugh!' she said, and grinned. I knelt on the kitchen floor amongst the sand and the dog hairs and for several minutes we indulged ourselves in the pleasures of the flesh, Drew kissing away until I stopped him for fear that he would come to regard it as a chore. The hot climb, the irritation and the wandering patient were all forgotten. I was enjoying my children.

Barry began his fortnight of working the twelve-hour night shift. He had done this on his previous ward, during the long winter nights, and I had hated it. Not only had I been alone all evening and all night, but most of the day too, for he stayed in bed till about four in the afternoon. I appreciated his need to do this but felt I needed to do it myself quite as badly, for Drew was teething at that time and waking up several times a night, usually waking Becky too, and there was no-one to share the load. How on earth, I used to wonder, did single parents manage? And it was so *lonely*. Barry might not talk

180

much but the house never felt right when he was not somewhere in it.

This time I didn't mind at all. For one thing it was summer,
and everything was always easier in the summer. But the main
difference was in me, not in season or circumstances. For too
long I had been relying on Barry, and on Barry alone, for
everything: clinging millstone-like around his uncomplaining
neck, because there had been nothing else to cling to. It had
been the extrovert in me which had first attracted him (ours
being a case of opposites) – that, and my independent spirit,
but both had come close to extinction during the last couple of
years.

No more. At last I was less dependent on him. Now, on rehearsal nights, I packed the children off to bed at seven and
rushed straight to the mirror, taking out heated rollers as I
went, brushing my hair into some amazing creation and then
applying make-up. At quarter-past seven I cheerfully saw
Barry off to work. At twenty-past Francis came and I roared
away on the mo-ped, knowing full well that the moment I was
gone Becky would run downstairs again, and not minding at
all. Because I was free.

With a perfectly easy mind I would spend a couple of hours
at Massey village hall, enjoying now a comfortable and
humerous cameraderie with Don Last, and flirting instead
with Godfrey, who liked it; then, declining invitations to the
pub, I would ride back through the warm summer night,
between the high hedgerows where the sound of chirping
crickets was audible even through my crash helmet, and so
home to Francis.

He was usually deep in some book or other, but he would
put it down, plug in the kettle, lean against the kitchen
counter and talk. Or listen. Sometimes we took our coffee out
to the back porch and sat there on the step in the dying light,
breathing in the summer smells: new hay drifting from the
fields across the valley, freshly-cut grass from the gardens.
We didn't talk about his English A level books because
Francis wouldn't let me, except on Wednesdays, but we
talked about almost everything else: children, parents, marriage, travel, history, politics, education. Writing.
Canoeing . . . He told me about the weirs on the River

Tamar at Gunnislake, and the spectacular river bluffs there; about how he had once broken a canoe on a weir on the Dart, but escaped unscathed; and about the notorious "washing-machine", which he described as three flights of underwater steps running straight into the rock face of a cliff. To make the ninety-degree turn at the bottom, he said, you had to approach with speed and confidence, for there was no turning round or stopping . . .

I could have talked and listened for hours. But at about eleven o' clock he would go and I, sleepy but intensely happy and not a bit lonely, would go to bed and to sleep with the noise of rapids singing in my ears.

And so we came to our first dress rehearsal – and Francis' final night of baby-sitting, for after tomorrow Barry would be available again.

The dress rehearsal was less than satisfactory. The detective's moustache kept dropping off, Miranda's scarlet satin dress bagged horribly at the neck (several times I saw Don eyeing her thin little cleavage with unjustifiable lasciviousness), the lights were set at the wrong angle and refused to be adjusted, the curtain stuck halfway across, the tape recording of the police car's siren jammed and squealed, Miranda forgot her words, Godfrey forgot his words, someone dropped a glass of whisky when they were't supposed to, I cut myself on the glass and the library door fell off its hinges.

This time I was sure Peter had done it on purpose. His grin was too wicked to be interpreted in any other way. Dorothy went berserk, berating all of us and turning unbecomingly purple in the process. We were all glum, certain that the thing would be a disaster, and no-one went to the pub that night.

I had decided to take home and iron my slinky black dress, which I normally left at the hall, so as the night was warm I rode home in it. Unable to resist, I posed in the doorway when I arrived, hitched up the already short skirt to reveal a leg clad in black seamed tights. I was not disappointed. Francis stared, whistled, said 'Wow!' and laughed.

'You can't imagine,' I said, giving a little twirl, 'what a boost this thing gives me. I feel terrific in it.'

'You look terrific,' he said, as he had to, I suppose, but his expression suggested he meant it. 'I must buy a ticket,' he added, and we both laughed again. 'No, I mean it. I was planning to come anyway.'

I found a ticket for him and said, 'On the house.'

He was already digging through his pockets. 'Rubbish,' he said, 'I'll pay for it.'

I took his arm and pulled it away from the pocket. 'Francis,' I said firmly, 'I couldn't have done this without you.'

'But you're already paying me for baby-sitting.'

'Then count it as a present. From a friend.'

He looked gravely at me. 'All right.'

There was a silence. I stood there looking up at him. How big he was, how solid and good-looking and what a lovely nature he had. I had again forgotten that he was a schoolboy. I still had hold of his forearm, bare, the sleeves rolled up on this hot night, and I could feel the thick hair on it and the firm muscularity of it. I let go, but was somehow unable to move away. I wondered what he was seeing, looking down at me. Heavy stage make-up and lined, tired eyes, or . . .? I remembered the dream I had had about him, the first dream, and the yearning I had felt then grew in me again. Those blue eyes so like Drew's, with a smile never far away . . . But there was no smile now. I heard my breathing change and in the same moment heard his own and saw just how unsmiling those eyes were, and how close, suddenly, they were to mine.

A moment, that seemed like an hour. I was poised, motionless on the brink, but ready, very ready to hurtle down towards – what? (Approach with confidence. There is no stopping or turning back.)

And I remembered how young he was, how brutally subject to the demands, commands, of his body. I had to stop this now, before everything became spoiled for both of us. Whatever happened it would not be a beautiful thing to remember, it never was in such circumstances, it would be shameful and tawdry and if we ever met in the future we would look at each other with embarrassment. Francis was too important for that.

So I turned my back on him. Took a breath, and said in a voice that was not my own, 'I'll just check on the children. Back in a minute.'

I went quickly upstairs. I had never checked on the children before when I came in, but it was the best I could think of. He would understand. He knew as well as I knew what had been happening, what had been about to happen.

I pulled off the black dress, put on another, infinitely more chaste, and returned. His face was flushed but otherwise he was, superficially anyway, himself. The problem now was how to return quickly to our old footing. It should not be difficult, I thought nervously – if only we could both stop blushing . . . After all, nothing had happened, we had merely looked at each other . . .

Now, for a few minutes, we didn't look at each other at all. But I made coffee as usual, and talked too loudly, telling him about the disastrous evening, and made him laugh. After that it was better and we exchanged smiles, shy or sheepish, I was not sure which. It was past. Almost, I could have imagined it had never been. It was strange – like believing you had seen gold, and then finding it gone because it had only been a sunbeam.

'I went to see Caroline today,' Francis said presently. 'She's looking very fit.' He rinsed his cup under the tap, then took mine and rinsed that too. I watched him. I had not suggested, tonight, that we go out to the porch, so we had drunk our coffee standing up in the kitchen. 'Tell me, does your husband find that his patients grow dependent on him?'

I jumped, and said cautiously, 'Sometimes. Why?'

'Caroline seems to have built up a strong dependency on one of the nurses. He's leaving soon and she's in a bit of a state about it. Says no-one else understands her and she'll never get well without him.' He found a tea-cloth and dried the cups carefully and hung them on their hooks. I was leaning against the opposite wall, hands behind me, still watching him. 'I wondered,' he said, 'if it was a common problem.'

'I think it is.'

He turned then, and I moved away from my wall and took the tea-cloth off him and said thank you. I was grateful for the mention of Caroline. Somehow that had brought me back to reality and restored my equilibrium.

But, standing on the doorstep before he left, he looked at me with something in his eyes that I could not, now, identify – something sad, but also something shining. I remembered

184

those years when the slightest hurt cuts deep and the smallest happiness is joy, and knew that he, too, had experienced – something.

So much for equilibrium.

Is he? Or isn't he?

That is the question.

Is Barry Caroline's nurse, on whom she has become dependent, without whom she believes she cannot get well? Or isn't he?

But there was no real doubt in my mind. Barry had said weeks ago that he had a problem concerning his anorexic patient. Barry's problems were almost always unselfish. He was concerned for her sake, not for his own. That was why he had been so withdrawn lately.

Was it? Was that all? He had told me about other dependent patients. Why not this one? Could it be because the dependence was mutual? There is nothing more flattering (until time and familiarity turn it stale) than being needed. She was young, probably beautiful if she resembled Francis at all, and she was in trouble.

And so, I told myself grimly, are you. So are you, my girl, if your hypothesis is correct.

But, surprisingly, my mind did not dwell on that at all, but returned to the boy – to the man – who had just left. I slid down in the armchair until I was almost lying in it, and stretched my legs, my feet, my toes, feeling alive from top to bottom of me. I felt the breath going in and out of my body, I listened to it, I felt the blood pulsing through my veins; sensations, life. Francis Blake, you enormous half-grown thing, you have done this to me, this which neither Godfrey nor Don Last was able to achieve, nor Barry any more although I suppose I will always love and need him. And you will never know. You might guess, but you will never really know.

The second dress rehearsal. Barry, his metabolism all to hell, baby-sat in a stage of wakeful exhaustion. The rehearsal went like a dream. Oh for an audience, we all said! By now we were so united in this endeavour that it was as if we were all lovers,

185

or members of the same family, close and very deeply involved with one another.

The first night. And my period started.

No baby! No baby at all!

I had no time to be either elated or sorrowful. I had been twelve days late, later than I had ever been before, and convinced that Becky's prophecy had been right. But no. Here I was, with protruding tummy, painful cramps, back-ache, pimples, and more-than-ample padding (heaven forfend that the bulge should show, but I daren't rely on Tampax alone) going on stage to play a nubile and villainous nym-phomaniac before, at last, a live audience.

Of fourteen people.

It's always like this on the first night, they assured me during the intermission; the villagers don't like to come to a first night, they feel it's intrusive.

So we stoically regarded the performance as yet another dress rehearsal, and secretly I was rather relieved that the audience was so small. By tomorrow I would be feeling and looking much better, and tomorrow Francis was to come.

The second night. The hall was packed, humming with expectation, naïve old ladies, and small boys who sat directly below the stage and guffawed every time Godfrey and I made contract. Early in the first act I saw Francis. I was standing primly holding a tray, waiting for my lady and her brother to issue their orders to me, and I saw without moving my eyes the blond head in the third row, inches higher than everyone else's head. The effect was electric. Instantly I felt my acting improve tenfold, and right away this had an equally electrify-ing effect on the rest of the cast. We were better, far better than on the night of the second dress rehearsal, and so high did we raise the standard of the performance that even the small boys fell silent. When Godfrey threw me to the floor there were gasps of horror all over the hall, and you could have heard the proverbial pin drop when Don produced his gun and held it to my head. They were with us all the way, that audience, and actually gave us a standing ovation during the curtain calls.

Later I looked, shining-eyed, around the dressing-room and saw triumph in every face. How I loved them all – Don and Godfrey, the would-be lechers; slave-driving Dorothy; wicked Peter, who had mercifully refrained from practical jokes tonight; dizzy Miranda who had died with such dignity, and the ageing detective who looked so distinguished in his moustache – those and all the others who had worked together with enthusiasm and good humour and brought the audience to its feet in that moment of shared jubilation. I knew now why people said the stage got into your blood, why, once you had done it, you never wanted to do anything else. The University pantomime had not been like this.

And so – the final night. And we had to call on Francis again after all, so that Barry could come to the performance. I left before he arrived but received effusive messages of congratulations from him through Barry, who stuck his head into the dressing-room to deliver them. For a time these messages buoyed me up. But the evening was somehow flat. We had peaked last night, too early, and tonight we were merely going through the motions, mechanically and without fire. Massey audiences, however, were not hard to please, and this one applauded generously. There was a bouquet for the producer, and speeches and a party afterwards which Barry had to miss for we could not reasonably expect Francis to baby-sit till the small hours; and then it was all over.

'You didn't tell me,' said Barry in the kitchen the next day, 'that you had all those bedroom scenes.'

'Didn't I?' I was half-absent, still re-living the heady success of the second night, and still, too, slightly intoxicated in the alcoholic sense. Then I realised what he had said. 'What do you mean? There wasn't a single bedroom scene in it.'

He laughed. 'There might as well have been. You positively oozed lust.'

'Did I?' I was pleased. 'Did you think I was good?'

'Yes. You were all good, but the play was terrible.'

'I suppose it was. I'd begun to feel it was on a par with Ibsen or somebody, but yes, I remember thinking it was rubbish when I first read it.' My spirits fell slightly. It was not such an achievement after all.

'Chin up. You enjoyed doing it, that's the main thing.'

'Yes.' I looked at him. He seemed more accessible, more *present*, than he had been for weeks. A spell away from the

187

hospital was doing him good. Or perhaps after all it had been my involvement in rehearsals which had been bothering him, not Caroline Blake at all. I said gratefully, 'Thank you for not minding, Barry. And for baby-sitting while I flaunted myself in front of other men. Lots of husbands would have gone bananas if their wives had done that.'

'God knows you don't get much fun,' he said, adding, 'And I've been pretty poor company of late.'

It was an apology, but the tone warned me not to pursue the matter, so I just smiled. I put drinks and a snack on a tray, glancing at him from time to time as he leaned against the kitchen counter where Francis often leaned. We were now halfway through the first week of Barry's two-week holiday and I was not yet sufficiently detached from *Murder at the Manor* to appreciate the luxury of having him home every day. I didn't know if it was a luxury for him too or a mild ordeal. He found his work at the hospital so absorbing that home life probably seemed hideously boring and humdrum in comparison. As, of course, it was.

We sat on the step by the back porch and watched the children playing in the sand-pit. 'I suppose you're going to sink into depression now that it's all over.'

'Not yet. I'm still high.'

'From last night?'

'No. The night before. Last night wasn't very good.'

He gave me an odd look, but made no comment. 'Did you know Marjory was there?'

'No!' I gave an unladylike snort of laughter. 'So she came to see my nude scene after all!' I told him what I had said to her and he grinned appreciatively. Definitely he had become accessible again.

This was where a thoughtful, tactful and considerate wife should put the past behind her, be grateful for the present, and resist all impulses to pry, probe, nag or question. So I asked, 'Why were you poor company, Barry? Will you tell me about it?'

And was suitably rewarded by one of his silences. An unproductive one this time. He simply did not answer me, and I felt myself growing angry. Why couldn't he just say he didn't want to talk about it, instead of subjecting me to this verbal isolation? Why had he even mentioned it in the first place? But I suppressed the anger. This was my own fault, I should have left well alone. I said, 'Never mind, it doesn't matter,' and got up to take the tray inside.

But I had spoiled it, and a long walk and a picnic lunch with the children did not dispel the morose quiet that had again come upon him.

Anti-climax would certainly have made itself felt if it were not for Francis' exams looking ever closer. We worked repeatedly through old papers and I tried to teach him something of exam technique: jotting down the salient points to include in each essay before beginning the essay itself; planning on paper the shape the essay was to take; timing each one and leaving a few minutes to look through all of them at the end; writing the best one first; checking constantly to make sure that statements were being supported by evidence, that is, quotations or references to relevant passages; being aware of the dangers of straying from the set question.

He took it all in (I hoped) with his usual expression of fervent trust. The other expression I had not seen since the night I came home in my black dress, and knew that I would never see again. It seemed like a dream now. We worked steadily, methodically, going again over all his books until at last there was only one more Wednesday left before his exam, and on that night we were to take a last look at *Macbeth*.

He came. Barry was out, having recently begun meeting his fellow students at the social club on Wednesday evenings. He had put the children to bed for me and left with one of his distant blown kisses. I made an effort and put on some make-up and brushed my hair, but my heart wasn't in it. I knew perfectly well that I would never see Francis again after tonight, whatever promises we both made to the contrary.

'I've had a letter,' he said at once. He looked troubled, and I knew immediately what he meant.

'From Caroline?'

He nodded. 'Here. Read it.'

I hesitated, looking at the proferred page of small neat writing. 'No. You tell me.'

'She's left the hospital. Discharged herself and gone away.'

189

'Discharged herself? Can she do that?'

'Yes. She was a voluntary patient, you know, not – what's the word?'

'Sectioned.'

'Yes. She's gone to Scotland. The letter is postmarked Edinburgh, but there's no address. She says she wants to get right away.'

I thought about it. 'Well, if she feels she can cope . . .'

'I'm not sure that she can. Any kind of pressure and she'll probably go under again. But it's not that; after all, if the worst happens there are hospitals there too. It's just that she didn't really want to go, she was sort of driven, and I feel a bit sick about it. Also I don't know what to tell my father, she says I'm to tell him she's gone, but – '

'Just a minute, Francis. What do you mean, she was *driven*? How?'

He told me.

She was nervous of men, he said, very timid and highly imaginative, and recently she had begun to believe that a member of the hospital staff had developed a very strong attachment to her. Francis assumed the 'someone' to be the nurse on whom she had been so dependent, because, Caroline said, the attachment had initially made her very happy. But lately she had become frightened by it, feeling that something, she didn't know what, was being expected of her. She became confused about her own feelings, terrified of any kind of relationship, especially as the man was married, she had thought happily but now she wasn't sure. He was to move to another ward but she was afraid of bumping into him unexpectedly or of being pursued by him, although (she stressed) he had never done or said anything to upset her. Caroline herself admitted that she didn't know how much of this was imagination, how much was real, but she did know that she couldn't cope with it. She joked that it was not a lover she needed, but a father figure, and she commented with wry humour on the irony of that. So she had made up her mind, abandoned her treatment and left the hospital whilst the cause of all this emotional upheaval was on leave. She wrote that she had money, that she would look for work, and that she was not unhappy. And would Francis please tell their father, before the next family therapy session, that she had gone and that she was sorry if she had let him down . . .

So detailed was Francis' account that I may as well have read the letter myself. But the very details made his account lengthy, and that I needed. After only a few words I had found myself sitting very still, looking down at the pile of papers before me, and later I saw my fingers patting them carefully, steadily, into neat piles, levelling the edges, straightening them so that they lay parallel to the edge of the table. Patting and straightening, watching my fingers, all the time Francis talked. Wondering if my face showed anything. Saying 'Yes' at intervals, encouragingly, sympathetically. Feeling quite sick.

'Gosh, you're a good listener,' he said admiringly, when he had finished.

'Am I?'

'You do see how awful it is, don't you?'

'Yes.'

'That she should be driven away by the very person who was trying to help her.'

'Yes.'

'What shall I tell my father?'

'The truth,' I said sharply. 'There's been enough deception. Enough hiding of true feelings. Tell him the truth.'

He looked slightly surprised. 'You do get involved with people, don't you? That's why I told you all this, really, because you've been so interested in Caroline all along. And you're very – er, well, warm, aren't you?' He blushed.

'Let's get to work,' I said abruptly.

At heart Macbeth is as pure as the driven snow. It is Lady Macbeth who is the embodiment of evil.

I talked about Lady Macbeth. I talked about her discontented nature, her need to get her own way, her forcing of her husband along paths he would not, without her, have taken. Had she been supportive instead of ambitious, content to accept her good fortune instead of demanding more, had she recognised the good in her husband, his potential for greatness, he need never have taken those paths. But he, weakly or lovingly, allowed her way and all that he might have achieved was lost. It was her fault, her fault, for all the witches in the world would not have led him astray if she had been a better wife . . .

191

But didn't she pay? Wasn't the guilt, the unbearable burden of her guilt, a fair price to pay? Ah, but the others who were destroyed . . .

'You're getting quite passionate,' Francis remarked, lightly but with a peculiar glance at me.

And I remembered then what I was supposed to be doing, and did it. Omens, imagery, naked babes and slaughtered children, the whole blood-bath of darkness culminating at last in the light that was Malcolm. I demanded quotations, and got them. I invented essay topics and asked for a brief description of the shape the essays would take, and got them. I chose the section where Duncan arrives at the castle, there to be murdered, and told Francis to talk about it, to take it to pieces and explain its significance, and he did.

Enough.

On the doorstep he stood over me, huge; he took my hand, and then my other hand, and gave them both a painfully hard squeeze. And let go. 'Goodbye,' he said, 'and thank you for everything. You've been – Wish me luck.'

'I do. I do, Francis. And – I hope Caroline . . .'

'Thank you. Yes, I – '

'Send me your results, when you get them. And – keep in touch . . .'

'Goodbye, Amabel.'

''Bye . . .'

I watched him go, jogging steadily away, down the road with the pink-flushed hills before him – into the sunset, I thought crazily – out of my life – Then I shut the door and went back, as I always did, to gaze at the mess of books and papers we had left.

Francis. Gone.

Caroline. Gone.

Barry.

There seemed only one thing to do, and that was cry. So I did.

Part Three

Chapter One

At the end of July, while he was still on holiday, Barry went to the hospital to collect his pay cheque. He came back with a stern expression on his face and stood in the doorway, looking from the living-room to the dining-room, I watched, rather alarmed. He said, 'These floors are filthy. We're living in squalor.'

Something about the tone told me this was not a criticism but some kind of introductory speech – to what, I could not imagine – so I did not suggest that he crawled round the floors himself, manipulating dustpan and brush and fighting off children as he went; I said, 'True,' and waited.

'You need a vacuum cleaner.'

'True,' I said again, and saw his face. 'Barry!'

He waved the cheque at me. 'Nights,' he said. 'Sixty pounds extra for working nights.'

'Sixty pounds! But you only worked for two weeks!' Then I remembered Don Last's fabulous pay cheques. 'Oh, Barry! But don't you want to – I mean, you deserve – '

'Vacuum cleaner,' he said firmly. 'We'll go and buy one tomorrow, and we'll pay off the balance quickly before next winter's fuel bills start. All right?'

'All *right*!' I said joyfully.

So the next day we went on a mass expedition to the large seaside town which we hardly ever visited because the bus fares were so prohibitive, and Drew climbed inside tumble-driers and Becky programmed home computers while Barry and I chose a vacuum cleaner. It was to be delivered the following Tuesday. Until then I should hardly believe it was mine. The expedition took most of the day and Drew missed his sleep and was as grizzly as any small bear by the time we arrived home, but it was worth it.

For me the day out was like a week's holiday in itself. Apart from a brief visit from Barry's mother the previous week, absolutely nothing had happened during his holiday and we had scarcely left the village. All along our road people were going away or coming back, roof-racks laden with luggage. Every day mothers packed children and buckets and spades into cars and zoomed off to the coast with them, whilst we stayed put, filled the paddling pool, cut the grass, and walked to the local wood or the hospital rose garden. My own mother, brought up in the age of female humility, lectured me when I complained in a letter to her. Motherhood, she told me, meant Self Denial, and I must just put up with it.

It didn't, not these days, but I did put up with it because there was nothing else to do. And when my new vacuum cleaner arrived I was as excited as any child and for several days scarcely noticed our incarceration. I cleaned the whole house, under furniture, behind cupboards; I cleaned ceilings and window frames, I pushed nozzles behind bookshelves and bathroom pipes and inside wardrobes and under beds; I changed attachments and did curtains and upholstery. I even went in the shed and cleaned out all the old spider's webs. It was a positive orgy.

And after that –

After that – Nothing.

Barry went back to work, where he started his new placement on a Geriatric ward. The days were hot, drought threatened and we were asked to use water sparingly. Drew was still demanding frequent middle-of-the-night drinks, although he had been persuaded to part with his bottle, and I was perpetually short of sleep. Nursery school holidays had several weeks yet to run, playgroup was closed down for the summer, the drama group would be inoperative until autumn and all members were seemingly away; for no-one came to pay the promised visits and I could not get the pushchair over the hill to Massey to visit them. Francis was, I supposed, off canoeing somewhere. There had been no word from him.

Nothing.

196

I gave myself a stern talking-to about self-pity, ingratitude and discontent. It did not help. I wrote to Rayner and Patrick – When are you coming to visit? – but got no reply, and learned when a postcard of the Brenner Pass arrived that they were spending part of the summer with friends in Austria. I tried to resume my novel, but it would not come to life, and what little research I had been able to do into Extra-Sensory Perception would not pad out my dismally thin plot.

Nothing.

Becky splashed more and more grumpily in water which was turning thick and green in the plastic pool, and finally even she conceded that we had to tip it away. Then there was nothing for her but mischief because there was a limit to the number of hours I could spend walking, reading stories or otherwise entertaining her. Gradually my own behaviour deteriorated again, into apathy or intolerance and ill-temper, and soon I was once more shouting at both children, often unjustly and simply for my personal release. I recognised what was happening and tried to rectify it, gave Becky small but responsible tasks to do, and she did them – for a while. But she too was bored, horrendously bored. In desperation I put a notice in Ivan's window calling on all mothers enduring similar states of purgatory to meet at my house, with offspring for morning coffee. I even bought an extra-large jar of coffee (which I could ill afford) and ordered extra milk, but nobody came. Marjory said she *would* have come, but it was so difficult with the shop . . . Marjory had never said a word about my performance in *Murder at the Manor*, nor even mentioned that she had been to see it, but she had given me several very odd looks for days after. Whether this was because I had disappointed her in the matter of the nude scene or because she was thoroughly disgusted by the amount of lust I had oozed, I could not decide, but my feelings towards her were now distinctly cool. It seemed mutual.

Nothing.

Every night Barry came home full of the day's events, exuding vitality and a lively interest in his work. There was no shortage of anecdotes, even from him, on this ward. Most of them concerned a combination of bodily functions and con-fusion, and most were hilarious – if you could disregard the basic tragedy. You could, since the patients themselves were mostly unaware of it.

Funny stories were all very well, but I seemed to be back where I had started, months ago, and I did not like it. It was all the harder because during those months I had remembered how to live, and now –

But I was not, I knew, back where I had started. Things had happened to me, they could not unhappen. I had realised certain fundamental things, I could not unrealise them. Or could I?

Much of the difficulty, I saw at last, stemmed from my efforts, and presumably Barry's too, to go on as if nothing *had* happened. I realised this when Francis (finally) sent me one of his A level English papers. The letter was postmarked France, and he wrote in his brief accompanying note that he was canoeing and camping there with friends. (How on earth, I wondered, had they got their canoes to *France*?) The exam had gone well, he said, and he promised to let me know the results. There was no mention of Caroline.

The exam paper was crumpled and extremely dirty. If it had been posted in France he had evidently been carrying it about with him for ages – meaning to send it to me, and forgetting – until one day, in a fit of stricken conscience over his half-forgotten tutor, he had made a noble effort . . .

I shook my head irritably and turned to the paper. Within seconds I was laughing aloud in incredulous delight, for I might have designed these questions myself. There was one about the respective culpability of Macbeth and Lady Macbeth, one about the nature of freedom in *Kes*, a rather nastily-phrased question concerning duality in the Chaucer poem (but Francis' jottings in the margin told me that he had understood what was wanted) and, on *Tess*, one about Hardy's fate theme and one which asked, virtually, for a comparison of the characters of the two men in Tess' life. I could not tell from the scribbles on the paper which of these he had chosen but I had covered the material for both more than adequately.

Gleefully I tucked the paper away with my literature notes. My spirits had leapt an octave or so, and I got out the dolly mixtures. It was only fair that the children, who bore the brunt of my downs, should also get the benefit of the ups. I lined them up in a row on the (clean) dining-room floor, Becky, Drew and Gin, and doled out a smallish handful to each. Gin's were gone in an instant and then she hung around trying to scrounge everyone else's, until I sent her to her basket. Sometimes I felt I had three children.

That reminded me of my fears of a few weeks ago, and I grimaced. How near I had come to having an affair, or at least committing adultery, just because of hurt feelings over Rayner's old letter and a belief that I was pregnant! I had put too much weight on Becky's prophecy when all she had caught was my own thoughts on the subject. She had known no more than I did myself. And for that I might have destroyed my marriage!

I recognised something melodramatic and not quite truthful in these thoughts, and pulled them up to examine them, much as one pulls up water from a well. Down at the bottom, below the clear clean water, is a lot of murky stuff. You have to keep dipping to get at it.

That was when I saw that I had made a mistake in going on as if nothing had happened. Things *had* happened and the murk was down there to prove it. Hearing from Francis, now that I had got over his exam paper, had brought me face to face with it all over again.

The children had gone back outside, naked as usual. Now Becky came in, exaggeratedly tip-toeing, and whispered, 'That man is at the gate.'

'The old man with the hat?' He was a frequent visitor now, and I had grown used to his silent comings and goings. 'He's all right, Becky. Quite a sweet old thing, really. You needn't worry, so long as he doesn't open the gate.'

'Drew is talking to him.'

I nodded. Drew had got over his terror of strangers and was quite as gregarious as Becky. Some day soon , I knew, I would have to start warning both of them not to talk to strangers. Especially Becky. Hurtful, when they had such a clean belief in people's goodness, to have to shatter it.

I went to look through the window. The patient was moving away, Drew cheerily waving to him, unregarded. The gate was still fastened.

Becky padded away and I returned to my thoughts. There was a rather unpleasant feeling inside me as I looked again at the things I had suppressed since that last night when Francis was here. The first thing I had to acknowledge was that I had *not* nearly committed adultery, either with Don Last or Francis. (Dear Francis.) I had lied to myself about the reasons, I thought now. When the moment had come I had not been remotely tempted by Don's physical charms, but not necessarily because Barry was the only man for me. I *had* been tempted by Francis – I could recall easily the wave of sweating desire that had come over me for him – but again, I had not turned from him solely for his sake or the sake of our friendship. I had kept both Don and Francis at a distance for the same reason that I had often, physically anyway, kept Barry at a distance: because I had wanted to survive. Me, Amabel Dennell. I had wanted at least part of me intact, possessed only by myself. All day, all night too sometimes, there were demands, I want I want I want, and I was the sole and supposedly the inexhaustible supplier of all those wants. Emotional, physical, mental, intellectual. Hugs, cuddles, smacks, praise, discipline. Meals, drinks, sweets, dropped spoons, spilt milk, grazed knees, hairy lollipops, dog's dinners, wet towels, wet knickers, lost toothbrushes, sore tummies, dirty washing, clean underpants, shopping, food, food, food. Drinks in the night, bad dreams in the night, Mummy, Mummy, Mummy. Demands, a continuous stream of them and a continuous stream going out from me to meet them, and nothing coming in, no replenishment, all of me being gradually eroded, goodbye Amabel Dennell you are being consumed; nothing left.

Sex. The last, the ultimate demand. Total obsession of. No longer a person but a supplier. Demand and supply. Everything, everything expected from me. Even the birth control pills. My responsibility.

Call it loss of libido, call it survival instinct, call it wrong. Whatever, it had been a sign saying Keep Out.

That was the first thing I had to realise.

The second was that, given a wife with such hang-ups about retention of identity, almost any husband, however understanding, would be ripe for plucking.

200

I was lucky: Barry had not been plucked. But if the girl in question had not had far more serious hang-ups, he might have been.

So what does one do? Sink one's identity? And what if it refuses to be sunk?

I shelved the question and went back to Barry. He had, of course, fallen in love with Caroline. A man of his type did not indulge in idle sexual encounters like Don Last did. There she was, young, clever, half-starved, unhappy, a misfit. Exactly the type that always called to Barry's heart, exactly the type to recognise the compassion that lived there. And so, a drawing together of souls, a mutual dependence, and at last, because wife Amabel was simultaneously clinging and cold, an intense need which was ultimately greater on Barry's side than on Caroline's. But Caroline could not take pressure, could not even bear expectations from others. And Caroline was terrified of sex.

I saw it from Barry's side. Knowing her intimately, probably more closely than any friend she had ever had, knowing exactly what she could and could not bear and at some point realising that his own feelings, and therefore expectations, were the thing she could bear least of all. Barry, who was supposed to be helping her to cope with pressure, involuntarily applying it by the ton. He must have known. He must have seen the awful irony of it, realised that she felt his intensity and was being harmed by it. He must have suffered, feeling as he did the need to *help*.

And whose fault was all this? Mine. Or so I believed. Mine.

And the girl with the phobia, had he been half-falling for her too, until Caroline usurped her? Would *any* girl do, any girl who needed him and did not resent his infringement of her private territory? Just how far *had* I driven him?

I had thought I knew guilt before, but this was a hundred times worse. I had had a glimpse of it once, the night I talked to Francis about Lady Macbeth's guilt, and it had been dark enough to make me push it well down and slam the door on it. Now it rose again.

Things unresolved. Should I try to resolve them? Bring them out into the open, have an honest talk with Barry? But I knew those honest talks, we had had them before about other subjects. I talked and he listened. I paused and he said nothing. So I talked again and he listened again. Then I, at least, was left with a refreshed feeling, as if we had aired everything, and only later would I realise that Barry had aired nothing at all. It would be just the same this time.

Well then – become an understanding wife, sweet-tempered, loving, always available? Easier said than done, and I had tried that before too.

Go back to the drama group, rehearsals, coaching as soon as the summer was over? Become again that happy, interested and interesting person I had so briefly been (hadn't I?) and spread sweetness and light about the house as a result? Maybe. Last time had not been a fair test, for I had been half in love with Don and with Francis, and Barry had been in love with Caroline . . .

A small gleam of humour appeared in the situation and I found myself faintly smiling. The English were never any good at bedroom farce, I thought. Too reserved by half. Always teetering on the threshhold, worrying about their image and their pyjama cord. All this emotion and no sex!

I felt better then, and went to check on the children. They were not outside, nor were they anywhere downstairs. I realised just how long the abnormal silence had been going on. It could mean only one of two things. Either they were dead or they were doing something evil.

I went quietly upstairs. They were standing in the bath, smearing each other with toothpaste. It was a new tube, giant-size, with Ivan's usual generous profit margin on it.

I shut my eyes for a moment, then wearily opened them again. Both children were quite oblivious to my presence. It wasn't just toothpaste, I saw now. The toilet was covered in what looked like blobs of cotton wool but proved to be shaving foam from Barry's aerosol can. The wash basin had turned pink: calamine lotion. And in the bottom of the bath, half covering four bare feet, were the complete contents of my bottle of hair conditioner.

About a fiver in all, I calculated grimly, and started forward. Becky looked up and her striped face broke instantly into an apprehensive wail. Drew merely smiled beatifically. Rule by terror never bothered him until he actually felt the jackboot. Unimaginative child.

I didn't apply the jackboot, because two smacked and sobbing children would not have functioned well. And they were going to function. I gave them a bucket of warm water and a cloth each, and told them to clean the bathroom. Every inch of it. And themselves. Then I shut the door on them and left them to it. I knew that they would not do it properly, that there would be floods everywhere, but I reasoned that half an hour's hard slog would deter them from a repetition and also keep them out of my hair. But after a few minutes I began to regret the move, so merry were the sounds of splashing and laughter. The punishment, I reflected sourly, probably seemed like a reward to them. They would want to do it every day. Perhaps I ought to write a book about mother and child behaviour. What to avoid. *Every Wrong Decision You Could Possibly Make. And More.* By Amabel Dennell.

I went downstairs and banged the kettle on to boil. Outside the sun blazed down and the grass lay half-dead, parched and yellowing. Through the spindly hedge I could see the woman next door sunbathing, bikini-clad, on an expensive upholstered lounger. Her small child played contentedly nearby, not bothering her at all. I stared resentfully through the hedge. Sun-bathing was not allowed in our family, nor was anything that involved sitting, lying, relaxing in any form, or being absorbed in any pursuit of one's own.

I drank my tea, grimly determined to hear nothing of what was going on upstairs. When it began to sound as if the Victoria Falls had been relocated in our bathroom, I gave in, trudged up again, waded into the bathroom and sent the children out while I continued the cleaning-up operation. Within a minute agonised howls issued from Drew's room. I rushed in to find him being slowly bisected between the side of the cot and its frame, which Becky had dismantled and was now attempting to refasten, with him halfway inside. I rescued him, getting a hefty kick in the process from his flailing feet, and swore. Drew said, 'Harry.' Becky said, '*What* a clever boy, learning to talk!' I said, 'OUT!'

Life? Don't talk to me about life.

I put the cot back together again and had a despairing lean on it. If I could only crawl in there, curl up, foetal position naturally, yank a blanket over myself and remain hidden. How could I possibly *think*, how could I deal with anything of a serious nature while all this was going on? And on. And on . . .

I wanted to cry, but didn't. I wanted to lose my temper, but didn't do that either, though I thought that I probably would quite soon. I hadn't lost it yet today and it was already mid-morning. I supposed that we ought to go out, but quailed at the thought of dressing those toothpastey bodies. Should I bath them? The water wasn't hot enough.

I went downstairs. 'Shut the fridge door!'

'Me?' That, innocently, was Drew. He now had a dozen or so mono-syllabic words which he used with devastating effect.

'Yes, you,' I snapped, foolishly. Hooked again. He extracted his fingers from the margarine, licked them, shut the door. I put the kettle on again, intending to wash the children at the kitchen sink. (How very working-class, Rayner would say.)

'*Shut the fridge door!*'

'Why?'

I flew at him and he shut it, fast. 'Don't say "why?" to me! Now leave it alone!'

He flung himself carefully on the floor, emitting unconvincing screams, but got up again almost immediately. Cold tiles. I began to clean the sink.

'*Shut the* – !'

'NO!'

This time I let him have it. Drew, my baby, my beloved. But he wasn't my beloved at the moment, although penitence threatened when I saw my handprint emblazoned on his dimpled buttocks. His world came to an end for all of two minutes.

The doorbell rang.

A miracle! There was instant cacophony as we all jostled to get there, Gin too, and for a moment it was impossible to open the door. My heart had leapt ridiculously. Of course it couldn't really be Francis, he was still in France, it was probably a Jehovah's Witness but at least it was *somebody* –

Godfrey.

'How lovely!' I exclaimed. 'Are you on holiday, Godfrey?

What a nice surprise, come on in.' I flung the door wide, with some difficulty, and beamed at the impeccable Godfrey. His glance moved from me to the naked smeary children pushing to get a look at him, and I saw his own smile falter. 'Lovely kids,' he murmured, and cleared his throat.

'Do come in,' I persisted.

'No thanks, I'm – er – just passing. Dorothy asked me to give you a message. You don't seem to be on the phone?'

'No.' I gave a sigh and let go of the door. I could hardly blame him for refusing to come in, I thought, watching his eyes nervously switching back to Becky and Drew. It wouldn't have been so bad if the toothpaste were white. 'Are we starting another production already? I thought – '

'No, it's not that. Quite the reverse, in fact. The group's breaking up – for this year, anyway. Dorothy wanted every-one to know as early as possible so that you can all make other plans for the autumn, join other groups if you want to.'

Disappointment swept through me. 'But why? What's happened?'

'Nothing much,' he said evasively. 'Dorothy doesn't feel like doing another production, that's all.'

'But someone else could produce, couldn't they? What about Don? Or yourself?' Or me, I added silently, hopefully.

He bit his lip and looked down. I said, 'Look, Godfrey, do come in, it's silly standing here.'

He took no notice. 'I may as well tell you. You'll hear anyway, sooner or later. Don and Dorothy have separated. He – well, he left her.'

'Oh.'

He said with sudden passion, 'He's moved in with Miranda.'

I stared at him. 'Miranda!'

'Yes,' he said bitterly, 'old enough to be her father. Well, that's fashionable now, isn't it? Anyway there it is. Sorry.'

He turned away and I did not press him further. I shut the door on the wafting scent of his aftershave and looked gloomily at my children. Moved in with Miranda! Godfrey had been smitten with Miranda. I saw it now. That evening in the pub, when he had looked at the two of them and remarked on Don's marital freedom . . . Thank God *I* had not been involved in all that – the break-up of a marriage – Oh, why couldn't people try *harder*, stick together and work out their problems?

'That man smells,' said Becky.

Try harder, stick together. Work out your problems. It was easily said. But when you didn't know what the problems were . . .

Did Barry know that Caroline had gone? Did he know why? He would guess, of course. I imagined how it would make him feel. Barry, the great healer, driving his patients away from their treatment. If he knew, what a terrible sense of failure he must have had, perhaps had still. All his ideals ashes. He *must* know, he had met staff from his previous ward, he had even told me how the phobic patient was getting on so he must have heard about Caroline. He had kept it all quiet, all hidden inside him, he was so good at keeping things hidden. I supposed I must do the same. But then I would never know if he still loved her – if he *had* loved her . . . I would never be certain that he loved me. But how could I be certain anyway? He would not say that he didn't.

That evening, while the children were rioting over the tea table and Barry was drinking his homecoming cup of tea, I put my arms round him and he put down his cup and responded warmly. I said into his ear, 'Sometimes you seem to love me and sometimes you don't.'

It was the closest I dared get to 'Do you love me?'

But my cowardice was repaid, for he merely chuckled softly down my own ear. As if I had made a small joke. And that was all.

Nothing.

Chapter Two

I had a day out. Alone. Barry had worked eight days in a row
and now had four days off. Two of these had been taken up as
usual by catching up on sleep and going shopping, but on the
third I decided that I would have my own day off. I would go
and look at the sea.

It seemed that it was no longer possible to do anything,
anything at all, without an accompanying sensation of guilt.
Today the guilt was caused by three things: I was going to the
beach without Becky and Drew, who would have loved it; I
was leaving Barry to babysit all day; and I was spending
money on bus fare which ought to have been spent on food or
put towards school fees or having the bike serviced or new
shoes for Drew or paying off the vacuum cleaner. . .

But I need a *break*, I told myself viciously. It's only a few
pounds, why *shouldn't* I?

As soon as I got off the bus I forgot about the guilt. There
were other things to occupy my mind. The town was crammed
full of tourists – lobster pink or golden brown and sporting
shorts, bikinis, halter tops, bare feet, bare chests, sun-hats –
and babies in pushchairs. I lost count of the number of babies
in pushchairs after only a few minutes. They were everywhere
and almost all of them were crying. Some were whimpering
softly, some wailing loudly, unbecomingly. There were red
open mouths, waving fists, silently coursing tears, but all, all
had their eyes screwed into slits. 'Damn you,' I wanted to say
to their mothers, 'damn you, can't you see it's too hot, can't
you see the sun is too bright? Can't you see you've been
hauling them around for far too long and they want rest and

cool, they want to be picked up and held and loved?'

A great lonely sadness invaded me then, for wasn't that what we all wanted? I had once thought, If only we were all children . . . But we *were* all children, we all wanted to be picked up and loved, and nobody did it. People went past, unheeding, while we whimpered or wailed in our various ways. We were all babies, wanting what seemed so simple and was somehow so impossible.

I yearned over those babies. All the way to the sea I yearned over them, but when I got there it was diffcrent, for the sea breeze cooled the air and children large and small were paddling with delicious abandon as the tide came in. I leaned on the wall above and looked down at them. A tiny blond boy wearing only a t-shirt tottered perilously over some slippery stones, his little buttocks trembling with effort and concentration. From the back he could have been Drew, and I held my breath as I watched him. His sandals protected his feet but nothing would protect his knees if he went down. He didn't go down. He made it safely to the point he was aiming for and then turned round and grinned triumphantly at someone out of my line of vision.

So much for having a day out and a break! If all I could do was agonise over small blond boys who might get hurt I may as well go home again.

I went to a spot I had visited once before, where there was a nearly-natural swimming pool formed out of cliff face and a little concrete. The tide was washing clear and green into it, and it was full of suntanned children, confidently diving and swimming in the salt water. I settled down there with my sandwiches and Thermos flask. The sun was hot, but pleasantly so, and all around were the sounds and sights of freedom: space, water, warmth, laughter. Dogs dashed up and down the rock steps beside lithe brown legs. The dogs barked, the legs vanished upside down in the pool. Presently I noticed that one dog, a small terrier, was playing with a pebble, tossing it down the steps and chasing it, running up again with the pebble in its mouth and tossing it down, over and over until eventually the inevitable happened and his pebble splashed into the pool.

Disaster. The little dog sat down and howled. Then he

peered down through the clear water to where the pebble sat on the concrete bottom, and barked repeatedly, urgently. I watched entranced, waiting for someone to notice, or for the dog to give up and find another pebble. But he didn't give up. Bark, bark, bark, bark. Over the noise of the sea and children's shouts it penetrated only faintly, but his persistence paid off. A child swam up, then another. Soon there were half a dozen of them clustered at the edge of the pool, making a fuss of the dog, while he tried to explain his problem. And at last someone understood.

A flash of legs, spray rising and settling, a gleam of limbs underwater and up came a child with the dog's pebble. The dog said thank you, took it and trotted away.

I discovered tears in my eyes. Marvellous children! If only we were all children!

But other children, at another time or in another place, might not have helped. Other children might have beaten the dog, slashed him with a knife just for the hell of it. It was no good believing that all children were good and kind, because they were not, any more than all adults were good and kind. If they were kind to dogs, they were probably rotten to their kid sisters or to the school weakling.

Nevertheless it was a satisfactory ending to my picnic and I left feeling considerably less desolate than when I arrived. The children and the sea had done their work, as had the sails of distant dinghies and the heat haze over the harbour and the gentle sucking and hushing noise of the shingle under the swell.

I went back up the rough cliff steps, while the sea fell away beneath and I remembered anew why I hardly ever brought Becky and Drew here. You could come the long way round by bus, but by the time you had changed buses twice, heaving on and off children and all the necessary impedimenta, half your day was gone, not to mention your money, and you were in such a state of exhaustion that lying down in the middle of the road seemed the only sensible thing left to do. If only we had a *car*, I thought for the thousandth time, as I arrived, panting, at the top; if only I could write a novel that would sell, so that I could buy a *car*.

If only I could write a novel at all!

209

I left the bay shimmering behind me and walked through the heat of the town to see what Oxfam had to offer.

'Presents, children!'

Exultantly I opened the large brown Oxfam bag. Everyone crowded round, even Gin. 'For you,' I said to Becky, and gave her a horrible painted thatched cottage made out of cheap pottery. It was about four inches high and had a bit of the chimney missing, but she was thrilled with it. 'Drew, this is yours. Don't suck it till I've washed it.' His present was a polythene plate bearing two improbable ladies in tall black hats and the inscription WALES. 'I said *don't* suck it! Yours, Barry.' A battered plastic record-rack, but nobody would notice the rack once his records were in it and I was sick of them lying all over the living-room. So really it was a present for myself, but I didn't say that.

'And I've got a blanket – rather holey, but that doesn't matter. This, however,' delving again into the bag, 'is my *pièce de résistance*.' And I produced sandals for Drew.

Barry frowned. 'I thought we agreed we weren't going to buy secondhand shoes for the children.'

'We did. But they're Clarks, in super condition, and you can still read the size *and* the width fitting. They're exactly right for him now.' I put them on Drew. His face shone with that joyous glow I always envied, and he adopted a self-conscious stance while we crawled round him, prodding at his feet. Barry was satisfied.

'Tell me about the children who had all these things before,' said Becky, and waited expectantly.

I looked ruefully at Barry. Poor Becky. She always assumed that someone else had had her things first, and usually she was right. But it was not altogether a bad thing. Last winter we had sent off a lot of our old baby clothes, via a charity, to Poland, and since then Becky had developed a great concern for children who had nothing. If we had not been hard up ourselves we might never have thought of doing it, and Becky would have started to expect life's shiny goodies to land unearned before her. Well, there was not much chance of that.

She was already inventing her own histories for the bits of

210

rubbish I had brought. I went into the kitchen to scrub Drew's awful plate while her high-pitched voice described articulately and in great detail the child who had previously owned the pottery cottage, and Drew walked ostentatiously about the house, smiling at his feet. They were not so bad really. An enjoyable day out, some freedom, and they seemed like different children.

'Did you meet anyone today?' Barry asked, after we had put them to bed.

I glanced up from dish-washing. He was drying. 'Hundreds of crying babies. What do you mean, did I meet anyone? I don't *know* anyone.'

He stacked some dishes neatly in the cupboard. 'I just wondered.'

'Who did you think I might be meeting? Did you – ' I stared at him, half appalled, half amused – 'did you think I had a *date*?'

'No,' he said huffily. 'But you never go to the coast, so – '

'I never go anywhere. That's why I went,' I said logically. 'Come on, admit it, you thought I had a date. Who with? Don Last?' I didn't wait for him to answer, for I had suddenly remembered Godfrey's startling news. I told him about it and to my astonishment he nodded.

'Yes,' he said placidly, 'I heard.'

'You heard? Where? When?'

'At work, about a week ago.'

I slammed down a plate, cracked it, and glared at him. 'And you didn't tell me! You never tell me *any*thing, Barry!'

'I didn't realise you were so interested,' he said mildly.

'Of course I'm interested! I'm interested in anything that happens to someone I know. I'm interested in *people*. I want to *know* things!' I stopped. He didn't say anything. To my horror I found that I was on the verge of tears, without in the least knowing why.

He said casually, 'If you really want the truth, I thought you might be meeting Francis.'

My head jerked up. 'Francis!' I could hear the guilt in my voice.

'Innocently, of course. You liked him.'

211

'Yes . . . He's in France.'

'Oh?'

'I had a letter. Well, just a note really. He sent me one of his exam papers.' I told him about that while we finished the dishes, and he was interested and seemed pleased about the questions that had been set. I said, not knowing I was going to say it, 'You're right about my liking him. I – sort of loved him, you know.' I looked at him and he smiled.

'Yes, I did know.'

'*Did* you? How?'

'Oh . . . You came alive when he was here. When he was coming, even.'

I could hardly believe my ears. 'You're – incredibly understanding,' I said. 'I don't deserve you.' And the damned tears came.

He took me into the living-room and sat on the arm of my chair. 'I don't know why I'm crying – Sorry – I know you're – I couldn't ask for a better husband, but – I miss him, and it's all so *dull*, and the bloody kids . . .'

He murmured things, and after a few minutes I blew my nose and managed a smile. He said gently, 'It wasn't Francis you were in love with, you know.'

'Do you think not?' I said it hopefully, not sceptically, trusting him but wondering what on earth his interpretation could be.

'You were in love with his youth – and his spirit of adventure, and his freedom. All the things you've had to say goodbye to. Why, even his name . . .'

'Free. Yes.'

'And another thing. Who does he look like?'

I smiled at him. 'Drew.'

'Drew.'

'Now you're suggesting that I have incestuous tendencies.'

He laughed. 'Not incestuous. Francis allowed you a communicable, non-maternal form of adoration. But the adoration was for Drew.'

I remembered the dream, the yearning love I felt. Maybe Barry was right. Maybe. But I didn't think so.

I got up, ruffled his hair and said lightly, 'You read too many psychiatry books.' Then I bent down and dropped a kiss on

212

his brow and said, 'You're good to me, Barry Dennell. Not many men . . .'

I didn't finish, because he knew the rest. I had said it before.

That was one of our better love-making nights. We had them from time to time now, mostly when I had had some variety in my day, something to make me less bad-tempered and less self-obsessed than usual. Sleep had a lot to do with it too. Last night Barry had seen to the children's night calls and I had slept uninterrupted for eight glorious hours. Such small things, but so much hung on them.

Afterwards we turned over for sleep almost right away, and immediately doubt jumped out at me again. *Did* he love me? I had cried, I had needed him, I had not resented his closeness, I had talked about my emotions; in short, I had acted like a dependent patient. So he had made love to me and I happened to be able to reciprocate. But did he *love* me? Wouldn't he really rather be in Edinburgh with Caroline – or back at University, writing poems – or up north with his family – anywhere, in fact, but with me?

The trouble with a good husband and a good father was that, even if he grew to hate every minute of family life, he would never, never admit it.

Just as I was falling asleep I realised that he had done it again. He now knew everything, almost everything, that was inside me. And I still knew nothing at all about what was inside him.

'What shape is the sky?'

Silence, while I thought desperately.

'It isn't an oval, is it?'

'No,' I said thankfully.

'It's not a triangle, or a rectangle. Or a circle. Is it a circle?'

'We-ell . . .'

'It's not star-shaped or diamond-shaped or banana-shaped, is it?' There was a little pause. Becky was standing on a chair at the window, scrutinising the sky. '*I* know. It's *sky*-shaped!'

For this relief, much thanks. I went on working out my shopping list and consulting my purse, trying to co-ordinate the two, while I waited for the next unanswerable question. We had already had 'Why have icicles got no wheels?' and 'Why does the wind blow all on its own?' and 'Why do things fall on the ground when I drop them?' ('It's called gravity,' I had said tersely, in reply to the third question, and surprisingly that had satisfied her. I had opted out of the second altogether.)

Question time, however, seemed to be over for today. Becky became absorbed in tucking her teddy bear into a makeshift bed on the couch. The kitchen towel was commandeered. 'Becky, I think we'll have to manage without dessert at tea time – unless – ' I chewed my pencil, wondering if I had enough spare margarine to make apple crumble.

'That's all right,' she said stoically. 'I'll eat my upper lip for dessert.'

I choked on the pencil. Drew goose-stepped in from the garden, still proudly parading his new sandals, went immediately to the unsuspecting Becky, and gave her a smacking kiss. Becky screamed. Drew kissed her again and Becky fell to the floor in a crumpled heap of outraged dignity and infringed territory. I hung on to my chair and laughed till my eyes streamed while Drew crawled about kissing every accessible bit of Becky and she screamed blue murder. It was a revelation. The battle, so one-sided for so long, was finally to begin in earnest.

I swept Drew into my arms. 'You little love. You little treasure. Kissing her into defeat! I would never have thought of it! Kiss me instead, Drew.'

He did, long and noisily on the cheek, the sort of kiss to make your toes curl. I got out the dolly mixtures and Becky recovered. While the two of them munched I found a Mozart horn concerto on the radio, diligently told them what the music was, and returned to my shopping list. All was peace.

'But what *sort* of horns?' said Becky, after a long and puzzled pause.

'Not that sort. I think it's a French horn. A sort of trumpet. Half a minute and I'll draw one.'

I turned over my shopping list and drew. But drawing a French horn, especially when you are not intimate with the wretched things, is not easy. We all surveyed the result in silence. 'It's a bicycle,' said Becky at last.

'No,' said Drew supportively.

We went to the shop.

''Morning, Annabelle,' said Ivan. 'How are you today?'

'Fine,' I said dutifully, as I always did, even in the middle of winter when I had to break into a hacking cough halfway through the word. When we first came to Lottabridge I used to take the daily enquiry literally and tell him how I was, but I soon realised that Ivan was not interested in listening, only talking.

He gave me some squashy tomatoes, free. They would do for cooking, he said. As if I ever *cooked* with tomatoes! They were far too precious to waste like that, squashy or not. I was grateful, but wished he would not be so obviously pleased with his own generosity. Why did he and Marjory, who had done me a hundred small favours like this one, always make me feel so *prickly*?

Marjory and Tommy were out, so the children made a nuisance of themselves around the shelves while Ivan told me we absolutely must go to the Wildlife Park near Andover, and recounted in great detail their visit of the previous Sunday. I could have said that Andover may as well be on the moon for all the chance we had of getting there, but forebore. If he didn't know by now . . . I listened with half an ear, and kept an eye on Drew and the Vaseline jars, and made occasional dashes towards Becky, who had found the birthday candle holders. It was all quite normal, and only when we were on the point of leaving did Ivan drop his bombshell.

'Terrible thing about Gloria,' he said in a deep voice.

I checked, my hand arrested in mid-air as I reached for the door. I said, 'What?'

'Gloria. Gloria Griffiths. The, er, dramatic lady with the Labrador.'

'Yes. Yes. What's happened?'

'She's dead.'

I just looked at him. My hand fell slowly to my side. Beside me Becky sang 'Twinkle, Twinkle, Little Star', quietly.

'I thought you'd have heard,' said Ivan.

'No.'

'She fell downstairs a couple of nights ago. You know

215

where she lived, don't you, in one of those big old houses down the hill? Have you ever been inside Gloria's house?'

'No,' I said.

'Very steep stairs, a straight flight. She broke her neck. Gone, just like that.' He snapped his fingers. 'Makes you think, doesn't it?'

I just stood there, like a fool, staring at him. Someone edged past me into the shop and Ivan greeted her jovially. ''Morning. How are you today?'

I went out, guiding the children and clutching my shopping, and we set off up the hill. I felt quite numb, stupid with the shock of it, as if Gloria Griffiths had been someone I was very close to, when in fact – I turned and scanned the hill road, looking for her, expecting to see the vital, over-made-up face and the obese dog waddling beside her, expecting to hear her clear *'Hello*, darlings!' But the road was empty.

The sense of loss was disproportionate, I told myself. I hardly knew her. But. She had represented – something. She was warm, she was not afraid to show her warmth, she cared about other people. She was *real*.

She was dead.

And the dog? What would happen to the dog?

All day I thought about her. The morning's comedy was forgotten and I was back again in the mood of yesterday: yearning over all the babies in the world.

216

Chapter Three

Dark dark dark beside the wind.

It was one of Becky's little poems. She often experimented with words until she found an arrangement that pleased her, and then she would repeat the phrase time and again. This one was echoing knell-like through my head as I stood at the dining-room window and watched the tractors at work on the far hills. It was evening and the sky was flushed pink. On the horizon the pink was darkly hazy where farmers were burning off the straw. It was strangely surrealistic and I stood there for some time, watching, imagining dark figures moving in that smoke and remembering the scene in *Tess* where Alec, silent and unrecognised, tends the bonfire with his pitchfork before uttering his words of temptation.

Yesterday, Barry's day off, I had seen Francis. He had not seen me. I had ridden into our local town on the mo-ped and seen him walking leisurely along the busy pavement, his hair bleached by the French sun, his face deeply tanned, his arm round a girl. I had gone straight past, rendered anonymous by my crash helmet and his own absorption in his companion, and lost myself in the crowded supermarket.

I felt quite sick. Seeing him like that – the girl could not have been more than seventeen – I realised suddenly and with a stab of hot shame just how mistaken I had been that night, when I thought . . . I understood now that what I had taken for suppressed passion or desire or infatuation had been nothing but embarrassment. How could it have been otherwise? There were years between us, he had a young girlfriend, a lovely girl, long-haired, long-legged . . . What a

217

fool he must have thought me, how panic-stricken he must have felt when I started breathing heavily all over him, how relieved to make his getaway!

Standing in the supermarket, my whole body had blushed with humiliation.

It was only now, watching the smoky pink fields, that I wondered if I had again leapt, as Barry often accused me of leaping, from one extreme to the other, from one extreme conclusion to another. There had been a moment. We had had a moment. I had believed that and there was no real reason now to disbelieve it. If I chose to feel humiliated, better to pick a more tangible reason: that Francis was back and had not been to see me. But this too was no cause for humiliation, for I had known that he would not come. I was no more than a stepping-stone on his path to higher things, and that was as it should be. If I had put more weight than he on our brief friendship that was my fault. I had done it involuntarily because I had so few friendships.

Dark dark dark beside the –

Oh, balls! I shook my head impatiently. Feeling sorry for myself again! I had been in a strange mood lately. The sense of being unloved and having to live with it, to pretend, was doing odd things to my perceptions. First there had been that business over the crying babies – then my contemptible feeling of insecurity after love-making – the sense of loss over Gloria – and now this degraded sensation concerning Francis. I knew it was all nonsense, all of it; at least I thought I did; but that old lack of confidence, in myself, in my judgement, had returned. The only secure thing in my life seemed to be the children, and they – well, they were independent entities, or soon would be. Ultimately one was alone and I would do well to remember that and not go clinging to superficial relationships. The people at Massey, for instance. They had not bothered about me once the euphoria of the production was over, apart from Godfrey's abortive doorstep visit, and I knew that I would not now bother about them. The thing was to stand alone and not mind it. Like my courageous man who still, somehow, fought his lone battle against Huntingdon's Chorea. I had seen him too, yesterday, standing motionless in the High Street, his face grey and streaming sweat, like a walking dead man, and self-disgust filled me now as I remembered that I had been more affected by my glimpse of Francis than of him. And yet if there was a moral here at all it was embodied in him, in his brave determination not to fall prey to self-pity. Whilst I, who had everything, became more and more bitter . . .

I did have everything, I reflected, turning from the window. Everything that mattered in Maslow's Hierarchy of Needs. It all depended how far up the triangle you aspired. We were fit and healthy, we had enough to eat, none of us was likely to end up in the psychiatric hospital, unless I put myself there in an excess of introversion. Barry, whether he loved me or not, was marvellous to me, to us, and any difficulty or uncertainty in our relationship was my own fault. It was time I pulled myself together and stopped acting like a baby. Just because the days were so lonely . . . and the evenings . . .

Quarter to eight. Barry came home after a twelve-hour shift and I put the kettle on and took his not-quite-burnt dinner out of the oven. This was Wednesday, the evening he had been spending at the social club, but he had stopped that again now. I assumed he no longer felt the need to drown his sorrows over Caroline, if that was why he had started going in the first place. But I didn't really know.

'Sorry it's a bit dried up,' I said, hovering anxiously.

'It's fine. Sit down. How was your day?'

I grimaced. 'Awful. Becky kicked Drew. So Drew kicked Gin. Everybody screamed at everybody else.' I shut my eyes at the memory. How do you describe it, that head-bursting noise, the nerves all taut, yourself screaming 'STOP SCREAMING!' at the top of your voice?

'Poor old Amabel,' he said, meaning it, and immediately I felt guilty for making such a fuss. Other people, whose nerves were not merely taut but snapped, deserved that sympathy, not me.

I said, 'Sorry. How was yours?'

'Normal,' he said laconically. 'One of the patients strolled into the office eating a banana and dropped the skin on the floor, so I told him he couldn't do that here; whereupon he said indignantly, "All right, I'll smoke it outside," and went.'

He grinned at me. I was laughing now, and he said, 'That's

219

better. You were looking very glum when I came in.'

'Sorry,' I said – for the third time? – and uttered a mental warning to myself against becoming too apologetic, obsequious even. Nothing more deadly. 'What are you doing tonight?'

'*Senile Dementia: Reality Orientation*,' he said promptly. 'Followed by a quick dash of Yoga. Want to join me?'

'You never give up, do you?' I said sourly.

'Is the immersion heater on? I'll have a bath after the Yoga, and an early night. I'm whacked.' He pushed his plate away and yawned hugely. 'Nice meal,' he added untruthfully.

I said desperately, 'Can't we do something tonight?'

'What sort of something?'

'Oh, I don't know.' I looked round the room, seeking inspiration. 'Something creative. Constructive. Put up a shelf – or – a bracket for a hanging plant – '

'Look, I've been working for twelve hours – '

'Something *together*, Barry. That we can discuss and share. *Not* Yoga. We never do anything together, we never even – ' I thought wildly, grasped something at random – 'we never even decorate a room together. Decorating's fun.'

'We can't afford,' he said grimly, 'to decorate a room.'

'Let's get Becky's powder paints out and paint a picture for her bedroom wall. Shall we? Something modern, with lots of squirly bits.'

'I'm sorry,' he said, quite gently. 'I really don't feel like it. You do it.'

A pause. 'I suppose I'm being unreasonable.'

He said nothing.

'Well? Do you think I'm being unreasonable?'

He drew a breath. 'Look, it doesn't *matter* – '

'But it does matter. I want to know. I want to know what you *think*.'

'Ah,' he said. 'That one again.'

'Yes. I'm sorry, but – I feel so isolated sometimes. I wish you'd criticise me, I wish we could have a flaming row and hurl insults at each other and then I'd know where I stand.'

'I'm not very good at hurling insults,' he said slowly, and gave me a long look. 'Amabel. What's all this about?'

But I couldn't. I just couldn't. I said, 'Sorry. I know I'm

getting neurotic. Remember that sexy maidservant, oozing lust and self-confidence? She's gone. Again.'

'Things will improve when school starts,' he said encouragingly. But I thought he looked worried. Or irritated. I wasn't sure which. 'Next term you can start coaching some other poor sod for the November re-sits. In fact, you'll probably have to, because God knows how we'll pay Becky's school fees if you don't.'

'Yes,' I said.

'Is there any more tea?'

'Yes,' I said.

In the kitchen I counted to ten. I poured his tea. I made an effort and called, 'I asked Ivan today if he knew what was going to happen to Gloria's dog. I thought we might take him.'

'Oh.' I sensed him looking apprehensively at Gin. 'And are we taking him?'

I came back and leaned in the doorway, balancing the cup and saucer on the palm of my hand while I studied him. 'Would you mind?'

He gave a little sigh that said yes, and shook his head. 'I wouldn't mind, if you think we could afford to feed the great brute. But you've got enough to do without another dog. Why not let someone else have him?'

I watched the liquid slop gently around in the cup as I rocked it. 'Some kind of atonement, I suppose.'

'You're going to drop that in a minute. Atonement for what?'

I gave him his tea. 'Not asking her round for coffee. Not asking – someone else round for coffee. Not appreciating my life. My sanity.'

He raised his eyebrows at me. 'You know what Rayner would say to all that?'

'Oh, Rayner would think I was mad. She'd say "You worry too much".'

'Well, you do. What about the dog?'

'Someone else got in first.'

'Thank God for that.' And he went off to his book.

I had never doubted, I realised, his acceptance of Gloria's obese Labrador. So sure had I been that I had not even consulted him before asking Ivan. Such was the measure of the man. He was generous, understanding, co-operative, tolerant. Not many men . . .

But.

I walked quickly into the living-room. He was already deep in *Senile Dementia: Reality Orientation.* And they said television killed conversation. Right now Barry didn't even know I was in the room.

'What happened to your anorexic patient?'

'What? Oh, she's gone. Discharged herself several weeks ago.' His voice was absent, his eyes still on the page. *Tell me,* damn you! 'Whatever made you think of her?'

'I think of her quite often.'

He didn't answer. I stood there, obviously supernumary, and hated him. Becky woke up and shouted for water in that voice that woke the dead and I walked out of the room. By the time I had seen to her and come back downstairs I knew that I was very tense indeed and that the only sensible and safe course for me was to go to bed at once. I didn't. I sat in my chair in the living-room and held my library book in tight fingers before me, and thought.

But 'thought' is the wrong verb, implying as it does some slow, peaceful and ultimately fruitful process. Whereas what I was doing resembled water crashing over Niagara Falls – or heavyweight boxers battering each other. Endless mental violence. I remembered the beautiful young man screaming at his voices on the hospital verandah and wondered if this was just a fraction of what he endured, but knew that it was not. It was not given to me to experience what he experienced, nor to understand. Nor to help. I could do nothing, receive nothing to relieve someone else, give nothing, not even friendship. On the one occasion when such an opportunity offered, I had failed. I had failed because I lacked the confidence to succeed.

I must have been putting out very strong vibes indeed for Barry had raised his head and was staring hard at me. He said, 'Spit it out,' and put down his book.

'Are you sure you can spare the time?' Cheap sarcasm, and it took even me by surprise. I saw Barry's face register equal surprise, and then it closed. Like a door. This was not the way

222

to approach anything and I knew it.

'Sorry,' I said. And was suddenly furious. 'Look, why don't I just make a tape-recording of myself saying "sorry" every fifteen seconds and play it continuously?'

'What the hell,' he enquired, 'is all this?'

'I'm sick of being in the wrong all the time.'

'But I haven't said – '

'I *know* you haven't said anything. That's just it. You never *do* say anything.'

'If you're referring to my conversational powers – again – '

'I'm not. Well, I am.' He gazed coldly at me and I demanded, 'Do you know why I'm so bloody boring and feeble? Yes, I know we've been through all this before. The kids, the daily trivia. But it's more than that. It's you.'

'I make you boring and feeble.'

'Yes. You do. Look at yourself, sitting there reading your damned psychiatry books – night after night – then disappearing upstairs to stand on your thumbs or whatever it is you do. It's a whole bundle of fun for me, isn't it? Wildly stimulating, isn't it? You never even *talk* to me, not properly, not real conversation. You were altogether different when Rayner and Patrick were here. But with me – You don't shine your light for me, Barry. I live in the dark.'

'A very picturesque metaphor,' he observed, and I gritted my teeth. 'But this is all old stuff. What's really bothering you?'

'Don't come the psychiatric nurse with me,' I snapped. 'You and your bloody intuition and your bloody understanding! That's what's bothering me, as you put it. You know everything that goes on inside me, because I *tell* you, but I never know a *damned thing* about what's inside you.'

I was on my feet now, pacing, infuriated by his calm. He said quietly, 'I find it difficult to talk about myself. As you know very well.'

'Well, *try*! I'm shut out here on my own, it's like – like being in a library full of sealed books.' I flung my own library book into a chair, and a page ripped.

'What do you want to know?'

Here it was. But again I couldn't. I turned my back on him and walked about for a minute, trying to crush down the guilt that was already rising within me. But the guilt was the last straw, and I said resentfully, 'You always behave so well, don't you? So reasonably. Sitting there coolly, not getting angry, not even showing whether you're hurt or not. I've spent years admiring you, do you know that? Of course you do, I've told you often enough. Years, saying how good you are, saying I don't deserve you. Trying to emulate your self-control, your patience, your ability to forgive, and feeling guilty because *I can't*!'

'Amabel,' he cut in, 'don't do this.'

But I swept on. 'I'm always trying to live up to you, to attain your standards. Every time I lose my temper I feel like some little crawly thing afterwards, like one of those wood-lice behind the sink. Because you never lose *your* temper, do you? Oh, you go away and brood and shut me out, and that's bad enough, that's rotten, and why the hell should I admire you when you do that to me; but you never lose your *temper*.' I paused, breathing hard. He said nothing. 'Now, for instance. I've just told you that you're dull and boring and utterly selfish and inconsiderate, and you're still CALM! Barry, it drives me crazy, I can't live with your damned nobility or whatever it is, it makes me feel so bloody *guilty*, and I run myself down, and I've run myself down for so long that there's nothing left. Do you wonder that I have no confidence in myself any more, that I'm not even lovable any more?'

I stopped. 'I see,' he said, after a moment. He had gone rather pale. 'It's all my fault.'

'Yes,' I said defiantly. 'I don't see why I should keep blaming myself for everything. I'm sick of apologising. You're not a saint and I'm sick of treating you like one.'

'I hadn't noticed,' he said dryly, 'that you did.'

I bit my lip, suddenly doubtful, but he was silent. Marshalling his thoughts. Marshalling his damned thoughts. But now that I had said all that – and heaven knew it was unpremeditated, I had not known I felt those things until a few moments ago – now that I had said it, I badly wanted to retract it. Because he *was* a kind of saint, and all that I had said was not the real reason for my hurt and anger. That had remained unsaid. And even Barry, for all his intuition, could not guess at it.

I wanted to cry, preferably on his shoulder. But it was too late.

'You mentioned Rayner.'

'Yes,' I said huskily.

Another pause. 'Becky kicked Drew, you said. And then Drew kicked Gin.'

'Yes,' I said again, bewildered.

'It's taken you a long time. But you did it in the end.' He got up and went to the door. 'Think about it,' he said.

I crept into bed hours after he did, red-eyed, wretched and ashamed. All the tragedies in the world, the hungry people, the sick patients, all the crying babies that no-one cared for, these I saw and anguished over. But my own husband, who cared more than anyone I knew . . . Just because I was hurt and jealous and felt rejected . . . When would I *learn*?

I lay very still, tensed up, while the summer night came gently through the open window and crickets sang in the garden. In the next room Becky laughed in her sleep. I lay there, frozen with misery.

Barry's hand reached out, found my shoulder and gripped it for a moment. Slid up and round, over my head, finally resting on my hair.

Comforting me.

Amazing, incredible man. Barry Dennell.

Chapter Four

I felt happier the next morning that I had felt for months. No, not happier – but steadier, more levelly contented, more contentedly level. I played with the words in my mind as I stood in a blaze of sunlight at the kitchen sink, washing up the breakfast dishes and half-listening to Becky singing in the back porch. We had slept last night as we used to sleep in my narrow bed at the University residence, curled up together like baby rabbits, just one thin sheet over us and the summer air stirring in the room. It had been very loving. It's just the kids, he had said, over and over, it's just the kids doing all this to you, hang on, a couple more years and it will all be different. That, when I might have destroyed him, as Rayner had nearly destroyed me. Oh, I loved him. Why he loved me I could not imagine.

It was another hot, golden-blue morning and I pottered gently about in the kitchen, feeling mellow, as if I had drunk Drambuie. I was not going to calculate just how many years had passed since I actually *had* drunk Drambuie. I got out my one and only cookery book, shiny with unuse, and decided to make toad-in-the-hole for lunch. Even I couldn't make a mess of that, and it would be a pleasant surprise for Barry, who had promised to eat his midday meal at home today. Now, if I only knew which lunch hour he would be on . . .

I hummed softly to myself, smearing the cookery book with flour so that it looked quite professional and thinking the while about Barry. How could I have doubted him? He had never doubted me, even when he knew that I was – whatever I was – over Francis. I must have equal trust in him and not become foolishly insecure whenever I remembered that he had been – whatever he had been – over Caroline. What a crazy pair we were. Mad as hatters, both of us, with our complicated emotional needs. No wonder Lottabridge didn't think much of us.

One last look at the recipe, and I left the batter to stand and got out my vacuum cleaner. Right on cue the children came in demanding drinks and biscuits. I gave them a snack and put shorts and t-shirts on them so that they would be ready to go to the shop as soon as I had finished cleaning, then I heaved the vacuum cleaner upstairs, fell cursing over the raccoon (who was always where you thought he wasn't) and set about the bedrooms.

'What on *earth* is all this grass doing in here?'

I stood aghast in the doorway of Becky's room, which looked as if the village fête had recently been held in it. Handfuls, armfuls of long coarse grass, the sort that grew in the jungly part of our garden, were strewn about the floor, the dressing table, the bed. I groaned and, settling my hands on my hips in time-honoured fashion, looked grimly at my children. Drew pointed to a small bulge beneath the grass and uttered a sentence of explanation. Becky said, in the reverent tone of one in the presence of great art, 'It's a little garden for my little house.'

'What little house? Oh.' She had delved into the sileage and unearthed the bulge: the pottery cottage I had bought her from Oxfam.

'It's not supposed to be covered,' she said severely, addressing Drew. 'Drew, you mustn't cover my house or it will sufforate. Do you know what sufforate means, Drew?'

'Suffocate,' I said automatically, then, 'It can't breathe so it certainly can't suffocate.' Then, 'I think I'm going mad. Take all this grass out. All of it. No, on second thoughts you can keep just a few bits for the house to sit on. Go on. Start.'

They looked dolefully from me to the Psyche's task before them. Heaven alone knew how they had brought it all in – and without my noticing. It was the Drambuie, of course.

'Can't you use your bee-eautiful new vacuum cleaner?'

'No. It'll block.' They stood, unmoving and glum, and I relented slightly and sent Becky for a couple of carrier bags from the kitchen. 'Fill these. Then you can take one each and empty them at the bottom of the garden and come back for the rest. I'll help,' I added resignedly.

Picking up the grass was not half as much fun as strewing it around had been, and they soon mutinied, though Becky managed to keep her temper. I was close to mutiny myself, but between us we got the bags filled and they trudged off downstairs with them. I started to scrape the remainder into a pile, then Becky came back alone, bearing the empty bags. 'Drew doesn't want to help me.'

'I don't blame him. I don't much feel like helping you myself.'

'But it was a *lovely* idea,' she said in her gushing stage voice. 'Very – very *creative*.'

She had even pronounced it correctly. I gave a non-committal grunt, but she knew that I had softened. 'Do you like that word? Creative? I'm saying it properly, aren't I?'

Precocious child. I had never been able to stand precocious children, and here I was, the mother of one. Nevertheless I was impressed and said so, and wondered whether I, or Barry, or the excellent Mrs Thompson was having this undoubtedly good influence on Becky's vocabulary. If it was me it was double-edged for I had also heard her shout, in one of her enraged moments, 'OH BALLS!'

'I think that'll do,' I said at last, getting grassily to my feet. There were bits of the stuff all over our clothes but they would brush off outside. The room was relatively clear of them, but had I now got time to vacuum it? '*Don't* do that again,' I pleaded.

She gave me one of her wicked laughing looks and tossed her nimbus of red hair at me. I picked her up. 'Let's go and see what your lazy brother is doing. It's ominously quiet downstairs.'

'What does omi . . .?'

I carried her down, spoiling her shamefully at a moment when I should (I supposed) be administering stern discipline, and she wound her legs round my waist and had a little burrow into my neck as we went. Becky and Drew, when they were not being utterly unbearable, were gratifyingly affectionate; especially Drew, who was still at the baby stage and loved nothing more than a long session of kissing and tickling and cuddling. I experienced a wave of devotion for both of them, and decided that I would postpone our trip to the shop until this afternoon, after Drew's sleep. There was my toad-in-the-hole for lunch. I would put the fat in the oven to heat up and then we would all sit on the couch and have a story.

'Drew? Where are you?' I set Becky down and stuck my head into the various rooms. Kitchen, dining-room, living-room. No Drew. 'He's gone down to the sandpit,' I decided. 'Run and get him, love. Tell him I'm going to read a story.'

She ran off with alacrity, to return almost immediately. Drew was not there.

My goodwill turned to exasperation. 'The little wretch. He's hiding.' I went to the back porch and looked behind a row of old macs. This was one of Drew's favourite hiding places, but he wasn't there. 'Drew! Story-time!'

'Read me the story,' Becky said heartlessly.

I frowned. Awful tales came into my mind, of people who had hidden somewhere and got stuck and not been found till ten, twenty years afterwards. There was that chilling one of the bride who had teasingly run away from her husband during the wedding reception and slipped inside a hollow tree. And couldn't get out. They had searched for days, weeks. Was it a century later that her skeleton had been discovered? I couldn't remember. And the child who had hidden in a large roll of sponge rubber under a bed and suffocated.

I became agitated. 'Stay here. I'm going to look in the wardrobes. He might have come back upstairs while we were . . .' I was already running back upstairs as I spoke. Becky's room? No, we had been in there. But I checked it anyway. Under the dressing-table. Only grass. Becky had no wardrobe.

Drew's own room, then. There was a big built-in cupboard, the most likely place for him to hide. I went right in, pulled out stored suitcases and cardboard cartons. No Drew.

Our room. We had an old-fashioned, iron-frame bed with lots of space underneath it. But he wasn't there. I pushed back the clothes in our wardrobe. Nothing.

The bathroom? You couldn't hide a moth in the bathroom.

But I looked, in the bath, behind the door.

Thoroughly alarmed now, I ran down the stairs again. Looked under them. Shoes and more shoes, mostly unwearable. Barry's old rucksack, squashed flat. My ancient hand-operated sewing-machine. No Drew.

The kitchen cupboards. No. The gate-legged table in the dining-room. No. Behind the living-room couch. Behind the curtains.

The toilet! What an idiot I was. Of course, he was in there playing with the forbidden water. I strode to the door and opened it.

He wasn't.

In the kitchen Becky was standing very still, her eyes following me every time I passed her. 'He *must* be in the garden,' I said at last. 'He's playing down at the bottom in the jungle, where you emptied the grass.'

Becky brightened, but then said, 'It's all brambly.'

'Well, there you are. He's eating blackberries.'

'That's naughty,' said Becky virtuously, and I was in no mood to remind her of the times she herself had been caught eating blackberries. We went outside and across the grass, searching the wilderness of brambles with our eyes. It was clear immediately that no-one could have forced a way into them, even someone of Drew's size. But I pushed in all the same, calling his name now, thinking that perhaps he had fallen and somehow got covered, even lost consciousness. I came back, scratched and bleeding for my pains but certain that he was not there.

'The shed?' said Becky, but she knew as well as I that Drew could not open the shed door. Nor could Becky herself. But we went back up the garden and checked the shed and checked behind the shed.

No Drew.

There was only one other place to look. And I knew, sickeningly, that it should have been obvious from the beginning. That we should have looked there first, not last. And fleetingly I wondered if something dreadful, I did not yet know what, might have been avoided that could not now be avoided, if we had looked there first.

Becky said it. 'Mummy, the gate's open.'

It was not open, but it was not fastened either. It was resting gently against the gatepost, where its own weight had returned it after Drew went through. I did not stop to think that Drew could not unfasten the gate and that Becky would not have unfastened it, I just flung myself out and up the steps to the road, our quiet little road with hardly any traffic, please, hardly any traffic, and I shouted: 'Drew! Drew! Drew!'

Becky was behind me, white-faced, and Gin, her tail wagging. I looked in both directions. Nobody. Oh, all that *time* we had wasted, picking up grass, searching the house, searching the bloody *brambles*, for God's sake! But I had never dreamed of his opening the gate. *'Drew! Drew!'*

'It must have been the man,' said Becky. Her lips were quivering and tears stood in her eyes. She knew all about roads. 'The man must have opened the gate.'

'What man? *What man?*' She began to cry and I realised that I was practically shaking her. I picked her up, my eyes still searching, and said, 'Sorry, sorry love. But what man are you talking about?'

'Drew's f-friend.' Her voice rose. 'The one who comes. In the *h-hat*.' She sobbed uncontrollably. I waited, I tried to wait, but at last I had to ask, 'Was he there? When you took out the grass?'

She nodded violently against me and I shut my eyes. Why didn't you tell me, oh, why didn't you *tell* me.

The patient. Drew had walked away with the patient.

Chapter Five

When Drew had cut his lip and bled so dreadfully, the first thing I had done was panic. The second was to run to the phone box with him in my arms and phone Barry. I did exactly the same this time, though I did manage to summon just enough presence of mind to shut Gin in the house first.

There was no sign of Drew, no old man loitering at any of the gates, no sign of life anywhere. It was always like this in the mornings: so many people worked nights, so many curtains still drawn. Useless to start banging on doors to use someone's telephone. I ran on breathlessly, my eyes searching everywhere, arms already aching with the weight of Becky. It was like one of those awful dreams in which you try desperately to wake up and cannot.

I reached the post office and swung wide the door of the telephone kiosk. Changed my mind abruptly and ran into the shop and straight through the door marked PRIVATE.

'Marjory – ' My voice was a croak. She was ironing in the kitchen and looked surprised and annoyed at the sudden intrusion. 'Marjory – will you have Becky please – *now* – '

I was panting. She stood the iron on its rest, her annoyance gone. 'What on earth's the matter?'

I told her in two short, choked sentences, and before I had finished the second she interrupted me. 'Go and phone. Of course I'll look after Becky. Phone from the shop.'

But Ivan was busy with customers and I could not reach the shop phone unless he passed it over the counter. I ran outside again.

These stupid *delays*! Explaining things, looking for loose

change – while Drew might be – But at least I *had* some change, it just happened to be in my pocket, I had not even thought to bring any . . .

'Hello?' I was through to Barry's ward, and Barry himself was speaking. I said his name; then found that I was dumb.

'Hello? Amabel?'

'*Drew*,' I managed, and again foundered. But somehow he understood.

'All right,' he said quietly. 'Take your time. But – look, give me your number there. I'll call you back if your money runs out.'

The matter-of-fact instruction calmed me, and I was able to read out the telephone number. Then I was all right again and could tell him.

'*Gone?*'

'The gate was open. He's vanished.'

'He can't have got far, surely. How long ago?'

'Ages. Barry, *ages*. We looked all over the house first – and – down the garden – ' My voice threatened to give way again and I broke off.

'Stay there,' he said. 'I'll come.'

'Wait!' I shouted it, before he could hang up, and just then the bleeps signalled that I was about to be cut off. 'Call me back!'

I put the phone down and waited. Minutes, precious minutes. Had he heard me? But he had to go through the switchboard, and switchboard was probably having its damned coffee break . . .

At last it rang, and I said without preliminaries, 'He's gone off with that patient, the old one who comes and looks over the gate. I've told you about him.'

Silence, and I turned cold. 'Barry?'

'Describe him. Slowly. I'll write it down.'

I did my best but was conscious of time ticking away, time in which anything, anything at all might be happening to Drew. And I was not even looking for him.

'At least half of the old men look like that,' he said flatly, when I had finished. 'Isn't there anything else? Some distinguishing mark?'

'*No*. Surely one of the staff will know who it is? After all, he's missing.'

'He isn't. Drew's missing. The patient has merely gone for a walk and so have dozens of other patients who fit that description.'

I couldn't stand it any longer. 'Hurry *up*. We're doing *nothing* . . .'

'I'll be there in five minutes. Look around but stay within sight of the shop.' He hung up.

Look around! Madam, would you care to view this very desirable residence? I was close to hysteria as I came out of the phone box and the heavy door swung slowly shut behind me. Look around. But where? Up the hill, down the hill? In all the cottage gardens? Along the main road at the bottom of the valley? Down all the little entrances behind the gardens? *Where*?

I ran down the hill on one side of the road, looking, calling. Arthritic Rose stood in her doorway. 'Have you seen my little boy? The little blond boy?' Startled, she shook her head. I ran past, looked over Gloria Griffiths' gate. Gloria would have known something, where the patient was likely to go. Gloria would have encouraged him to talk and probably even found out his name.

I reached the main road, heavy lorries roaring past, stood on the kerb and looked in both directions. In the distance was a figure with a child. I could not tell if the figure was male or female. I ran. Two hundred yards further on I could see that it was female and that the child was the wrong shape and size. I turned and went back, slower now because of the pain in my side.

Back up the hill, on the other side of the road. Stay in sight of the shop, Barry had said. But I couldn't. I went along a little entry beside the old railway cutting, looked over walls and inside a half-collapsed garage.

On up the hill, but there was nowhere on this side to hide or lose oneself. A hedge atop a high bank, fields behind it. I hauled myself up the bank and half into the hedge, and looked. Cows. I climbed down again.

'Lost him, have you?'

It was Rose, still in her doorway, and concerned now, as Marjory had been. Her dog, the cause of our old estrangement, tried to snap at my ankles through the bars of

234

her gate. I scarcely noticed. I said, 'I think he's wandered off with a patient.' I described the man, and she pushed out her cracked old lips in thought and shook her head. 'There's a dozen look like that,' she said at last.

I left her, and saw Barry standing by the telephone kiosk and looking down the hill at me. I shook my head as I climbed up towards him, and saw his shoulders slump. It had probably only now come home to him, I realised, as he saw me alone. I was hardly ever alone.

'I've phoned the police,' he said when I reached him. 'They'll have the Pandas out. The hospital is instituting its own search. There'll probably be helicopters too. We'll find him.'

I looked dumbly at him. For once it was he who was taking refuge in speech, I in silence. 'I want to check on Becky.'

He nodded, and I left him there and went through the shop and into the living quarters. I was instantly reassured. Becky and Tommy were sitting facing one another in an enormous cardboard box, one wearing a colander, the other a saucepan, and nautical phrases were being bandied about. I backed out quickly before Becky noticed me, but Marjory saw and came with me. 'Anything?'

I shook my head.

'He'll turn up. Don't worry.' I looked at her and she gave a nervous laugh. 'Silly thing to say. Of course you're worried. I'd be going out of my mind if it was Tommy. Can we do anything?'

I told her about the police and the helicopters. 'If you could just keep Becky for a while . . .'

'Of course. Tommy's delighted. I'll give her her lunch if you're not – I mean, if you haven't – '

I went out again. Barry was in the road, stopping people, asking questions. Nobody had seen Drew. A police car whizzed past and shot up towards the hospital.

'Becky's playing pirates. Happy as a sandboy.' At least it was one worry less. An hysterical Becky was the last thing we needed right now. 'I didn't know Tommy could play imaginative games like that,' I said, conversationally, stupidly. 'Maybe he's not as bad as I thought.'

'Hardly anybody is.' As bad as I thought? Or as bad as

other people thought? I didn't pursue it. We were postponing the moment, or I was; pretending that if we stood here talking the thing could not have happened. My own swift hunt up and down the hill had warned me what that moment would be like, when we had to start looking in earnest.

'I think you'd better wait at home,' Barry said.

'No!'

'Someone should be there. What if he manages to find his way back and there's no-one there?'

I stared at him. I pictured Drew standing on the doorstep, unable to open the door. No-one there. Fighting it, I said, '*You* wouldn't want to go home and wait. Would you?'

'No.'

'No. And neither do I. I'd go mad. Watching the clock.'

He said nothing. A moment. A precious moment.

'All right. I'll leave Becky here.' Tears were again perilously close, for this was the hardest thing of all. To wait.

He gave me a quick hard hug. 'Good girl. I'm going down to the woods.'

We separated, I stumbling home on legs that were still shaky from my run down and up the hill, he to the area around the stream where we often took the children to play. Looking through the trees that surrounded the hospital I thought I could see unusual activity, numbers of people moving about the grounds. A chill went through me at the sight, distant though it was. How much more chilling to be the one sought. How frightening, how panic-inducing. What might a panic-stricken patient not do under such circumstances?

But it was reassuring too. People were looking, even if I was not. Other people would find him, even if I did not. (But he would want *me*!)

I went into the house, to a welcome from Gin, and wept a little into her thick coat. She was puzzled, half distressed, half delighted at such unwonted attention. I thought wildly of getting her to follow Drew's scent, but she had never been trained to such skills, she was not even very intelligent, it wouldn't work.

On the kitchen counter my batter for toad-in-the-hole stood waiting. There was a fly struggling in it and I fished him out. I put the kettle on, made tea, drank it standing up. The irony of this struck me forcibly. How often had I yearned for an empty house that I might sit down and enjoy a proper tea-break! Well, I had my empty house. It was like a mausoleum.

I looked at the clock. Ten minutes had passed since I came in. It seemed an hour. I tidied up, folded a pile of clothes, put Drew's favourite trousers on the top and looked at them. They were faded red denim and they had a zip. Drew was thrilled by that zip and had spent hours playing with it, often risking more than he knew.

I gave a little half-laugh which wanted to turn into a sob. Another five minutes. I *could not* do this for – however long it took. Surely if I didn't stray too far from the house I could join in the search?

I went out of the front door and up the steps to the road. It was less than an hour since Becky and I had made our mad rush up those steps, less than two since Drew had climbed up them with his companion. But a lot could happen in two hours. A very great deal could happen.

I moved about, peering crazily into crazy places, behind bushes in people's gardens, inside someone's aviary. I even, stupidly and sick at heart and angry with my own imagination, lifted the lid from a dustbin that had been left out after the collection. (Kes! Kes! Kes!) I paced to the end of the road and back again. Questions started to pile up in my head.

Suppose Drew had not gone with the patient at all? Suppose the patient had unfastened the gate and then gone away and Drew had spotted it later and toddled off alone?

No. Drew would not have gone far before he became frightened, and then he would have stood still and howled. Even if he had gone a fair distance someone would have scooped him up, realising he was too young to be out alone.

Supposing he had been scooped up by – ? Blind foolishness to think that country villages were safe. Nowhere was safe any more. This particular village was not far from the motorway and it was the holiday season. All sorts of people were in the area, maybe the sort you most dreaded your children coming into contact with . . .

I shut off that train of thought. If Drew had been found by someone good and decent, what would they do? Phone the police, of course. And, if they were local people, go straight to the village shop and tell Ivan.

So he had not been found by someone good and decent.

But why was he not screaming his head off? A search party might not see him but they would surely *hear* him?

And if he was screaming, that too would panic the patient.

If he was still with the patient.

If he was still alive.

'Excuse me. It's Mrs Dennell, isn't it?'

I turned, and met the anxiously enquiring face of one of my neighbours. It was one of the playgroup women who were usually so cool. I could not remember her name. 'I'm so sorry about your little boy,' she said.

The houses swung about me. I heard myself gasp. 'Why? Why?'

'Sorry – Did I say – ?' She was embarrassed and rather alarmed. 'I thought he'd gone missing. Isn't it your little boy then? They were saying in the shop . . .'

Relief made me faint and I sat down suddenly, on the kerb, not caring how odd it looked. 'Yes. Mine. I misunderstood you.'

She stood over me, kind and worried. 'I saw you wandering around and I thought you must be hanging about in case, well, in case – '

'Yes. I am.' My head cleared and I got up slowly. 'Someone has to stay here.'

'That's what I came to say,' she said eagerly. 'You go and look for him and I'll sit in your house. I'll take my little girl with me and she can play with your children's toys. I expect you wouldn't mind that, would you? Would that help a bit?'

'Yes,' I said blankly. Then, 'Yes. Thank you. Thank you.'

And I set off, leaving her standing there.

At the corner I stopped, for I had not the faintest idea where to go. The hospital grounds and presumably the hospital itself were being thoroughly combed. Even as I stood there I heard the deep clacking hum of a distant helicopter and traced it to the sky over the open hills, a mile or two away. My throat tightened. All these people, people who didn't even know us – helping –

238

Down the hill I saw Barry talking to a uniformed police officer, and resisted the impulse to run down to him, just to be in his presence. His comforting presence. Other things were far more important than my being comforted.

Why did these police have no tracker dogs? Surely that would be the method to use, the quickest method? Why, even Gin, if she had been properly trained . . . But maybe the dogs were on the way, I thought, maybe they were being sent from some other town, and if so that wonderful woman was on duty at the house and would find something of Drew's for the dogs to sniff. In the meantime –

There was only one other way to go, and that was on up the hill. Past the hospital the road levelled out quickly and it would be easier walking here for an old man and a toddler. I walked fast, thinking of those feeble old legs and those short unsteady legs. They *couldn't* have gone far, even a mile would tax Drew's strength to the limit, and the patient could not carry him, frail as he was. Yet was he so frail? I remembered the deaf and dumb man, Mr Howarth, who had appeared ancient until you looked closely at him. It was hospital life, the institutionalisation, that aged these people prematurely. Drew's friend might be even now striding ahead of me with Drew securely seated on his shoulders.

I went another half mile or so and knew that it was not true. The slope was less obvious here but slope there was and my own legs were aching. He could not have done it.

I turned back. This time I climbed the bank every time I came to a fresh field, and scoured each one with my eyes. They would be lying behind a hedge somewhere, worn out, asleep in the hot sun. And it was hot. It was high noon and the sweat was dripping from me, soaking my light dress. I tried to remember what Drew was wearing. Shorts and a t-shirt, I thought, and thanked heaven that I had dressed him this morning. If he had gone out naked he would have been terribly sunburned.

He must have wet his pants by now.

I realised this suddenly. He would have wet his pants because he could never manage to pull them down without help, and the old man would not have known what he wanted. He would have held on and held on until he could hold on

239

no longer, and afterwards he would cry, it would upset him, he was always so proud of using the potty . . .

This tiny thing, this having no-one to help him with his call of nature, reached into me as nothing else had so far. It was real, it was accessible to me, it was everyday stuff and I understood it well. The other had been nonsense, a nightmare which would, surely, presently end.

I suddenly desperately wanted Becky. The eccentric normality of Becky. She at least was safe. I went on looking into the fields but I moved faster now and by the time I came level with the hospital again I was almost running.

The activity there had stopped.

They had found him!

I flew home. The woman and her child looked up from the contents of the toy box and at the sight of my face the woman's own brightened. 'Have they – ?' she began, just as I started to ask the same question.

Both of us broke off. I said, 'Oh – I thought – They don't seem to be searching the hospital grounds any more.'

'They'll be searching somewhere else now.'

The matter-of-fact voice helped. 'Yes.'

'I've made some tea. I didn't think you'd mind. Have a cup before you go out again.'

'No, I'll – Have whatever you want,' I said, and went.

God, but it's hot. And he hasn't got a sun hat on.

Again I stood at the same corner, feeling helpless. Again I looked down the hill but there was no Barry this time. There were, however, about two dozen people standing in the road. Jumble sale? Wedding? But they were not dressed for a wedding. Even as I watched they dispersed, some going further down the hill, some into the little alleys I had explored earlier. And I understood that Lottabridge was looking for Drew.

Damned bloody tears.

I sniffed, and wiped them away with my bare forearm. I realised that I felt weak, exhausted as much by fear as by physical exertion. The fears I had mostly suppressed. I had been able to think the phrase 'if he is alive' but it had been so remote that it barely meant anything. Other fears were more real. Fear of sexual assault. Better not to imagine what might

240

happen to that beautiful little body. Fear of the insane. Despite education, knowledge of drugs, knowledge of hospital policy, knowledge of the dear old harmless things who wandered about the village, knowledge of the extent of our ignorance, the exaggeration of our misgivings – despite all that, fear of the insane.

But if I was exhausted, how was Drew feeling? He had not had his lunch, he would be hungry, he should be curling up in his cot for his afternoon sleep soon. I would not undermine what little courage I had left by allowing the fears free rein. I would go and see Becky and then I would carry on searching.

I picked her up and pressed her face against my own sweat-grimed, tear-streaked face. Terms of endearment filled my head. My red-haired beauty. My lovely unruly girl. (My sweet-tempered smiling blue-eyed boy.)

Now that I had stopped, for the moment anyway, a huge weariness came over me and I sat down in one of Marjory's armchairs, Becky on my knee, and wondered how I was ever to get up again. I was ravenous, certain I could not eat, aware that I needed food if I was to keep going.

'I'm not hungry,' said Becky. 'We've been eating chocolate biscuits.'

'I'm so sorry,' Marjory said quickly. 'I'm a little behind with the lunch so I'm afraid I gave – '

'That's quite all right. Thank you.' Manners. How one retained one's well-bred politeness, even now. Drew had not had chocolate biscuits. Drew had not had anything at all – not even a drink – and in this heat . . .

I closed my eyes. Becky said impatiently, 'Why can't *I* go and play at the hospital, Mummy?'

A pause. I opened my eyes. 'What did you say?'

'I want to go to the hospital where the long white path is, and run along it. Drew can, so why can't I?'

I stared at her for a long moment. Very slowly, never taking my eyes from her, I lifted her off my knee and set her on her feet. Tommy stood with his thumb in his mouth and watched. Marjory looked at my face and a question appeared on her own. But Marjory did not know what I knew about Becky.

241

I said in an odd, high voice, 'Stay here. I won't be long.'
Then I bent down and gave her a hard kiss and turned and ran.

Back up the hill, my knees shaking. Along the lane, the short-cut, the way I had taken Rayner. The entrance to the cemetery.

I stopped there, breathing hard. I took a few steps forward and stopped again, looking. The grass that grew over the graves was yellow and parched now, but hydrangeas, not minding the lack of water, grew in a riot of colour along the edges of the enclosure. And there, running the length of the cemetery, was the long path which Becky had referred to.

But there was no one running along it. There was no-one here at all. I could see that at a glance, for the whole place was wide open, fully visible, and it was empty. Except for the dead.

Becky was wrong.

I stood, absolutely desolate. I had been sure, *sure*. From the lane there came the shouts of children playing, and I remembered that it was a favourite place for roller-skating. One of them burst into loud tears and the weak tears came again into my own eyes. I had been so sure of her.

I turned away. After all, they had searched the grounds, they would have seen him immediately if he had been in the cemetery. I should have thought of that when Becky said it, not leapt instantly to this most joyous of conclusions, only to be so bitterly let down. But she had been so impatient, so casually sure herself.

I turned back again, swiftly. *Trust her.*

'Drew!'

I began to work my way around the perimeter of the place, thoroughly, searching the bushes while I trod on the unseen graves and the metal plates with their anonymous numbers.

'Drew! Drew!'

The children in the lane, invisible from here, played on, exuberantly and loudly. I thought suddenly – If he was here, and crying, they might not have heard him – if he was hidden – They would just have glanced in, as I did –

'Drew! Drew!'

I found them behind an immense mass of hydrangeas in the

242

farthest corner. My shouting had woken him up, for I heard the whimper first, the sort of whimper he always gave when I woke him from a deep sleep, and then he started to cry in earnest.

Movement. The hydrangeas trembled, a lovely, shimmering, swaying motion of most delicate pink and blue petals, and the serrated green leaves shone warm and eager in the sunlight, as if it were the first real sunlight they had ever known, as if it were a benediction.

I crawled forward under the bush and paused, on hands and knees, just looking. There they were. Both of them, half crouched, half lying in the green shade between the thick lower stems and the wall, Drew and his friend, and both were crying. The old man cried perfectly silently, tears pouring down the creased cheeks, the mouth open wide in a grin of anguish. His arm was tight round Drew's shoulders and his veined hand entwined in Drew's t-shirt as though he would never let go. I saw that hand and understood it, and knew then that all my fears had been groundless, for my own hand took exactly that clutching grip on Drew's clothes whenever any sort of danger seemed imminent. It was not the grip of the warder, but the guardian.

God knows what memories, what associations were there in the confused old mind. Somehow he had got muddled, thought himself back fifty years perhaps and his own son in jeopardy. Now he did not know himself what he was doing here or why he had the child. He knew only that he was frightened, and Drew was frightened, and so they cried. Two babies.

Drew saw me. For a moment he did not react, then recognition came into his eyes. He whispered, 'Wee-wee,' and pointed down at his soaked shorts, and sobbed.

'It doesn't matter. It doesn't matter. It doesn't matter.' I said the words over and over again, rocking him, crushing him against me, and the old man let me do it. 'It's all right, it doesn't matter my love, silly old wee-wee, it doesn't matter.'

After a while he quietened and relaxed against me. I stayed where I was, squashed uncomfortably under the branches, and let him take his own time. The old man's trilby hat lay on the dry peat earth and I picked it up and placed it gently, one-handed, on the grey head. There was no reaction. The patient was clasping those thin, pathetic ankles, huddling into himself and staring at the ground. His tears had stopped.

I wondered what he was thinking about, if he comprehended enough to be relieved that it was all over, if he was still distressed. I put a tentative arm across his shoulders and patted the bony frame. 'It's all right, it wasn't your fault. You just got mixed up, didn't you, and Drew liked you and wanted to come with you. It wasn't your fault.'

He turned his head slowly then, and looked at me with that blank look that I had seen so often. Then his eyes moved to Drew's face, and back to mine again, and the faintest ghost of a smile appeared. He gave a kind of sigh and leaned against me and put his face down on my shoulder.

We sat there, close together, the three of us. Bridging the gaps between the generations, between the found and the lost, the sane and the confused. Connecting the different worlds, the different experiences; the expectations – and the realities.

And presently Drew returned to normal.

He sat up and attempted his usual grin. Then he remembered that he was wet, hungry, thirsty and in a very odd place indeed, and howled. Green thoughts in a green shade were not for him. Not at the moment.

'Come on.' I took the old man's hand and gave it a gentle tug. 'Let's get you home again. The whole of Lottabridge is looking for us.'

He came docilely and we crawled out into the dazzling sunlight of the hospital cemetery. I put Drew down while I helped his friend climb stiffly to his feet, and suddenly Drew realised where he was. And laughed.

Freedom. He started to run, turning and laughing at me. Then his brown legs sped, straight to the long white path and down it.

Chapter Six

It was a week later, the first week of September, and I was fighting yards of red crêpe paper, which fought back, and some well-chewed Sellotape. 'Becky, may I borrow your head, please?'

'You can't,' she said, alarmed, 'it's stuck on.' I advanced, she retreated. 'It'll *hurt*!'

'Stand *still*!' I struggled with the crêpe paper, swathing her in the stuff and swearing under my breath.

'I can't see,' she protested in a muffled voice.

'Sorry. Better?'

She squinted up at me. 'Mummy,' she said, in the sorrowful, pitying voice she adopted on these occasions, 'what are you trying to do?'

'Make hats.' I slapped on some Sellotape. 'Party hats for Drew's birthday.'

'But it's not till next year.' She disappeared again.

'That's too big. Next week, you mean.' I hoisted up the mess of crêpe and re-stuck it. 'I'm being a caring and well-organised mother, Becky. Preparing everything well ahead of time. Remember your last birthday party?'

'It was very very splendid,' she said loyally. 'You cut all the burnt bits off.'

I took the hat off her head and discovered too late that I had Sellotaped it to her hair. There was a Scene. The hat ripped in several places. I lost my temper, Becky lost hers, so we both had some chocolate drops and a love and 'The Walrus and the Carpenter'. Drew was in his cot having his afternoon sleep. After that I went outside into the endless, rainless heat, and when I came back with the washing Becky was sitting cross-legged on the couch, stark naked as usual, with a large blue hydrangea jammed between her thighs. Where the stalk was I daren't imagine.

'If it would rain,' she said wistfully, 'if it would rain we could have the paddling pool out again.'

'I'm afraid there's no chance of rain at present. Why have you got a hydrangea in your groin?'

'It was on the window ledge. Mummy, why have we got *all* these hydrangeas *all* over the house?'

It was no exaggeration. They stood in milk bottles in every room. I stole them by the armful from the hospital cemetery whenever they needed replenishing. 'Well, you remember when Drew was lost?'

She nodded. 'A long time ago.'

'Last week. He was lost under a hydrangea bush and he was very sad.'

'Crying.'

'Yes.' I paused, wondering how to avoid the word 'association', which I would certainly not be able to explain. 'I don't want Drew to remember, whenever he sees hydrangeas, that he was sad. I want hydrangeas to be happy things for him. So I thought that if we put them around the house he would remember, later, that hydrangeas made him feel happy. They'll remind him of being at home with us, you see, instead of being lost.'

Silence. I could not tell if she had absorbed it or not.

'I think I'll go and catch a grasshopper.' Not.

'You won't be able to. Bet you.'

'Alison catches grasshoppers.'

'*Does* she?' Becky had made a friend, the little girl whose mother had come to my aid when Drew disappeared. I thought that I might have made a friend too, but I was not sure yet. No more rushing at friendships for me. Patience.

Becky proffered and I accepted, dubiously, her bloom. Then she went off outside, purpose in her step, and I sat and looked at the hydrangeas. I was not sure how effective this disassociation exercise would be. It was just possible, I supposed, that the constant proximity of the things would even defeat the purpose and serve as a reminder to Drew of

246

his ordeal. Certainly their presence reminded *me*, but he was just a baby and probably already had no conscious memory of those few hours. It was the unconscious I had been worried about. Barry felt that Drew had not been harmed by his experience any more than, say, a child lost for an hour in a big store. But then he did not have to contend with these damned female hormones, namely the ones that produced anxiety by the fluid ounce.

But if ever a child seemed serenely unconcerned, it was Drew. After I found him he had fallen ravenously upon a peanut butter sandwich (the fastest thing I could produce) and fallen asleep after three mouthfuls. He had slept the afternoon through and awoken his normal amiable self. It was all over as far as he was concerned. Barry had taken him up to the hospital then and had one the doctors examine him, but he had apparently not been molested in any way at all and was pronounced quite fit.

And now – absolute normality. No nightmares, no insecure clinging. It was as if the incident had never occurred.

Becky glided in carefully, her hands folded over something and her tongue sticking out in concentration. She shuffled through the toys on the floor, watching her hands all the while in case whatever was in there crawled out, and headed for the couch where I sat. Somewhat apprehensively, I waited.

'I've catched a grasshopper.'

'You've caught a grasshopper?' I was pleased with myself: never correct grammar, merely set a speedy and discreet example. I believed it and hardly ever achieved it.

'Do you want to see it?'

'*No*. It'll jump.' I eyed her closed hands curiously. 'Is it really a grasshopper or are you teasing me?'

Before I could stop her she opened them. It was a grasshopper all right, and equally curious about us. I had never seen one at such close quarters before, nor known that they would sit tamely on one's hand like that, beadily enquiring as to whereabouts but apparently quite unafraid. I was fascinated. So intricately made, all those little knobs and joints. So *green*. So trusting, as if it was waiting to be stroked.

'Close your hands again, *carefully* – ' as amputation threatened – 'and let's take him back outside.' I went with her and watched him spring effortlessly into the freedom of the long grass in the jungle. 'Why, there are hundreds of them!' My heart sank.

'Yes,' she said happily.

Well, it would keep her occupied. And meanwhile, I decided, I would take the opportunity of reading through my novel, all four chapters of it, and planning tonight's work. The wretched thing had still not got off the ground, Timothy Walthers was a whining little toad and his mother a grinding bore, but I pressed on. If I did not write now I would never write again. The necessary egocentricity was almost gone as it was. The diary, I had abandoned long ago.

I checked that the gate was fastened (we had a new latch: child-proof, Amabel-proof and even Barry-proof when he was tired) and deposited the slim (very slim) pile of scrawled-on sheets on the dining-room table. First I had to push to one side the bundle of red crêpe paper. Should I continue making the hats instead? But the blasted things wouldn't *make* – and it was several days yet before Drew's birthday . . .

Out of the Mouths of Babes.

By Amabel Dennell.

Chapter One. Unconvincing.

Chapter Two. Melodramatic and unconvincing.

Chapter Three. Absolute rubbish, but oddly convincing. Why?

I looked at it more closely and realised that Becky had somehow crept inside Timothy in Chapter Three, and that while his adventures were totally implausible his personality had suddenly come to life. Interesting.

Chapter Four, and he was comatose again.

I sat there, chewing ruminatively on my pen while a germ of an idea crept into my brain. Maybe if I based these characters a little more firmly on the characters of people I knew – knew well – and maybe if I threw out all this ESP nonsense –

Nonsense? I looked at the hydrangeas.

'Mummy! Wee-wee! Why?'

Because what goes in has to come out, I answered mentally, running upstairs. In some form or other.

'"Why",' I informed Drew, as I dumped him on to the potty, 'is the most useful word you could possibly have learnt.

It is only three letters long and yet it's the biggest word in the English language. Or in any language, come to that.

'The only trouble with "why",' I continued, hoisting up his pants, 'is that no-one will ever know the answer to it.'

'Oh, *Drew*'s awake! Drew, I've catched lots of grasshoppers, come and catch some with me.'

'No,' said Drew, and followed her.

I went upstairs to tidy the cot, and then I leaned out of the bedroom window and watched my children creeping silently forward in the sunlight. They pounced. Drew caught two blades of grass. Becky caught another grasshopper and generously offered it to Drew. He bent forward to give it an experimental suck and just as I opened my mouth to yell it leapt to safety, or so I assumed from the simultaneous movement of their heads.

Lovely red-gold head, tousled blond head. How beautiful they were, how lucky I was really. I held such crazy views on my life, such conflicting or inconsistent views, about whether it was rewarding or not, whether I was happy or not, whether Barry was the right man for me or not. Sometimes I felt it had all been a terrible mistake, sometimes that nothing else would have done, for me or for him. I would probably never know, never be sure, which it was. Perhaps both. I had learned recently that what I had was very precious, but I knew perfectly well that I would forget it again. There would again be boredom, frustration, restlessness. The children would drive me insane when the long winter days entombed us, Barry would have his silences, and I my tempers, followed by my usual guilty humility which was too extreme to be constructive. One day things would change: more money, more freedom, a car, a different environment, and hopefully a less fraught me. But until then – it would all be much the same as before. Much the same.

But not quite. There were some mistakes I would not repeat. That new environment, for instance: it would be Barry's choice this time, not mine. As for our present environment . . . Well, Lottabridge had helped me when I needed help and I would not forget that. More people had spoken to me in the past week, asking about Drew, than in the

249

previous twenty months. Perhaps they did things slowly here, perhaps I had expected too much too quickly. I would give Lottabridge a chance in future. I would even give the W.I. meetings and the singing of 'Jerusalem' a chance. Well, maybe. Then there was Alison's mother, who might or might not become that humorous and sympathetic coffee-drinking confidante I had longed for. And certainly there was Alison, whose grasshopper-catching prowess had so captured Becky's imagination.

But it was all so *small*.

I sighed, hearing already the note of discontent slipping back into my thoughts. Never mind, I comforted myself. One day . . .

And when that day came I would yearn for the days I was experiencing now. I knew it. I would want them back again, my babies, dependent on me, needing me, making their demands. I would remember how adorable they had been and forget the rest, the wretched rest. Damn Mother Nature. One simply couldn't win.

I looked down into the sunlit garden where the grass was perishing for want of nourishment. The children had gone into the house now, but in my mind's eye I saw them still playing there, as I would see them some day when they had gone, when they were on the other side of the world perhaps and forgetting to write home. It was a strangely poignant moment. The poignancy of the present is the nostalgia of the future, I thought tenderly . . . Then, What a good line! I must write it down!

I shot downstairs, muttering 'The poignancy of the present . . . The poignancy of the present . . .' and rummaged in the kitchen drawer for a pen. From the dining-room scuffling, rustling sounds came abruptly to a halt and Gin slunk in and licked my knee.

'It was an accident,' Becky called hopefully.

'Oh Lord, what was? Half a minute while I write this down.' I scribbled furiously on the back of the electricity bill. 'Did you catch lots of – ?'

I stopped.

'Accident,' said Becky again, with less conviction.

Just inside the dining-room lay a great pool of blood. When

250

I looked again it was not blood at all, but shredded red crêpe paper. And beyond it, snowflakes.

I reached the dining-room door in two strides. Becky had inched away but Drew was still sitting amongst the red and white confetti. I turned and looked at Gin, who smiled nervously at me from under the kitchen counter. A shred of party hat hung redly from her chops.

'Becky, how *could* you? Gin would never have done that on her own. You must have encouraged her.'

'She was sad,' Becky said defensively. 'She was ever such hot so I gave her a temperature to make her feel better and put one of these bee-eautiful red blankets over her and she liked it. Also it tasted.'

'I can see that. Oh well, I wasn't much good at making party hats anyway . . . But what's the other stuff, the white – ?'

I bent down and picked up a scrap of paper. My own handwriting covered it and I didn't need to read the words to know what it was. Or had been. 'My novel!' Frantically I looked round the room, trying to locate that pile of papers I had left on the table. 'My novel! My novel! It can't all – surely – Not *all* of it? *Ohhh!*'

Becky walked rapidly backwards. Drew looked concerned. Gin rushed outside and was sick.

How long, oh Lord?

Over the tea table I recounted the tragedy to Barry. We were eating salad with the children, or had been until I introduced this most delicate of subjects. Then Becky decided they had both had enough to eat.

'I'm surprised they're still alive,' observed Barry.

'It was a close thing.'

'How fortunate,' he said gently, examining his lettuce (Becky had washed it), 'that it was not a very good novel.'

I glared at him. 'Whatever do you mean by that?'

'Surely,' he said, maddeningly, 'it was not an ambiguous remark, or even a particularly obscure one.'

'You said it wasn't a very good novel!'

'Well, was it?'

'No.'

'Well then.'

'But how do you *know*?' I was exasperated. 'You haven't read the damned thing. And you never will now,' I added bitterly.

'I know because I know you.' He found a decorative caterpillar, admired it, dropped it carefully out of the window. 'You grumped my head off every time you came away from writing it. If it had been going well, you would have been high.'

Damn the man. 'You may be right,' I conceded. 'All the same – '

'I know. Awful.'

'I wish you'd stop examining your food. You're putting me off mine.'

'Sorry.'

'As a matter of fact I realised just this afternoon how bad it was. I wondered about re-writing it, or, better still, writing something altogether different. A sort of domestic tragi-comedy, perhaps, with characters based on – er – the children.'

'Now that's a much better idea. Loads of material close at hand.' He glanced furtively at his plate. 'As a matter of fact I've used the kids myself. In a poem.'

'Barry! I thought you'd stopped writing poetry.'

'It's not a real poem. Just an adaptation of a bit of T. S. Eliot. I'll show it to you later. I did it ages ago.'

Becky and Drew sidled back into the room and stood eyeing my Victoria sponge. It was the only sort of cake I could make and they liked it and didn't mind at all what shape it was. 'Are you going to make one of those *lovely, lovely* cakes for Drew's birthday?' enquired Becky, taking the devious route.

'Yes. Barry, if you're going into town tomorrow will you get some balloons?'

'Good God, have I got a day off at last? I'd forgotten.'

'Drew,' said Becky, 'you must never go up to a hedgehog with a balloon. Can I have some cake?' We looked at her. 'Please,' she added.

'You said you'd had enough,' said Barry sternly. A pause. 'But I like hedgehogs. You may.'

252

'Me?' asked Drew.

After Barry had taken them up to bed, I got out my notepad. And thought. I must, I *must* write something. I would not give up. There would be no drama group till next year, no Francis, probably no students at all this term although I had advertised. I had to make some money somehow, but more than that I had to have some activity and preferably the kind of activity that would give me back my self-respect as a literary person.

Barry came back and said, 'Hello, writing again already?' Our eyes met and I gave a rueful smile. (It's really stimulating for me, isn't it? It's a whole bundle of fun for me, isn't it?)

'I'm thinking. I ought to be able to use all these experiences with the children somehow. The chains of motherhood. You know.'

He raised his eyebrows. 'Not more repressed female stuff? The market's groaning with it. What you want is the good red meat of emancipation. Women are crying out for it.'

I pulled a face. 'The market's groaning with that too. Besides, it's not really relevant to most women's lives. I know it's *fun*, we've all read Erica Jong, but honestly, can we relate to it? Most of us? Orgasms and intellect. Anyway, that's not emancipation.'

'No?'

'No. Furthermore I don't think you *need* erect nipples on every page. It gets boring.'

He was silent and when I looked up I caught a peculiar expression in his eyes. 'What's the matter? Don't tell me you're embarrassed!'

'No. Just surprised to hear the word "nipples" coming after the word "erect".' He paused. 'I suppose this qualifies me as a male chauvinist.'

I considered his half-grinning face for a moment. 'Why don't you show me your poem?' I suggested sweetly.

Maybe it was the nipples. Maybe it was the exotic atmosphere engendered by hydrangeas all over the house. Or maybe it was just that I was, temporarily anyway, appreciating my life. Whatever, I made one of my efforts that night and joined Barry in his Yoga session. And after fifteen aching, muscle-wrenching minutes I decided that an eiderdown on the floor could be put to a better use than this.

Spontaneity at last. And, astonishingly, no interruptions. Yoga wasn't so bad after all.

So I woke up with an unwonted glow, only to find that it was One of Those Days.

Barry slept blissfully through the usual manic awakening. Drew climbed on to a chair at his bedroom window, and I checked that the windows were securely fastened and hauled Becky off to the bathroom. We emerged, and it was Drew's turn.

I stood behind him for a moment, silently adoring his luscious little legs and round bare bottom. Then I saw what he had done.

'Oh *bother*!'

'Has he fallen out of the window?'

'No, he's torn the blasted curtains.' I examined them. 'Irreparably. Oh, Drew!'

'Dear dear,' said Drew.

They had been in use since the time of Methuselah so I couldn't really complain. I had bought them from Oxfam a few years before and they had been threadbare then. So frail were they now that a determined finger could punch holes in them, as Drew had discovered. Repeatedly.

'Drew doesn't need curtains,' said Becky comfortingly. 'He's a boy.'

I did not attempt to follow the logic of this, if logic there was. 'He'll need them soon enough when the winds start to sweep in from Spitzbergen.'

'Where's Spitz – ?'

After that it was the snail. We had not even eaten breakfast, and after I had extracted a mess of crunched shell and glutinous green jelly from Drew's mouth I felt I might never eat again. 'Drew, what's the *matter* with you today?'

'Me?'

'Yes, you. Oh, never *mind*!'

When I was not dwelling with morbid horror on the fate of the snail, I was lamenting the fate of the curtains. A fine life it is, I thought gloomily, shoving sheets in the washing-machine, when you can't even replace a pair of moth-eaten old curtains. And how were we to pay Mrs Thomson's fees for the next half-term? Becky had blithely presented us with the bill on her first day back, and Barry had looked at it and shut his eyes quick.

I hooked on the tap fixtures, turned the taps full on and set the machine going. That at least was paid for, but I hardly dared use it at present, with the water shortage.

Music. Soothe the savage breast, Amabel. I switched on the radio and found some Vivaldi and immediately felt better. I made my shopping list for the day, using my habitual method, which was to list the things I wanted, then cross out the things I could do without if I really tried, then estimate the cost of what was left; then cross out the other things I could do without if I tried even harder. Vivaldi helped a lot.

Then I stood by the dining-room window and watched the children doing ballet. It was not intentional ballet, they were pretending to be house martins, but accompanied by such music they would have graced any stage. They ran and swooped, flapped madly and glided, wings out, wings in and shoulders prominent. Almost you could hear the muddled trilling note that martins make, and see the early evening sky behind them.

Becky ran into the kitchen, flushed and delighted. 'Did you see us, Mummy? Did you see us?'

I turned and smiled at her through the doorway, praise ready on my lips. The note of the washing-machine changed as a great jet of water shot across the kitchen.

'Oh,' said Becky, whom it had narrowly missed, and gazed interested towards the sink. I ran. But by the time I got there several gallons, or so it seemed, had crashed against the opposite wall and were now cascading down on to the floor.

'OH BALLS!' I shouted, wrestling with the tap. Disastrously deflecting the jet, the tap fixture hung by its chain at the point where I had failed to hook it tightly enough.

'Drew, come and look at *all this* water!'

He did, at the run, and the pair of them stood enthralled; then paddled. 'Out! Out!' The thread of the tap seemed to go on forever, but at last the torrent eased and finally ceased, and I stood drenched and panting.

255

'You're all wet,' said Becky admiringly.

'I told you to go out!' I hit the switch on the washing-machine with one hand, the switch on the radio with the other. Blessed silence. Except for the drips.

'Shall we help you to mop it all up?'

'*No*! thank you.' A pause, while the flood gently worked towards the furthest corners. 'Go and catch some more grass-hoppers. *Please*.'

I mopped and mopped. (If seven maids with seven mops mopped it for half a year, Do you suppose, the Walrus said, that they could get it clear?) While I was mopping I managed to knock over a bowl of gravy. Furiously I swiped at it, casting malignant looks at the ceiling, above which Barry slept in peaceful ignorance. Outside Becky was singing,

> 'Ohhh
> I've never
> Never
> Never
> Seen a tap
> Do
> That.'

Just as I was finishing they edged back in.

'Is that grasshopper blood?'

'No,' I snapped, 'it's gravy.' I threw the mop out through the back porch to dry anyhow in the sun. They looked at me sympathetically and I felt suddenly small and mean. But before I could give them an apologetic hug the doorbell rang and three bodies hurtled into the hall to answer it. I followed, squelching.

'Mrs Dennell? Interflora.'

Interflora! I gaped at the woman and she smiled under-standingly, evidently well-accustomed to disbelieving house-wives. Slowly I shut the door and looked at the little bouquet in its cellophane wrapping. It was a humble enough selection of flowers within but I didn't care about that, it could have been dandelions and I would have been just as thrilled. I had never, never in my life received flowers through Interflora, I probably never would again for Barry was not that sort, and this was one of those tiny golden moments that come some-

imes, sunbeams through the grey, and flooded kitchen floors
meant nothing at all.

I didn't hear Becky's remarks, though I was aware that they
were many. The card read:

> 'History: C
> Sociology: C
> English: A
> Thank you, Amabel Dennell.'

Later, Barry got up, looked at the flowers, looked at the card,
and looked at my face. He said the right things, as I might
have known he would, and took himself off to town for one of
his periodic rummages round the secondhand bookshops. I
was not sorry to see him go. I wanted to stay inside that small
sunbeam for a while.

It was not to be. Becky rode her pram frame into the shed
wall once too often, and it collapsed, with her inside it. She
wasn't hurt, but infuriated, as I gathered when I paused on the
doorstep to assess the situation. 'This blasted thing! Drew,
help me! Pull that bit – No, *that* bit! Why do I have to say
everything three times! DON'T KISS ME!'

I let her endure Drew's kisses for a few minutes and then
went to extricate her. By that time she was in a towering rage
so I sent her off to her bedroom with a book, to cool down.
Then the postman came, bringing a letter from Rayner and one
in an unfamiliar hand. I sat down next to Francis' flowers and
opened Rayner's letter first.

Pages of it. Her handwriting was bold, shapely and confident like herself. I scanned it quickly, before Becky should
come back. They were in Oxford, she said, and had bought
the most fabulous house, horrendously expensive, and
Patrick had a job at a most exclusive school full of terribly
intelligent pupils, children of Oxford lecturers she assumed,
and they were enormously happy. There were details about
the house and the new furniture; about trouble with the fitted
carpets and delays in getting bidets plumbed into the two
bathrooms; details about the enormous garden, about the
neighbours and other friends they had already made; details
about concerts they had been to, plays they were going to,

lectures they hoped to attend on the history and architecture of Oxford; and they were going to buy 'some sort of boat because it would be such a tragic waste not to use the river.'

Not a word about a forthcoming visit, but an open invitation to 'come any time'. Sure. Walk there perhaps, pushing the pushchair and carrying the cot under one arm, and eat our sandwiches at the side of the road on the way.

I pushed down my momentary envy and bitterness. They had worked for all this, they had earned it, they had the right to it. It was just that they always landed on their bloody *feet!* They never got in muddles like I did, they were never lonely or frustrated or unsure of themselves, they had no money problems, no anxieties other than those concerning fitted carpets, they just skated serenely and successfully along on the top of life; always on top of it.

Whilst I . . .

But there was no point in going over all that again. I was glad to hear from them and would be genuinely pleased, in a minute, when I had recovered myself, that things were going well for them.

At the end of the letter was a PS. 'Amabel, please phone me. Reverse the charges.'

Yes, I would certainly reverse the charges. I turned to the other letter, glancing up for a moment to check on Drew. He was dismantling the coffee table – more efficiently than usual, I was pleased to see.

'Dear Mrs Dennell,
    Could you please coach me for my A level Engish exam, which I have just failed? I will be taking it again in November. Francis Blake says you are ace.'

I smiled, and looked at the signature. A boy. 'Thank you,' I said to Francis' flowers.

Becky's gorgeous red head appeared round the doorframe. 'Are you still alloyed with me?'

'No. You were the one who was annoyed. Come on in.'

She approached. 'Would you like a butterfly?'

'Oh Becky, no, you mustn't catch – '

'It's a pretend one.'

'Oh. Yes, please.'

258

Out came the round brown arms. The small hands lifted, thumbs entwined, and fingers fluttered. Gently, tentatively, the butterfly came towards me, danced slowly from side to side in an exploratory movement, and then settled with the utmost delicacy on my wrist. The wings closed.

'Hello, Rayner? Thank you for your letter.'

'Amabel! Patrick, it's Amabel! Amabel, I'm so glad you called, I'm wildly excited and I was dying to tell you but I didn't want to do it in a letter or I would have missed your reaction. Amabel, I'm pregnant!'

I looked at the receiver. 'Congratulations,' I said.

'Do you mean it? Isn't it exciting! I'm about a month gone, so I don't look any different yet, but I *feel* different. I knew even before I had my test. You can tell somehow, can't you? The timing is perfect. Here we are in this enormous house – Amabel, you must come and see the house – and I've already started decorating the baby's room. Listen, if you've still got any baby clothes – I mean, you're not going to have any more children, are you? We've ordered a pram because they didn't have the model we wanted, and of course later we'll need – oh, all sorts of things. Loads of expense! I can't imagine how we'll manage on one salary! Amabel, you remember talking about baby books? I've got simply tons of literature on pregnancy and child care and I'm wading diligently through it all so I won't be caught out by anything unexpected like you were! Just a minute.' A pause, and muffled voices at the other end. 'Patrick says I'm talking too much. Amabel, you've hardly said a word. Now tell me the truth. I know you've been a bit disillusioned now and then, but don't you think it's wonderful really? The truth now. Are you pleased?'

'Rayner,' I said, 'I'm absolutely delighted.'

And meant it.